WINTER

ONCE MORE WITH FEELING

ALSO BY THE AUTHOR

Fiction
The House on Sugarbush Road
Nightwatching

Poetry
A Fine Grammar of Bones
Toward a Catalogue of Falling
Slovenly Love
A Walker in the City
Monologue Dogs

Essays
Writing Lovers

ONCE
MORE WITH
FEELING

MÉIRA COOK

ANANSI

Published in Canada in 2017 by House of Anansi Press Inc.
www.houseofanansi.com

21 20 19 18 17   1 2 3 4 5

Library and Archives Canada Cataloguing in Publication

Cook, Méira, 1964–, author
Once more with feeling / Méira Cook.

Issued in print and electronic formats.
ISBN 978-1-4870-0296-1 (softcover).—ISBN 978-1-4870-0297-8 (EPUB).—
ISBN 978-1-4870-0298-5 (Kindle)

I. Title.

PS8555.O567O53 2017   C813'.54   C2017-902292-X
                    C2017-902293-8

Book design: Alysia Shewchuk

Canada Council   Conseil des Arts
for the Arts   du Canada

ONTARIO ARTS COUNCIL
CONSEIL DES ARTS DE L'ONTARIO
an Ontario government agency
un organisme du gouvernement de l'Ontario

*We acknowledge for their financial support of our publishing program
the Canada Council for the Arts, the Ontario Arts Council, and the Government of
Canada through the Canada Book Fund.*

Printed and bound in Canada

RECYCLED
Paper made from
recycled material
FSC® C103567
FSC
www.fsc.org

To Mark, once more and always

And in the turning lane
Someone's stalled again

— The Weakerthans,
"One Great City!"

ONE

GOODWILL

MAX BINDER'S MANY friends tend to exaggerate the dozens of half-full glasses — and some of them considerably less than quarter-full, it's been pointed out by a couple of the more sour and dill-picklish ones — that he has eagerly poured one into another until presto, not only is the glass full but it runneth right over. But for Max, hope is not merely a feathered thing, a bird, or an equation for water and glass. Hope is where he lives, where he hangs his hat and unbuckles his belt.

At the moment, hope is a place called Arrivals where he notices that, once again, the girl's flight has been delayed. He buys a newspaper and a coffee and settles down to read and sip his way through another empty, irrationally heated half hour. In the time he's waited he's already greeted a university colleague and waved to a Magnolia Street neighbour. *Hi there stranger, are you coming or going? Just meeting someone. Ha, thought you were sneaking off on us, Binder. Nope, you know how I'd miss you. Yup, yup, take care.*

It's a city with only two degrees of separation, according to the old chestnut. The idea of those couple of variant degrees is what the inhabitants want to believe about themselves, and like all fond myths it's mostly true. Not the separations so much as the connections, the way strangers meet up at weddings or funerals, at summer festivals or fall suppers, waiting at the bus stop or in line at the movies. *Your face is so familiar, where do I know you from? Didn't you used to go to Ridgehaven High? Were you ever a Girl Guide? Let's see, do you know the Binders, the Tergussons, the Boychuks? Yes? I thought so. Small world, eh, small world.*

The truth is Max has never visited the airport without running into someone he knows, however tangentially. It's not a cliché; it's where the cliché comes from, his mother used to say, as if there exists a repository of truths so original they can't possibly be squandered.

Is an airport such a place? Max wonders. A temporary place, a place of such transience that everything is always new again.

Apart from going away to university, he's lived here all his life, so he's used to running into friends and acquaintances at the convenience store or the bank machine. He has one of those perennially familiar faces — warm, well-used, kindly — people always think they know him. But more and more lately, all the long-time-no-see faces from his past seem to parade by him: a classmate from North Point High, one of his mother's mahjong-playing cronies, a dad from his son's long ago soccer team, a kid he went to summer camp with, a girl he once had a crush on, a customer from when his parents still owned the shoe store. Max Binder — This is Your Life!

Now, from across the terminal a sprightly old fellow hails him. The fellow saunters over to pass the time of day and

Max recognizes the man whose name he can never remember because of his mother's ironic habit of referring to him as Grace of God, on account of his vast wealth and the resulting perception among his coterie that God had been rooting for him from the start. And on account of his having grown up in the North End like the Binders — practically neighbours, his mother insisted — but where Max's father made a living, more or less, the other man made a fortune. Good luck to him, Minnie Binder always said. We should all be so lucky. The man had God on his side, was her point. It was as simple as that.

Today Grace of God, natty in his leisure wear and Panama hat, is setting forth to winter in Florida but stops to shoot the breeze with Max and share a meandering joke about winning — or perhaps failing to win — the lottery. "There's this old Jew haranguing God. 'I'm so poor, I'm so luckless. Grant me a favour, just this once let me win the lottery,'" he begins. Grace of God — who, famously, won a bundle on the Extra with his very first ticket — chortles on. If the man has a flaw, it's his inability to deadpan. He guffaws his way through the punchline, playfully punches Max on the arm, and waves goodbye. Max is stymied.

Poor, luckless, favour, lottery. And then what?

He gives up and returns to his paper but the news he has purchased is not good: prospective flooding this spring, another missing woman, a fatal collision out on the highway. Two confirmed dead but the driver of the Hydro truck seems to have escaped unharmed.

Hydro truck drivers lead charmed lives, he thinks. Must be all that electricity whirring through the muscle and flex of their high-wire lives. He's still thinking about the effect of positive ions on the goofy good fortunes of union workers when he notices that the girl's plane has arrived. "Flight AC 732 from Toronto," reads the screen, the flight status changing directly from "Delayed" to "Disembarking," without appearing to pause at the grounded equanimity of "Arrived." In his haste, he overturns the last of his coffee and accidentally tosses his newspaper onto a moving baggage carousel where it revolves grandly for a couple of turns.

The girl's journey has been beset by difficulties, so many and of such varied complexity that by the time she appears at the gate — late, bedraggled, tearful — Max is perversely certain that her visit will be a riotous success. He hastens toward her but she thrusts a travel sickness bag at him and sprints for the ladies' room. Dreamily tossing the sealed bag from one hand to the other, Max admires her grace, her speed, her unerring instinct for intuiting the whereabouts of washroom facilities in foreign cities.

When the girl emerges, he sees that she has scrubbed her face and dried her eyes, but her colour remains poor, a grey pallor of fatigue patching the brown skin. Beneath the airline blanket that she clutches about her shoulders, he glimpses a black skirt and white blouse that, in cut and colour, imply a crispness sadly lacking in their present incarnation. Indeed, the shirt is badly stained about the collar and a fairly important button — from Max's somewhat bashful perspective — is missing. The skirt, too, is awry, its ragged hemline guiding the eye down a pair of bare legs that end in clattery white sandals.

"Where's your coat, darling?" he asks. He advances, arms outstretched, but she backs away, appalled.

Max takes rapid inventory, comes to a decision. "Oh, this?" He tosses the travel sickness bag into a nearby receptacle, not noticing that it's been allocated "for glass and aluminum only," and tucks the girl's hand firmly under his arm.

"Let's go find your suitcase, darling." He hauls her off to Carousel 3 where they watch the river of other folks' luggage gradually diminish to a trickle of oddly shaped bags and duct-taped boxes. After a while even these misfits are claimed. Max and the girl stand before the empty baggage carousel, watching it revolve until, somewhere in the depths of the airport's baggage handling facility, a switch is thrown and the conveyor belt hitches and stops.

Max, who had been temporarily hypnotized by the soothing rhythm of moving luggage, comes to himself with a start. "Whoops," he says. "Looks like we have a claim to file."

Undaunted, he turns and strides toward the Baggage Services counter and almost makes it when he is halted in his tracks. Somewhere between a stifled wail and a whimper — it's the first articulate sound he's heard from the girl, and it is such a hopeless small cry, such a hiccup into the whirling void, that he swivels, the over-polished granite of the airport walkway shrieking in sympathy.

Who, if I cried out, among the hierarchy of angels would hear me? Max kneels beside the girl. She has slid to the floor as if disconsolation has rendered her boneless and is weeping into her cupped hands. All he can see is the top of her small head, the hair clipped close to her skull. He puts an arm around her shoulders and tries to recall the rest of Rilke's elegy. It's only a distraction, a way to forestall the pity that runs through him as marrow through bone. He's just gotten to the part where *every angel is terrible* and the poet is trying to restrain himself from *the luring call of dark sobbing.* But he's in no mood to admire the high-spirited romp of life chasing art, a dog and its tail.

The girl is bereft — she is a broom-swept heap of sadness and goosepimply flesh and all that has gone awry between home and here. So many borders to cross, so many forms to fill out, so many boxes to tick, so much blamelessness to declare.

"There, there, darling," he murmurs. He's not used to soft-hearted girls, being the father of two hard-hearted boys and the husband of a woman who prides herself on being a tough cookie, not the weepy sort. Even his mother, a widow of twenty years, is a fighter with plenty of snap left in her garters. His professional experience has made him wary of mishandling young women, but the girl is such a forlorn bundle of unclaimed despair that he throws caution to the winds, comes down firmly on the side of "what the heck," and puts his other arm around her.

Oh, but there is nothing to her. Skin and bones! Beneath the threadbare fabric of the airline blanket and the girl's thin cotton shirt, he can feel the row of bumps that is her spine, and the *bump bump bump* of what is knocking against it. She's shivering with cold, so he wraps his winter coat around her. Vast and cumbersome, the coat envelops her once, twice, three times. It is a coat that has swallowed a girl and, for a moment, he is tickled at the sight.

The girl looks up and catches him laughing. Unexpectedly, she laughs too. "That's better, sweetheart," says Max. He's feeling flustered, though. He can't keep addressing her by these endearments, and in the flurry and dismay of their first meeting he has somehow forgotten to introduce himself.

"You know who I am, don't you?" he asks. "And you must be Pat."

*   *   *

MAGGIE ALWAYS MAINTAINED that she'd been hoodwinked by those World Vision hucksters. When the door-to-door salesman came around with his full-colour pamphlets and his talk of mere pennies a day to feed a hungry child, his slippery, glittering words, a pen tucked behind his ear ready to be whipped out at a moment's notice, she fell for it.

"Choose your country," he said, unrolling a map of the world coloured in the strident shades of national emergency. "Any continent you like — Africa! Asia! South America! There are needy children everywhere."

Maggie closed her eyes and stabbed her finger down and around. When she opened them again she saw that her finger had landed on a red-for-danger blood splatter.

"Ah, Zambia," the gentleman said, apparently delighted. "Wells! Irrigation systems! Schools!"

"Yes, all right," she said. "But I want a girl."

The travelling salesman looked startled, as if she was accusing him of being a child slaver, a trafficker in human souls. "Girls, boys," he started to say, triangling his arms in a God-bothering gesture. "All children are precious, all children are —"

"Yes, indeed," she interrupted him. "But I already have two of the other kind and I want to see if girls are any better."

He was a professional, that man, and looked only slightly shocked for slightly longer than the blink of an incredulous eye, and then he said, Ye-es, well, why not ma'am, and he thought it could be arranged, by jingo. And please sign here, and here, and initial on this page, and right there at the bottom, thatagirl.

Hence Pat. Pat Ngunga came to the Binders in the form of a blurry headshot and a nine-digit registration number, along with a magnetized photo frame into which Maggie inserted the photo. Then she stuck Pat on the refrigerator.

"Would've thought you'd have chosen a girl," Max said when he came home that night, the mail fanned out in one hand, the other hand yanking at the refrigerator door in search of a snack to steady him for the long ride out over the hungry plains of six o'clock.

"She *is* a girl," Maggie snapped. "Her name's Pat." Her blood fizzed through her veins, every nerve shorting.

Max looked at his wife. She had curly auburn hair (curls: genuine; colour: natural but enhanced) that she wore piled on top of her head and secured in place with whatever was handy (hair clips, pencils, bobby pins, chopsticks). Complicated, bright eyes, eyebrows like a couple of Spanish virgulillas so that she often looked like a comically troubled child when she was merely thinking deeply, a wide mouth and a general air of flashing energy that veered toward exasperation but could simmer down to natural good humour if circumstances were conducive.

She tapped the photograph, *Look!* Obediently, Max looked at the photograph inside the magnetized frame on the refrigerator door. *Greetings From Your World Vision Child.* She *could* be a girl. With cropped hair and deep-set eyes and a gamine, unisex smile. Maggie cut him a look but Max wisely said nothing on the understanding, strenuously earned, that it was better to be happy than right, or married than burn, or happily rustling through a refrigerator in search of German potato salad than arguing with your wife. But by the time the Binders received their September plea for extra funds necessary to "a successful school year for your World Vision child," Maggie was distraught.

It was as plain to her as the enclosed snapshot of young Pat Ngunga sprawled in the front yard of the family dwelling that the longed-for daughter was a son. Maggie blamed God (instinctively), World Vision (peripherally), Pat (predominantly).

"Come now, Maggie. How could the kid possibly know he's been pretending to be a girl inside a photo frame on our refrigerator all these months?" Max chided. "Or she," he hastily amended.

Max, the sole inhabitant of the tiny principality of Hope, still believed that Pat could be a girl, but Maggie was an honorary citizen of a town called Unconvinced. "She's a boy," she repeated. "A boy called *Pat*."

A boy called Pat. And Maggie was the Patsy who'd fallen for it. Oh those were dark days.

"I KNEW YOU were a girl," says Max. "I knew it. My wife went through a period of, of despondency but —" He breaks off, uncertain of his ground. Pat, who has had no reason to suspect that she is not a girl, remains silent on the subject of her disputed gender.

They're driving east to the Goodwill Store on Ellice in the old family Pontiac to procure a winter jacket and boots. It's February, and the poor girl has come too far to freeze to death in a foreign land. Max cranks up the heat and laughs to see her small frame engulfed in his voluminous coat.

"Thank you, Mr. Macks," she says.

"Just Max," Max says. He used to request the same of his students. "Call me Max," he'd say, but only the bravest or the most precocious would oblige, and the rest would call him Prof or Dr. Binder or even Sir (the rural kids), although most studiously avoided addressing him at all. She doesn't look brave, though all he can see beneath the swaddling folds of his winter coat are her thin wrists and her thin neck and her compact, elegant head that at times looks like it's been poured from some liquid metal and at other times droops sleepily, her skin clouding, turning matte, as exhaustion swoops in. She rouses herself to gaze out the window as the unfamiliar landscape plays out its continuous, repetitive loop: cloud, bird, building, boy. Cloud.

He asks her about her journey and she turns sideways to address him.

"Mr. Macks, it was a boon," she says. "My thanks."

"A boon!" He is delighted.

Pat nods with emphasis. So much emphasis, in fact, that it engages not merely her head on its long question mark of a neck, but her shoulders too, and even her hands. "Because I have never travelled by jet airliner before, Mr. Macks. It was very tight and hot in the airplane, and I did not feel well. But Father Michael says, 'What is the good of remaining on the ground when we have been given wings to fly?'"

Well, why not? he thinks. For a moment he lets himself imagine the winged nature of airline travel, as well as the enigmatic spectre of Father Michael, with whom he had conducted a somewhat terse correspondence on the subject of Pat and what Father Michael persisted in calling "Pat's Voyage Broad." After some cogitation, Max decided that Father Michael must have meant "abroad," but when Pat replies, he becomes less sure.

"You see," says Pat, "Father Michael, says travel broadens a person. When my mother says she does not want me to come to Canada, Father Michael says to her, 'Mrs. Ngunga, do you want your daughter to remain narrow as a row of beans or would you prefer her to return to us broadened by all this travel she will be doing?'"

"So that's how the old — So that's how Father Michael talked your mother into letting you visit us!" he exclaims.

"My mother, she said: 'Father Michael, I would prefer my daughters to remain narrow,'" Pat says with a sigh.

"And how many daughters does your mother have?" Max is aware that he should know the answer, but he is charmed by the girl's air of quaint submission to the Word according to Father Michael, or at least what he imagines the good Father to represent: a gaunt man on a stick, a scarecrow.

"We are five now. Once we were seven but two are late."

"Oh, how sad."

"Yes, my father is often sad. He looks at us and shakes his head. 'Oh girls,' he says, 'how am I to marry you all off?'"

Startled, Max glances at the girl but she appears to share her father's view, shaking her head sadly at the economic rigours of patrimonial responsibility. "And you, Mr. Macks? How many daughters do you have to marry off?"

"I'm a lucky man, Pat. I have no daughters at all." But he doesn't feel lucky. Sitting beside her, he longs for what he's never even known he's been missing. A girl of his own, a little Pat-a-cake. Well, well.

"That is lucky," Pat agrees. "My father would be most envious of your lot in life, Mr. Macks."

Max laughs. He doesn't want Sams and Lazar to come as a shock so he tells her about his sons. "There is Sams," he explains, "and then there is Lazar." As always he falters, at a loss to apprehend his boys.

They drive past the last of the airport hotels owned by Grace of God. "Back in the day, that hotel was the site of some shady dealings." Max hooks his thumb over his shoulder and assumes the voice of a tour guide but trails off when he remembers the charges: solicitation, along with drug trafficking and bare-knuckle cage fighting. For an establishment with such an imaginatively criminal past, the Airport Inn is a bland-enough place now, newly renovated and catering mostly to business conferences and trade shows, although a neon sign that reads "Automatic Off-Track" blinks on and off in a second-floor window. It looks like one of those video horse-racing places he's heard about. Max thinks of himself as a lucky sort of fellow, but he's never placed a bet on a horse or a dime in a slot machine. Why is that? Something tugs at his memory, some joke he's lost the thread of. *Poor, luckless, favour, lottery.* He could swear he's heard it before but still can't remember the punchline. Ah, shoot! When he gets home he'll ask Maggie. She'll know.

Up ahead a level crossing looms. Max, who swears he has a sense for these things, feels in his bones that a train is approaching. He floors it, the Pontiac jumping forward so that they jolt across the tracks seconds before the light turns red and the boom descends. The freight is nowhere in sight, but it's out there, Max knows, clattering down the tracks toward him.

Ha! He punches the steering wheel in delight and turns onto Route 90. They're driving through an industrial area of warehouses and storage lockers and half-abandoned strip malls, many of the buildings already in receivership. It's a grey flannel day, rumpled and ill-fitting. The only splashes of colour are the Day-Glo orange and fluorescent yellow banners draped over buildings — *Liquidation Sale! Clearance Sale! Moving Sale!* — and the maple leaf pennants snapping above a used car lot. He notices that the snow banks on either side of the road have shrunk to grimy honeycombs oozing slurries of dirty water beneath a winter's weight of traffic exhaust and pollution.

"It's not usually this bad," he tells her. "When the sun comes out —"

But she interrupts him. Her small head is canted toward the sky. Something is falling in flurries, spinning earthwards on wind currents and downdraughts. Are these the wings of which Father Michael spoke? She rolls down her window and puts out her hand.

MAGGIE, WHO WAS about to turn forty, claimed that the Christmas card from their World Vision brat was snarky. When Max asked how, she hit the flat of her hand against her forehead and drew her brows together as if to mime, *Jesus who is this fool?* But in the end she just snapped: February. She meant that the card had arrived much too late to have had any effect on the Binders' Christmas celebrations, always conflicted occasions anyway on account of Max's divided loyalties and Maggie's ongoing grudge against God, not to mention his son.

"You'd think a Valentine's Day card would be more to the point," she said. "Or something for Easter. But no, there it is, 'Seasons Greetings from Your World Vision Child in Zambia.'"

"Perhaps Pat didn't send the card, exactly," he felt compelled to point out.

"Perhaps there's no such person as *Pat*," said Lazar, lifting his eyes from whatever Xanadu of the dispersed mind he was currently scrolling through. "Perhaps *Pat* is just a front for a Russian mafia–owned offshore pharmaceutical company."

Max was struck by his younger son's eyes which, he suddenly realized, he hadn't glimpsed for months because they were always narrowed over a screen. Lazar's eyes were roughly the same as he remembered them — colour: blue; shape: eye-shaped; size: in this case enlarged by devilish advocacy — but he looked for too long and somehow got entangled in the spokes of the boy's dreamy irises. Lazar swerved his eyes back to his unfolding, palm-held universe and his father felt bereft. For something to say, he asked about Pat.

"Seems to be thriving, actually," Maggie said. "Whole bloody village of Nakonde seems to be thriving. Ever since the Mission brought in the water system and Mr. Mwenyi returned from his pig management course. So hooray! And since our Christmas card was two months late, they saved postage by tossing in his report card early, so that was a bonus."

"Oh-ho, how's young Pat doing this term?" Max asked in the appeasing tone that he'd not yet learned was an elbow to the ribs of Maggie's composure.

"Not too bad for a Third-World, fifth child, only son of struggling subsistence farmers, and a damn sight better than either of your sons are doing. Let's see — he 'excels' in language and health studies, whatever they are, and achieves 'good to excellent' marks in everything else with the exception of art. And, if the crappy sketch of what I suspect was some sort of hut-type dwelling was anything to go by, I'm not sure I agree with the optimistic conviction that he 'could do better.'"

"Still think it's a girl," said Lazar. "Or at least a girl bot." He smiled without bothering to raise his head.

"Well, there you go," his mother replied. "The oracle has spoken. The Oracle of Angry Birds has had his say." But she managed to tousle his head before he escaped the room and the beaky peck of her love.

THE WOMAN AT the Goodwill Store, at first undecided, has thrown in her lot with young Pat.

When the two shuffle through the door — Max half-carrying the girl, whose stockingless, sandalled feet are awfully cold; a combination of shock and freezing temperatures, not to mention the Pontiac's dodgy heater — she stares at them from over her bifocals for a long Geez Louise moment. Something or someone is being nastily interfered with, the Goodwill lady seems to be thinking, and she is uncertain whether her own good nature is the victim.

But Max immediately stumbles over a rack of dresses, setting the wire hangers clattering, and his helpless clumsiness mollifies her.

"Zambia!" she exclaims. "Well, well. Must be hot in Asia this time of year, poor child."

Pat stares at the rows of jackets and winter coats, their weight dragging at the flimsy hangers. Sweaters flap their woollen arms out of bins as winter boots march off into the distance, measuring the length of the store in their stride. Over the pervasive smell of disinfectant there is the strident note of what is not quite concealed. Pat sniffs, sneezes.

Her feet, which have been tingling unpleasantly, turn red and cramp in agony. Pat tries not to mind. Mr. Macks has been so kind to her, and Father Michael has charged her with being of good cheer, no matter where she finds herself. Where she finds herself is in Hell. Her feet are the fiery coals of everlasting damnation, and the pins and needles of the Lord's displeasure are radiating through her toes, her ankles, her heels. Pat stumbles to a chair and hunches there, watching Mr. Macks and Mrs. Goodwill hold up winter coats to their chests and say, "Hmm?" and "Too puffy!" and "Just a slip of a girl, so..."

"I wish my wife was here," Mr. Macks says. "She's the shopper in this family." Mrs. Goodwill looks at him pityingly, as if to say, *Really, your wife is a remarkable shopper? How extraordinary!* Then Mr. Macks tells the woman about his wife's really extraordinary shopping talent, but their voices are far

away because now the pain is a hornet that stings and stings.
No, Pat has had hornet stings before and they have always sub-
sided, but this agony shows no signs of abatement. On the contrary, it increases with each breath.

Oh! she thinks. *Oh Mama! Oh Father Michael! Oh wings
seen for the first time!*

Mr. Macks and Mrs. Goodwill have finally found a mutually
agreed-upon winter coat. "Look Pat," says Mr. Macks, and he
holds the navy jacket to his chin and prances comically for a
moment.

Mrs. Goodwill laughs. Pat would laugh too, if she could.
She is not crying, quite, but her eyes are bulging with refused
tears. There is no mistaking it.

"Oh," he says. "You don't like it." The jacket, he means. It's
true, she doesn't like the jacket but why would she cry about a
jacket? No, it is —

"It's her feet!" exclaims Mrs. Goodwill suddenly. "Her feet
are beginning to unthaw."

"No such word," Mr. Macks begins to say, but catches himself. "What have I done?" he wails instead.

After that, things get better. Mr. Macks wrings his hands
the way she has often seen men wring their hands in the village,
poor fellows, but Mrs. Goodwill knows what to do. She brings a
towel and rubs at Pat's feet, first gently and then firmly. Feeling
floods back (more pain), and then warmth. Mrs. Goodwill
brings Pat a pair of thick socks and hiking boots that fit. Also
jeans and a sweater. Mr. Macks kneels on one knee before her
to zip her into her new jacket and she is all set.

Oh my, she thinks, catching sight of herself in a full-length
mirror. *Who is this somebody?* Her eyes are bright and so wide
that she can see the white rim all around the irises. She narrows

her eyes and straightens her spine, hangs tough. She hardly recognizes the fierce traveller who stands before her in hiking boots and navy jacket. Also, she has never worn so many clothes before. In fact she feels tighter and itchier than she has ever felt before, even in the jet airliner.

Mr. Macks sees her struggling to breathe and says, "Out, my girl, go stand outside while we ring this lot up. You need to try out your new duds."

She pushes open the door and gulps in the cold outdoor air. From the bottom of her heart she thanks him: Mr. Macks. He is the kindest man she has ever met. Not as wise as Father Michael, perhaps, but kinder. She wants to thank Mrs. Goodwill but can't bring herself to return to the odorous, wool-stuffy store. Instead, she offers up a prayer of thanks to the goodness and willingness of Mrs. Goodwill.

Pat stands in the cold in her new coat and boots. Such a coat and such boots of which even that remarkable shopper, Mrs. Macks, would approve. It is a day in late February, flipped inside out, cold side against her skin. For a moment the weather exactly coincides with her protection against it. It has taken thirty-five hours of travel and strife but she is finally, perfectly comfortable.

The snow is falling faster now. Harder and faster. Pat looks up into a sky of flying wings.

MAGGIE HAD SAMS when she was ludicrously young. He'd been a mistake but a good one.

"What's a good mistake?" Lazar asked the first time he heard the story.

"It's something you don't even remember regretting," she'd told him, although the truth was she did remember, vividly.

She could hear Lazar turning that one around in his eight-year-old head and before he could offer his own examples of a life lived on the Édith Piaf plan (no regrets about punching Sams or sneaking cookies or disobeying Imee, no regrets at all) she said, "You have to know you made a mistake, though."

"Come here, kid," called Max from the other room where he was watching a college basketball game. "A good mistake is like a good foul, which is basically any foul that prevents the other team from making a basket." Together they watched a player who had just gotten fouled by an aggressive point guard line up on the free throw line.

"Swish," said Lazar. And then a moment later, "Double swish."

"Them's the breaks, kid," Max told his son.

"D'you think that guy regrets his mistake?" Lazar asked.

"Damn straight," Max said, watching the coach yank the point guard from the court.

That had been more than six years ago but Maggie was still thinking about that point guard and his misjudged foul. "There's no such thing as a *morally* good foul, Mags, it's all just strategy," Max told her when she brought up the game a little while after, but too long after, apparently, to convince him of her sudden interest in basketball stats. The truth was that Maggie *was* interested in statistics by then, if only to calculate the ratio of free throws to fouls in her maternal standings.

Sams must have been about eleven because he'd just started compiling the first of his lists: "A Select Guide to Cigarettes in the Movies." She remembered him sitting quietly on the living room sofa, absorbed in the black-and-white movies he loved, taking notes on cigarettes: hand holds and brandishings, the amount of smoke generated and the way the cigarettes were extinguished. The *method* used. He watched *Double Indemnity* five times because in the final scene Edward G. Robinson lights a match for Fred MacMurray by flipping the tip with his thumbnail. It was a good trick, but in the end Sams had to exclude the movie from his list. It was about lighting cigarettes, he explained, rather than smoking them. He was strict but fair. For hours after watching *Gilda* or *La Dolce Vita* or *Casablanca*, he'd scribble cigarette notes, his head bent so low over the page that a dark brown lock of hair touched the paper.

The truth was that Sams was the best mistake Maggie had ever made. Sometimes, as she stood in the doorway, watching the light from those old movies play across his features, she wondered how the hell she'd gotten so good at free throws. So *lucky*. But how much longer could her luck hold out, given that the average free throw percentage was right around 75 percent, at least in a league game, which left the other 25 percent in which a person could foul out to no avail? In a game like that you might trade the chance of giving up a couple of points for getting two free throws and *still* not make a goddamn basket.

DISASTER STRIKES WHEN they return to the car.

"Perhaps it would be more accurate to say, 'Disaster struck when they returned to the car,'" says Mr. Macks, because it happened while they were in that blasted store. But while he is working on her tenses he sees that he has wounded her feelings and, supremely kind man that he is, he says, "Not to worry, dear. How were you to know?" and "Who's to say?" and "We'll sort this out in the morning."

What happened is that someone — "Some Godless rogue," Father Michael would have said — jimmied open the passenger door of Mr. Macks's superb automobile and snatched Pat's travel

purse from where she had carelessly left it, heaped on the passenger seat. In her defence: she was jet-lagged, confused, hungry, cold, out of her element, entranced by wings. On the other
hand: she should have known better. Her mama had made her
that travel purse; it was just large enough to contain her passport, her return ticket, and a single Citibank Zambia traveller's
cheque in the amount of ten scraped-together, penny-pinching
dollars.

"To buy a birthday present for Mrs. Macks," Pat tells Max.
"Something wonderful." In fact, Father Michael had said
"Something useful," but although she has been in the city little more than an hour, Pat has had occasion to measure the
useful (coat, boots) against the wonderful (wings), and she has
made her choice.

Max smiles. He can't help himself, although he would certainly like to. The girl is a whole bowl of trouble: delayed flights,
lost luggage, tears, frostbite. And now a stolen passport. Ah, but
she is also dauntless and brave as she stands beside the Pontiac,
hopping from one foot to another in her agitation.

"Oh, who would do this?" she cries. With her upturned face
and her right fist raised to the heavens, she seems to be addressing the falling snow.

"Must be someone who needs a new travel purse," says Max
phlegmatically. "Don't worry about the passport, darling. We'll
go and see about a new one in the morning." His heart sinks,
though, to his boots.

But the girl is inconsolable. She stands there forlornly, her
new jacket flapping about her knees. Max notices there's a button missing from the cuff of the jacket, and that she has pulled
the sleeves up over her wrists, as far as they will go. *Oh, mittens!* he thinks, but is loath to dart back into the Goodwill

Store because he has the irrational fear that when he returns, something else will be missing. The car, the girl. Pat, he now realizes, is the sort of young woman to whom nothing can be added without something else being subtracted. Buy her a jacket and boots and presto, her passport and traveller's cheque will disappear.

Strangely, the memory of kneeling before her and zipping her into her new jacket assails him. It's an oddly freighted memory, as if it's still about to happen. A memory not of the past but of the future. Such nonsense, Max shakes his head hard as if he has water in his ears.

He glances at her, at this girl whose self-sufficiency is unaffected by what she has or lacks, what she owns or loses. She is Pat, and the snowflakes catch like white burrs in her hair and on her thick dark lashes. She's beginning to look like the ghostly imprint of a girl he once knew. A long ago girl in a place called Arrivals. As he watches, she starts to transform: she's a photo negative, a snow sculpture, the winter afternoon spinning forever in place on the tips of its skates.

"Come on, darling," he urges. "Let's go home." He hurries around to her side of the car and ceremoniously opens the jimmied door, then hands her in. Once inside he watches as she drips repentantly upon the Pontiac's stained upholstery. He cranks the heat and turns the radio to a country music station. Some guy is singing a song about honky-tonk bars and pickup trucks and cheating hearts. About moving on and messing up. *If you want to bring me down better get in line.* Max knows how the fellow feels.

"Mr. Macks?"

Max startles. He feels as if he's just dozed off, but Pat is still talking, lost in a rush of words. She slows some when he turns to look at her, his big hands gripping the steering wheel as if to give himself ballast.

"But so you see my quandary, Mr. Macks?"

He doesn't, quite.

"It is the wonderful something which now I cannot acquire for Mrs. Macks. How can I visit this lady, this wife, without a gift to offer? Father Michael said 'useful,' and Mama said 'well made,' but now that I have met you, Mr. Macks —" The girl falters, at a loss to express her thoughts. But Max, who knows himself to be neither useful nor well made, finally understands.

"You see, it is not every day that one celebrates a birthday," the girl explains.

"Quite right," Max says. "You want to buy my wife a birthday present?"

"A wonderful something," she assures him.

"But my dear, *you* are her birthday present," Max says before he can stop himself.

WHAT IS A *good* mistake? Over the years Maggie had pondered Lazar's question from every angle, even taking suggestions from the peanut gallery. Her mother-in-law told her about the time she ran out of butter for her pie crust dough. "I substituted margarine," Grandma Minnie said, "and I've never looked back." (It wasn't technically a mistake, thought Maggie, but as close as Minnie would ever come to admitting domestic liability.) As for her boss, he just shook his head: "There's no such thing as a good mistake in the newspaper business, Maggie. You should know that."

"Original sin leading to free will," Max offered another time, winking at her over a stack of third-year *Paradise Lost* essays, and Lazar, still hooked on his father's sports analogies, cited the time he'd taken a soccer ball to the head, gone down, but immediately leapt up. "The crowd went wild," he reminisced fondly. Once she even asked Imee, but the poor woman, who could barely speak English, said she had never eaten a good steak.

Only Sams took her question seriously, or at least sensed the panic behind it, though she thought she sounded lighthearted enough when she asked, "Ever come across a good mistake, Sams?"

He barely paused. "You know that scene where Charlotte and Jerry are talking for the first time and he lights her cigarette?" He'd been watching *Now, Voyager* over and over, making notes. "There's four or five main cuts and each time the camera goes back to Charlotte, she's holding her cigarette differently. At first you think it's just camera angles, but no. The most important mistake comes after the third cut when Charlotte balances the cigarette between her middle and index fingers and then, after the cut, she's twirling it between her thumb and pointer like she's playing a tiny flute, a piccolo almost." As he talked Sams demonstrated, puffing on his pencil, twirling and gesticulating.

Maggie sat down beside him on the sofa. "That's certainly interesting, Sams. Sort of a continuity error, right?"

"No, see that's what people think, but the cuts show that Rapper isn't interested in continuity. He's cutting time into little pieces and Charlotte is trying to blow the pieces together again. It's like a battle over who gets to control time."

"Why, Sams, that's beautiful. I'll have to watch that movie again. It's certainly an interesting mistake."

Sams didn't reply. He'd thought of something else — direction of smoke exhalation or a way to measure time differentials on the in-breath — and he was bent over his notes, scribbling. Maggie leaned back, her eyes closed. She was thinking of Bette Davis, her lips pursed in *o*-shaped awe at the pleasure of that first good draw. Charlotte Vale and her cigarette holds! It was certainly an interesting mistake but it was only later that she began to wonder why Sams thought it was a *good* mistake. For a long time she couldn't work it out, until one day it came to her. Sams thought that all mistakes were good mistakes. They reminded him of who he was.

PAT CHEERS UP considerably after Max explains that she's been brought out on a birthday visit.

"So I am Mrs. Macks's gift?"

Max thinks of Maggie's terrible mood these last few months, her sense of injustice, her yearning for a daughter. Maggie is turning forty, but forty has got Maggie all bent out of shape, and she was always a mite angular to begin with. He's talking metaphysical shapes, here. Max loves the shape Maggie's in, the Maggie-shape, so familiar he could find her in the dark if there were a million others to sort through.

By the time he breaks the news that Pat is to be Maggie's birthday gift, the girl is already vastly enlivened on account of the drive-thru window they've just negotiated and the Happy Meal she is clutching. That a meal can be "happy" appears to strike her as the perfect coincidence of the gleeful and the edible. Max sips his coffee and enjoys her delight — hasn't she ever had a takeout burger before? She has not.

"Go on, open it," he urges. The salty, meat-greasy smell of fast food fills the car with an almost audible *thwock*. Pat closes her eyes. Her lips move as if she is praying. She is, in fact, praying, he realizes.

They're parked at the far end of the mall, Max looking on as Pat grapples with her Happy Meal. At last Max, who has ordered his own burger, stuffs it into his coat pocket so that he can help her. But his native klutziness is no help at all, and after a moment he throws up his hands. Valiantly, Pat grapples on, drops her burger, catches her fries, fumbles both, but eventually manages to steady herself between the various components of her takeout meal — burger and fries, bright, warring packets of ketchup, mustard, and vinegar, wads of paper napkins, and a pink plastic puppy that lurches about when placed on the dashboard, yelping halfheartedly. Pat finishes her meal in the time it takes for the world-weary animal to jerk itself to the furthest reaches of mechanical exhaustion.

Devours, actually, thinks Max proudly. Pat: 1; Happy Meal: 0! The only evidence of this instant moveable feast is the wrappers and boxes, transparent with grease, that he bundles up and lobs out of the car window into a garbage can before swinging a left out of the mall parking lot. That and the ketchup licks on the girl's face. Oh, the poor hungry child!

Now that she has squared matters with her dinner, Pat turns her attention, once again, to Maggie's upcoming birthday.

"So I am to be Mrs. Macks's birthday gift?" she asks.

"We'll put you in a box tied up with ribbon," he says. "Or would you prefer to jump out of a cake?"

"A box," says Pat seriously. "I have never been inside either a box or a cake, but I do not like to waste food even for such a cheerful occasion as the birthday of Mrs. Macks."

Chastened, Max promises her that neither a box nor a cake lurks in her immediate future. For the first time he feels the impropriety of what he's been planning. *How can a girl be a birthday present?* he wonders. And why has this thought never occurred to him? The truth is, he was taken up by the idea and then overtaken by the idea's execution — he's barely given propriety a thought. And then there were all the arrangements to make: the Byzantine web sites and conflicting instructions on how to obtain a travel visa, the bureaucracy and hoop-jumping, the forms filled out in triplicate (and the immediate disappearance of those forms somewhere in the system), the greasing of wheels and wiring of money orders and transferring of funds, all undertaken in the interest of uxorious love.

Of course the World Vision people were at first incredulous and then suspicious — he would have expected no less from such an earnest crew — but they put him in touch, at last, with Father Michael who was neither incredulous nor suspicious but instead exhibited a coldhearted efficiency that chilled the blood.

"And you would like the girl when? And for how long?" he had inquired, before calculating a handling fee, half of which, he assured Max, would go to the girl's parents.

There were visas to arrange, a task complicated by the last-minute intelligence that Pat didn't own a passport although, he thinks, why should she? Indeed she didn't even have the identity photograph necessary to acquire a passport (briefly Max remembers the smiling girl inside the magnetic photo frame). Through all these details, as numerous as trees in the forest he could no longer see, Max was patient, persistent, buoyed by optimism. And when the passport was finally issued, the airline ticket purchased and painstakingly delivered by bicycle messenger, he had nothing to do but look forward to the girl's arrival and Maggie's wonder.

Today is his wife's fortieth birthday and Maggie has not, so far, approached even the outer rim of wonder. All the better when it comes, thinks Max. He is hopeful.

According to her passport, Pat is seventeen years old, but she looks younger, slight and girlish. She dozes on the seat beside him and Max, loath to wake her, finds himself driving aimlessly west on Portage. Her head lolls to one side and he tries to prop her up so that she won't get a stiff neck. Her face, at rest, is pliant and childlike; it lacks the commotion of her lively waking self. He fishes his handkerchief out of his pocket and wipes the ketchup from her lips. The white cloth comes away stained red and he curses himself for a fool but stuffs his handkerchief back into his pocket. He's approaching the horseracing track at the perimeter of the city when a familiar excitement overtakes him. He wants to keep going, to hear the hitch of wheels on highway, the breath-hitch of a hurting song on the radio, to feel his fond old heart take flight.

"Would you like to take a drive?" he asks the girl. She's asleep but nods at the sound of his voice, smiles and murmurs. Max doesn't notice. He's already turned the car around.

MAGGIE IS NOT in the mood for a birthday but she has one anyway. She is not in the mood to turn forty but she does. Ob-la-di, ob-la-da, as they say.

All morning her friends phone to wish her happy birthday. Happy fortieth, old gal! "How's it going?" they ask. "Are you having fun yet?"

"I'm old," she says. "Other than *that* —"

Other than that, she wants to snap, Mrs. Lincoln and I enjoyed the play, thank you very much.

But the horror of her fortieth birthday turns out to have little to do with the baggy misery of ageing. The drift, the dwindle, the drag. In fact, for reasons unrelated to birthdays, this is unquestionably the worst day of her life. Hands down.

So far and henceforth and forever after. As the years pass, she will manage to grind down the edges of this terrible day, sheer pluck wearing off the corners, one by one. When that finally happens, Maggie will be able to laugh: "Well, at least it wasn't a leap year." The implication being that pain has a season, can be discarded as one tears a page along the perforated edges of the kitchen calendar.

She is confused when the police arrive to tell her there's been an accident. "Not Sams," she cries.

"I'm sure Sams is fine," the officer says, looking at his note-book. So she knows it's not Sams. Someone is dead and the present tense is her ally.

"Sit down, ma'am," says the officer who looks like he would rather be anywhere else but here. Anywhere else in the world, quite possibly the universe. But the poor fellow's not about to shirk his death-knock duty. "Can we get you a glass of water?"

"Lazar!" she cries. "Where? What?" She is all interrogatives, cycling through "How?" and "When?" and "What the hell?" although, for some reason, she does not ask "Why?" Perhaps she is saving *Why?* for the days and weeks and years to come, the everlasting proof that pigs can't fly, the crooked letter that no amount of wishing can straighten. *Because* is why.

"But Lazar is at school," she keeps repeating. "Why isn't Lazar at school?"

"I'm sure Lazar is fine," says the officer. "We can send a car to collect him, if you like."

"Sit down, ma'am," he says again. "Can we call someone for you?"

"Call my husband," Maggie says. The officer tells his part-ner to get this lady a glass of water stat, and suddenly Maggie panics. Why does she require water? Why is she being called a lady? Why the goddamn hurry? She begins to run in tight, comical circles (no one laughs), she pulls at her hair. She has wet her pants although no one seems to notice until she jumps up from the sofa. Then they all stare at the sodden patch and the officer's partner hastily snatches back the glass of water as if loss of bladder control is a function of too much to drink rather than a siren going off in her head, rather than her heart crashing through her ribs, rather than the rush of adrenalin swerving through her racetrack veins.

"Call my husband," Maggie says.

"Someone else," says the officer.

So she knows.

Bizarrely, she remembers a joke Max used to tell, badly but with gusto. Private Schwartz's wife dies while he's away on active service and his sergeant volunteers to break the bad news. "Line up, men," he says. "Now, all those who are married, take a step forward. Not so fast, Private Schwartz."

"Someone else," the officer repeats to Maggie.

So she knows.

For a moment that's all she knows: the knockout punchline of a shaggy joke. The old one-two. Then the officer begins to fill her in on all the things she doesn't know. "There was someone with him," he says. "No, we don't know who she was, ma'am. There were no identifying documents at the scene."

"No, we don't have a photo, ma'am. She wasn't wearing a seatbelt, you see." His voice is low and steady as if set to the thermostat of *Keep calm, lady*, but he stretches out his hands in a helpless gesture. *Do you understand?* he seems to be asking.

She understands nothing. Nothing!

"Yes, a female," he confirms.

"Yes, a female," he confirms again. "I don't know why she wasn't wearing a seatbelt, ma'am."

"We don't really know why she wasn't wearing a seatbelt," he repeats. "They were both still in the car when we got there," he adds, as if this is the final clue he is at liberty to provide.

"Yes, ma'am, the Jaws of Life," he repeats.

"Prone across the front seat," Maggie will later read when she demands a copy of the police report. "At the time of impact the adult male, later identified as Max Binder, was in the driver's seat. The unidentified adolescent female victim was prone across the front seat. The male victim's fly was disengaged."

"Yes, ma'am, paramedics," the officer confirms in his thermostat voice, but with an odd emphasis made odder by his attempt to banish oddness from his tone. *Nothing going on here, folks. Move along, please.*

THAT YEAR, FEBRUARY has only twenty-eight days, but March has thirty-one and April drags the usual wheezing train of thirty days behind it, so.

"So what?" asks Lazar. "What's your point?"

Counting is her point: mental arithmetic. Days adding up to months divided by money in the bank. Cigarettes multiplied by the square root of insomnia. One sleepless night she perversely decides to count her blessings. There is only one and it has stalled on the lucky eight ball of "could be worse." *At least it isn't a leap year,* she thinks. *Other than that…*

Other than that, she rages when her friends call to say, "How's it going, honey?"

Other than that, Mrs. Lincoln and I enjoyed the play, thank

you very much. Other than that, Mrs. Kennedy and I appreciated the motorcade.

Actually, she tries not to be such a goddamned bitch. "We
have to take it day by day," she comforts her devastated mother-
in-law. "One step at a time, Minnie. Remember to breathe."
Blood, war, famine, flood, she thinks. *Kill, kill, kill.*

The forensic report comes back negative. "No semen was
found in the interior of the automobile. No semen was present
upon or near the body of the middle-aged male victim. No
semen was present in the oral, vaginal, or anal cavities of the
adolescent female victim."

"No semen" seems to be the consensus, but Maggie knows
that the presence or absence of semen has nothing to do with
the intention to commit hanky-panky. That unspeakable bastard who didn't even buy her a birthday present and the cunty
bitch with her Electrolux mouth were undoubtedly up to no
good. She doesn't give a fig about the girl but she wishes that
she could bring her low-life, despicable, no-account husband
back to life so as to have the rare pleasure of killing him again.
Slowly and with painstaking attention to detail. Once more
with feeling.

Some days she wants to share the joke with him, and some
days she wants to snag his penis in his disengaged, adulterous
fly. She wants to run him down and reverse over what's left
of him but, sadly, this is no longer possible. It seems the old
Pontiac has been totalled.

This too shall pass, some damn fool tells her. One of her
buddies at the paper, most likely. *La-la how the life goes on.*
Nobody loves a platitude or an old Beatles' song better than a
journalist. It's true though, probably. Passing being the primary
attribute of time, that crazy assassin. One day she'll glance out

of the window and it will be February again. A year will have
passed, her forty-first birthday approaching, the *dwindle* setting
in. Twenty-eight days and an extra day to leap over.

Not so fast, Private Schwartz.

BETTER GET IN LINE, Max sings. His wife is seldom far from
his thoughts and this is especially true today. Today is Maggie's
fortieth birthday, a day she's accepted as the fulfillment of all
the cranky displeasure with which she has anticipated it. Max
admires her simple talent for outrage.

Max's talent is for forgetfulness. All day he's been tugging
at a joke he can't quite get to the end of although the refrain —
poor, luckless, favour, lottery — runs across the bottom of his
mind like a news crawl. And now he remembers how, birthday after birthday, he always seems to get his wife's gift slightly
wrong. The wrong shape, the wrong size, the wrong colour.

"This must be for your other wife, kiddo," Maggie says every
year, rolling her eyes. Now Max has brought her a girl.

The girl is sleeping beside him, her head lolling forward no
matter how he tries to prop her up. He worries that Pat will have
a stiff neck when she wakes; he worries about her lost suitcase,
her stolen passport. Unaccustomed to such varied and sustained
anxiety, Max wonders if this is what it's like to have a daughter.

But the highway is an arrow shot into the future, and the
sun is low and wintry yet hanging in there. The familiar wobble
in the Pontiac's front axle is a comfortable nudge, a reminder
that life is just another commodious but flawed vehicle to get
from here to there. Along the highway, telephone poles slam
past, their lines converging on an artist's sketch of perspective. Some way out of town, the fields lay down and spread
out a little, get comfortable. They pass the Joliecoeur Motor

Hotel, its "Vacancy/No Vacancy" sign flickering indecisively. Somewhere between "Full up" and "Come on in." Somewhere between "Keep on trucking" and "Welcome home." High above them the sky is crammed with silence and space.

All that drive-thru coffee has dripped through and now Max's bladder is full. There's no traffic coming or going so he pulls up on the shoulder of the road, dives down into the ditch, and signs his name in the snow. He's damn proud of his signature too, a young man's autograph, although when it comes time to close up shop he finds that his zipper is broken. The little metal doohickey won't snag the two pieces of cloth together but runs vainly up one side and then the other. He makes a note to get rid of his trousers before Maggie sees.

Back in the car the girl has somehow wriggled free of her seatbelt and is slumped across the front seat. Max surveys her tenderly. At least she won't wake up with a stiff neck, he thinks. He remembers her astonishment at the drive-thru window, when the disembodied voice suddenly crackled through the speakers. "Can I take your order, please?"

"Wonders!" she'd exclaimed, so overcome that he'd had to order for her. He smiles at the memory and casts a weather eye about him.

A couple of sun dogs, one on either side of the sun, catch his attention. A lucky sighting. The snow in the fields and all three suns in the sky are flashing light. Far away a Hydro truck is coming toward them, flashing light off its windscreen. Max knows he'll have to turn around and head home soon but, by God, not yet.

A BREAK IN
THE WEATHER

TWO

THE RIVERVIEW NEWS

HALF PAST MARCH and the earth was hurtling toward spring and thaw, whirling out of control. The staff at the *Riverview News* felt the season's bilious pitch and yaw as if the entire office had been set spinning.

To his surprise Shapiro found that he missed Maggie. He'd grown accustomed to her face, even to the ones she pulled at him behind his back. Without the whetstone of her stroppy presence he felt shaggy and unkempt. But when he finally phoned to ask how she was doing, she insisted on telling him all about a movie she'd seen, or maybe it was a play. The point seemed to be that someone had gotten shot, as unlikely as that seemed. Shapiro couldn't be sure. The connection was bad and Maggie's voice sounded uncharacteristically hoarse.

"Come in whenever you're ready," he told her, ringing off hastily.

Like Maggie, the time was out of joint. Miss Leonard, the ancient bookkeeper who had once worked for Shapiro's father, rattled her swear jar and wondered aloud at its relative emptiness.

"Good work, people," she said, without conviction.

Shapiro, too, was feeling oddly unstable these days, restless and unmoored. He'd wake up most mornings with an oily stomach and a tongue like a chamois cloth, his head clumsily wired and much larger than he remembered it being. It was your classic hangover, minus the alcohol or the sense of being justly shriven for his sins. But if he was being punished, Shapiro had no idea what he'd done wrong. Time seemed to be skipping tracks, a favourite song played once too often on a scratched disc. One minute he'd be staring into the mirror applying shaving cream to his jaw and cheeks, the next he'd come to with a start, his eyes blank, the razor clogged with stubble. Added to which, his wife seemed more remote than usual, the weather was anything but remote, and the atmosphere at the office, much like the weather, was subject to all manner of advisories and watches, alerts, warnings, and moderate to severe risks.

Something was awry, but what? And when had it all begun?

As near as damn it, Shapiro reckoned that it had started with his first sighting of the man he'd come to think of as the kidnapper. If he had to stick a pin in a calendar, that's where he'd stick it. Since this made no sense at all, Shapiro was encouraged. Given the course his life was taking, no sense made the only kind of sense there was.

Meanwhile, the city roared with the sound of meltwater running in the gutters, everything dissolving, transforming from one element to another. From solid to liquid, from ice to water. From indifference to its opposite, whatever that was.

* * *

SOME WEEKS AGO, Shapiro spotted a man using a public pay phone on the corner of Broadway and Sherbrook. Oddly, he'd never noticed the pay phone before, but there it was, grimy and unimposing, on the windswept street. The man wore a long black overcoat and braced against the wind as he tipped a Slavic river of swiftly flowing anguish into the receiver. His dilapidated bike leaned against a nearby lamppost, untethered. After all, who would want to nab such a beat-up machine? The man was gesturing so violently that he kept yanking himself away from the steel cable of the pay phone and then being yanked back in like a fish. For a moment he looked slightly sinister, but the moment passed.

"Why sinister?" asked Shapiro's wife that evening at dinner. Allie prided herself on being able to zoom in on the beating heart of the matter without flinching.

"I think he was a kidnapper," Shapiro said.

"How so?" she asked, zooming.

"Who uses pay phones these days?"

But Allie was shaking her head and tapping her fork on the side of the plate like a United Nations diplomat calling for order. But not a very diplomatic diplomat: Khrushchev with his shoe.

"Kidnappers always use disposable phones," was her assessment.

Shapiro demurred. He remembered the man's glossy black beard from which the winter sun had picked out a scattering of wiry silver strands. He wanted to tell her about that beard; surely there were few beards of such lustrous angora weave. The kidnapper looked young and old, youthful in his posture and imprecations yet old in all the ways that a beard confers gravitas — wisdom, solemnity, the high-collared mantle of good stewardship. Shapiro felt certain that the fellow wasn't the sort to squander the earth's resources in the way of disposable cell-phones and getaway SUVs.

"I suppose he cycles from pay phone to pay phone making his fiendish demands," his wife taunted, reminding Shapiro how much he preferred irony to sarcasm. One had an andante touch; the other was a hand in a wooden glove thumping out "Heart and Soul" in double time.

As the din of his wife's irritable after-dinner cleanup commenced, Shapiro dawdled beside her in the kitchen, dishcloth in hand, his eyes distant and unfocused. He was thinking of his kidnapper cycling furiously through the melting city — head down, the lapels and cuffs and hem of his long black overcoat slamming against the wind. Time sped up and blurred like revolving bicycle spokes. From pay phone to pay phone he raced, laying down his terms and hedging his bets and threatening to rough up his limp, sock-mouthed victims.

THE KIDNAPPER WAS one thing, but what was wrong with his colleagues at the *Riverview News*, not to mention his readers? So many letters of pique and complaint. In all his publishing career Shapiro had never encountered such readerly ire. Such nitpick-ing insistence that he'd gotten everything wrong and ought to apologize, now, this very minute; there wasn't a moment to lose. But what was at stake? Shapiro liked to think of himself as a newshound, an inky-fingered hack, his necktie permanently askew and his cuffs smudged with newsprint.

"Not so fast, slick," his old man would have said. "Don't pretend to sell yourself short, boychick."

He was right, of course. Shapiro was the publisher, manag-ing editor, and hinky dog's body of a community newspaper with a subscription list of almost thirty thousand, a number that had fallen by half since the plummy peak of the market days when his late father ran the paper. Lately, though, many of their long-time subscribers had been dropping off the list and reappearing on another kind of list entirely. Indeed, these days, the *Riverview News* seemed entirely composed of salutes to old friends and bygone patrons, edged out by the usual birth and wedding announcements, congratulations to special graduates, notices of socials and garage sales, along with the various bureaucratic shenanigans of city councillors, school board trustees, and traffic court judges.

Sometimes Shapiro wondered how one city — medium sized and moderate in most things — could sustain such a flurry of earnest-minded commerce: the buying of outboard motors and selling of bread machines and lawnmowers, of gently used wedding dresses trailing their homey melodramas of desertion, divorce, and general hard-up-edness. The same old stories of "Shouldn't oughta," and "Gone done and did it, anyway," and "Will again, most likely." Sometimes he forgot that the citizens were known for their glittery-eyed individualism and that the city itself was situated inside a province that resembled the outline of a raised freedom fist.

Perhaps it was simply that Shapiro still felt guilty about the story they'd run following Max Binder's accident, his *tragic death*. In deference to Maggie, they'd forgone idle speculation about her delinquent husband's supposed tomfoolery and concentrated instead on the mysterious young woman who'd been in the passenger seat. "Who Was The Mysterious Hitchhiker?" ran the headline, above a photograph of frozen fields lashed together with yellow police tape, behind which the blurry shape of a savagely crushed motor vehicle could be glimpsed.

As always, opinion in the newsroom had been divided. Miss Leonard pointed out that the *News* (as she called it) was a community paper and therefore not obliged to concern itself with current affairs. In rebuttal, Stan Brodsky, copy editor and sometime columnist, pointed out that Miss Leonard was a bookkeeper and therefore not obliged to offer her lousy two cents.

In the end it came down to an editorial decision and Shapiro, running his eye down last month's balance sheet and the previous year's shoelace-narrow profit margin, handed down his judgement. We'll pitch it as a public service thing, he consoled himself. "Who Was The Mysterious Hitchhiker?" Perhaps someone would come forward.

But no one, it seemed, knew the answer to the question the headline had posed, and no one phoned in to the tip line they'd provided (although it later transpired that a couple of digits in the tip line phone number had been transposed, so who the hell knew). And since the slight uptick in that month's sales figures could be attributed to the inclusion of the annual Bridal Supplement, the whole incident could be filed under the usual sleeping dogs clause, Shapiro was forced to conclude.

A big hoo-ha, his father would have called it. A right old howdy doody.

But, as always, there was more than one fire to piss on. Reader's complaints and corrections had reached an all-time high and matters were not improved by the slipshod style, the touch-and-feel go-luckiness of Aunt Betsy's Country Recipes. She was the most popular food columnist they'd ever had but also the most erratic — outrageously careless of weights and measures, inclined to omit essential ingredients, and over-fond of folksy idioms. She sent her recipes in on time but they were seldom free of query and puzzlement. "Add a peck of cinnamon to a bushel of apples, honey," was this week's conundrum. "What the fucking expletive is a bushel?" yelled Brodsky. In deference to Miss Leonard there was a zero tolerance swearing policy in the newsroom, but Brodsky always got it slightly wrong. Perhaps they ought to change their policy to "low tolerance" or "amber alert," thought Shapiro. "Try your best not to," or "Don't, if you can help it." In all honesty, zero was an intolerant number: it was a knothole in the Tree of Life, a wormhole in the wind, a dense black hole swallowing all the starry numerals to the left and right of it. It was the pursed mouth of God withdrawing from the world, whistling Dixie.

Shapiro shrugged sadly. Brodsky ought to put a quarter in the swear jar but these were exceptional circumstances. Shapiro was sympathetic to the man's outrage. What, after all, was a bushel? What was a peck? A biblical measure of subsistence farming or the best way to gather a harvest of pickled peppers? A small ornamental shrub or an unenthusiastic kiss?

The fact of the matter was that Brodsky was bitter about pies, all kinds and all fillings and all spices, on account of last week's Saskatoon Berry Rhubarb Pie, which unhelpfully avoided any mention of rhubarb. Readers wrote in imploringly but Aunt Betsy was unresponsive. It was the chocolate-less brownie debacle all over again. As a matter of fact, Shapiro was pretty sure that "Aunt Betsy" was an inventively crafted cipher wreaking her culinary mayhem under an assumed name. He suspected that Aunt Betsy's real name was Miss Leonard, although it occurred to him that even Miss Leonard must have another name. Not Betsy, but Maud perhaps, or Jane. But whatever her real name, the avatar called Betsy sent in her country recipes then, like the tiny dot at the centre of a TV screen after you clicked off the remote, she disappeared until the next month's issue with its skinned-teeth deadlines and skimpy, digressive copy. "Who are we and what are our dreams?" asked the sportswriter every year during Grey Cup season.

Enraged, Brodsky stamped out, flinging a quarter into the swear jar. It was an unremorseful quarter, so who knew if it counted? He was angry at Betsy, angry at Shapiro, but mostly he was angry at himself. Ever since last year's lucky Thanksgiving save ("Here it is, folks — 'The Best of Cornish Game Hens!'"), he'd caught every no-show turkey, every inadvertently cheese-free pizza, every boomeranging fruitless pie that Betsy had thrown at him. But he wasn't the same since his parents' divorce.

WHERE WERE THEY? March? No, middle of February, it must have been. It was the week Shapiro took Brodsky to lunch at Resnik's Diner so that his buddy could unburden himself, relate the next installment in the epic maternal saga entitled "Alienation of Affection." Shapiro frequently ate lunch at Resnik's. He appreciated the two-handed heft of three-inch sandwiches stacked with interleaved layers of deli meat cut thin enough to turn transparent. You could almost read the *Riverview News* through a slice of Resnik's pastrami. Mustard so sharp, so yellow, so like a warning light blinking through the fragrant steam of hot brisket on rye.

And then there was Resnik himself. Resnik the showman, Resnik the vaudevillian of smoked meats and Russian dressing. Resnik the keeper of the flame, who'd loved Shapiro's father like a brother and tolerated his son like a slightly disappointing nephew. He met Shapiro, party of three, at the door and ushered them to the usual table, ousting the poor slob already seated and about to bite into his Reuben, the saliva springing to his mouth.

"Get along there, my friend," barked Resnik. "Shapiro eats here."

They were three because Maggie had insisted on joining them.

"You barely pay me so you might as well feed me," she told Shapiro.

She cracked up over the advertised Valentine's Day "tasting menu," ordered the Bachman Turner Over-Easy Platter, then stabbed a couple of plastic forks through her wild auburn top-knot in an attempt to keep her gravity-laden curls in check. Mostly, though, she distinguished herself by failing to act with the appropriate sang-froid on discovering that Brodsky's baleful mother was pushing eighty-five. (And winning. Winning!) The old girl was in the middle of her second round of chemotherapy yet appeared anxious to shrug off her husband of sixty-odd years.

"Very odd years they must have been," Maggie giggled.

"I'm too old for this," Brodsky lamented. "Now I've got to adjust to being the child of divorced parents. The guilt, the divided loyalties. The whole broken home shebang."

Maggie shook her head. "Nah, they'll both be showering you with stuff — taking you to the movies, buying you baseball gloves and hockey cards." She patted him kindly on the arm. "Um, it's a cancer divorce, right?"

Shapiro hadn't heard of this sort of divorce but Maggie didn't have time to fill him in.

"Hey, maybe it's something I can write about!" She looked flushed and absorbed, the way she always did when she thought she'd found a topic for her slice-of-life column.

"What kind of cancer did you say it was?" she asked sweetly.

But Brodsky was enraged. He broke open the swear jar inside himself and let it all spill out.

IT WAS ODD, yet all that month Shapiro couldn't shake the memory of the man on the pay phone. The image disturbed him in ways he didn't understand, got under his skin and made him itchy. Who was he? What was he saying? And why did it matter? Every day Shapiro walked to the bus stop, and every day he passed the public pay phone on the corner of Broadway. The kiosk with its hooded Perspex windbreak and its torn directories chained to the post was innocent of human use, no kidnapper. Where had he gone with his glossy pelt, and his global conscience, and his urgency? Perhaps he was holed up somewhere with his hostages, playing Russian Roulette and Stockholm Syndrome. Sluicing down lemon tea from a samovar or slipping a single bullet into a six-chambered revolver. *Come here,* lyubov moya. *Come here, my love.*

As Shapiro walked, he brimmed with melancholy — he'd lost something, but what? February was the coldest month, the city a cheap snow globe shaken by a lunatic child. Inside the sealed globe, snow shrieked like Styrofoam, the air smelled of freezer burn. Kids pulled terrible faces and stayed that way when the wind changed. It was the shortest month of the year but it felt like the longest, was what people said. And every year they said it again because February was a jig played on a cracked fiddle. The timing was off, and the fiddler's hands were much bigger than his instrument, and each note that sawed from his crooked bow curled away like wood shavings. He played his heart out, his eyes watering and his fingers bleeding. But nobody could hear him above the wind.

Shapiro hunched into winter, pulling up the collar of his astrakhan coat. An early birthday present from his elegant wife. Again and again, he tried to find purchase in the season's frictionless slip and fall, the solipsistic intimacy of cold, the little cough of hope sucked thin as a throat lozenge as he wandered through the cumulonimbus of his own breathing. What had he lost? His keys, a stray thought, the thread of a conversation he'd had years ago? He checked his pocket, his phone, his wallet, his watch. Everything was in order. He snatched a glance at his driver's license and, for a moment, thought he was gazing at his father's face, but no. Instead, Shapiro stared out at Shapiro from the laminated blank flash of his driver's permit: brown hair, brown eyes, brown pullover. He studied himself, his monochromatic middle age. He was the proud possessor of a street address and a phone number. He wore prescription spectacles and was licensed to drive a standard vehicle.

Gingerly, he felt himself all over. Heart, check. Lungs, yup. Kidneys, liver, courage — check. He ran a hand over his scalp sensing the grey busyness of his brain inside the skull's honeycomb. But something was missing — some organizing principle, some unified field theory, some queen bee fattening in her cell. His brain was present but his mind was absent.

This, then, was the shape of his days, but Shapiro couldn't help thinking they were the wrong shape. An impossible shape. A four-cornered triangle or a circular square.

THE LAST TIME Shapiro saw Maggie before the accident was in late February, a blustery day. She was waiting for him when he got to the office, blowing Nicorette bubbles and flipping through her anxiety channels.

"He's struck again," she announced. "The Fucker."

She mouthed this last word, chary of Miss Leonard's sensibility, not to mention her everlasting swear jar.

Maggie called the fellow "the Fucker" to distinguish him

from all the other fellows she had to deal with daily (fuckers all). He (or *she*, Brodsky interrupted smugly) was a prankster whose letters, while sporadic, were addressed to "Miss Belief," Maggie's advice column *nom du guerre*. They turned up in her inbox every couple of months, although only once — alas, on Shapiro's watch — had one actually been printed. Maggie could quote that letter verbatim, as if every word had been tattooed upon the hidden flesh of her credulity. The peek-a-boo part of her that once gave a damn.

> Dear Miss Belief,
> I love my husband but am frustrated by his typically masculine attitude. He is rational to a fault, a real problem solver, but he lacks spontaneity. He has common sense but no sense of joy. How can I convince him that love is magical?
> Yours sincerely,
> Mrs. Samantha Stephens
> P.S. He also dislikes my mother.

As always, Maggie had counselled "honest dialogue," an air-clearing "heart-to-heart," a renewal of "physical and emotional intimacy." Make a date night, take up a hobby together! Why not sign up for a ballroom dancing class? Have you thought of couple's yoga? Cunningly, she'd taken issue with the man's churlish attitude to his mother-in-law which, she advised, had to be addressed as a prelude to "the new era of marital magic."

Since the disastrous publication of that letter and its ribald aftermath, Maggie had come to suspect every letter signed "Sleepless in Seattle" or "Play Misty for Me" or "Likes Piña Coladas," as being yet another taunt from the dastardly Fucker. The Fucker, true to his name, had responded by becoming even

less subtle, as if to goad her with the implied assault upon her
pop cultural naïveté.

Dear Miss Belief,
I am an astronaut who enjoys all the perks of the swinging
singles lifestyle. The other day I stumbled upon a bottle con-
taining a female genie…

Dear Miss Belief,
I am in the process of grieving the loss of my dear mother. Do
you think it would be inappropriate, or otherwise foolish, to
purchase a 1928 Porter automobile?

The current letter concerned the misadventures of a close-
knit family of friendly monsters.

"Why do folks react so strangely to us?" the letter writer
inquired plaintively.

"If he would just *try* to fool me," Maggie fumed. "Would it
kill the bastard to give me the benefit of the doubt?"

Dutifully, she mouthed the word *bastard*. She'd been bon-
ing up on the unlikely plot lines of quirky seventies sitcoms,
unfortunately by watching them. She knew that one day the
Fucker would stop patronizing her — she was banking on it.
Instead he might throw her a curveball, an easy lob with a subtle
top spin, and she wanted to be ready for it. She was halfway
through the slapstick misadventures of a blended family living in a split-level bungalow and was dreaming of the day when
she would receive a letter from a spunky housekeeper about the
infuriating mysteries of meatloaf.

But how could Shapiro appease her? "That's a lot of Nicorette
gum," he said instead.

It turned out that Maggie wasn't trying to quit smoking so much as attempting to achieve a sustainable blood nicotine level between smoke breaks. She couldn't go cold turkey, she told him, on account of her rotten kids and her aggravating husband. She'd been experimenting with patches too, she confided, tugging her shirt out of her trousers and flashing him a view of her nicotine-patched stomach. Shapiro nodded sagely. *Yup, uh-huh.* But Maggie was in one of her hot-tin-roof moods, as she called them and, raking a hand through her hair, she grabbed her bag and told him she'd be outside.

Smoking, if he really wanted to know.

"Effing March wind be ding danged!" she yelled over her shoulder.

But a moment later she poked her head around the door to clarify that she would be sure to stand at least fifteen metres from the entrance to any public building. Miss Leonard, a stickler for scofflaws, waved her on. *Get out of here, you!*

Maggie having taken her cranky leave, Shapiro was free to return to his computer terminal where hundreds of emails were already queued up, awaiting the benediction of his higher education, his perfect understanding.

Dear Editor,

As a high school social studies teacher who believes that accuracy counts, I feel compelled to draw your attention to certain errors in last month's edition of the *Riverview News.* With all due respect, the recent town hall meeting that you reported as having taken place on February 17th actually took place on the 19th, the speaker's name was misspelled, and the excerpted words of Councillor Buhler (not "Buler") were misquoted.

I have included a full transcript of the meeting so that you might include it in a subsequent edition.

Yours truly,

Catherine Boychuk

There were fewer letters in his father's day, but enough even then for the old man to feel compelled to dismiss them with one of his characteristic zingers.

"This fella's sharp as a matzo ball," he'd murmur, running his eye over letters signed "Concerned" and "Long-Time Reader."

Naturally, all Shapiro's readers were long time, eagle eyed, alert to typos, grudgy. They had an exaggerated sense of grammar and held no truck with contractions. He suspected that the lure of misinformation was what kept them reading.

Some were plaintive: "For pity's sake, I have baked Aunt Betsy's butter raisin tarts four different times —"

Some were belligerent: "What gives you the right to editorialize on the Israeli question? You self-hating Jew, you hemorrhoid swelling in the anus of your people's history!"

And some veered giddily between passive-aggression and its more active form: "You might be interested to know that your photograph of the Saint Dominic Craft Fair incorrectly identifies me as Rachel Schellen. And it incorrectly identifies my prizewinning toffee pudding as a 'delicious second-place apple pie.'"

But all, in the end, were vaguely litigious: "Shapiro, did you even taste my sticky toffee pudding?"

WHEN SHAPIRO FINALLY saw the kidnapper again, two weeks to the day since their first encounter, he realized how much he'd been missing him. The world shifted subtly on its axis, as if aligning itself with all's well, and Shapiro drank him in. His shoulders were braced, as if he was preparing to heft the sky on his back, and his ancient bicycle was still leaning against its lamppost. Once again he was hullaballooing into the pay phone. He cocked his head for a moment, angling the receiver to his ear. Shapiro imagined his lips touching the mouthpiece that was smudged with other people's lips and words, their confusion, their pain, their stale morning breath. In a mere fourteen days the man's beard seemed to have greyed.

It was almost March, the sky flashing sunlight and shadow in a series of grand mal seizures. A full rigging of clouds scudded overhead, their sails stiffening in the breeze. When the sun wheeled through again, Shapiro saw that the silver threads glistening in the kidnapper's dark scarf of a beard had inexplicably multiplied. Once he could have poked his doubting finger right through those slipped stitches, once he could have counted them, but now they were as infinite as the snowflakes that fell all night over a prairie city. Stars! Cells!

A feeling of joy and homecoming overwhelmed Shapiro. How happy he was to see that man! The happiness was a little corkscrew twist into the heart's sweet wine. It reminded him of how long it had been since he felt the spiky joy of nothing he could name. A stiff breeze engaged the edges of the man's overcoat and he rustled in his sleeves seeming, for a moment, to caper, to dance. The man no longer resembled a kidnapper. Instead he looked like someone Shapiro knew or had known. Perhaps even someone he had yet to meet. But what is resemblance? Only wind moving over the surface of water. Only nothing.

As he stood there, watching, he had the strangest feeling that the past was a locomotive barrelling into the present, derailing the future and scattering boxcars across the rails. The past, the present, the future. But not necessarily in that order, so that Shapiro, poor goon, remained confused. *"Tak kak zhe vy zhili, kol' net istorii?"* the man yelled into the mouthpiece.

Those were his exact words — Shapiro read them as they emerged from his mouth and hung in the cold air. For a moment he even believed he understood what they meant, that he'd overheard them somewhere. *But how could you live and have no story to tell?* The man turned to face him, his eyes blank with the effort of listening, and Shapiro finally recognized him.

Rabbi Zalman, none other. As always the old man's trousers were knee-sprung, his overcoat battered about the elbows, but the rabbi was not entirely grey, not yet. Indeed, viewed from a distance, a backward glance, the rabbi's beard still appeared mostly black, a dark thumbprint against the sun.

From apparently nowhere snow began to fall. Thick snow-flakes, fluffy as lamb's wool, gamboled about the rabbi's shoulders. The wind started up again and the direction of the snow changed abruptly. Now it spun around the figure in long, whirling strands. Suddenly, Rabbi Zalman was caught in the double helix of his people's self-replicating history, yet he remained oddly serene. The motionless centre of a clock face, the still point of a child's spinning top. For the third time the wind changed, turning the snow to static, flipping the weather channels of the world to interference and white noise.

Shapiro gave up on his bus and stared at the rapidly transforming snow, at the figure stranded in his once-black overcoat and fedora, his once-black beard fading to white, like the end of an old movie, before the titles roll and the theatre lights are turned up.

* * *

"RANSOM HASN'T BEEN paid yet?" Allie asked politely.

She was referring to their *folie à deux*, their shared fantasy of the pay phone kidnapper. Shapiro wanted to tell her about Rabbi Zalman, but what could he say? His parents had once been congregants at the rabbi's North End synagogue, frequent attendees and generous donors to the Sisterhood fund. When Shapiro's mother died, Rabbi Zalman had delivered her eulogy, selecting for the occasion the proverb about a virtuous woman's price being far above rubies. Less than a year later, he officiated at her husband's funeral, blessing the memory of the man who was so fortunate as to have married a woman whose price was far above rubies. So many rubies, Allie had murmured at the time.

His wife would certainly remember Rabbi Zalman, but Shapiro was reluctant to mention his parents even though he and Allie were eating scrambled eggs for dinner, which Allie prepared by adding a dollop of mayonnaise to the eggs after she took the pan off the burner, just the way Mrs. Shapiro had taught her. The taste of the eggs, at once fluffy and creamy, reminded him of his childhood, of shovelling food into his mouth on winter evenings while beleaguering his parents with the miniature blackboardland of his school days. Bookends, those parents of his: once they'd held his world in place but now that they were gone, Shapiro tended to slip sideways.

Perhaps marriage was just another *folie à deux*, he thought. He imagined telling Allie about his day. The ruby merchant called, he would say. He wanted to know if I'm finally ready to sell. Out of nowhere, it occurred to Shapiro that the rabbi was angry with him.

Allie picked at her eggs and rambled on about the bicycling

kidnapper and his pay phone ransom. Could one have a *folie à deux* alone?

"Things are heating up," he conceded, playing along.

"He's quite a wimpy fiend, isn't he? Always pleading and getting tangled in telephone cables."

Allie possessed the kind of beauty that was difficult to ignore, but Shapiro had been married to his hothouse orchid for long enough that her pale, watercolour allure had become routine, nothing more than the cultivated scent of a tea rose and sometimes, when he was distracted, she was merely a border flower. A marigold!

In short, Shapiro frequently ignored.

But Allie was no silently falling tree. Allie was no cat in a box. Allie was objectively beautiful, whether or not she was centred in the opprobrium of her husband's eye. Starting from the bottom and proceeding upward, she had long, shapely feet, legs, fingers. A Modigliani balance of extremities, an Audrey Hepburn tilt to the neck, an oversensitive Woolfian nose. In contrast, her hair was cut short and on the bias. Complicated modern tufts stuck out all over as if to mime the passage of thought intercepted by impatient fingers.

She pulled absently at a lock of her hair: "Ears should be turning up in the mail soon."

The ruby merchant called today, Shapiro imagined telling his wife. *I told him I was finally ready to sell.*

To distract himself he asked Allie if she'd heard of a cancer divorce. Of course she had; she was a crack attorney, the best there was. Grounds for divorce included adultery, cruelty, abandonment, mental illness, and criminal conviction, she told him, rattling them off as if she'd recently been turning them over in her mind. Cancer was a no-fault circumstance that did not, ipso facto, constitute grounds but rather established a precedent by which similar cases might be resolved.

Cases of what? he wondered. Terminal illness? Existential despair? Failure of the imagination?

A cancer divorce was the worst, Allie explained, because it combined elements of all other divorces. To wit: betrayal, alienation, malignancy, and lies. It was about failing to balance the odds, she reckoned. It was a teeter-totter swinging crazily between love and love's beautiful corpse. Someone fell ill and someone else fell out of love. The way she looked at him she might as well be coughing up the old one-syllable spitball, the single word-phlegm of disgust. *Men!*

The unspoken curse still ringing in his ears — *Men!* — he wanted to tell Allie that the cancer divorce in question had been initiated by the wife.

"What's cancer good for if you can't lose the extra weight?" Brodsky's mother would like to know.

Shapiro longed to ask his wife if she would rise to the occasion if he got ill. Or would she fall instead: out of step, out of sympathy, out of love. Out of the clear blue sky with its patina of melting wax wings?

And if she still wanted him, would he want her back? The older he got the more he realized that what he had was never as beguiling as what he thought he'd always wanted. Was all of adulthood merely a couple of turns on a kid's merry-go-round, each horse focused on the one in front, all the riders changing places when the canned music stopped? Ah love, that creaky old carousel horse! How like this penny-ante world to set such store by it.

*   *   *

THE DAY BEFORE the tragedy, Maggie finally turned in her slice-of-life column about Brodsky's mother's cancer divorce (names and circumstances changed, naturally), to which she had perversely appended a trigger warning alerting readers to graphic content. She'd also included a spoiler alert on the grounds, she claimed, that no one enjoyed a surprise ending anymore.

"Every day should come with trigger warnings and spoiler alerts and age restrictions! Not to mention helpful advice from the goddamn Surgeon General," she yelled, banging out of the office.

The following day her husband, together with a young woman — "the Hitchhiker" — was killed in a highway collision. There had been no warning signs.

But Brodsky was unmoved by Maggie's bereavement and responded to her copy by editing out every last syllable but one. His red pencil moved swiftly over the page, scrawling out phrases and lines and eventually whole paragraphs. In the end, only the half word *can* was left intact, briefly parting the Red Sea of "What if?" and "Why me?" and "Who knows!"

In Maggie's absence, but presumably in sympathy with her tragic loss (not to mention the news staff's commitment, equally, to freedom of the press and wasting time), the office divided into anti-censorship lobbyists and cancer advocates, neither faction realizing that they were basically on the same side. Brodsky tried to toss a dollar into the swear jar just to give himself some leeway but Miss Leonard fished it out again.

"You don't get to cuss on credit, young man," she chided.

But even without Brodsky's prepaid contribution the swear jar filled up then brimmed over. Miss Leonard clapped her hands in delight; she was relentlessly good. As good as she was homely, Shapiro's father had always maintained. She volunteered at the Mission on weekends and stuffed envelopes for World Vision in her free time. Now she turned her gleeful attention to the brimming jar, which she planned to run down to the credit union first thing on Monday morning.

"Enough money for a goat!" she sang out. "I know of a certain Kenyan subsistence farmer with limited access to grazing pasture and no clean water supply who is going to be pleasantly surprised."

ON DAYS WHEN his aged parents' custody battle got the better of him, Brodsky walked the four blocks to Shapiro's house. The neighbourhood was made up of Tyvek-covered condo conversions, thirties-era apartment blocks, and baggy old, energy-leaking houses that neither man could have afforded in today's market. The shops on the main street reflected the residents' preoccupation with yoga and nostalgic vinyl records, knitting yarn, hemp products, and fair trade coffee, a takeaway cup of which Brodsky was now staring into glumly. Today he was in mourning for his childhood and hadn't put razor blade to face for three days.

"Neither of them wants me," he complained. "They're fighting to waive custody."

The bottom half of the copy editor's face had come in nicely, but with an unexpected nod to the red-headed Cossack who must have inveigled his way into the heart of a long-ago female Brodsky. Shapiro wondered how it must feel to wear your family's shameful past emblazoned upon your lower lip, but before he could inquire, his wife came in to offer her condolences.

"No one died," Brodsky protested.

Allie gestured at his nubby ginger cheeks, pretending surprise. But her malice pre-empted her surprise and it was an unsuccessful subterfuge. After Allie had been ousted from the company of men, Brodsky pretended to comfort his friend for having married such a savage woman by wondering aloud at the quality and hue of Shapiro's future beard.

"For when you have to sit shiva for the fishwife," he explained.

The two men mooched about, drinking beer and watching SportsCenter while discussing stubble and second-day-itch and the verdant, manly bushel that represented a full week's mourning. Although he would later attempt to assuage his conscience over his wife's premature death, at least — momentarily — her death in his heart, Shapiro was intrigued by the prospect of his shiva beard. So much so that in no time at all he grew resigned to his bereavement.

But the truth was, Shapiro had more than a passing acquaintance with the rites of mourning. His mother and father had died within a year of each other. One day, almost without warning, Shapiro, an orphan, found himself standing at his father's graveside, his shirt ritually torn, his hand on a shovel, ready to throw the first clod of earth on the coffin. As Rabbi Zalman began to intone the mourner's prayer, Shapiro remembered his father in the throes of his final illness, his frail body shaking with the effort of words that had jammed in him like rotting river ice. How many words and for how long had they stopped up the flow of his love?

An editor, a reader all his life, a *poetry* lover, it was ironic that the old man had always used words so judiciously, so sparely. And it was words that deserted him in the end, as everything had already deserted him: his wife, his sight, even his faith. His blind eyes blazing at the confluence of speech and silence, the terrible fork of that unnavigable river, Shapiro's pious father raised his fists in the air and shook them. *Take that, God!*

In the days that followed, Shapiro lost his voice. It was as if his voice had pursued his father into the grave. For a month he couldn't utter a word. Rabbi Zalman visited and instructed him to come to the synagogue and say Kaddish for his father. Even a whisper was permitted in extraordinary circumstances, the rabbi explained. But Shapiro was too sick to whisper.

MARCH CAME IN like a lamb, a bleating flock chasing through the streets in soft billows of drifting snow. But by the evening, opinion and the wind had changed, the last bearing down hard and fast from the north. Nope, it was the lion all right, people agreed, hurrying through the blustery, darkening city, herding their kids into minivans and white-knuckling it home through fish-tailing skids, past cars stalled at intersections and pedestrians canted awkwardly into the wind. All night, that crazy lion bounded between city blocks, behind suburban lanes, and across parking lots, roaring his damn fool head off.

At night the mercury plunged and the sidewalks froze into jagged contour maps of their former fluencies. All over the city the distinctive sounds of falling could be heard, the sound of hipbones breaking and ribs cracking. One night the weather, too, broke with an audible crack. The next day meltwater rushed through the drains and dripped from the eaves. Overnight the world had turned to water again.

It was nowhere near Grey Cup season but the sportswriter seemed to have grown restive. Apparently abandoning his dogged allegiance to the CFL he got carried away for the first time ever, grew a playoff beard, and staked his reputation on his March Madness bracket.

"Who are we and what are our dreams?" he asked.

Shapiro found himself growing irritable at Maggie's absence. How could he be expected to run an office with no staff? One thing he didn't miss about his errant Girl Friday was the way she raided the stationery supply cupboard to keep her messy hair in place. Pencils and bulldog clips and rubber bands! But her hair's failure to be subdued was much like the rest of her, her upstream-swimming contrariety, her willingness to storm hell armed only with a bucket of water. Now and then the image of her taut, nicotine-patched stomach flashed into his mind, unbidden. The ruby merchant called, he imagined telling Allie. He wants a refund.

The river was melting, ice breaking off in rotting chunks and chugging heavily downstream. For once the muddy slide into spring was uneventful. For a couple of days the waterway was clogged with greasy, exhausted-looking ice floes. Then the current picked up and the river cleared itself. There was no flood, although talk of one overflowed newspaper columns and engulfed local radio stations for weeks. Speculation about the on-again off-again flood churned upstream from North Dakota where it could usually be guaranteed to swell the banks of the Red with American bombast. But not this year.

After some consideration, Shapiro ran Brodsky's story: "City Says No To Flood." After more consideration, he decided to punctuate the headline with an exclamation point indicative, he hoped, of the relief folks must feel at having escaped what they might not otherwise realize they were in no danger of experiencing. "City Says No To Flood!" But it was a feint in the direction of relevance and fooled no one. Every spring the readers grumbled at the this-thatness, the humdrum finger twiddle of what passed for news in this prairie city. Even Aunt Betsy had taken to sending in her own retractions.

Dear Editor,
Some foul copyist has edited the blueberries and raspberries right out of my famous Three-Berry prairie Muffins. There's nothing but bananas left. It's a tapestry!

"She means travesty," Miss Leonard translated helpfully.

Dear Editor,
Kindly replace the ground elk meat in my traditional recipe for Wild Bison Burgers. If your staff continues to play fast and loose with my sacred ancestral heritage I shall be obliged to prostitute.

"Prosecute?" ventured Miss Leonard.
What heritage? Shapiro wondered. As far as he knew, Aunt Betsy was a hearty Mennonite lass who lived near Lac du Bonnet. Of course she might also be Miss Leonard, despite that good woman's frequent protestations that she couldn't cook for toffee. Except for cheap bulk meals, she hastily amended, referring, as she so often did, to her volunteer work at a downtown soup kitchen. She certainly knew her way around poor man's soup and potato hashbrowns, she told Shapiro, but anything else was beyond her. A no-toffee deal.

Shapiro was growing increasingly impatient with disguises. It seemed that no one was who they seemed and the only emperor was the emperor of ice cream, as his father frequently declared when he ran the paper. For the first time in a long while Shapiro wondered what his old man would do in his place. He'd go out for Dairy Queen, that was for sure, but when he came back?

He decided to confront the problem head on. No more disguises!

"Who are you?" he emailed Aunt Betsy.

For three weeks she didn't reply to his query, and when she eventually did it was in the form of an obituary: her own. Aunt Betsy wrote a splendid eulogy, a paean to a much-loved wife, mother, community activist, sustainable organic farmer, philanthropist, and culinary innovator. Dearly loved, sadly missed, always remembered. Donations could be made to the Mission soup kitchen although flowers were also welcome and should be delivered to the offices of the *Riverview News* where Aunt Betsy had spent many a busy hour.

"What a liar!" Brodsky exclaimed in admiration.

The deceased was especially fond of lilies, confided the anonymous eulogist.

With her customary irresponsibility however, Aunt Betsy neglected to include information about her funeral and its accompanying memorial service. As always, the most important ingredient was missing. Nevertheless, Shapiro ran the notice in Passages and the floral tributes soon began arriving. The heavy-breathed odour of lilies made everyone feel hungover but Miss Leonard walked around with a pollen-yellow nose, looking happy.

"Aunt Betsy will certainly be missed," she murmured, lining the vases along the windowsill.

Meanwhile, the condolence cards piled up on Shapiro's desk, tipping over every time someone slammed his office door.

The most recent door slammer was none other than Maggie Binder, who had interrupted her bereavement leave in order, specifically, to come to the office and rail at her boss. She looked pale and sick, thinner than Shapiro remembered, her bright hair flaring out like a neon halo around her wan face. Her lips were cracked and dry, and the circles beneath her eyes were as dark as the nights she must have spent acquiring them. She looked like a fallen angel, not so much brought low by sin as fallen on hard times. Is this what grief looks like? Shapiro wondered. This burnt-out woman with feverish eyes? This *widow*?

He tried to imagine Allie in mourning, but imagination failed him. His wife had an air of irreducibility that grief could not embellish. She was always exactly herself: no more, no less. In contrast, Maggie looked as if she'd been boiled down to her essence. Impressed, despite himself, at her theatrical decline, Shapiro pulled out a chair, an uncharacteristic gesture that appeared to goad Maggie to fury. She hadn't come to be patted or pitied. She glared at him, tapping at his keyboard with such vitriol that the condolence cards once again toppled and this time hit the floor where they scattered in disarray. Still tapping furiously, Maggie brought up a recent email.

Dear Miss Belief,
How can I explain to my wife, Carol, that Mister Ed is not just any horse, no sirree. The wife thinks I love Mister Ed more than I love her (which I don't). It's just that Mister Ed talks sense — horse sense, ha ha — and the missus talks no sort of sense at all.
Yours truly,
Wilbur Post
P.S. They say that marriage is an institution. But who wants to belong in an institution, eh? WP
P.P.S. The above is not my own joke. Just wanted to let you

know, on account of copyright concerns. WP

P.P.P.S. Although, come to think of it, it *might* be my own joke. I've been around a while, ma'am, is the problem. WP

"Seems to love his wife," teased Shapiro. "Whoever he —"
"The Fucker!" yelled Maggie, punching the air so hard that she swivelled around on the pivot of her anger. "The fucking Fucker!"

She was using the word as a noun, an adjective, an honorific, an exclamation, an expletive, a curse, and a proper name. Clearly she believed that that goofball was all things to all people, all tenses, all times, and all that was wrong with the world. The ineffable Fucker.

Maggie didn't even bother to mouth the word. Because, frankly, fuck Miss Leonard.

SHAPIRO CAME HOME early from work to find Brodsky in his bed. He paused in the doorway, watching Brodsky and his wife, who were too absorbed to notice him. Brodsky was either sitting on a spread-out section of last month's *Riverview News* or was reading the newspaper in an unconventional manner. His wife was kneeling between the other man's feet, her fingers busy. She seemed to be massaging both halves of his face with her exquisite, extraterrestrial fingers. As Shapiro watched, silent, on the threshold, Allie tilted the copy editor's face toward the light, the extra ten percent of daylight savings time tacked onto these late afternoons like a sales tax. Brodsky's chin and cheeks were covered in foam whipped to the friable stiffness of meringue topping on a slightly wobbly pie.

Allie ran Shapiro's safety razor down Brodsky's cheekbones and began to shave off his beard. Shapiro imagined his wife's face as he had so often seen it, engrossed in concentration. Her eyes, he knew, would be half-closed, her mouth half open.

She turned when she heard Shapiro, glancing back at her husband over her shoulder. It was a Giaconda look, imprecise and disputative. Her eyes might have been secretly following him around the room. The notional curve of affect that didn't quite reach her lips might have been the beginning of a smile or its slow chiaroscuro fade. She looked her calm, catastrophic look. *Who do you think you are?*

"Whoops," Allie said. She was embarrassed at having been caught using her husband's razor on another man's whiskers. It was an unhygienic practice. Careless, unworthy of her.

WHEN THE SNOWS melted, the grass was dun-coloured and mangy as the fur of a stray dog. Spring was always a terrible month on the Prairies: belated, belaboured. Perhaps everyone resented having survived winter, coming out of hibernation only to find themselves at the intersection of Flat and Dusty again. Right back where they'd started. One day Shapiro saw Brodsky in the neighbourhood, walking his beagle and once more peering into his takeout coffee. *Oh Brodsky, why always so glum,* thought Shapiro, *so disheartened?* As ever, Brodsky gave the impression of being on the wrong end of the leash but perhaps that was just the beagle. An alpha sort of dog. Brodsky, on the other hand, was looking down-at-heel, shabby, decidedly beta. After Allie's intervention he'd started coming to work clean-shaven and sweet-smelling, spruce as a pine. Now Shapiro noted that, once again, the other man hadn't even bothered to shave.

"Hey, buddy." Shapiro tapped his copy editor jovially on the shoulder. "Who died?"

Even the beagle seemed to rear back in dismay.

Later, at Resnik's Diner, Shapiro ran his hands through his hair. "But how was I supposed to know?" he implored.

"What, an eighty-five-year-old woman?" Miss Leonard scolded. "In the middle of chemo? Going through the stress of a cancer divorce? You didn't think that the spectre of mortality was hovering over her?"

"How did she go?" Shapiro asked.

"Terrorists," Miss Leonard chortled, cracking herself up.

Resnik hovered, torn. "At least have something to eat," he coaxed. "A bite."

But Miss Leonard, looking as if biting was precisely what she had in mind, waved him away. She was unusually snappish because Brodsky, in his grief, which he claimed he had the right to express as fulsomely as possible, had flung the swear jar out of the office window.

Sixth floor, concrete sidewalk, quarters everywhere.

ANOTHER WEEK PASSED before Shapiro encountered Rabbi Zalman again. Once more he was standing on the street corner, yelling into the phone.

"*Chem glubzhe skorb', tem blizhe Bog!*"

Once more his words hung in the air, cursive and inscrutable. Once more he was snarled in the telephone cable of his tangled preoccupations. Then his words flipped from one language to another, rearranging themselves like fridge magnets. *The deeper the grief, the closer is God!* Shapiro thought he heard him cry. Was this the answer to all the questions that had been churning through Shapiro's mind for months?

What would his old man do? Who are you? Is this what grief looks like? What's cancer good for if you can't lose the extra weight? Shapiro, did you even taste my sticky toffee pudding? Who do you think you are? But how was I supposed to know? What the hell is a bushel? Who was the mysterious hitchhiker? But what is resemblance? If she still wanted him would he want her back? How can you live and have no story to tell?

As always, Shapiro was stymied, at a loss. Lost. The rabbi whirled around and Shapiro noticed that the man's beard had turned pure white. Driven snow. Fleece of the lamb. Last page of the world's last book.

Who are we and what are our dreams?

The rabbi glared, shook his fist at Shapiro. The wind parted his beard in the middle, the two halves blowing over his shoulders like a break in the weather, like a frothing stream diverted from its course, like the veil of longing that hangs between the world's riches and man's hapless desire for them. In a flash that was like resemblance glancing off a mirror, Shapiro recognized him for the third time. He was neither Rabbi Zalman nor his pal, the kidnapper. Instead he stood there roaring, an Old Testament patriarch, a reluctant messiah, thumping his fists against indignity in this fifty-cents-a-call world.

Scalded, Shapiro cried out. A single word. The word sounded like a measure of distance but it was simply a measure of relationship. *Father* — the distance between an only son and his responsibility.

Half sobbing, Shapiro covered his face with his hands and began to rock back and forth, chanting his prayers for the dead.

SPRING

THREE

THE MISSION

DOWN AT THE Mission folks were idling on the sidewalk, smoking and waiting for the metal shutters at the kitchen counter to clatter up so that lunch could finally be served. *Folks* was what Miss Leonard called the men spinning on their worn-down rubber heels in the weak iodine sunlight of early spring. Miss Leonard volunteered all her free time to the Mission and consequently had a proprietary attitude. She called everyone *folks*: the old-timers sipping coffee and playing checkers in the dining room, the born-agains who came for breakfast and stayed for Christ, the teenage boys with their wire-hanger shoulder blades angling through their "Born to Rock" T-shirts.

Sometimes a woman would sidle or shuffle or strut into the Mission, her gait keeping pace with her disposition, her mood the coin tosses of bravado or despondency that saw her through her days. Singly, or in spindly little groups, the women would wait in line at the lunch counter, their hunger for food or companionship rendering them bold. And they were *folks*, too.

Five or six men were idling outside the Mission when Annunciata arrived, a thin brown girl clutching at the balloon-string of her occasional buoyancy. The snow had finally rotted away, winter rushing through the gutters and gurgling down the drains. A couple of the men were smoking, coaxing a last puff from their burnt-down cigarettes, holding each breath until their eyes bulged. The Mission opened its doors to the city's jobless, the street people, the panhandlers, the squeegee kids, the homeless ones, although once, when she'd wondered aloud at these poor doorstep ghosts, Senior Admin had corrected her.

"We don't say *homeless* here, Anna. We say *persons experiencing homelessness.*" Senior Admin was a stocky girl with a permanent furrow above her brow. A little asterisk in the arid homelessness of her face, although what it bore witness to, Annunciata couldn't exactly say.

Experiencing homelessness was meant to convey the temporariness of the condition, the vagrant hope that poverty was merely a refugee camp on the way to permanent citizenship. A waystation.

"They're just folks who've fallen between the cracks," Miss Leonard would say.

"Or gotten hooked on crack," Lolleen Magary would add, always the thorn in Miss Leonard's corseted side.

"Morning, Isaac, Donny, Bodo," Annunciata called, stepping through the men who obligingly allowed her passage, sucking back their smoke and paddling at the air in front of them. "Morning, Nachos and Mr. Wilson." Weary of being told what not to call the Mission people, Annunciata had decided to learn as many names as she could and use them accordingly.

"Mornin', Mr.... Um." His name wasn't really Um but the old fellow had been uncooperative when asked, and Mr. Um was the best she could do. Annunciata thought that perhaps he was secretive about his name because it was the only thing he owned. On the other hand, maybe he'd just forgotten it — drink did that to a fellow, and crack, and the dog-eyed loneliness that eats its own paws. Rain or shine he always wore an oversize duffle coat. His eyes were yellowish and his few remaining teeth were grey. He never smiled and seldom spoke, but when he was hungry he rapped out "a shave and a shoeshine" on the metal shutters of the kitchen window, and when he was feeling sprightly he did a soft shoe shuffle in the dust.

Annunciata stopped to watch and applaud. "Bravo!" Mr. Um made jazz hands and blew her a kiss. He had a heavy, stumbling gait but a perfect pitch for imaginary music. "Nice weather we're having," she replied.

An early thaw had cruelly widened the distance between the end of the snows and the beginning of the rains, and the city was a horrifying dust bowl of migraine-inducing winds, mould-fed allergies, grass as mangy as a sick dog, and the return of all the repressed objects that always floated to the surface after the snow had melted. Fat sausage links of dog shit, predominantly. Water-heavy mittens and filthy socks rummaged from the bottom of winter's grab-bag of a closet. Styrofoam takeout containers, plastic beer can rings, and Big Gulp cups drooling the thawing sludge of last year's neon-coloured Slurpees into the earth. Cigarette butts and broken glass and bank statements peering through the windows of their red-stickered envelopes. Hello, sunshine! Good morning, spring!

Whenever she lied — even social lies, even weather lies — Annunciata felt terrible. Now she stood with her head bowed, dabbling her toe in the dust. She was nothing, less than nothing.

She was gum on the shoe of the world's smallest flea. But Mr. Um was unfazed.

"Pizza, chicken," he confided. Something like that. At least she thought he said "pizza," and then some other kind of food. Possibly chicken. It was going on ten and she had to hustle to report for kitchen duty. So did.

"Heavens, child, I'm glad we're not waiting for you to make any big announcements," cried Miss Leonard when Annunciata came into the kitchen, tying an apron around her waist and tucking her hair beneath a hairnet. She meant the miracle of the Lord's birth which, if she was an angel, Annunciata would have been in charge of. Sometimes Miss Leonard said, "Hallelujah, young lady!" and sometimes just, "Hurry, you!" but it was always to do with Annunciata being half a minute behind-hand and two thousand years too late.

It was a pity, this inclination to tardiness, because Annunciata had so much to do on any given day and knew from experience that the first five minutes of being late could never be retrieved. In fact those five minutes seemed to replicate, adding themselves to every errand, every chore, every drudgery so that by the end of the day she was likely a whole week behindhand.

"Any faster and you'll catch up to yesterday," her papa would remark when she got home.

What she had to do today after her shift at the Mission was take the bus to her mama's cleaning job because Imee had woken up too dreary to get out of bed.

"Don't worry about it," Mrs. Binder had said over the phone. "In fact, since I'm home these days, you can tell Imee to rest up for the next month." Mrs. Binder was only being kind, Annunciata knew, or thought she was. But they couldn't

afford to lose her mama's cleaning job money. Imee had worked
for the Binder family since the boys were babies and her name
was Imelda, she liked to say. It was the oldest boy who'd begun
calling her mother Imee. Although Imee would never admit
it, Annunciata thought that her mother had loved those two
baby boys. Well, why not? Just because you love two little
boys, not your own, doesn't mean you don't have room in your
heart for the two little girls you started with. There was room
in Imee's heart for all the children in those days: boys, girls,
sons, daughters, her own and another woman's.

The boys grew up but Imee still went round to clean for Mrs.
Binder, who loved Imee and didn't want to lose her. Perhaps she
felt sorry for her or perhaps it was only that she, Mrs. B, as Imee
called her, was a slovenly housekeeper. Imee had a terrible time
trying to keep the house in the Heights clean, but Mrs. Binder
was a good employer. She was both generous and careless, occasionally paying Imee for the same day twice. Imee called these
windfalls her two-timing money but, to her shame, Annunciata
always deposited the cheques in her mother's savings account
even though she knew it was wrong and that she was taking
advantage of a grieving woman and would likely end up in hell.

"Needs must," Miss Leonard would often say, adding water
to the lunch soup. Annunciata tried to think of the family
income as a pot of this soup, so thin and watery to begin with
that the addition of a couple of extra ladles of whatever was
going would hardly make a difference.

The kitchen was at a rolling boil by now, the regulars at
their stations, and Chef Charlie sweating through his ban-
danna as he listened to Christian rock on the radio he always
kept beside him on the counter. Why Chef Charlie listened
to Christian rock was a story in itself but one that could

be boiled down to his claim that it inspired him not to sin because the music of the saved was so goddamn awful. Long story short, Chef Charlie could still count the years of his sobriety on one hand and, as he told Annunciata, he didn't want to take any chances by letting his *other* hand, together with the *rest* of his body (his words), settle into the hard-luck rhythms he truly loved. If Christian rock was a poor substitute for the blues, well the Mission folk knew all about poor substitutes, having made their peace with margarine and powdered milk and instant mash.

"Am I right, Anna Banana?"

"Darn tootin', Chef Charlie."

He was the only one who could make her joke around, coax her small face to shine.

"Which way, which way, which way is home?" he was singing now, sounding distracted as he rifled through the cutlery drawer.

Annunciata began organizing the volunteers into an efficient serving line. Most were old hands, coming in early to chop vegetables for soup, toast bread cubes for croutons, and mix up batches of red sauce for poor man's lasagna or lazy halloumi. The adjectives were misleading, though. In Annunciata's opinion the lasagna was fit for a king and the halloumi was a time-consuming endeavour requiring nimble fingers and a tightrope disposition. Cabbage was a demanding mistress, the blanching and cooling and rolling of it. But there it was again: "poor man" and "lazy." Angel for cake and devil for eggs, as her mama said. All the lying words made Annunciata feel hot and uneasy as if she were, once again, zipped into that ill-fitting parka, that immigrant coat of lapsed languages.

"English, she is a bitch," her papa always said. It was one of the few phrases he'd learned in twenty years of reluctant citizenship, and the others didn't bear repeating.

Beyond the step-and-fetch-it of her shopping, cleaning, cooking life, Annunciata's mama hadn't even bothered to make the bitch's acquaintance, although she was charmed by the bizzaro jauntiness of idioms, every last one of which, she maintained, meant the opposite of what it set out to prove. "Because pie isn't easy, eh, and mice aren't quiet and babies — ho, babies never sleep."

Her mama knew all about babies, that was for damn sure. Because babies were what Annunciata and her sister, Maria, had been when they arrived in this country. They had been "babes in arms." Their parents had carried them off the plane in a winter blizzard, the whole flapping prairie as blank as the fluttering pages of this new country. Her parents still spoke to one another in Tagalog, their looted mother tongue. It had become a language of curses and lullabies, of blessings and terrible haphazard losses. And although Annunciata and her sister had once bobbed about in the amniotic fluid of this language, they had made it a matter of some urgency to claim ignorance and, by elementary school, had achieved it.

Annunciata was still messing about with the volunteers because, along with the regulars who knew the score, there were the usual shiny do-gooders who had to be ushered into place, reminded to wear hairnets and to wash, wash, wash their hands. Herding cats!

"Our friends in Christ," was what Chef Charlie called the Mission people who gathered behind the metal shutters that divided the kitchen from the dining hall. Men and women were already lining up at the food window, two and three deep, crowding into the Mission or hurrying down the street, bandy-legged in their haste.

"No hair in the soup for our friends in Christ," Chef Charlie yelled, slamming an enormous jar of sweet pickle and garlic onto the counter. Most of the friends in Christ loved sweet pickle to distraction. They stirred it into their hambone pea soup, they spread it thickly onto their Co-op buns, and, God help them, they arranged clumps of sweet pickle like a corsage upon the pastel frosting of the slab cake that Miss Leonard was, even now, apportioning. The cake, along with a platter of butter tarts and a plate of iced fancies, had been donated by Glory Funeral Home. When a family overestimated the number of their mourners or the appetites of their guests, the Mission was the happy beneficiary and Reverend Tremblay, bless his heart, was diligent about delivering the funeral baked meats.

Miss Leonard was humming like a generator as she cut the cake into precise squares. Geometry was her sanctuary when it came to the Levitican abomination of different foods piled on the same plate: colours and odours and courses all jumbled together and devil take the hindermost. Annunciata herself hated the way that the bowl of soup inevitably slopped over, soaking dinner rolls and turning dessert squares into vegetable glop. But what could they do? Every weekend the Mission welcomed hundreds of customers but there were only so many dinner plates to go around.

"It all ends up in the same place anyways," Lolleen Magary said. Lolleen had several bones to pick with Miss Leonard: there were the ones in her hambone soup, and then there was the soup itself, which Miss Leonard had boasted was a family recipe. An heirloom, no less. But Lolleen insisted that she'd seen just such a recipe reproduced in the cookery column of a local paper — Aunt Betsy's Country Recipes — had Miss Leonard heard of it? This was a sneaky, underhanded jab since surely Lolleen Magary knew that Miss Leonard worked at the *Riverview News* and had for nigh on thirty years. Thirty years was longer than most folks' marriages, Miss Leonard often said, Lolleen's bitterly acrimonious divorce after thirty-two years notwithstanding.

Notwithstanding what? Lolleen snapped. And by the way *had* Miss Leonard heard of that cookery column she was talking about? No, Miss Leonard replied serenely, she had not.

Truth be known, Lolleen Magary had more than a couple of bones to pick with her supervisor. A whole turkey carcass of bones, more likely, an articulated dinosaur skeleton of bones. But she contented herself with returning to her initial point: "It all ends up in the same place anyways," she said. "And it looks even worse when it gets there." This was true if a little vulgar, but Lolleen wasn't allowed to say "Beggars can't be choosers" anymore.

"Customers" was what Lolleen now called the men and women on the other side of the metal shutter.

"Customers, eh?" Miss Leonard scoffed. "So they have the right to complain and demand better service and threaten to take their business elsewhere, do they?"

"Couldn't have said it better myself," said Lolleen, who clearly believed she could have said it better than Miss Leonard, could indeed say anything better than Miss Leonard, who had seniority and was her sworn enemy and also a dried-up old prune that no amount of soaking could plump up. The truth was that everyone complained, everyone demanded better service. Giving stuff away — food, clothing, the proverbial fish — was the shortest route to whatever the opposite of gratitude was, which in Lolleen's book included a whole chapter on complaints. Teach a man to fish and he'll only develop a hankering for rump steak, she was fond of observing.

In this cynical observation, Lolleen was not far wrong. It was the Saturday before Easter Sunday and the kitchen had been barraged all week with anxious questions regarding Sunday's lunch menu. Chicken or ham? What kind of soup? More than a single helping of dessert for once? The building across the street, vacant for some time after Sturgeon Investments folded, had recently been bought by the Salvation Army, which had moved in and set up shop. The rumour was that they were going to serve turkey on Easter Sunday. Turkey and all the trimmings! It was an unseasonal offering but undoubtedly a competitive one.

"Whoa, girls!" said Chef Charlie, as always a day late and a dollar short.

"Girls, are we?" said Lolleen. "Well, I guess everyone's got to be called something. They're customers and we're girls and you're a no-good line cook." She knew she shouldn't bait Chef Charlie but Lolleen was snappish and sour at being called a girl by a man with no sense of flirtation.

"Heh, I'm a proud indigenous warrior," Chef Charlie said. He brandished his chopping knife to demonstrate his fierceness and winked at Annunciata. *Chin up, Anna Banana!* Someone on the other side banged at the rolled metal shutters and a trip line of laughter caught and rippled through the dining hall.

"Our friends in Christ are hungry," Annunciata said as loudly as she could. The odd little phrase was a gift to Chef Charlie, whose feelings, she feared, had been hurt.

"Whoops! Let's not keep our friends in Christ waiting, people," said Chef Charlie, turning off his radio and looking Annunciata in the eye, although this time he neither smiled nor winked. Oh, did he think that she, too, was baiting him? What was the matter with everybody? But even as her arm-pits prickled with mortification, she knew that nothing had changed. Every Saturday it was the same — Miss Leonard and Lolleen Magary scrapping daintily, Chef Charlie throwing his sharp-edged words this way and that, although he always managed to sheath them in the butcher's block of his sturdy good humour.

As for the volunteers, they remained oblivious to everything but the satisfying slow burn of their charitable fellowship. There was a tongue-in-groove neatness to the way their selflessness meshed with their self-regard. They had come to do good and were consequently obliged by their own goodness.

"How are the March sisters?" Lolleen asked Annunciata. She always called them the March sisters, as if they were one entity and not two separate women: Lolleen's good friend, Rose March, and Rose's elderly sister, June. Rose worked long hours as a receptionist at Thiessen's Tiling and Flooring, and her sister was sickly and reclusive. Since the Bautista family lived in the same neighbourhood as the sisters, Lolleen frequently asked Annunciata how they were, by which she meant to inquire: Have you looked in on June March recently?

Everyone called her Aunt June, even Annunciata who had grown fond of the old woman, enough that she no longer begrudged the unpaid services she performed: making tea and keeping Aunt June company as she drank it, dusting the old woman's room and turning her mattress. If Lolleen had ever had a mind to pay Annunciata for her trouble, she had long ago misplaced it — the thought and not the mind — but Aunt June always pressed a little something into Annunciata's hand when she left. Not money, unfortunately, she was poor as a church mouse (another Miss Leonard-ism), but a piece of lace she'd been hoarding, or one of her late mother's famous dinner bracelets. The bracelets were cheap and gaudy, only costume jewelry, but Annunciata presented them to her own mother in the hope that they would cheer her up.

But before Annunciata could reply to Lolleen's pleasantry, Miss Leonard rapped on the counter to bring the kitchen workers to order. Somehow she contrived to rap in a leisurely manner so as to indicate that she would not be influenced by Chef Charlie in the painstaking molasses drip of her duty. As if pulled by strings, the volunteers jerked into place at their stations on the line, Lolleen behind the thirty-litre vat of hambone pea soup, her ladle at the ready. The soup was lukewarm but hearty looking, with fingernail-size chunks of meat bobbing in it and croutons piled on top. In addition to the soup, every plate got two pieces of garlic bread, a spoonful of coleslaw, an apple or a banana, a square of iced slab cake, and a helping of sweet pickles bleeding their bright yellow liquor.

"A word from our sponsor," said Chef Charlie.

Miss Leonard glared at him. "For what we are about to receive, Lord Jesus Christ, and for what we have already received from your bounty. For the strength to help others and the strength to request help when help is needed. For the compassion that we give and the compassion that we seek…"

She was well and truly launched on her breezy sea of scruples, and wouldn't be back for hours.

"Seems Miss Leonard's been kissing the blarney stone again," Chef Charlie would often say. But fortunately, he once explained to Annunciata, her chattiness only affected her during prayers.

Lolleen, however, was of the opinion that Miss Leonard had been bitten by snakes and that the outcome was grave and inconclusive.

"That's tongue speak," she sniffed, whenever Miss Leonard

got going. "I've got no patience with a snake-bitten fool who lets her tongue run away with her."

Annunciata couldn't help it — the image of snakes like flickering tongues bearing Miss Leonard away beset her. She put her hand in front of her eyes so that she could open them and banish the terrible picture. Surreptitiously, she watched Chef Charlie's expression of implacable, tolerant skepticism. He had his chin sunk deep into his chest and his eyelids closed, just so. These eyelids were like perfectly composed drapes over the windows to his soul. They neither wrinkled with effort nor fluttered with impatience, both *effort* and *impatience* being words that sprang to Annunciata's mind at this moment, her body constrained by Miss Leonard's dire God while her thoughts raced on.

Sometimes Miss Leonard would give minute thanks for all that had been bestowed and sometimes she would give the Lord a gentle nudge in the direction of the pantry. Pancake mix was a blessing, she would point out, but one of which they were generally in short supply, and milk — even powdered milk — was always a welcome contribution. Mostly, though, she lost herself in the lulling give and take of her own splendid gratitude.

"For what we may fashion with our hands and what we may fashion with our hearts. For the love that we give and the love we are granted," said Miss Leonard. "For —"

"For Christ's sake," yelled Lolleen, riled beyond bearing, but Chef Charlie, without opening his eyes, intoned "*A—men!*" breaking the single word in two and transforming Lolleen's runaway curse into the end of a prayer.

"Praise the Lord and pass the ketchup," Chef Charlie said just for good measure, and the volunteers broke ranks, chuckling. Lolleen cranked open the metal shutters and called

"Grub's up, folks," her thistly disquiet when forced into close quarters with the Lord and Miss Leonard always coming out as this canteen boisterousness.

For an hour and a half a steady stream of men and women passed by the kitchen to hand in their meal tickets and pick up their lunch plates. And for the next half hour the stream still flowed but it was more on the tributary end of the spectrum. After that it was trickle, trickle, halt.

Miss Leonard took up her position at the head of the serving line, inspecting each plate that came her way and clicking her tongue against the roof of her mouth. "*Tcha*, too much soup slopping about again, Lolleen. Remember, one ladle is a delight, two is a deluge." Often she would comment on coleslaw skimp or sweet pickle distribution but her bone of contention was, and always had been, the soup — too much, too little, never just right.

"Sorry, Goldilocks," muttered Lolleen. *Hey little princess, hey little pea,* she'd sometimes sing in her hoarse, oddly tuneful voice. *Hey little princess, hey little pea. Come down from your tower and dance with me.* Occasionally Miss Leonard would send a lunch plate back for correction but mostly she was content to rattle about in her easeful disgruntlement.

The thing about Miss Leonard, though, was that she was damn good at hospitality. The kitchen staff — from Chef Charlie to Annunciata, his *sous*, and even Hermano, the dishwasher — all agreed that this was so. She specialized in making folks feel welcome. For all her curmudgeonly this-and-that, she overflowed with the milk of human kindness, and her smile was genuine.

"Yeah, genuine leather!" her sister Maria would have joked, regarding the smile. She'd probably also have pointed out how quickly milk curdled when it was left out too long. But that was Maria for you, and it had nothing at all to do with Miss Leonard, who spent her weekends at the Mission, who remembered names and stories, who asked after people's job prospects, their housing situations, even their children, which was a fraught subject since most of the children were in foster care, or missing, or otherwise destroyed by their parents' love, which around these parts often took the form of something crooked and ingrown.

"You can't love if you've never been loved," Miss Leonard explained.

"Why not? *You* seem to love them," Lolleen muttered, because even she had to acknowledge that if Miss Leonard loved anyone it was these lost creatures.

But Miss Leonard just smiled at Lolleen, taking her sarcasm as the compliment that it was surely never meant to be.

In the Mission's Mission Statement, ha ha, talk of children was discouraged, along with discussions about sex and drugs. Blasphemy, too, was strictly verboten. Only religion was encouraged as a topic of endless fascination. Yet strangely, the friends in Christ were eager to talk about their children. Annunciata was always surprised at their eagerness, as if the stars had stopped in their lonely orbits and consented to discuss astronomy. Some folks carried dog-eared photographs — overexposed and blurry — of kids with gap-toothed smiles and wary eyes. But most had nothing to display except memories and stories, forgetfulness, blunder and prevarication, all mixed together like cheap rum and Coke.

"Good afternoon, Mr. Johnson," Miss Leonard addressed an older gentleman with arthritic hands. "Can I tempt you with some hambone soup?"

"Certainly, Miss Leonard. The hambone is my favourite of all possible bones."

"And how do you find yourself, these days, Mr. Johnson?"

"Creaky in the joints, Miss L. Cold all the time. Used to take a couple of hours to warm up in the morning, now it takes a couple of months. But I reckon I'll be thawed out by July so how's about I meet you back here and take you dancing?"

Miss Leonard smiled like a girl and although the years did not fall away, they teetered somewhat, and her eyes — which had never grown old though the rest of her had thickened in some places and thinned in others and generally crinkled all over — shone out like good deeds in a weary world. Blue eyes too, the most pursuant kind. She tapped Mr. Johnson briskly on the wrist and he knocked a couple of fingers against his head, a ceremonial doff of the hat brim in the absence of a hat.

"You look nice today, Marleen. Wearing makeup and a new scarf, I see," Miss Leonard greeted a newcomer.

"Betty-Ann here did my makeup. Hides my big black eye." Marleen giggled as if the black eye and what had caused it were nothing, a trifle, an excuse for dress-up, although she took the trouble to complain, on behalf of her friend, about the coleslaw.

"Repeats on me," Betty-Ann explained.

Cabbage was a problem, however you sliced it, ha ha. Many of the friends in Christ were dubious about coleslaw in general, cabbage in particular. Gas was the main bugaboo but there were reports of other gastrointestinal tribulations: slow-downs and accelerations and uncomfortable bloating. One fellow reported that whenever he cabbaged-up, he disgraced himself.

"You need regularity when you live on the street," he explained. "No surprises."

"Can't do anything about the coleslaw today, Betty-Ann.

But I'll alert catering," Miss Leonard promised, dashing a note to herself on her pad. She always kept paper handy and doodled away for all the world as if she were taking notes and making resolutions and drafting proposals. Under cover of refilling the sweet pickle jar, Annunciata peeked at what Miss Leonard had scribbled. *Coleslaw, slow caw, low saw, sole claw*, in her full, curvy handwriting with its fat top and bottom loops like so many balloon animals bobbing across the page.

"That's all right, Miss Leonard. I know you got a lot on your plate, ha ha." Marleen was still laughing when a woman came up and grabbed her by the arm. Annunciata had never seen the woman before and she didn't look hungry. Or rather she looked famished — and tired and sick — but Annunciata knew that no lunch plate in the world, no hambone pea soup, no garlic bread, no helping of slab cake and sweet pickle relish, was going to feed her. And this was unusual because, despite what people said about the deep-rooted problems of urban poverty, and the Band-Aids of charity and good intentions, and the giving away of fish instead of handing out those damn fishing rods, Annunciata had seen what a cup of coffee and a bite of food could do to keep heart and mind and spirit nesting together like dishes in a kitchen cupboard.

No, *uh*-uh. That woman was not going anywhere until whatever had been taken from her was restored.

It was a child, of course. It was a daughter or a sister or a niece. The woman showed Marleen and Betty-Ann a photograph and when they shook their heads she began making the rounds of those diners who'd lingered, sipping at the four-hour coffee and sopping their fingers around the rims of their plates. Annunciata turned away and did not look up again for a long time. She helped Hermano with the lunch dishes, she sluiced the counters down with ammonia and the grill with vinegar. She promised Lolleen that she'd look in on June March before she went home that night, and then she poured a bleach solution into a bucket and began to mop the floor. She did not want to think about missing girls, and for the next hour, at least, did not.

"Take a break, child." Miss Leonard was always jaunty after lunch. She had fed the hungry and welcomed the stranger to her table. She had harried the volunteers and riled up Lolleen Magary. What more could she accomplish in a day?

Annunciata untied her apron and slipped out the back door. She seldom felt like eating after she'd helped cook and serve lunch, but Chef Charlie had fixed her a ham and sweet pickle sandwich, so she sat down on the back steps and ate it. Tried to, anyway. She'd only achieved a bite or two when Mr. Um came stumbling over, his tread heavy as if he were wearing horseshoes. He held out his hand so she gave him the rest of her sandwich.

"Pizza Chicken," he said.

"Yummy," Annunciata replied.

But Mr. Um would not be appeased. He came closer. "Pizza Chicken Dentist," he insisted, giving each word equal weight. "Pizza Chicken Dentist," he said again, as if it were the answer to a riddle. He did a sort of Bob Fosse shimmy in the dusty street, popping his imaginary top hat and sticking out his bottom as if he were wearing tails.

She put her head in her hands and closed her eyes. She sensed Mr. Um and his conundrums go spinning off in the wind, his hooves sparking at the iron rim of the world. Tomorrow was Easter, blood of the —. Flesh of the —. On her way to catch the bus this morning she'd passed advertisements in store windows proclaiming the yeast of the rising, unsaved world. "Spring is sprung / The bread is risen," in pastry font cursive at Heartstone Bakery, and Mr. Lube had a banner that read: "Spring is sprung, the grass is riz / I wonder how your sparkplugs is?" Then there were the neighbourhood window displays of chocolate bunnies and chickens, the arrangements of silk daffodils and plastic tulips in their fake grass tubs. Real flowers wouldn't take root until next month, at least. Not in this city.

The United Church near the hospital had a sign display that asked, "Got God?" and the one outside First Baptist read, "Conversational English for New Immigrants!" Only Holy Faith Evangelical seemed to display a sober attitude to resurrection. The white signboard with its unevenly spaced black lettering was forthright and joyous: "He is coming!" Sometime in the miracle-ready night before Easter Sunday, the letters would shuffle around so that when the congregation arrived at church that morning, shivering in their early spring frocks and lightweight suits, they'd be greeted with the Good News: "He is risen!"

It never failed. One day rising, the next risen. He was a loaf set to prove in the ovens of the faithful.

"Risen?" asked her mama, the first time she saw the Sunday sign.

"It means erect, Mama," Maria told her. "Today our Lord is erect." She threw back her head and laughed at her mother's puzzlement. "English she is a bitch," she giggled, mimicking her papa's formula for assimilation and spite. None of the Bautistas attended church anymore. It was just one more empty building with a sign beside it.

The woman with the missing child was coming down the street, carrying a stack of posters. Annunciata watched as the woman struggled to affix one of her posters to a hydro pole. That's not going to work, she wanted to tell her. Come the weather, any weather, and the paper would turn to paste in the rain, or fly away like a wish on the wind. The last of three wishes. One, come home my sister. Two, never get lost again. Three, down comes the rain.

What Annunciata and her mother found was that a staple gun was essential. You stapled the Missing Girl poster to trees and fences and telephone poles all the way up and down the street. And when the street was full, you moved on to the neighbourhood (the city, the world, the universe, oh my heart). If coloured paper made you feel better then use it, by all means. You centred your pink or green or yellow poster then, with four quick hitching clicks, you secured the corners, being particular not to run the bottom staples through the Missing Girl's throat. In the beginning, her hands shaking, Annunciata had done just that.

The woman was limping along the street, stopping at hydro poles and community bulletin boards, even the odd stunted tree that remained, fenced in its little black cage. As she walked she fumbled at her stack of posters and her roll of sticking tape. Once or twice a door opened suddenly and someone — a storekeeper or office worker — would call out to the woman. Then they'd catch sight of the poster and stop. Shrug sometimes, sometimes wave a hand as if to say, *Well, if you have to,* or *Hurry up, lady,* or *I hope you find her, honey.*

Annunciata went to help — she was good at centring the posters, holding steady.

"Go away, white girl," yelled the woman. Then she took a closer look at Annunciata and corrected herself wearily, "Fuck off, you filthy Pino."

Some things still hurt, like remembering the staple glinting through her sister's throat, or seeing other posters of Missing Girls with their once-and-before smiles that no never-after could erase. All the Missing Girls were the same girl but every girl was different. Meanwhile, the family waited as April melted into an impossible river that flowed in both directions at once. He is coming! He is risen!

What could halt the river? For her father, nothing, though he tried to dissolve his pain in various solvents. For her mother, nothing — she slipped into the soft noose of her sorrow and hung there. Yet Annunciata never stopped looking for her sister. *Maria, Maria!* But where could you find a young woman — a small-boned, soft-skinned, almost girl — in the immensity of the city, its concrete factories and railway bridges and smoke stacks, its vast post-industrial fields. She was never where you looked and Annunciata had still not come upon *the last place she would have thought to look*, that hidden pocket in the world's lining where you could always find your bus pass and your change purse.

The police lacked conviction and after a while they stopped coming. Now her sister was a cold case.

"Cold means dead," sobbed her mama. "Dead and buried in the snow."

"Not the case, at all, ha ha," said her papa, drunk.

Cold wasn't dead, explained Mrs. Binder. It was just a waiting place. Not as good as warm, admittedly, but soon Maria would come in out of the cold. Mrs. Binder was angry, though, and she promised the Bautistas that she would agitate the police until they found Maria.

There was talk in those days of many young girls who had disappeared. But where did they go? People began to avoid the river. They would not walk past or stare too long into its muddy brown waters. The river had become a place of misfortune, but Maria wasn't found in the river.

What did it matter where she was found? One day, two officers came to the door, their hats in their hands. I'm sorry, they said. Her papa went to the city morgue to say, Yes, this one is mine.

Cold was cold. Case closed.

After the funeral, Annunciata's parents continued to decline in their separate but interesting ways. Annunciata had to look after them; what else could she do? She dropped out of college where she was learning to be a business manager and went to work at the Mission where chores were as infinite as the mercy of the Lord, as Miss Leonard would often say. One meal was scarcely over before preparation for the next began. In Annunciata's dreams the homeless marched toward her, their mouths wide open.

Blue with cold.

A door banged behind her and Miss Leonard staggered out of the kitchen, dragging a garbage bag in each hand. "Go home, Angel. You've got a lot to do tomorrow." She meant announcing the resurrection of the Lord, ha ha, but also Easter dinner which was going to be chicken *and* ham. Surprise!

Annunciata buttoned herself into her coat and walked to the bus stop. She stood there for some time, staring blankly across the road at the new downtown gym, reading the words "Mr. Big Guy" over and over until they made no sense. The gym had a basement boxing ring, people at the Mission said. But when the 99 bus finally arrived she remembered that she'd promised to collect Imee's housekeeping money from Mrs. Binder and that she must find the bus that would take her to the Heights instead. The words to a song — *Which way, which way, which way is home?* — ran through her head although she couldn't remember where she'd heard it.

On her way finally, she stared out of the bus window, past the pale imprint of her doppelganger face with its hollow cheeks and eyes, out into the city. On Main, the dusty storefronts flashed by, one after the other, desultory and grimy with the dregs at the bottom of winter, that old cracked mug. The boarded-up Railway Hotel, the methadone clinic, the Healing Circle Collective. "Come In We're Open For Business," entreated North Main Denture Centre although, unlike the grinning dentures in the window, the office had been closed for years.

The bus stopped outside the Neon Factory to let off a couple of passengers. In the wide storefront windows Annunciata watched the neon signs pulse on and off: "Pizza" "Chicken" "Dentist." Each word singly and in turn, then all together, like the answer to a riddle. Like a lost language she'd once understood and might again some day.

FOUR

RIDGEHAVEN HIGH

EVERYONE KEPT ASKING Lazar how his mother was. A lot of people and a lot of asking and a lot of shaking their sorry heads when he said, Not too good, I'm afraid, Hariharan — or Bernie or Grandma Minnie. One day Mrs. Boychuk, his homeroom teacher said, "Um Lazar, how is your um mother doing um nowadays?" Her voice was phlegmy, as if she'd accidentally swallowed a raw egg and was too polite to hawk up the yolk. That was just her voice though — she always sounded like she was gargling eggs. Lazar stared her down, high noon style.

"Good, Mrs. Boychuk, she's doing good, thank you for asking," Lazar said because:

a) Politeness counts (Maggie a.k.a. Lazar's mom).
b) Don't let the bastards grind you down (Max a.k.a. Lazar's dad).
c) Irony (Lazar, what he really thinks).
d) Blink, blink (Sams a.k.a. Lazar's brother).

Maggie was the least polite person Lazar knew, and Max was possibly the most ground down, and Sams had his own problems, so Lazar was inclined to go with (c) Irony, etcetera. He narrowed his bounty-hunter eyes and stared down Mrs. Boychuk just so they were both clear that this stupid junior high corridor lined with rackety, swamp-green lockers was the wasteland at the end of the world where one day he was going to kill her. Snap her chicken neck, just like that. Cut out her heart and pick his teeth with her bones.

"She's doing good, Mrs. Boychuk," he repeated.

"*Well*, dear. She's doing *well*," said Mrs. Boychuk, as if the only thing that bothered her about the whole business of Lazar's dead father and his zombie queen mother was the scandal of Lazar's bad grammar. Everyone knew about the Binders, everyone in the whole city, probably the world. Just don't get him started on the kids at Raging Hormones High.

"Sorry, yeah," he yelled at her rapidly retreating but still prominent backside. "She's doing *well*. Really really really *well*." Visibility-wise Mrs. Boychuk's butt was like the Himalayas. You could be standing on the moon and thinking, holy moly, what *is* that extraordinary natural outcrop? Lazar didn't even want to think about what was going on beneath the polyester rub of her triple XL tent dress. Chafing, probably. Stinkiness, for sure.

Mrs. Boychuk was getting divorced, was the rumour, and Lazar envied Mr. Boychuk, whoever he was. The other thing he knew about Mrs. Boychuk was that she had a son called Frankie. Frankie was only eleven years old but he was already a soccer star, according to his mother. The king of Grover Park Fields FC she always told her class. Lazar used to love soccer when he was young but, despite the unknown Frankie's much-vaunted athleticism, he most certainly did not envy that kid.

For one thing he'd probably end up at Ridgehaven High one day, where his mother would point him out to all her students.

"Have you met my son, Frankie? He's the king of Grover Park Fields, you know."

Ridgehaven High (Go Ravens!) was one of those high schools that parents sent their kids to because they were "lucky enough to live in the catchment area." The catchment area was the Heights and the school district was South Central, and the luck was because nobody had been stabbed on school property or died during grad, in recent memory, and nobody'd been busted with anything more dangerous than weed in the last twelve months. Most of that was true if you didn't count the crosswalk outside the gym as school property (stabbing incident), or the grad after-party of 2011 (permanent brain damage due to DUI). The part about drug busts was true, though. Ever since Gary Woo set up shop in his Camaro outside the 7-Eleven on Academy, none of the kids needed to exert themselves to procure speed or opioids (Gary could hook you up with weed too, but he was having difficulty with quality control).

Lazar's theory was that the school retained a certain retro glamour on account of this kid who'd grown up to be a famous rock star after spending one term as a mediocre student at R. H. High, before his parents moved to the States. Not right after, obviously. His parents moved first and lots of stuff must have happened in between, but that was the rumour, anyway. None of the kids listened to Neil Young, for God's sake, and most of them didn't even know who he was, but every time "Harvest Moon" came on the car radio, you knew that some dad somewhere was congratulating himself on being smart enough to live in the right catchment area.

Anyway, back to Mrs. Boychuk. The thing about Mrs. Boychuk — who always signed her full name where most teachers just scribbled their initials (it killed Lazar) — the thing about Mrs. Catherine Boychuk, was that she wasn't the kind of teacher who let a kid goof about, or mouth off, or fool around all on his own. No, instead she jumped right into the idiot pool with him. So next thing, of course, was that Lazar ended up in Mr. Bubel's room for a chat, young man, nothing serious. Mr. Bubel was his real name, if you can believe it, but they were supposed to call him Mr. B, for obvious reasons. Actually, nobody but the grade sevens cared about his dumb name anymore because:

a) Some things are too easy.
b) Some things are too damn easy.
c) How many jokes can you make about some poor dude called Bubel?
d) Plenty.

An alternate way of expressing this equation would be:

a) b but not d
b) c if b
c) all of the above
d) except a

Lazar went with (c) and (d), an apparent contradiction that proved the exceptional rule. In other words: Mr. B was the school guidance councillor and sex ed teacher. He was also in charge of high school soccer (where they were supposed to call him Coach Bob) and intermediate drum line (where they were free to call him dufus because nobody could hear a thing above the racket). Those were all his "hats," as he called them. Sometimes he wore one hat and sometimes he asked permission to "change hats." "In the current job market you have to be flexible, people," he often said, flexibility being key to soccer drills and synchronized drumming but not necessarily to sex ed, unless you ignored all that stuff about *No* meaning *No*, and just saying *No*, and what part of *No* don't you morons understand?

So, really, not that flexible. Thank you very much, Courtney Segal ("My Slutty Dress Does Not Mean Yes!"), for pointing that out.

The first time Lazar did his patented Mr. B impression for Grandma Minnie she practically laughed her head off. But then she sobered up and said that flexibility was good advice, all things considered. She was just speaking as a grandmother, though. Wearing her *grandmother* hat. Then she yucked it up so hard that the only way to describe her would be "lolololol!" But that was long ago. Grandma Minnie was too sad to laugh much anymore.

It was difficult not to draw the conclusion that if you named your kid Bubel you set him up for a lifetime of demonstrating how to fit a condom onto a banana (roll don't pull), or the correct way to insert tampons (slide don't push). This one time, Lazar confided his theory about the destiny of names to his dad and Max looked thoughtful for about five minutes. "In that case perhaps you'll become a bookbinder," he eventually replied. "And your brother can work with mummies or, um, corpses." Lazar had no intention of becoming a bookbinder but he wouldn't rule out embalming for Sams. His brother already had a mortician's stoop.

Those were some of the random-shaped thoughts that fell
into the wrong places in the Tetris game of Lazar's mind as he
waited for Mr. B. He was slouching against the wall outside
Mr. B's room where kids were supposed to go if they were having problems at school "or even at home, guys, you know you
can always blah blah blah," was what Mr. B said every year at
general assembly. In the history of the school, the world, the
twenty-first century, no one had ever voluntarily gone to see
Mr. B because:

a)   He's a guidance councillor, for one thing.
b)   Ditto, for another.
c)   Some animal has laid down and died in his gut is what
     his breath smells like.
d)   He hangs cheesy poster art on the walls of his room.
     "If You Love Something Set It Free" and "Today Is the
     First Day of the Rest of Your Life."

If Lazar really believed that today was the beginning of
another whole rotten life to get through, he'd hang himself,
which is what a kid called Tony Aiello did. Problem was, Aiello
took a moment to text his ex-girlfriend, so they managed to cut
him down in time. Sort of in time — he ended up brain dam-
aged and inclined to seizures with pop-out Kermit eyes.

But why make it so difficult? Lazar reckoned he could swipe
his mom's vast supply of Ativan, cut it with a handful of whatever kids were currently into (fentanyl, oxy, diet pills), and wash
down the whole jumpy cocktail with his late dad's favourite
single malt. Minus the Scotch and the meticulous planning, he
knew a girl who did just that. Brittany Lam was her name and,
guess what, still is, because she texted a bunch of her friends

to say *Later, peeps. Goodbye*, and *So long*, and *Life is brutal*. *LMAO* and *YOLO*.

"Question," said his dad after that little episode. "What did suicidal kids do before there was texting?"

"They died," said his mom.

If Lazar ever saw his mom for more than two blurred minutes a day he'd like to ask her what she meant. Did she think that dead kids could live on in virtual reality, surviving as a billion pixels of shimmering light? Did she mean that, even if you deleted your profile and your tweets and your Instagram account, you still existed on someone's timeline or screen grab or the Facebook page that stayed up forever after you actually died? Or maybe she just meant that without technology, without being *connected* to some digital life force, kids died. It was as simple as forgetting to charge your phone.

Sometimes he wondered if all the new electronic identities, the hundreds of ways to be yourself or someone else, were confusing death. Maybe death just didn't recognize anyone anymore. Because the fact was that kids were certainly having trouble dying these days. It was slightly spooky, something in the wind or the water, but the kids in this city were having real trouble going down and staying down. There was a guy in another school, Matthew Somebody, who tried to shoot himself with his dad's hunting rifle and missed, mostly, and although hardly anyone knew about it, even next-door Bernie once tried to cut her wrists in the bath (too little, wrong direction, some neat scarring though, she told him), and a chick in band knew someone who stepped in front of a train.

"Yeah, that might work," Lazar said.

"Are you fuckin' kidding me?" she yelped. "A freight train in the middle of the day? In the middle of the after*noon*?" Her name was Sami Fisher, one of the cool kids. Lazar knew the names of all the cool kids and all the suicidal kids but hardly any of the others. Maybe "cool" and "suicidal" were his specialties, but then they were probably everyone's, even Sami Fisher's. She definitely didn't know Lazar's name though, because she gave him a *Who do you think you are?* look.

They were all hanging out behind the gym, waiting for Mr. Dubchek to finish smoking and let them back into the band room where they'd continue to fishtail their way through the swoopy skids of "Louie Louie," a perennial favourite of beginner band. But Lazar was the one who said, Yeah that might work.

"They saw him from ten miles down the line," Sami said. "They saw him from like Saskatchewan. Someone had to get down from the train and *hike* to where he was. God, how embarrassing."

"Yeah well, that's life in the big city," Lazar's dad used to say. He complained all the time about how the trains stopped traffic dead. His dad turned out to be an expert on dying in the end, but who could have known? Once Max had been voluble on the subject of how traffic was the only thing those trains stopped dead.

"Take it from me," he'd say, "don't bet your life against the two-fifteen Prairie so-called Express."

Lazar was beginning to notice a pattern. It seemed to him that the kids he knew were lousy at dying. At best, inefficient. They kept killing themselves and rising up from the ashes and yes, some of them lost an eye in the process (Matthew Somebody), or a rep (Brittany Lam), or a ton of blood (Bernie), or what was left of their minds (Tony Aiello), but he couldn't remember the last time a kid went down and stayed down. Zombie-wise they had a lot going for them, he thought.

He imagined the movie of their lives: the burnt-out, wasted city. The trains hanging off the broken-in-half bridges. Silhouettes of the ruined Ferris wheel and dangling rollercoaster cars at the Exhibition Grounds. The carousel still cranking out the syrupy canned music of an innocent time which, since it had never existed, lent the scene a terrible, deranged nostalgia. And in the distance, the river chugging its freight of zombie body parts and gnawed-to-death pets, half-consumed cattle spinning in the current. The army of the walking dead was on the move, pitchforks in their entrails, their eyeballs revolving in their sockets like ball bearings.

He was so lost in his end-of-days scenario that he barely heard Mr. B calling him into his room with its accelerating goofiness (posters and window plants and cozy corner padded with beanbags, so freaks and losers and kids who hadn't adjusted to their meds could kick back and zone out). There was a soccer poster behind Mr. B's desk featuring Cristiano Ronaldo leaping up to head a ball into a net. It was a new addition to the resource room but Lazar wasn't surprised. Ronaldo was Mr. B's favourite soccer star because he played with his head *and* his heart, as Mr. B often told the stoners and burnouts who wandered in there and couldn't get out again until he'd lectured them on how anything was possible if you jumped high enough or ran fast enough or worked hard enough. The Ridgehaven JV soccer team hadn't won a game in, like, *ever*, but if they did it would for sure be because of some phony poster that had probably started out life as an advertisement for Nike.

"Where would you like to sit, young man?" Mr. B asked, eyeing his padded corner hopefully.

Lazar told him he'd prefer to stand, and Mr. B's mouth went *oh* and he started to cycle into a REM episode, blink-wise.

"Oh," Mr. B said again, this time out loud, and he searched the room for a place where they could do their standing together. Eventually he just decided to stay where he was, although he kind of hunched down as if to say, *Any minute you're going to want to sit down, Mr. Binder, any minute now. And when you do, I will be ready for you.*

So there they were, the two of them — Mr. Bubel and Mr. Binder — hanging out in the middle of the afternoon under the flickering resource room lights, which made everyone look sick as hell. Mr. B was wearing his "Let's rap, pal" hat, and his "I hear you, dude" grin, which along with his Monday meme T-shirt ("Saskatchewan! Easy to Draw, Difficult to Spell!") completed the outfit of a natural born halfwit. Lazar suddenly remembered how once, while delivering a public service announcement about teen suicide, Mr. B began to tear up. The grade nines listened in silence, but not a good silence. Perhaps they'd grow out of their callous ways, or perhaps they'd always remain hard at the centre: rows and rows of them like a box of the sort of chocolates nobody really wants to eat.

"Blah blah blah," Mr. B said, and Lazar took a step back because, the truth was, Mr. B's breath reeked. In fact, Mr. B's breath was so revolting that actually Lazar was kind of impressed.

At least twenty cups of coffee a day went into the making of the halitosis cloud that surrounded Mr. B. It killed Lazar, really it did, to witness what a sorry bunch those teachers were. If you thought about it, any eleventh grader with a learner's permit could walk into school with a Grande in hand while his teachers, poor demented souls, had to guzzle whatever dripped out of the staff room coffee machine. In a movie, it would be the liquefied brains of their students. In a movie, the teachers would sip the evil coffee all day long and it'd be like a sort of blood transfusion only it wouldn't make them younger, just crankier and paler and ever more inclined to gaze thoughtfully at the adolescent necks of their innocent students. In a movie, the coffee would be a sinister, bubbling elixir of brain chunks accompanied by oozy-stew sound effects: *THL—RR—UP! URP—GLUNK!*

"So, um. Just um —" Mr. B finally asserted himself. Lazar snapped out of the movie of his life and into some other dude's movie where nobody was going to die of fright, although they might succumb to the decaffeinated *drip drip drip* of boredom. Stale coffee was the top note of Mr. B's terrible breath, but there was also bouquet of tuna fish sandwich in there, and the remnants of however many cigarettes had lived and died in his airways between homeroom and fourth period spare.

"So any time you want to, em. Or just, um…" Mr. B trailed off. "Mmmm?" He beamed at Lazar hopefully.

God, he was such a cretin. Lazar grinned right back, showing all his teeth: "Right on, Mr. B. Cool beans." Any time I want to talk about my lousy father and my zombie mother and my crazy brother I will come and breathe in your stinky breath, he did not say.

"What?" went Mr. B, startled.

Oh, okay. So perhaps he did say it. Whoops! Lazar had been losing control lately because:

a)   The circumstances.
b)   The dog keeps eating his homework.
c)   Actually, come to think of it, he's in perfect control. Crisis brings out the best in some people (a.k.a. Lazar Binder, boy wonder).
d)   Control is bullshit, anyway. For example, Mr. B is

shortly going to lose control and disappear right out of the story. Lazar is getting bored with that chucklehead. Goodbye, Bubel!

Some days Lazar shuttled so swiftly between his comic book superhero powers of control and the apocalyptic chaos of his life's lack of control that he got motion sick. He suddenly remembered one of his dad's favourite jokes: This guy lent his friend a kettle but when his friend returned the kettle, it was broken. "What gives?" said the kettle's owner. His friend replied:

a) What kettle?
b) That kettle was broken to begin with.
c) You never lent me a kettle.
d) I returned that kettle in perfect condition.

Although Lazar's dad loved jokes, he couldn't remember any of them except for the kettle joke. In Lazar's opinion, his dad was a consummate master of the lost art of lame joke telling. But despite his hard-won status as the world's worst comedian on account of being terrible at beginnings and forgetful of endings, Max could still crack himself up with his rare brand of corny meta-humour. Just thinking about those jokes made him lean back in his grimy, dad-smelling La-Z-Boy recliner and smile fondly, like a harmless loon on revved-up loon tablets.

Here are some of the late Max Binder's favourite jokes:

a) To get to the other side!
b) One to hold the light bulb steady and the other six to turn the room around.

c)   Not so fast, Private Schwartz.
d)   Dwayne the bathtub, I'm dwowning!

Here are some of the things Lazar's dad said while trying to tell a joke from beginning to end:

a)   Wait, have I mentioned they were in a bar at the time?
b)   Okay, let's go back a bit. I need to fill in some stuff.
c)   Did I say Irish? I meant Polish.
d)   Here's where it gets a bit tricky, so concentrate.

And here are some of the things that Lazar's dad said after he finished telling one of his jokes:

a)   Think about it: a chicken!
b)   Think about it: a light bulb!
c)   Pretty sick, eh? The part where he —
d)   Dwowning — I'm *dwowning*! Get it?

A couple of months after the accident, Sams made a list of all their dad's jokes. Except for the kettle joke it was a list of punchlines. Fifty-seven punchlines in order of importance, Sams said. As usual, Lazar didn't have a clue. But Sams went ahead and put the list up on the fridge, held in place by their World Vision child. All that evening he kept yelling out numbers, until Maggie finally joined in, the two of them sounding like bingo callers at the Legion Hall.

"Fourteen!" Lazar shouted finally ("Seven *ate* nine!"). Sams and Maggie gazed at him sadly.

"Twenty-one!" he tried. "Fifty-two!" "Thirty-eight!"

"Kiddo," Maggie said, "you need to work on your delivery."

Then the two of them — Beavis and Butt-Head — yukked it up for about an hour because "You need to work on your delivery" was actually one of his dad's all-time favourite punchlines. Who the hell knows which number.

After Lazar's failure in the humour department, Maggie went into a coincidental decline. In other words, not his fault ("I returned that kettle in perfect condition"). When her bereavement leave ended, she began going into work so early in the morning that she was gone before the school bus came.

"Gotta hit the dusty trail, kid," she'd say out of the corner of her mouth.

Lazar had no idea why she was pretending to be a cowboy. It remained an intriguing question though, and one to be filed under "Who the Hell Knows?" Most evenings she didn't get back until long after they would've eaten supper if anyone had bothered to make it. The status at the Binder residence was pretty much delivery or die.

"Pizza or fried chicken? Your call, boys," read the note his mom left on the kitchen counter every morning, along with a twenty and some finicky wrapped toothpicks whose meaning was difficult to interpret. They might have been her way of saying, *I love you*, or *Watch out for food in your teeth*. They might have meant, *Take care of the details*, or *Don't sweat the small stuff*. The fact was those darn toothpicks expressed everything and nothing at all. As with most things in his life, Lazar just didn't have a clue.

To tell the truth his mom had always been a lousy cook and the only two people who seemed to enjoy her Signature Tuna Casserole with Potato Chip Topping were Bernie (who sometimes ate dinner with the Binders when her parents were at odds) and his dad.

"Lord, Maggie, you are a marvel," Max would say, sighing and shaking his head over her Shake and Bake Chicken Surprise. As if to say, *I wish I knew how you manage to achieve such an even crumble.* As if to say, *Moist and tender on the inside but golden crisp on the outside.* As if to say, *There is more than one surprise in Chicken Surprise and not the least of it is you.*

Seven minutes. *Seven minutes* — Lazar timed her once — was all it took for his mom to rustle up one of her Chicken Surprises, the surprise being tomato soup sometimes and onion soup at other times. But mostly it was the surprise of managing to produce his dad's undying admiration, in under ten minutes, by the simple trick of ripping open a couple of boxes and yanking around a Ziploc bag. *Et voilà!*

She was always on the phone in those days, yakking to her girlfriends about her job and making fun of Shapiro, her patriarchal son-of-a-bitch pissant boss at the *Riverview News* where she was an assistant copy editor as well as the advice columnist and writer of the monthly slice-of-life column. This last was a creative channel for her spleen, Max used to say. She'd been trying to break into features for some time, though, and back when the Binder family was merely peculiar rather than disastrous, rather than shocking, rather than pathetic, she'd been agitating to write her own copy. So far she'd pitched a series of local business features, any number of human interest stories, and an investigative feature about a human rights group who were proposing to drag the Red River in the summer.

"Okay," said her patriarchal son-of-a-bitch pissant boss, "restaurant reviews it is." Maggie said her boss was just trying to psych her out and ordered Lazar to quit laughing. "You don't have to be a chicken to appreciate a good omelet, *n'est ce pas?*" was her point.

In fact that's exactly what she wanted to call her column, You Don't Have to Be a Chicken, but naturally her boss said, "No way, Maggie, how much space do you think I have for a headline?" According to Lazar's mom, her patriarchal son-of-a-bitch pissant boss had some suggestions of his own:

a) Yum Yum
b) Yum! Yum!
c) Good Food
d) Foodie Goodie

To which she replied:

a) Am I reviewing food or opera?
b) Punctuation can't save you, Dumb! Dumb!
c) Bad Idea.
d) So I'll be specializing in all-day Chinese buffets, then?

God, you are such a cretin, she didn't say to her boss and then, what the hell, did.

That's when he told her to "Get lost fancy-pants," which made Maggie howl with girlish glee on the phone to her friends and then again later over family dinner and her version of Pineapple Chicken Surprise. "We ran out of pineapple chunks so I used Cheez Whiz — surprise!" His mom should have called it Pineapple Chicken Shock, thought Lazar after taking a bite. Maggie was still laughing so hard that she almost forgot to tell them she had just one night to pitch a name for her non-existent column. Otherwise, no go, kiddo — she was back to her red pen, her dangling widows and lonely orphans.

"Way to bury the lede, sweetheart," Max told her.

The thing about Lazar's mom was that she was funny and digressive as hell, she smelled good, and she loved basketball (NBA, college, high school, even kids shooting hoops in the back lane). Naturally she expected Lazar to share her ardent interest. He'd have preferred her to take a direct interest in him but he instinctively understood the roundabout routes that families have to travel just to stay in one place. The other thing about his mom was that she needed *in*put. So then the Binder family had to put their heads together and come up with some suggestions for the name of her column. Maggie scribbled them on her grocery pad, one after the other, no matter how dumb they sounded, which in Max's case was considerable. The dumbness, that is.

"A Moveable Feast," Max offered. "Gatsby's Party," "Mm, La Madeleine."

"And *who* is Madeleine?" Maggie snapped right back.

Lazar's dad fell right into the trap, explaining that a madeleine was a French cookie with an amazing smell that reminded Marcel Proust of his childhood, over the course of seven volumes and thousands of pages. You could tell that Sams was quite taken with the idea of this cookie-sniffing French dude because his eyes brightened as if he was already figuring out where to score this madeleine-huff. Maggie was still going on at Max since he'd implied that she didn't know what a madeleine was, which made him the most condescending prick she'd ever come across. And, as she'd spent most of the morning veiling her insults in strained pleasantries to her patriarchal son-of-a-bitch pissant boss, that was really saying something.

"Think, people," she urged.

They all thought some more, the Binders sinking into deep cogitation. Maggie clicked her pen, then her cigarette lighter, and finally one of her clip-on earrings. Sams gnawed on his cuticle and Lazar ran his fingers compulsively over an archipelago of acne that had risen to the surface of his chin, wondering (again) why all his growth hormones went into pimple production rather than the breadth of his shoulders or the depth of his voice. As for Max, he slowly chewed his way through another helping of Pineapple Chicken Surprise seeming, for the first time, to register surprise at the absence of pineapple chunks in the Cheeto dust–orange sauce. He appeared deeply interested, as if he was on the verge of working out the solution to a complicated language problem: the surprise inherent to Pineapple Chicken Surprise is the ratio of pineapple to chicken-Cheez Whiz. Which is to say unequal at best. Which is to say dicey vis-à-vis pineapple representation. Which is to say none at all.

Ergo: Surprise!

Therefore the name did not have to say it all. *Au contraire.*

"What about *Au Contraire?*" Max suggested.

"And why?" snapped Maggie, but she wasn't really mad. Lazar's mom didn't mind being called contrary or perverse or even hardhearted (she was). What she minded was being called pretty (again, she was), or nice (she wasn't, at all), or well-mannered (not even close), a problem only for her poor deluded husband who clearly believed that she was the most beautiful woman in the world. Rose of Sharon, he called her, Star of My Firmament, Peg of My Heart. Lazar's dad used to sing these lame-assed songs every morning while he shaved. "January Girls" and "Xmas in February" and "April Love." Belting them out in the bathroom mirror, a song for every month of the year. If his dad was alive today he'd be singing "Maggie May," gelling his hair into Rod Stewart spikes, and gravelling up his voice.

Wake up (mwah) *Maggie I think I got something to say to you* (mwah). The kissing sounds were his own invention.

Lazar didn't know anything about being married and sure, music had changed in the last hundred years since his dad was young, but "January Girls" and "April Love" and "Maggie May" were the reasons that he and Sams plugged in their ear buds early and turned up their music loud.

The thing about his mom being pretty was something that other people said. He didn't have an opinion on the subject because:

a) She's his mom, so.
b) He never looks at her.
c) If he thought she was pretty he'd have to put out his eyes, so Oedipus-wise he's just going with popular opinion here.
d) That's all.

Max used to steal all his lines from *The Goon Show* and his moves from Benny Hill. God help them, but he'd crack up Lazar's mom with his fake cockney accent. Sometimes he'd even chase her around the kitchen with a frozen fish fillet stuffed down his pants. Lazar remembered those times — the fish fillet beginning to thaw, his dad's fly blooming a dark stain, his mom holding herself and yelling that she was going to pee, oh god. Some chick in an old song that Bernie used to play on guitar said you don't know what you got till it's gone they paved paradise and put up a parking lot. But Lazar knew. Kind of. Mostly.

That was all before, though. Before his mom threw his dad's computer out the second floor window and it smashed to pieces on the sidewalk. Before she packed all his clothes into boxes for the Salvation Army to collect and got a guy to come and haul away his dad's recliner. Before she instructed his department head to donate all his books to deserving students — or undeserving ones for that matter. Illiterate football louts or gumsnapping coeds: anyone, anyone, she didn't want to know (Lazar heard her yelling on the phone). Before she threw all his papers in the recycling bin: files and folders and every loose piece of scribbled-on paper cluttering his desk. Before she locked the door of his home office, the tiny room beneath the eaves, and tossed the key into the garbage where Lazar retrieved it because *you never know*. Having the key to his father's office jingling about in his pocket made Lazar feel closer to his dad in an odd way but more distant from his grief-stricken, slightly deranged mom. *Them's the breaks, kid*, his dad would have said with one of his wide, goofy grins. *You win some, you lose some.*

Max might have said those things but it was a cinch he didn't believe them. His dad used to say that the Binders were the luckiest unlucky family he knew: unlucky because of poor Sams, lucky because of everything else. They were the Binders (four against the world!) and they lived on the Street of Flowers. Magnolia Street, he meant, that exotic flowering plant nestled between rows of earnest local tree-streets — Elm, Oak, Ash, and Birch. Nobody knew why Magnolia Street had been named so absurdly, but naturally Max took it as one more sign of exceptional good fortune.

His mom would probably have put it the opposite way: they were the unluckiest lucky family that she knew. They both had the same reasons in mind but Maggie's way sounded sarcastic and a little forlorn, as if they'd somehow had the luck rubbed off them. Max's version, on the other hand, didn't sound sad at all. Starting off with luck was like hitting the genetic jackpot: being born with perfect pitch or athletic ability or a natural immunity to mosquito bites. Beginner's luck wasn't a fluke; it was collateral.

The difference was that Max *believed* in luck. In fact he believed in it more than he believed in God, country, country music, gravity, academic freedom, or good intentions. (Not more than love, though, never more than love.) The problem was that he only believed in one kind of luck (good) and not the other kind (bad). "Lord, Max," Maggie would say, "haven't you ever lost a coin toss?" Then Max would get quite dreamy eyed telling her about all the coin tosses he'd won. His dad was the only person Lazar knew who got excited when the phone rang in the middle of the night. His mom always blanched and went, *Sams!* His gran and Imee straight off thought that someone had died, and Lazar himself assumed that one of his deadbeat friends had gotten drunk and was phoning to shoot the 3 a.m. breeze.

"Who the hell would be phoning you at three in the morning?" Maggie would ask, watching her crestfallen husband replace the receiver on a wrong number from Kyoto. But they all knew the answer: it was the lottery. Max was certain that a congratulatory bureaucrat from the Liquor and Lotteries Commission was on the line, phoning to tell him he'd just won a million bucks.

Here are some of the reasons that this could never happen:

a) No one phones to tell you that you've won the lottery. They just don't.
b) Nobody actually *wins* the lottery. Lazar has looked it up and the odds aren't good.

c) Maggie's crummy attitude is the antidote to any good luck that might be floating about.

d) Max has never bought a lottery ticket in his life.

But his dad's hopefulness buoyed the Binder family, made them feel special and, yes, lucky. It would be years before Lazar would realize that the song Bernie used to sing in her deep, tuneful voice was a melancholy song, a song about living in a fool's paradise which was still a paradise because at least it wasn't the parking lot that it was one day destined to become.

Sometimes Lazar wondered what their story would be called, the story of the Binder family. If anyone cared. He had some thoughts on the matter, naturally.

a) "Fifty-Seven Punchlines"

b) *"Binder peculiaris"*

c) "One to Swallow All the Light Bulbs and the Other Three to Hold the Room Steady"

d) "Lucky Unlucky"

e) "That Kettle Was Broken to Begin With"

He favoured (e) but would probably have gone with (d) just to be tactful. The trouble was there were so many possible contenders it was difficult to choose the right one.

f) "Multiple Choices"

Whoa.

"Big Night," said Sams suddenly. No one was expecting a suggestion from Sams, and the Binder family went quiet. *They fell silent.* This does happen and not just in books. Actually, the falling silent didn't happen that often in their family because Maggie was a yeller and a talker and a laugher and a weeper, so most opportunities for reticence were lost in the crackle and roar of her, but occasionally she was what is called *taken aback* and then a blessed feeling of peace descended and spread over the Binders like bread upon the waters.

"Why Sams, I am quite taken aback," Maggie said. Maggie and Max and Lazar stared at Sams. Sams gazed at his plate. He looked past the point of there being any point to his looking. Paint dried, grass grew, worlds collided, stars died and were born again. The remaining Binders waited him out because the thing about Sams was that he definitely wasn't any of the things other people called him. To wit:

a) Thick as a brick.
b) Mad as a hatter.
c) High as a kite.
d) Dead as a doornail (zombie-wise).

Although, like most people, he was some of those things some of the time: crazy, dead, dumb, and stoned being relative terms.

"What he *is*," said Lazar's father, "is lacking in ambition, volition, stick-to-it-ness. He'll never change."

"What he *is*," said Lazar's mother, "is eighteen. He'll grow out of it."

Imee said something about the devil (but softly) and Grandma Minnie said something about upbringing (even more softly) and after that — after everybody had had their bloody two-and-a-half cents (Maggie, not at all softly) — the jury was still out. In Lazar's opinion they were all wrong. Sams was about seven feet tall and thin as a wire. Double the height of anyone else in the family and a quarter the width. The postman, Max used to say when anyone asked who Sams resembled, but he stopped after a while because everyone knew Hariharan, and anyway Hari was short too.

Lazar's dad had read tons of books and he did the daily crossword in minutes flat and the sudoku even when it was rated "diabolical," but about Sams he was just purely bewildered. It was Maggie who'd always been partial to Sams, who tried to get him to stop biting his nails and eat protein and air out his room occasionally. She worried about drugs, but the fact was that his hands had always shaken. (It's just a tremor, the doctors told them when Sams was twelve, a physiological tic, means nothing.) And despite the two or three nerves he lived on and the way that he hardly seemed to talk anymore, not to his family anyway, and being out all night and asleep half the day, Sams was an amiable fellow. He never laughed (shy maybe, maybe sad), or seemed to eat (faddy), but he was always willing to help out around the house when he returned from whatever Middle-earth he inhabited, to stumble around in the kitchen dropping things and trampling small creatures underfoot.

His brother was anxious, Lazar reckoned. More so than anyone he'd ever met, including:

a) Weird kid in world events class who still can't say his name without stammering. (It's D-Daniel.)
b) Kid behind the counter at the 7-Eleven whose fingernails bleed they're so bitten.
c) Franny Glass, this girl in a book he's reading.
d) Lazar Binder. (Surprise!)

Sams was more anxious than any of those people, probably more anxious than any two of them combined. Sometimes
Bernie or Imee could calm him down but mostly he looked
like a dude who was saying the Jesus prayer in his head *all the
time*, he looked like someone returning a kettle that was broken
to begin with. He looked as if he was trying to remember to
think of other things, which he always was anyway, but furiously. Not furiously in the sense of angrily, but furiously in the
sense of *applying himself with great concentration*, which most
people didn't do, thought-wise, but there you go: Sams wasn't
like most people.

You could blame it on his height or his goofy way of loping about on the backs of his heels, thought Lazar. You could
point out that he was practically seven foot and skinny and
had always been the kind of kid to just about jump out of his
skin every time a car backfired or a dog barked its rotten head
off, but Lazar's theory was that if you went ahead and named
your first-born son Samson then you were asking for trouble.

Here are some of the names that Maggie and Max decided
not to call their eldest son:

a)   Not Adam created in the image of God.
b)   Not David or Jonathan or Saul, all men of royal blood.
c)   Not even Noah who got drunk and was a jerk to his
     daughters but in the end saved all those animals.
d)   Not Lazar short for Lazarus (they were saving that one).

On his first day at Bible Thump Elementary, Samson was
beaten up by some kids who held him down and shaved his
head. After that they beat him up and shaved his head whenever they saw him coming although, to their credit, they also

went out of their way to search for him. Sams stopped talking halfway into September and wore a toque all the way through the end of June. Lazar's dad tried to chivvy his son along but Sams was helpless against the bristly little gangs of preschoolers who roamed the hallways armed with safety scissors, disposable razors, a literal imagination, and a devastating grasp of the Book of Judges.

"It's your fault," Maggie yelled at Max. "You're the one who wanted to name our son after some motherfucking idiot in a poem by that cunt-bubbling excuse for a shit-faced fuckety rhyming loser." That was how Lazar learned that Samson was named after a character in a story by some guy named Milton instead of being named after some guy in a story by — well — God.

On the positive side, Lazar's mom was brilliant at swears. The best he'd ever heard. Here's how good she was; she could swear:

a) Alphabetically, *A* through *Z* and back without repeating herself.
b) In iambic pentameter.
c) In twelve different languages (three of them dead) and five different alphabets.
d) In American Sign Language and Morse code and semaphore.

Of course (a), (b), (c), and (d) were all fancy swears — party pieces, Maggie called them. Most of the time she just did her ordinary, everyday swears as they fell trippingly off the tongue. Max was a great admirer of her talent.

You there, you with the stars in your eyes, he'd often sing.

Quoting something nobody ever heard of, as usual. Some song.

"It's your fault, you Jackass! You Knucklehead! You Lummox!" Maggie yelled at him that day (the day of Sams's biblical haircut).

Max, who had the normal amount of guilt, shame, and pity molecules zooming through his bloodstream, was downcast. But what could he do? The boy had been named, his name had been witnessed, signed, and sealed. Max was a professor of literature, for goodness sake.

"You can't suddenly rename a character in the middle of the story," he told Maggie. "Imagine if Shakespeare had changed his mind halfway through Act III and renamed the old guy King Cheer?"

"I don't care about shit-eating Shakespeare," said Maggie, "or motherfucking Milton or, if it comes to that, *you*."

The argument raged all evening and most of the night. Max slept on the living room sofa although actually he didn't sleep a wink, he said. Just lay in the dark while all around him the wind blew on a lonely moor and his eyes watered and his cheeks cracked, which was a reference, Lazar reckoned, to something that had gone before or to something that was still to come and that he would understand much later and have the satisfaction of saying, Aha! His dad called it the Loony Tunes effect.

Of course Lazar was only a toddler at the time. So how did he know so much about Samson's hair and where Max slept and how Maggie swore and all those private *conjugal* conversations? Here are some distinct possibilities:

a)   Lazar is an old soul, a time traveller.
b)   Maggie is a compulsive storyteller.

c) Max is an unreliable narrator.

d) Sams is a pod person implanted with a human brain.

But Max wasn't the only one who didn't sleep. The next morning Maggie, who had hatched a plan, took her still silent, still balding son firmly by the hand, walked him down the block and through the park and up the hill to school, and deposited him in the kindly hands of his first-grade teacher, Mrs. Bender-Pollock.

"Meet Sams," she said. "He's new in town."

Mrs. Bender-Pollock nodded. She was old. Too old to argue or look surprised or not know better. So, okay. Sams.

It was a bloodbath, it was a massacre, it was a crazy playground brawl. These were some of the names that the other kids called Sams:

a) Sams-I-am

b) Green Eggs and Ham

c) Baldy Stupid Head

d) Yo Mama's Got a Fat Ass

All that year the teachers called Sams *dear* sometimes, and *um* sometimes, and *oh dear I didn't see you sitting there off by yourself,* most of the time. But by then the Tergussons had moved in next door and Bernie Tergusson — who understood all about names and the trouble they caused — had taken Sams under her wing. She was Bernie (*not* Bernadette) and he was Sams, and she would beat up anyone who said different. She was a skinny, dark-haired kid with long legs, a slip of a girl who punched far above her weight category and kept punching until somebody yelled uncle.

She was also ornery as all get out, Lazar's dad said admiringly. On Heritage Day when the kids were supposed to bring in traditional foods, Mrs. Bender-Pollock suggested that Bernie ask her mom to fry up a pan of bannock to represent her mother's people. *Uh*-uh, said Bernie, unconvinced. Instead she hauled in a can of Red Bull spiked with vodka and a jar of green M&M's, which she claimed were the traditional food of rock stars and roadies, her *actual* people. Lazar was crazy about her.

As for Sams, he remained silent and put all his energy into growing. Growing up, growing tall, growing his hair back to its righteous Samson locks. Growing the hell out of there. By the time Lazar was in junior high, Sams was back to speaking — or as much as he ever would — and the length of his side locks made up for the brevity of his commentary, as his dad would often say, who clearly had just the opposite problem. Twice a year Sams allowed Bernie to trim his hair with a pair of nail scissors, only she wasn't allowed to go above his shoulder blades. But he'd never pulled his hair back into a crummy ponytail and Lazar was proud of him for that.

Quite a ways back now, Sams made his unexpected suggestion and the Binders fell silent, and peace descended upon the family like bread cast upon the waters. In another sort of family, Lazar reckoned, peace might have lasted a while longer. A father might have *cogitated*, a mother might have *mulled it over*, and dishes might have remained on the table and not gone crashing to the floor. But they were not that sort of family.

"Hmm, 'Big Night,'" said Max. "Oops!" (That was because of the Surprising Chicken sliding off the table and splattering on the kitchen floor in oily lumps of curdling cheese.)

Maggie was super excited, though. "Oh Sams," she said,

"what a wonderful name! What a wonderful non-literary name!"

That was to get at Max, of course, but they all knew that Sams's suggestion didn't come from a book. It came from a movie because that was what Sams did: he watched movies. Even when he wasn't sitting hunched over his computer, Lazar had the feeling that his brother was downloading movies from an unverifiable cosmic source and live-streaming them inside his head. That would explain his blank gaze, at least, and the way his foot was always tapping in time to some unheard but urgent oddball musical score.

When he wasn't watching movies, Sams worked in a retro video store. The Celluloid Museum it was called, where "Sams's Picks" had collected an unexpected cult following. There were these freaky fans that turned up at the store on the first Wednesday of every month when "Sams's Picks" came out, Bernie told Lazar. To witness the magic.

Sams liked old movies and zombie movies best because black and white was his favourite colour (old movies), and the subtle gradations of existence between being dead, being undead, being immortal, and dying slowly of being eaten alive his favourite theme (zombie movies). The way Sams saw it:

a) Zombies can't die, that being the first principle of zombie-hood.
b) You can't kill what was never alive unless...
c) But they do. Apocalypse survivors and vigilantes and hot girl warriors blow their heads off.
d) ...unless you are killing the death in them.
e) So that they can finally die.

What happened after Sams made his surprising contribution was what always happened with the Binders:

a) Maggie says, "Oh! 'Big Night,' tell us all about it, Sams" (excited as hell).
b) Sams goes quiet, hangs his head and shakes his hair into his eyes. Gnaws his thumbnail (skittish).
c) Max says, "Your mother asked you a question, son" (is there a word for "wants Maggie to be happy"?).
d) Lazar goes, "That wasn't really a question, Dad" (is there a word for "leave Sams alone"?).
e) Max says, "That wasn't really any of your business, Laz" (snappish).
f) Maggie goes, "Sams?" (hopeful).

But Sams was already gone, swift and sweet as sugar lightning and Maggie too (after him), and then there was just Max looking at Lazar, and then there was just Lazar.

After he cleaned up the mess on the kitchen floor, Lazar googled *Big Night* and it was just as he thought: a movie about these brothers who owned a restaurant and all the crazy, exciting things that you wouldn't necessarily think happened to guys who owned a restaurant. Sometimes life hummed along for the restaurant brothers, and then suddenly there were broken dishes and people yelling and, ho hum, food on the floor. It was a "lyric to the love of food and family," a "feast of friendship," a "delicate repast about our recent past." Strangely, there were no zombies in the movie but apparently it featured a poignant scene involving risotto. Lazar didn't know anything about risotto but he was pretty sure that his mom couldn't make it and his brother wouldn't eat it.

He would've shown his mom the movie reviews but really, why bother? The moment Sams spoke she'd made her decision — Big Night! — and Lazar couldn't blame her. It wasn't such a bad name, quite good in fact, but even if Sams had come up with Salmonella.com or Botulism Today, she'd have fought for it. That was just the way things were with his mom when it came to Sams.

All this was last year, though. Shortly afterwards, Lazar's dad got killed in his car with some girl the papers called "the Hitchhiker," and his mom went crazy for a while. That was when Lazar learnt the most important thing about death: when someone died they never came back, you could never ever see them again, they were gone forever.

After his dad died it was as if he could suddenly see again, as if he'd taken off the Coke-bottle glasses he'd been wearing for years. He began to notice things and what he noticed was that kids died, they had been dying all this time. Sure there were all the uncommitted kids he knew who had returned from the dead — broken some of them, self-important or embarrassed or depressed. But then there were the others, the boy that Mr. B tried to tell them about during Teen Suicide Awareness Week, and Imee's daughter, and a young girl who had just washed up on the banks of the Red.

All this time kids had been dying and it was the kind of dying that stuck. It wasn't like zombies or vampires or this story his English teacher made them read where a girl was buried alive and came back to kill her brother. For a long time after the accident Lazar missed his father so much that he kept seeing him everywhere. But it was never his dad, just a man who looked like Max, a figment in his peripheral vision. Then one day he realized that he'd stopped seeing him and that was death too.

Bernie said that ghosts weren't lost souls like everyone thought. They were the sum of all the guilt and longing felt by the person who was left behind. Whoever saw the ghost was the real ghost, she said. Since Mrs. Tergusson had died last November Bernie knew the score, Lazar reckoned. His own mom must have been riddled with guilt and longing because she went around for months with a ghost-stricken look. There were dark circles beneath her eyes and she stopped eating or caring what anyone else ate. The three of them hadn't sat down to a family dinner since they got the news, which was fine actually because Lazar couldn't imagine what they'd talk about.

"Pass the risotto, please, Sams."

"Delicious risotto, Mom. Top notch."

Anyway, his mom went crazy for a while but she's better now.

"SHE'S DOING GOOD, Mrs. Boychuk," Lazar imagines saying the next time the teacher asked. Mrs. Boychuk would open her mouth to correct his grammar and Lazar would narrow his bounty-hunter eyes and blow her away in the swamp-green post-apocalyptic wasteland of the locker-rattling school corridor. Mrs. Catherine Boychuk's head would explode and her eyes would swivel in their sockets. Brains would spatter, and blood would gush, and nerves would short like fuses.

"What the heck?" Mr. B would yell, running from his room.

But it was too late. The posters were down and the window plants had shrivelled. Kids were standing at their lockers, watching: Courtney Segal and her besties, Jackson Riley and his gang, the cool chicks, the cute dudes, the loners, the stoners, and the losers.

What was left of Mrs. Boychuk would be twitching on the

floor when all the little zombie girls and zombie boys filed out of their classrooms and gobbled her up.

Lazar closed his eyes and tried to imagine the scene. But it was no good, it had never been any good. His imagination couldn't follow where his nerve wouldn't go. The only thing he could do was nothing, which he accomplished handily, standing there and staring into space for about an hour until Mrs. Boychuk lumbered up, her large, shapeless face hovering in front of him like a dirigible.

"Are you in there, Lazarus Binder?" she kept going.

He had to say something, didn't he?

That's how Lazar landed up back in Mr. B's office, back with the padded beanbags and plants and the poster of Ronaldo in his Nikes, heading a soccer ball. For once Mr. B was angry and out of sorts, as if someone had just yelled *Risotto!* and hauled him out of some other story. He didn't say "How can I help you, son?" or "Where would you like to kick back, buddy?" He just took a seat behind his desk and nodded for Lazar to lay ass in the chair in front of him.

"What's the story, young man?" he asked.

But Lazar had no idea why he'd suddenly begun ranting at Mrs. Boychuk in the school corridor, or what he'd said to make her eyes pop and her cheeks flush and her head spin. There was nothing he could say so he went on sitting there, gazing into space as if he were waiting for enlightenment.

SUMMER

FIVE

INSPIRATIONAL LIVING CENTRE

ON THE WAY back from the Inspirational Living Centre some of the girls said theirs were "cute," and Courtney Segal even said hers was "adorable." See, that's why I've gone off girls, and Courtney Segal most of all. Old is what they were, and wrinkled, mostly, and, every now and then, a bit yellow. Mine was the worst though. Even that lame-ass, Sami Fisher, couldn't have made a case for cute when it came to Mr. Morgenstern.

I started to tell Sami about Mr. Morgenstern, but Courtney leaned over the back of her seat and said, "Shut up, Daniel," so that was that.

The thing is girls are always going on about *cuteness*, posting pictures of puppies and babies on Instagram and writing cute notes to each other with their cute fluffy pencils about the cutest boys in the grade. So: puppies, babies, notes on scented paper, fluffy pencils, hot guys, and Holocaust survivors. Which of these is not like the others?

"Mine is so adorable. I just want to hug him," said that air-head, Courtney Segal, and guess what? Half the girls chimed in and claimed theirs were adorable too. There was even some thoughtful nodding on the part of the guys. Well, not all the guys, obviously. Just the cute ones.

For the record I'm not and never have been cute. Not the baby type of cute — just ask my mother (if you can find her, which nobody has, yet) — and not the hot guy type either. Not being cute is actually my secret superhero power, like being invisible, and even if you'd prefer a different superhero power, like say flying, which is totally the domain of the cool kids, you have to remember that you don't get to choose your superhero power. And, truthfully, being invisible helped a lot when it came to Mr. Morgenstern. In great bullshit lies great responsibility.

Why we were on the school bus, driving away from the Inspirational Living Centre, is a story in itself (world events class is why; Holocaust studies in general, and Mrs. Boychuk's particular conviction that if she doesn't repeat herself then History will do it for her). And I could tell you all the things Mrs. Boychuk told us about how to behave with the Holocaust survivors. The Protocol, she called it. No cameras, no phones, no devices of any kind, she said. Respectfully address your survivor by his or her last name during the interview, but when you write up your notes, for purposes of anonymity, simply refer to him or her as "my Holocaust survivor."

I could tell you about how much I hate Courtney Segal and every other girl in grade nine, but mostly Courtney. Hating her was like an arrow in my heart. I could tell you all these things, and what it felt like to be jerking through the city in the after-noon rush hour with the kids ramping up their sugar high from the iced tea and cookies that the volunteer from the centre had laid out for us to share with our Holocaust survivors. Her name, by the way, was Mrs. Harvey Silverstein but she said we could call her Mrs. Silverstein, no Harvey necessary. She said a lot of other things as well, about her late husband, her *Harvey*, and her daughter, Leah, who she didn't understand, God bless her, but loved anyway, which we'd all understand one day, for instance when we had children of our own.

Then she looked at us sternly over the tops of her spectacles as if to say: *But not yet, children. Don't go procreating just yet.* She was a real hoot, Mrs. Silverstein, and I would love to tell you all the other things she said because I really do not want to talk about Mr. Morgenstern except to say that was his real name. Mr. Bernard Morgenstern, for purposes of anonymity.

My dad was away on business for a few days, so I called out for a couple of pizzas even though I wasn't hungry, but I knew I would be later, after the weed kicked in. This kid I buy it from — the weed, not the pizza — always laughs and says his product is guaranteed to pack on the pounds, bro, which will be good for a featherweight like me. I don't say, Mind your own business, *bro*. I don't say, Looks like you've been firing up since your first wet dream, *bro*. I don't say, Get blazed, man. I just hand over the cash and grab the baggie. One thing I will say about my dad is that he's good about leaving me cash, and good about not asking where it's disappeared to, and good about clearing out of the place for days at a time, no questions asked. We're like army buddies, my dad and me. Don't ask, don't tell.

My supplier is called Gary, by the way. Gary Woo, pass it on. I'd be doing the dude an injustice by concealing his identity for purposes of anonymity because he's interested in promoting a solid business model by introducing all kinds of built-in perks, like offering "significant discounts to loyal customers for advertising a superlative product." Unquote, as he would say. Last year he began his "Introduce a Friend" incentive, which gets both you and your friend 10 percent off his best bud, the Zombie Reefer, and for an extra 15 percent off the bottom line on any purchase over the minimum, he'll deliver right to your door. He's not really into the drug scene, he once told me. He just needs to make enough dough to get into business school.

Okay, that's the end of our commercial break. You're very welcome, Gary Woo. Put that down in accounts payable.

After Gary left I could have called some of the guys to come over. I usually do. This place gets kind of empty after a while, especially on weekends when you can hear the neighbours mowing their lawns, and drinking out on their decks, and waiting for their barbecues to heat up. We don't have much of a lawn is the thing, and no deck at all. My dad says barbecuing is a fool's game, and waiting for meat to turn from one colour to another is like watching paint dry, but less of a head rush. You can probably tell that my dad has a problem with patience (hasn't got any), but that's okay. I haven't felt like eating meat for like ever, or much of anything else if it comes to that. In fact, if it wasn't for the weed, I wouldn't even be getting my daily pizza calories, so that's something.

I didn't call anyone, though. I turned off my phone and I lay on my bed in the dark with my headphones cranked to The Clash and my window cracked to let out the drifting smoke, and after a while I stopped feeling like myself (superpower: invisibility) and began to feel like one of the cool kids (superpower: flight). They say you can't *not* think — even if your mind is as blank as last summer, there's always something going on there. But it turns out that if the music is loud enough and the weed is strong enough and there's enough cold pizza to get you through the night, then a whole weekend can pass without one stray thought snagging on the chicken wire of your mind.

I KNEW I had to go to school after the weekend because, long story short, I'd fought the law and the law won. Basically, I'd run out of ways to avoid Mondays. I'd called in sick, pretending to be my dad; I'd forged doctor's notes, and my dad's handwriting, and my mom's signature, for Chrissake. I'd used every trick in the book but I'd been busted every time, and now I was on probation. Monday was my weak spot, which was why I found myself back at school, back on the bus, and heading for the Inspirational Living Centre with the rest of the grade nines, Mrs. Boychuk presiding. My head was bulging with pain and every lurch of the bus made my stomach contract, which you'd think would block out everything else, but Courtney Segal has this high, girly voice and I could still hear her cooing, "Oh, mine is so cute, mine's *adorable!*"

The survivors were all sitting around in the lounge, just as they had been the first time we'd been introduced. In the next room some old woman wearing stretchy leggings and a huge T-shirt that read #NeverForget was trying to get a group of even older women jiving to Beyoncé. Her T-shirt could have been a reference to the Holocaust or a shout-out to Alzheimer research, it was difficult to know. "To the left, to the left, to the left, to the left," she was yelling. But two of the women had entangled their walkers and the rest were just pointing and giggling. We all stood in the doorway and watched the instructor trying to untangle them, which was kind of mesmerizing in a zoned-out way. Like getting addicted to a low-budget game app created by some kid in Korea, featuring an angry fish trying to flip out of a fishing net. Whether you're rooting for the fish or the net you can't help enjoying the *bloop-bloop* of bubbles popping on the soundtrack.

The aerobics instructor finally got one woman moving backward and the other forward, and when she looked up and saw us she waved and blew a kiss.

"Right back at you, Grandma," yelled Jackson Riley, pretending to catch the kiss in his hand and rub it into his groin while making disgusting moaning sounds until Lazar Binder pushed him out of the doorway and said — although you could see he really didn't want to — "That's my *gran*, you asshole." A lot of us tried to catch a glimpse of Binder's gran then. The dude's whole family inspires a kind of rubbernecking fascination, to go with the car crash their lives have become (no disrespect, I'm just saying). But by now Mrs. Boychuk's super spidey sense was tingling, alerting her to trouble, and she hustled us all into the lounge where our Holocaust survivors were waiting for us.

I had a couple of seconds to observe them before the kids in my class crowded into the room and I tried my best, I really did. But they were just an ordinary group of old people, nothing special, no cutie pies there. Most wore long sleeves and trousers (the men) and skirts (the women), although here and there you could see a woman in elasticized pants, her stomach jutting out, providing a shelf for her breasts to lie on. All the women had handbags dangling from their arms, and the funny thing was that they never put them down, not once. Sometimes they'd open up their handbags to rummage: to show off a photo of a grandchild or offer a roll of Life Savers. The smell of boiled vegetables and meat came wafting over from the cafeteria, but the Holocaust survivors seemed unaffected. It'd been a long time since the camps, so perhaps the smell of food no longer drove them crazy.

I know this doesn't sound exciting; I'm just saying what I saw.

By this time everyone had found their survivor and I was still standing there, still watching.

"Is something the matter, Daniel?" asked Mrs. Boychuk in a voice that said there'd better not be, so I made my way to my survivor.

Mr. Morgenstern was sitting way in the corner, a skinny guy with a beach-ball stomach and a wispy tonsure. My Holocaust survivor. Like the first time, he was wearing a short-sleeved polo shirt and a pair of stained trousers.

"You vant to see my tattoo, boychick?" he cackled, thrusting his arm under my nose.

"No thanks, Mr. Morgenstern."

"Vhat, you *don't* vant to see my tattoo, boychick?"

"No, I mean you showed me last time, so."

"Oh, I see," he said. "You've already seen my tattoo, is dat it?"

I had, in fact, already seen Mr. Morgenstern's tattoo, but the aggression in his voice indicated that this was beside the point.

"Vhatsa matter, boychick? You only vant to see vhat you haven't seen before? My tattoon's not good enough for you, is dat it?"

"Okay," I said, "show me your tattoo."

He'd done this the first time, too — shoving his left arm at me as soon as I sat down beside him. This whole tattoo thing seemed to be his opening gambit. But as soon as I leaned forward to examine the numbers engraved upon his forearm, he turned churlish and pulled his arm away.

"Nah, I don't tink so, boychick. No tattoo for you today."

Everywhere the buzz of my classmates' enterprise rose and

fell. I heard kids asking the questions we had painstakingly prepared in class, their voices followed by the halting replies of the
survivors. All around us in the lounge, with its worn furniture
and shabby carpet, stories were being told, and they darkened
the young and old faces, casting their long afternoon shadows
across them. Here and there a survivor wept in the midst of a
tale of unimaginable suffering.

When Mrs. Boychuk first told us about this assignment,
she'd allowed that some of our survivors might break down,
but that as responsible witnesses we must bear the burden of
the story, *the tragic weight of history*. I had prayed not to get
a weeper; I knew myself to be callow and fidgety and wholly
unsuited to the task of silent witnessing. And my prayers had
been answered, for instead of being assigned Mrs. Horowitz
who dabbed at her red-rimmed eyes with a handkerchief while
Cindy Gershowitz silently held her hand, or old Mr. Salit whose
tears followed their well-worn courses down his cheeks, I had
been gifted Mr. Morgenstern.

"So, young man, vhat does your father do?" Mr. Morgenstern
inflected the question with an ancient lilt indicative of intimacy. He leaned closer so that I could smell his old man's breath:
the sour odour of mothballs, denture fixative, and empty mornings sagging beneath the weight of schoolchildren and their
impossible questions.

"He works for the Hydro, Mr. Morgenstern."

"Hoo-ha! You're telling me he veks for de gas man? Ha, dat's
a good one. Hey, Gittelman, did you hear dat — did you hear
about boychick's daddy? He veks for de gas man!"

Mr. Morgenstern had swivelled around and was addressing
the noisiest corner of the room. Courtney Segal and Sami Fisher
and a couple of other girls were crowded around this old guy

in a chair and all of them were laughing at something he'd just said — real laughter though, not the kind Mr. Morgenstern was doing. The more they laughed, the crankier Mr. Morgenstern became, until he was jabbing me in the side with his crooked yellow finger.

"Daddy veks for de gas man, hoo-ha! Daddy turns on de gas at night and all de little gels and boys turn green in dere sleep."

"Mr. Morgenstern —" I had brought my list of questions and was determined to ask a couple. Our last visit had degenerated into a series of jeers and taunts, but I'd come prepared this time and besides, Mr. Morgenstern reminded me of the Meisners' dog. I used to walk it for them when they were away. "Just put him on a tight leash," Mr. Meisner had said. "Show him who's boss."

"Mr. Morgenstern," I repeated, consulting my notes, "when were you born? And also, um, where?"

"Hoo-ha! Does de daddy's boy have a kvestion? Let me ask you somet'ing, boychick. Do you get your gas cheap, eh, on account of your daddy veks for de old gas man? Big man, your daddy, he must be. Big bad gas man. Must make your mama proud, eh boychick, vhen she svitches on de oven at night to make your supper. Hoo boy, all de lovely gas! And for so cheap. Must make your mama feel itchy in de pants, must make your mama vant to grab dat big bad gas man by de schwantz and get him on wit her. Yes? Yes?"

His crooked forefinger outstretched, Mr. Morgenstern accompanied each of these *yeses* with a jab in my ribs; it was like the yipping of an enraged dog on a leash. And I remembered that the Meisners' dog had not taken to me, had not in the end taken to his leash, and that the whole mess of a summer had ended with words between my father and Mr. Meisner. My mother had left us in the spring, and then it was the end of summer and I couldn't even get a lousy dog to heel (Mr. Meisner), but what d'you expect, the boy's small for his age (my dad).

"Yoo-hoo, boychick!" Mr. Morgenstern had left off his jabbing and begun snapping his fingers in my face. "*Vhen* vas I born, you ask? Ha, good kvestion. June eight, is de answer. Vot d'you say to dat? Say happy boitday, eh? Happy Boitday, Mr. Morgenstern! And *vere*, you vant to know? Vere vas Morgenstern born? Vell, boychick, I vas born in de middle of…I vas born in de middle of de wrong *century*! Hoo-ha! Did you hear dat, Gittelman? Gittelman, did you hear vhat I said to boychick over here? Da wrong *century*, da middle of da wrong *century*!"

"Many happy returns, Mr. M," I said. I wished him good health in the coming year because I knew it would piss him off, and it did.

Later, back on the bus, Courtney Segal glared at me. "Why can't you keep your Holocaust survivor from bothering ours?" she inquired before skipping up the aisle to join her friends, Sami Fisher and Dee Leblanc. The three of them began to yak about how *cute* their survivor was and how *lame* it was (glare) that some people couldn't leave other people's people *alone* (glare).

There was nothing to watch from the bus window except the way back, which made it seem as if we were all on rewind. There was nothing to do either, because we weren't allowed to bring our phones on account of showing respect. But, like I said, Courtney has this really high, girly voice, and when you almost hate someone it's hard to tune them out. It turns out Gittelman was a real sweetheart. Now I'm not saying he was *adorable*, okay, but from the sound of the girls' stories he was certainly no Morgenstern.

Gittelman had been born in a small town in Poland and he'd lost his wife and two sons in the camps. But he never lost his crazy optimism or his faith in human nature, which paid off in the end because even though he believed his entire family had been murdered, he met a distant cousin in a displacement camp after the war. Naturally, he went right ahead and married her. They immigrated to Canada and lived like newlyweds for forty-three years until she passed away last year.

"Like newlyweds," Courtney's voice wobbled as she repeated Gittelman's words.

"Adorable," the girls agreed. "*So* cute."

I could hear Courtney quoting Gittelman: "Man is wonderful and terrible," he'd said. "But God is always good. When people say, 'Where was God during the Holocaust?' I always say, 'He was in the camps with His people. He was in the gas chambers. He was in the mass graves. God never left our side in all those years.'"

Okay, so not too bright, but like I said, a sweetheart. Trouble was the old guy was a sweetheart with one last burning wish: He wanted to travel to *Ha'aretz* (his words, naturally), to stand before the Kotel, the Western Wall of his beleaguered people, and offer thanks to his God for — get this — a life of simple happiness. And he wanted to bless the memories of his first family, his darling Froike and their beloved sons, and the memory of his late wife of forty-three years, his newlywed.

By this time Courtney had given up trying to tell the story and was frankly sobbing, and Sami and Dee were trying to console her, and a whole mob of kids were leaning over their seats and craning around and saying, "Hey, what the...?" and, "Why is she...?" until finally Mrs. Boychuk came stomping up the aisle to disperse tragedy with intimidation. But like every teacher in the school, Mrs. Boychuk had a soft spot for Courtney Segal who — if you didn't know any different, and luckily I do — always threw out a nice line in big blue-eyed sincerity. So Mrs. Boychuk was all ears while Courtney explained how Mr. Gittelman — excuse me, her Holocaust survivor — couldn't afford to go to Israel, what with the price of a ticket and the exorbitant cost of medical insurance for someone of his advanced years.

"So I was thinking," she finished off, "maybe we could do like a fundraiser at the school. A car wash kind of thing."

"How thoughtful, Courtney!" said Mrs. Boychuk, evidently unapprised of the last car wash kind of thing we'd done, where a bunch of girls had shown up in their cut-offs and white Ts and had to leave ten minutes later when Jackson Riley hosed them down (his words), because they were like bitches in heat (more of his words). Jackson got sent home for swearing and the girls got sent home because their nipples were poking through their wet T-shirts. The rest of us had to slosh through the long afternoon of boredom and boners and hardly washed any cars at all, and we only had about fifty dollars to show for it in the end. Good luck getting to Israel on that, Mr. Gittelman.

MY DAD CAME home in the middle of the week and said, "This place smells like dead pizza and dead hippie. What gives, boss?" He had to meet a guy after work, but he said, "Why don't we go out after for a steak dinner, make a change from whatever crap you've been putting into that healthy young body of yours?" Sometimes he surprises me, my dad.

We still had two more weeks of school before the summer vacation and one more meeting with our survivors before we had to hand in our stupid assignments. I'd been failing social studies all term, and the last thing I needed was for Mrs. Boychuk to phone home, because I was so damn tired of telling her that my dad was asleep, and if you want to know the truth, I don't think she believed me the last time.

"Wake him up, Daniel," she'd said.

"He's really tired, Mrs. Boychuk," I told her. "I don't want to disturb him."

She cleared her throat: "Anything you want to tell me, Daniel?"

"Like what?"

"You tell me."

The thing is, my dad's away a lot for work. It's not his fault, and we have a deal about him *trusting* me when he's out of town, which includes me not blabbing to anyone about how often he goes away and how long he stays away. It's cool, though. I prefer being on my own, anyway, and like my dad says, I'm old enough to take care of numero uno.

But just to avoid the pointlessness of another conversation with Mrs. Boychuk, I sat down to write up my interview, despite the fact that Mr. Morgenstern had given me less than nothing to go on, and despite the fact that he was a giant turd that couldn't be flushed down the pipes of history. I don't care what the Nazis did to him. It's a mystery: You've got your Gittelmans that no cruelty can sour and you've got your Morgensterns that no kindness can sweeten. And in between there's Mrs. Horowitz dabbing at her eyes with her crumpled handkerchief and then folding the handkerchief into a tiny square to slip under her watch strap. And Mr. Salit, the tears forever running down his face as he talks and talks.

So, okay, Morgenstern.

My Holocaust survivor, I wrote, *was born in Lodz, Poland, in 1919. He was a young man when the Nazis invaded Poland, but an old man when he was finally liberated from Auschwitz at the end of the war. Not old in years, but old in experience and in the losses he'd suffered. This is his story in his own words.*

I didn't light up a cigarette or a joint or rummage for a slice of pizza. All I did was pop open a beer from the fridge and keep writing.

The light outside dimmed then darkened, and eventually the streetlights came on. I opened another beer and tried to drink it more slowly than the last one. The second beer took away my lame invisibility super power, but it was no help at all with flying. I was about to crack open the third beer — flying, guaranteed — when my dad phoned to say he'd been held up with this guy so I should go ahead and eat without him.

"You betcha," I said, which always makes him laugh.

"We can do the steak thing another time, right boss?" I could hear glasses clinking and some chick laughing in the background, so I asked him where he was and he said, "Breaking up, son," as if it was a place. The phone, I think he meant, although it could have been the laughing chick he was breaking up with. My dad likes to keep his options open.

"Okey-dokey, Dad," I said, hoping for another laugh. I don't think he heard me though; he was already somewhere else. Clinking glasses with some floozy in a strip-mall bar, eating his steak dinner and keeping his options open. I'm not being rude about the *floozy* — it's what my dad calls them and how he likes them. "A well-built floozy in a red dress is my idea of nirvana, son," he always says. "One day you'll find out."

I wasn't hungry, but I phoned out for pizza anyway because the pizza guy sometimes came in and played Xbox with me. But by the time the pizza came I'd forgotten all about video games.

The Nazi officer shot my father in the stomach. "Die, you dirty Jew," he said, "but slowly." He watched my father die, sitting and smoking his black cigar. My father took a long time to die, almost a day and a half, by which time the Nazi officer had departed. The ground where he'd lounged was filthy with cigar ash.

I knew it was crap writing. Don't worry, I wasn't kidding myself. Mr. Morgenstern would have laughed his head off if he'd seen it, and my dad would have killed me for making stuff up. Nah, probably not. He'd have likely just shrugged. "Oh well, whatever, never mind."

He says that all the time like it's our goddamn family motto or something.

THAT WEEK THERE was a lot of talk about the Gittelman Car Wash Fundraiser. All the cool girls immediately signed up for wet T-shirt duty and Courtney Segal got to flip her hair and tear up every time she "spoke out" for the rights of Holocaust survivors to visit the land of their spiritual rebirth, despite the reality of nominal medical coverage. There was so much talk, in fact, that finally even Ms. McNamara, our vice principal, heard of it, and she immediately nixed the whole thing. No fundraiser, absolutely *no* car wash, leave Gittelman alone, she told the steering committee, according to a tearful Sami Fisher.

Yeah, I could have predicted that one, if I cared, which I didn't, (insert family motto here).

For a while Courtney Segal and her besties returned to the absorbing business of snapping selfies and posting pictures of the food they were about to eat (and in the case of Dee Leblanc, eat and then throw up again) and texting each other how totally hot they looked. Then, suddenly, a light bulb must have gone on above Courtney's head and glowed with a cute yellow light because all the kids started talking about this Virtual Journey to Israel that Courtney and her friends had cooked up. They'd loaded a bunch of Birthright photos onto an iPad, along with some Israeli folk songs, bought white and blue balloons from the dollar store, and, the rumour was, they were going to bake Star of David cupcakes to take to our final meeting with the survivors. If we can't fly Gittelman to Israel then let's bring Israel to Gittelman, kind of thing.

Courtney even said that her mom, who was the president of the Sisterhood at some synagogue or other, was going to get their rabbi to come and make a blessing.

"A blessing on what?" I asked.

"Um, a blessing?" she said like I'd never heard of such a thing. But being a dumbass from way back never stopped Courtney Segal from doubling down on stupid, and the next day she announced that her amazing mother had gotten their rabbi to agree to come to the Inspirational Living Centre and "give his blessing." She really looked hard at me when she said that but I looked right back as if to say, *What the fuck, Courtney, I knew you back when you wet your pants in kindergarten.*

To absolutely no one's surprise, Mrs. Boychuk was totally on board with the whole Virtual Journey caper.

"I'm sure Mr. Gittelman will be touched, Courtney," she said, helping to load plastic containers of cupcakes onto the school bus.

The girls had made dozens of cupcakes, one for every kid and their survivor, but from what I could see through the plastic, they'd grown bored with the whole Star of David concept and just gone with alternate rows of white and blue frosting — an oddly intense blue that I could already imagine transferred in streaks to dentures and braces and tongues.

We drove north again, down Broadway and up Main and through downtown with its glass buildings that reflected the school bus in broken-up pieces as we passed. Sometimes, at a traffic light, if you were really quick, you could even catch your own stupid face staring out of the bus window. The first time that happened I didn't recognize myself, although the freak in the dark hoodie looked strangely familiar. Everything was exactly the same is what I'm trying to say: the stupid "Downtown Biz" flags that flapped from streetlights to advertise the city's summer events — *Come to the Folk Festival! Get ready for Nuit Blanche!* — and the panhandlers holding up their pathetic cardboard signs, and even the giant cookie outside Dough Nuts doing a sort of oatmeal raisin cookie shuffle in the street.

When we passed the new gym on north Main all the kids yelled out, "Mr. Big Guy!" as if they'd never yelled that before although they did every time we passed it, coming or going. The rumour was that Dee's father *was* Mr. Big Guy, a rumour she was trying to kill by yelling loudest.

"Mr. Big Guy!" she hollered. "Mr. Fucking *Huge*!" She got her lame laugh and Courtney patted her back and gave her a *You go, girl* look, as if to say, I *believe you, Dee. Thousands wouldn't but I believe you.*

By the time we pulled up in the parking lot of the centre the bus driver was steaming because of the yelling and the balloons, and the kids were hyper at the thought of all those crazy cupcakes. It was our last visit with the survivors, and Mrs. Boychuk made us sit in the bus for five minutes and breathe. "Breathe, people."

I looked out of the window and wished I could stop breathing forever. Only I'd probably pass out and have to get mouth-to-mouth from someone really terrible like Mrs. Boychuk with her moustache or Dee Leblanc with her stinky throw-up breath. Somewhere in the Inspirational Living Centre Mr. Morgenstern waited for me, his tattoo glowing in the dark.

When Mrs. Boychuk had decided that we'd had enough breathing, she let us off the bus, with Courtney and the other girls exiting first. Laden down with their trays of cupcakes and their balloons, they made an odd procession, solemn and festive at the same time. Courtney tossed her hair and led the pack, holding up her iPad cued to Mr. Gittelman's Virtual Journey to Israel, as if it was a flag.

The rest of us followed the girls past the fitness room where Binder's grandmother was still wearing her #NeverForget T-shirt because, obviously, that lousy T-shirt was the one thing she would #AlwaysRemember. She waved to us as we passed, still singing along to Beyoncé, still trying to get her ladies to move "to the left, to the left, to the left!"

The survivors were where we had left them — the men and women in their long sleeves and dark clothes, their sad, hooded eyes.

"Welcome, boys and girls," Mrs. Silverstein said, no one ever having informed her that we were meant to be addressed as young men and women, or — as Mrs. Boychuk would say — people, at the very least. "Sit down, children," she said as if she was in charge of story time at the local library.

We all sat on the carpet in front of the old people, crowding in close because there wasn't much room.

"We have a very special guest today," Mrs. Silverstein continued, pushing forward some old guy in a black coat and hat. "It is my great pleasure to introduce Rabbi Zalman who, you should know, has taken time out of his busy rabbinical schedule to talk to us." For some reason she looked distracted and worried, and the rabbi didn't help matters by shifting from one foot to the other and staring at the floor, although when Mrs. Silverstein called for a big round of welcoming applause he brightened and started the applause himself, clapping his hands delightedly and moving them around in a circle.

"*Big* round of applause," he beamed.

Everyone laughed because the guy was obviously a halfwit.

"*O*-kay," Mrs. Boychuk said. "Let's get this show on the road."

At first she tried to organize the cupcake distribution and keep the balloons from popping and giving the old people heart attacks or something. But Courtney waved her away as if to say, *Thanks, but I've got this one. Much obliged, Mrs. B, but I'm in charge here.*

I never noticed before, but Courtney looks a lot like her mom, who is president of the Sisterhood and chair of the PTA and a lot of other stuff too, like the Talk to Your Teen initiative and the Neighbourhood Watch. My dad says she'd be a damn fine-looking woman if you could put her on mute.

I tried to put Courtney on mute but it was difficult to tune her out completely.

"One cupcake each," she was saying and, "I couldn't have done this alone."

"You're the ones who've inspired *us*," she was saying and, "It's just our small way of saying thank *you*."

"A shout-out to Sami and Dee-Dee for always being there for me," she was saying and, "Snaps to *all* my girls, you know who you are."

The old folks were looking confused but patient. I think that was just their faces, though — life had proven to be confusing and patience was their response. As if they'd been waiting for someone to finally take control, the kids quieted, settling down beside their survivors, as Sami and Dee began handing out the cupcakes. I found Mr. Morgenstern in his corner, a polo shirt straining across his swollen middle. He was sitting on the edge of his chair and craning, too preoccupied with the impending cupcakes to glare at me with his usual commitment.

"Before we begin, though," Courtney said, holding up her iPad, "I've got something here for someone very special. Mr. Gittelman, we want to take you on a Virtual Journey, a Journey unlike any other!"

Someone cried out and immediately stifled the sound. I saw Mrs. Silverstein whisper in Mrs. Boychuk's ear and Mrs. Boychuk clap her hand to her mouth. The kids were still craning around, looking for Mr. Gittelman, but he was nowhere to be seen and, in the corner of the room that had once echoed with his laughter, some other old man was dozing in his chair.

All around us, the old people stared blankly into space as if Mr. Gittelman had never existed. Then the rabbi stepped forward.

"Excuse me, uh, young lady, the fact is, Mr. Gittelman —" he began. "Mr. Gittelman is no longer with us." The old rabbi stood there for a moment, rocking backward and forward on his heels as if puzzled by something he'd just said. "That is to say, Mr. Gittelman is not *against* us," he qualified, his voice singsong as if he was about to launch into a sermon. But he never even finished the sentence; there was nothing more to say. Gittelman had set off on his own journey, a pilgrimage neither virtual nor unique.

He had been taken ill the previous week, Mrs. Silverstein explained, flustered. She was terribly sorry about the mix-up.

"That's what you're sorry about?" yelled Courtney. "The mix-up?"

Mrs. Silverstein looked at her over the tops of her spectacles and said no, she was sorry about a lot of other things as well, and the rabbi finally roused himself and patted Mrs. Silverstein's hand.

"Okay, people. *People,*" yelled Mrs. Boychuk, reverting to crisis control. Everywhere, kids were exclaiming to one another, but I couldn't concentrate because Mr. Morgenstern was tugging at my arm.

"Hoo-ha, boychick. Still as ugly as ever." He had already pushed two-thirds of his cupcake into his mouth. It was a blue cupcake and, as predicted, inclined to smear. "Vhat you vatchin', young man? You ain't never seen a tongue before?"

I had not, in fact, ever seen one so long, so rapacious, or so blue. All around the room the survivors and my classmates were eating their cupcakes, but with an odd delicacy, with tiny bites and restrained licks and small pats of the cocktail napkins that had been provided. The happy rumble of conversation and story was absent, and most of the attention was directed to the chair where Mr. Gittelman had once sat and where Courtney Segal now crouched beside the sleeping stranger, weeping.

"Who's de cutie?"

"Um, that's. Her name's Courtney."

"I can see dat you fency her, boychick. You vant to suck her little titties, don't you? Vy you not eating?"

In truth, I had forgotten about my cupcake, but Mr. Morgenstern's words were mere bait and switch — he was already stuffing my cupcake into his bright blue mouth.

"So vy's de cutie cryin'?" he mumbled, chunks of sodden frosting spraying this way and that. "Come on, young man, out wit it. Vy is de cutie cryin'?"

"She's…um, sad, I guess. About Mr. Gittelman."

"Ooh, you don't say! Poor little cutie. Poor little cutie wit de little titties! Hoo-ha!"

I hadn't taken Courtney Segal's side since junior high when she wore braces and glasses and was a real girl, but I suddenly remembered how it felt to like someone a whole lot, so much that you were just purely glad to see them every day. And besides, Mr. Morgenstern was a real bastard. But even as I was telling him how hard Courtney had worked to make Mr. Gittelman's Virtual Journey a reality, I suspected that he wasn't really listening. .

"Um, and that's why she's sad. Because she wanted Mr. Gittelman to enjoy this, like this Virtual Reality Tour of Israel? And now he's dead, so."

When I stopped, Mr. Morgenstern was silent for a long time, watching me intently, all the while running his fingers over the numbers tattooed on his inner arm. Finally he leaned forward, his tone conversational.

"So, a Virtual Reality Tour," he said. "And Gittelman didn't get to see it. Poor fellow, eh, poor besterd. It vould've made up for so many tings dat dat goddamn sucker lost out on. Getting to see der ferkakte Holy Land. Living tru' de Holocaust. Seein' his family turn black in de ovens. Dying, even. Pfft. No vonder de cutie pie is cryin', eh. No vonder."

It was late and Mrs. Boychuk said we should start saying our goodbyes. I watched the kids around me hugging their survivors and giving them the cards that they had bought or made. Mrs. Greenbaum was handing around Life Savers, and Mr. Salit was teaching Jackson Riley and Lazar Binder a protest song from the Warsaw Ghetto, and the rabbi was pulling quarters out of Shiva Patel's ear.

"If you hear a ringing in your ears, don't answer!" he chortled.

Mrs. Silverstein was asking a bunch of girls if they were vegetarians, she certainly hoped not, but it seemed to be the fashion these days. For instance, her own daughter, her Leah, had become one recently, and she was still a vegetarian even after Mrs. Silverstein pointed out that if God didn't want people to eat animals he wouldn't have made them out of food.

Old Mr. Ostralov, whose family never visited anymore, had positioned himself at the door so that he could shake hands with each of the departing students. "Come any time," he kept saying. "Any time is where you'll find me."

By way of farewell, Mr. Morgenstern dug me in the ribs one last time. "No vonder," he chided. "No vonder." It was unclear whether he was addressing me or himself but in either case his position was indisputable: the world was a dark and lonely place; it lacked wonder.

And he was right. Mr. Morgenstern was a bastard, but he had a point. The terrible burden of Mr. Gittelman's life could not be lifted by a bunch of photographs on an iPad and a dozen party balloons, although he would probably have enjoyed the cupcakes. And how had he died, who was with him at the end, was he at peace now with his newlywed by his side? No one would say. The other survivors had closed ranks. Their history was one thing, but the humdrum tragedies of the present, their living and their dying, was none of our business.

We were on the road again, the day's loop winding back: the giant cookie, the panhandlers, Mr. Big Guy (no one yelled). The traffic lights, the festival flags, the glass buildings. The afternoon sun slanted in through the bus windows but when I looked out all I could see was the ghostly reflection of my face. In another week it would be the summer vacation, and I suddenly realized that I had nothing to do and no one to do it with. Most of the kids went to sleep-away camp over the summer or chilled at their parents' cottages. Last summer I'd hung out at the mall to get away from the heat and the Meisners' dog, but mostly to keep a lookout for my mom because I figured if she came back that'd be the first place she'd go.

The kids were quiet for once and kind of sad. Some of them were talking about their Holocaust survivors, but no one said "adorable," no one said "sweetheart." And maybe it was the light that blurred the edges and softened faces, but I wondered if the stories we'd heard had grieved us in ways we couldn't yet understand, and made us want to clean cars and bake cupcakes and blow up balloons. I don't know. I never wanted to see mine again, and I was glad that every city block was taking me farther away from him, but to hear some of those kids talk, they were really going to miss their Holocaust survivors.

SIX

THE EMPRESS MALL

KATSUMI PHONES UP and says, "D'you wanna go to the mall, Dee?"

"Nobody phones anymore, Kat," I tell her. "Haven't you heard of texting?"

She comes to pick me up in *das Auto*, which always smells of Angel perfume and cigarette smoke — the essence of Kat. Somehow she's timed it just right so that when I open the car door "Jerk" is blasting on the CD and I'm just in time to yell out the chorus. That's the thing about Kat; she's the whole 3D experience: sight, sound, smell. She hits repeat and we sing the song again, this time Kat playing ironic air guitar and improvising dance moves, both of which she somehow manages while revving down Empress Street so fast that she only narrowly misses a pedestrian. ("Ugh, old people," she says.) The street is a gridlock of roadworks and construction crews, as if we're in the middle of one of those early computer games with lame graphics and no plot. My dad always says there's only two seasons in this city — winter and roadworks. I'm just about to repeat something totally dorky like that when Kat takes up where we left off about an hour ago, which is kind of her thing.

"'Course I've heard of texting, Lamb Chop," she says. "I just wanted to hear your sweet fucking voice." We laugh for about ten minutes at least, because it's a joke, this not-texting kick she's on. Sometimes she says, "I can't think with my thumbs, Chop," and sometimes she says, "My goddamn phone died." Sometimes she says, "Texting is so not my thing, Lamb," and sometimes it's, "My fingers are tired, I think I've been wearing them out again." Kat has a high sex drive and a lot of jokes about tired fingers.

It's all a game and we both know it. Kat's older than me but she texts like a fiend when she wants to. Phoning is her new thing though, because it's hipster and cool and makes everything sound urgent, she says. Pluswhich she gets to talk while she's doing it, so win-win.

I met Kat at my dad's gym, where she teaches kickboxing. I'm fifteen and she's older than me by ten years so do the math. She doesn't look that old, though, because of her Asian genes. She's Japanese on her dad's side and something I can never remember on her mom's, but she gets her gorgeousness from her dad because have you *seen* her mom? The last time Kat saw her dad she was in pigtails and knee socks.

"Hey, you're still in pigtails and knee socks," I go.

"Yeah," she says. "It's my Catch-a-Predator look."

Sometimes I think Kat likes chilling with me because it gives her a chance to flip her crazy switch and act like a teenager again but, as my mom says, I am an old soul. What my mom actually says is, "Lighten up, Dee, you're not dead yet."

Anyway, we're hanging out at the food court, trying to

decide what to eat, or hopefully just what to eat first, and that's another thing I like about Kat.

When I used to go to the mall with my mom we didn't hang out at the food court at all, because my mom hates the hoi polloi, and fast food, and having to rub elbows with the one to line up for the other. "I don't believe in lining up for food, Dee," she once told me, like she grew up in the Depression or something, which she didn't, but not believing in lineups is *her* thing when it comes to food courts, concession stands, and all-you-can-eat buffets, even the ones with marshmallow salad.

"That's not a belief," I told her. "God is a belief, Buddha is a belief, Jesus Christ and Krishna and the Holy Ghost are beliefs."

My mom looked at me and narrowed her eyes to indicate that she was not in the mood for any of my guff, missy, but she only said, "I'd appreciate a little religious tolerance there, young lady."

The thing is, healthy food's a religion with my mom. She's super devout about not eating carbs or refined sugars or, my god, sat fats. And she's uber into cleansing, *colonic* cleansing, which is okay by me because, as my dad says, she's full of it. In some ways my mom's a total zealot, the kind they'd have burnt at the stake in the Middle Ages.

When I tell Courtney and Sami about my mom's obsession with her squeaky clean colon, they laugh and advise me to press the bitch button next time she calls but I can tell they're thinking, *Wouldn't hurt her to lose like ten pounds. Maybe fifteen. Wouldn't hurt her to pop a couple of poop pills or swallow a tapeworm.* It's a good thing they're away at camp all summer because going to the food court with Courtney and Sami is pure torture. First Courtney calculates the calories in a half-order of edamame beans on her Butt Burn CC app, and then Sami says, "Yeah but you got to remember the soy, girl."

Soy is the killer 'cause it's loaded with salt and we all know what salt does.

What salt does is retain water, so no soy, no sir. They do the whole calorie-counting, app-consulting, food-wanking thing for about an hour and finally get so hungry with all the *math* they're doing that they give in and get panic cheeseburgers from A&W. It'd be rude not to join them so I order a salad, no dressing, and a diet soda, no ice. It doesn't make any difference, though. Courtney and Sami each have a cheeseburger with fries and a chocolate shake and neither of those two puts on an ounce because, here's the kicker, by some magical property of fat-girl friendship, all the calories from their burgers and fries gets sucked into *my* salad, which I scarf down in about three seconds. God, you can actually watch my stomach pooch out.

But going to the food court with Kat is a whole other deal. "Okay, here's the thing," she says. "We can go frozen yogurt or fries, slushy or sushi. I don't believe in mixing my sweet with my savoury." Kat makes the international sign for gagging, complete with sound effects, and we both crack up. Kat stops first, though, in case I think she's laughing at my totally bizarre mother.

"Hashtag TotallyBizarreMother," I go. "Hashtag Starving ForMyBeliefs."

"Hashtag HungryAsFuck," Kat interrupts, and we end up splitting a yogurt smoothie (two straws), a salad (two forks), and a plate of fries (fingers, mainly). Kat calls it hedging our bets: fruit for energy, salad for being good, and fries because they're goddamn *fries*, girl. She only nibbles a few fries, though, because of being a fitness instructor. Pluswhich, she's decided to lose a couple of pounds. "Twenty-five's the tipping point, Chop," she tells me. Years, not pounds, she means.

I don't mind. I finish the fries before I've even noticed I'm eating them and, as usual, I'm still hungry on account of not being in touch with my appetite (Mom), because I don't eat slowly enough to experience that feeling of satiety (Mom), which comes with moderation and a healthy lifestyle (freaking guess who?). My dad doesn't say any of those things — he's not much of a talker.

Kat passes me a wad of paper napkins to take with me to the washroom and when I get back she hands me a stick of gum, already unwrapped. I give her the thumbs up and she tells me I'm the goddamn throw-up queen of River City.

"Ready, Lamb Chop?" she asks. And when I nod she yells, "Steady, Go!" and we both charge off for the upper mezzanine, on course for my favourite place in the world. I call it the Emporium of Everlasting Desire. It's got its own real-life name but I'm against product placement.

The first things I see when we walk in the door are the mannequins with their angel wings and their whorish bustiers and their remote, middle-distance gaze. Everything is whispers and feathers, lace and uplift, as if the Earth's lost its pull — this is a gravity-free zone, folks! — and the music that isn't a radio station plays from speakers that aren't speakers, or at least aren't visible, and the whole store is lit with the gentle pink glow of *No boys allowed*.

We're here to shop for a bra for Kat, and not a sports bra like the one we bought last week at lululemon. Kat wants an optical illusion — an undergarment that will showcase her amazing double Ds, but made of sugar and spice and French lace and dreaming. That's what she tells the salesgirl who comes up to ask if we need help.

"I need something that will make my boyfriend's dick super hard," Kat says. "Something that will put ding dong in his denims."

I know she wants to shock the salesgirl and make me laugh, but somehow our wires get crossed and the salesgirl — whose name turns out to be "Ask Kimmy" — giggles, and I'm the one who feels the prickle of embarrassment on my skin. Kat's like that: a live wire flashing through dry air.

Ask Kimmy, almost cross-eyed with wanting to please, looks at Kat's tits and says, "Double D — right?"

"No, *she's* Dee," Kat says, pointing to me, and the only thing that stops this from being the most hilarious joke in the best of all possible worlds is when Ask Kimmy looks at my tits and you can see her thinking: *Her! She's not anything. She's got a couple of infected mosquito bites, is all.*

Katsumi is beautiful, let's just get that out of the way right off. Most people only see her Amazin' Asian Beauty, which is like a perfectly fitting Spandex layer over legs (long), and skin (smooth), and lips (pouty, but in a satirical way), and the sort of hair that should be dark (it's platinum), but that mainly looks like shiny nylon. Today she's wearing a pleated Catholic school-girl skirt and over-the-knee socks and what she calls her fuck-me boots. Except even Catholic schoolgirls don't wear their skirts *that* short and her over-the-knee socks have little arrows along the side pointing up. I'm wearing jeans and a Ridgehaven Ravens volleyball hoodie and, truthfully, the two of us don't even look like we're the same species. If she's a girl then I'm something else, something not-quite-girl. An un-girl. Which is probably why most people can't believe she's my friend. You see them frowning and thinking, *Um, why?*

My mom is one of those unbelievers vis-à-vis Kat and me,

but then her beliefs are strictly food related. Also, she has this thing about elephants in confined spaces. She says the elephant in the room is my low self-esteem since the divorce and, not coincidentally, my dad's philandering ways, and my dad says he's got no elephants to pick with *her*, but if he did, if he *did* —.

My elephant is invisibility and not being anything special. I am not Kat, not all that, not anything really. I am the control half of Kat's experiment with beauty.

Dee. Lamb Chop. Lambie. Chop. I used to cry when the kids in elementary school called me Dora the Explorer, but I got over that in time to not cry when they started calling me Clitora, which isn't even a real word so fuck you, Lindi Jorgenson. I still won't answer to Dora, although my dad sometimes calls me Dor like I am something he can slam shut.

"What's your name?" Ask Kimmy asks Kat.

"Call me K, okay?" says Kat.

Ask Kimmy writes "Okay" on the chalkboard that hangs on the change room door and goes off to find more lacy double Ds on their miniature bra hangers, and Kat and I fall on the floor, practically, because Okay is by far the dumbest name for a totally hot chick like Kat to have.

Kat. Katsumi. Kitten. Kay. My dad calls her babe because she works for him and he is a jerk, but Kat doesn't seem to mind. Her ex-boyfriend called her Kit Kat, but no one, until now, has called her Okay.

"Oh Kay, oh God, O*kay*," I go.

"Kay and Dee!" she giggles, "Sitting in a tree. K.I.S.S.I.N.G!" She begins by blowing me kisses, then suddenly grabs my chin and, with her other hand, pulls the back of my head toward her. I am looking at her mouth (her beautiful mouth) and thinking, Oh? *Oh?*

But instead I say, "Um, Kat?" which is when Ask Kimmy comes back with about ten more wispy pieces of daydreams and underwire swinging from her index finger.

"Let me know if there's anything else you need," she says and Kat goes, "I need a plate of fries and a beer and a Lexus sports coupe and to lose five pounds." She's pulled her shirt over her head and snapped out of her bra and she's standing there in her gorgeous smooth skin that shines like it's been polished, which it kind of has been (Burt's Bees Cocoa Butter and Shea body rub), and her extraordinary double Ds, which are huge and yet self-supporting, if you know what I mean. And just for the record they do not look like melons and her nipples (small, dark) do not resemble berries.

If you take enough *Seventeen* quizzes you get to find out all kinds of neat stuff about yourself, like which Hogwarts house you belong to, or what your Girl Power Anthem is, or where your tits measure up on the secret *Seventeen* fruit-breast continuum. I'm a natural Hufflepuff, but I've never liked that Carrie Underwood song (my designated G.P. Anthem), especially not the words that go, "Wish you could see yourself the way I do." Most of the time, I don't want anyone to see me at all. Me and my "perky lemon" tits.

Kat is a Slytherin, of course, and her anthem is "Girl on Fire," but despite full marks for her "ripe honeydews," I am beginning to feel that fruit is not the way to go when it comes to Kat's bodacious boobs. Maybe inflatable toys, maybe party balloons. I don't know, but the truth is I've never seen breasts like hers although, actually, now that I think about it I haven't seen anyone's breasts — not bare-assed naked, not full frontal — since Lindi Jorgenson and I swapped training bras in sixth grade gym class because we'd pledged to be best friends and soul sisters, besticles for*ever*, which lasted until the end of the day when the weight of Lindi's post-training breasts snapped the frayed strap of my Playtex SportyGirl, and she told everyone that I was totally ghetto.

"Well, what about you, Chop?" Kat says, and I come out of my daze.

"Breasts," I say.

"Huh, good one!" Kat says. "You'll grow them, don't worry." She puts out her hand and, just like that, takes a fistful of whatever she finds on my chest (mostly hoodie). Straight away my nipples puff up, and I imagine two pouty little doll's mouths pursing up their lips for a kiss. A terrible red blush laps over me, my whole body tidal with shame.

"Hmm, nope, I feel a definite lift-off," Kat says, and I am so damn relieved that she's decided to pretend that a bright red girl is not wriggling in mortification in front of her that I find the courage to ask what I've wanted to know ever since the first time I saw her jiggling across my dad's gym in a lululemon fuchsia and turquoise crossover.

"When did yours, um, begin to grow?"

"God, are you kidding me? These aren't real. Here, feel."

Kat takes my hand and presses it against her right breast and I feel her warm skin under my hand, but behind that skin something is firm and inflated like a ball some kid has pumped up with too much air. Kat is looking at me in this encouraging way she has, as if to say, *Go ahead girl, be my guest*, but I can't decide what to do with my hand. My mom is a great one for etiquette, like setting your knife and fork together after you've eaten and not leaving them lying about like bloody great oars, Dee, and saying, "Pleased to meet you" instead of "Hi" or, as is my preference, nothing at all. But she has never instructed me on boob etiquette and I'm stymied. Luckily, Ask Kimmy knocks on the change room door with a kind of *how's-it-going-in-there-ladies?* knock, and we jump apart like we've been oh-so busted.

"Do you need a hand?" asks Ask Kimmy.

"Yes," says Kat. "I need someone to feel if my tits are on straight." Then she throws me a Gossard Dream Angel Bra to stuff in my mouth so I don't snort through my nose and embarrass us both. We hear Ask Kimmy flouncing off, her high heels clicking away, and Kat makes the international sign for *I-swear-that-girl-has-a-carrot-up-her-ass*.

"Yeah, no, I got them for my birthday from Mr. Special K, hottest DJ in the city."

That's what Kat called him when they were together. And now she sees no reason to change his *name* when she can change her *tone*, is what she says. Anyway, he is a total asshole scuzzball dickwad Super-Jerk, a revved up, steroid-puffed version of my dad who is just an ordinary jerk, no adjectives required.

Kat calls my dad Mr. Big Guy because that's the name of his gym and, take it from her, an accurate description of his physique. I turn away before she can wink, and suddenly wonder what she'll call him after she's dumped him.

Mr. Big Guy, I guess.

The problem with change rooms is that wherever you look, there you are. I'm not in the mood to look at myself (I never am), but today especially. I'm not even talking about how shiny my forehead is or how un-shiny my hair looks. What I really want to know is how a girl can be so pooched out practically everywhere except where it counts (breasts). I am all stomach and thighs and butt, yet my boobs are like tiny little footnotes to a thought that hasn't been thought.

Whenever I complain about my body, Courtney says, "I hear

you, cutie-pie," and Sami says, "Yeah, totally." But Courtney and Sami are somewhere else, jumping off a dock in their teeny-tiny string bikinis and shrieking as they hit the water so that the hot boy counsellor will jump in and save them.

What my dad would say if he could talk, which he can technically but reserves the right not to, would be: "You're fat, Dee — and lazy and greedy. But mostly fat." I try to twist around to avoid his words, but the change room mirror is playing catch and keeps throwing me these devastating glimpses of myself (overlapping thighs, little pad of flesh below my chin, second trimester stomach).

I notice that half my hair has already slipped out of the French braid I attempted this morning, probably because my hair is so fine but also because I am the clumsiest kid my mom has ever come across, bar none.

"I mean, it took you a year to learn to tie your own shoes, Dee," she still laments as if someone out there owes her a year.

If time is continuous and matter can't be destroyed and sound waves go on forever, which is something you pick up in AP Science, then somewhere there is a fat-fingered kid still crouching beside a kitchen chair, trying to tie knots and double loops and then actual bows around its leg.

"Nearly, Dee," my mom would say in her better moments of which there were hardly any because she is the worst bow-tying instructor in the world. Bar none.

"Okay," says Kat, grabbing my chin and waiting until I raise my eyes. "What's the problem, Lamb Chop?"

I shrug, and pudgy girl in the mirror shrugs too. Kat cinches her waist with her hands and taps her foot, which is the international sign for, *I'm waiting, Chop*, so I mumble something about being so fucking pale.

"I wish I had your skin," I tell her.

"Are you kidding me?" she totally shrieks. "God, Dee, look at yourself! You and your adorable white body!" She yanks me up and pulls my hoodie over my head so that I'm just standing there in my tank top and jeans. "You are so goddamn cute, Dee, I can't even believe it. Hey, girl, that's what I'm going to call you from now on: Adorable Dora!"

I wince because nobody's allowed to use that name. But the thing is, Kat is talking to the girl in the mirror and that girl is listening. That girl is loving what she's hearing; that girl is lapping it up. I watch her preen: *Adorable, am I?* I watch her poke out her tits and ass: *Maybe?* I watch her toss her hair as if she's finally made an important decision. As if she's come down firmly on the side of beauty.

"Any luck, ladies?" It's Ask Kimmy again, only with a different voice. Kat yanks open the door to see what's happened to our old friend. The woman standing there doesn't blink even though Kat is naked except for the upside down isosceles of her tiny bikini bottom, and the gold thong she's twirling around one finger like she's some sort of glitzy underwear cowgirl.

"Would you like to try a smaller size?" asks the woman, not blinking. She is old, older than Kimmy, anyway. I'm already beginning to miss Kimmy, the way I miss everyone I don't really know, except for Kat. I miss Kat all the time, even when we're hanging out.

"Where's Kimmy?" asks Kat, although she really means, *Who are you?*

"I'm Farida, if you need anything."

"Yeah, who are you if I don't need anything?" yells Kat, but the woman has already walked away.

"What a bitch," Kat says. But she isn't a bitch; she's just

old. Older than Kimmy, older even than Kat. She's seen it all, is what it is. There's nothing that two girls in a change room can get up to that will impress her. It kills the buzz, I won't lie.

After that we decide to leave, and Kat says not to worry, she'll pick up a sexy bra later in the week, in time for Saturday night. But when I ask her what's happening on Saturday night, she won't tell me and the girl in the mirror looks sort of hurt but she holds it together and makes a duck mouth with her fingers which is the international sign for *Blah Blah Blah*.

Then Kat uses the Gossard Dream Angel Bra to wipe away the purple chalk of her name on the door — *Okay!* — and we hustle out of there. Past Farida (ringing up a purchase), past the mannequin angels (watching), past the leopard-print and tiger-striped underwear sets (in case a girl suddenly wants to dress up as an animal), past the feather-trimmed negligees and the high-heeled slippers. Past the beautiful girls lost in their advertisements for beauty.

But I'm not really into Kat's crazy antics anymore, because suddenly I notice that everything's changing: the Emporium of Everlasting Desire is starting to fade away. The mannequins droop their wings and the music crackles into static. All at once the walls are just walls rather than the glowing pink lining of an expensive jewelry box. The creepy boys hanging around outside, listening to the gangsta rap that's pouring out of the next-door HMV, shove each other and whistle at us.

Kat stops for a moment to make the international sign for *Eat dick, dude*, which she has not invented but has certainly perfected. She pretends to push a penis into her mouth then pops her tongue in her cheek. In and out, in and out, hand steady, cheek popped. But Kat is a conceptual artist of the obscene; she knows she can do better. She goggles her eyes because her mouth is stuffed full, then she begins to moan. *Aah, aaah-ahh!*

All of a sudden she is choking because of this enormous, this *thing* in her mouth. *Ah, aagh! Ooh, ooOOH!* Her eyes roll back in her head and her whole body convulses. But before her final orgasmic death shudder, she makes one last valiant effort, managing to raise her right hand to her forehead, thumb and forefinger frozen in the international sign for *Loser.* The thing about Kat is that she has remarkable coordination.

The boys wolf whistle and catcall. One of them drops his pants and is about to shine his moon when Kat grabs my hand and we run, giggling and pulling one another, up the down escalator, bumping into shoppers and making babies cry.

"Show me," I say. And Kat pulls out her swag, the Seamless Beautyform with transparent straps that she stashed in her purse when we fled. Then she digs into her purse again and pulls out the smallest triangle of Valentine-red lace that I've ever seen. It's suspended on a complicated system of satin ropes and pulleys, and it's for me.

"What's the matter? Don't you like it?" Kat asks before I have time to react. "Hey, isn't that your boyfriend?" She points to this random dude passing by, his head swaying to his music. He's not my boyfriend (obviously), and I don't think Kat's ever seen him before but naturally, because it's my flipping lucky day, he turns out to be this kid from school, Daniel someone, who is a total stoner but also, apparently, something of a gentleman because he yanks out his earbuds as if to say, *Can I help you, miss?*

"Hey, what's your name?" Kat yells. "Hey *you*, do you like Dee's new panties?" Daniel doesn't say but his face turns the same colour as the Valentine-red thong, which Kat is now waving about in front of him as if she is a tiny matador.

"Fuck Kat, quit it!" I yell, grabbing the thong. I turn around to shrug at Daniel — *Sorry, dude, nothing to do with me!* — but he is so out of there. He's like Invisible Man, one minute there, the next who knows where?

"Nice one, Kat," I say because lame sarcasm is my thing, always has been.

"*Je suis désolée,*" she yells over her shoulder. "*Désolée, désolée, désolée!*"

She's not, though. Not sorry, not sorrowful, not *desolate*. Instead she's off and running, and as I trundle after her the crazy chemical happiness of being with Kat that's been flashing through me all afternoon burns itself out. The change room has changed nothing, I realize, least of all me. I am suddenly so low that I could howl like a dog. I want to fall down and press my cheek to the grimy, spilled-juice and chewing-gummy mall floor where people have been treading all day long. I want to climb to the top of this terrible place — this Mall of Desolation — and throw my adorable white body into the ornamental water feature outside Starbucks. Instead, I stuff the thong into my pocket and follow Kat, who is bumping into ugly people on purpose, then shrieking "*Je suis désolée, monsieur! Zut alors, mademoiselle! Je suis profondément désolée!*"

French is Kat's third language, she likes to say. She uses it mainly for sex and dramatic irony.

We're back on the mezzanine, on our way to get caffein-ated, which would kill my mother who'd rather I did heroin with a shared needle than drink an occasional moccachino. I swear. Kat is walking backward and I'm supposed to tell her when she's about to hit someone, but she never listens and we're getting serious side eye from all the people she's lurching into.

The stores are already getting in their fall fashions because it's July, duh. There's something depressing about looking at ribbed sweaters in summer, as if the Mall of Desolation is always one season ahead of you. It's my mom's birthday this month, which is a total rip-off because I hate her, and besides I'm broke. Anyway, what could I get her? I mean, let's say I was a salesgirl and she was a customer and I said, "I'm Dee if you need anything, ma'am — just let me know." She'd say: "Another kind of daughter, please. A different size, a better attitude."

When I was little and still loved her, I'd make a big fat fuss of her birthday. The whole macaroni art and potato print thing, and once I saved all my pocket money and bought her a jewelry box with a ballerina crouched inside. The ballerina stood up when the lid opened, and turned round and round to the tune of "Turkey in the Straw," which my mom found a total riot.

But now? I guess I could always get her a kilo of organic, free-range tomatoes. Or a couple of fair-trade, antibiotic-free chocolate bars. Or a gift certificate for a state-of-the-art colonic irrigation. There you go, Mom. Knock yourself out.

I start to worry about not having any money, like, *ever*, and having to rely on handouts from wealthy junk food addicts for an occasional plate of curly fries, and how I'll translate this whole not having money thing into a birthday gift for my mom. Then I remember that my dad will probably shove a wad of cash into my hand and say, "Buy something for the woman who gave you life, Dor."

"Watch out, Kat," I yell, because she's still doing her backward walking and this time she's about to whack into an ancient dude with a walker. Then, of course, she does and she's all, "Oh my goodness!" and "Heavens to Betsy!" and "Pardon my clumsiness, ma'am." The old man has his aluminum walker jammed against the mall railing and I'm trying to reverse him out, but he's clutching a paper bag and muttering about thieves, and Kat is like a drunk driver with three priors: she's already left the scene of the crime.

"Sorry, sorry, sorry," I mutter, but what I'm thinking is, *Damn, damn, damn*, because Kat's my ride home. Up aways I can see her crazy-shine hair rippling through the stream of shoppers, bobbing against this one or that one as the current takes her. The old man is fumbling at his chest, which is so not my thing — heart attacks, I mean — but it turns out he's only searching for his spectacles. Naturally, they're on top of his head but he finally locates them — gotcha! — and settles them on his nose. They are the biggest damn spectacles I've ever seen: cartoonish goggles with thick black frames and fingerprint smudges matting the lenses. *Good idea, Mr. Squarepants*, I think. *Right on.*

He takes a long look at me as if to say, *Who do you think you are?*

I take a long look at him and remember my plan to die before I turn forty.

"Well, young lady. And what's the big hurry?" he asks. "No, don't tell me. You were on your way to perform open heart surgery. *That* I can forgive. Or perhaps you were rushing off to give an address to the Supreme Court? The United Nations? The Nobel Prize Committee?" He goes on and on: "Maybe the Miss World pageant called to say they've seen your photo and don't bother turning up for the swimsuit competition? Why such a rush? Whatever it is, it can wait, believe me. Have you ever heard the expression —"

"Whoa," I say. "'Don't bother turning up for the swimsuit competition'? Really?"

The old man looks smug. "Swimsuit is tough. You're a pretty girl, if you don't mind me saying, but you don't look up to Swimsuit."

"You don't look up to, to... God what are you *wearing*?"

"Ha, you've never seen a smoking jacket, young lady?"

I have now, and it hasn't made me any wiser or happier or less inclined to push the old guy over the mezzanine. The jacket is sharp: red and velvety with a flashy green handkerchief spilling out of the breast pocket and a Shriners button on the lapel. He's wearing his jacket over tracksuit bottoms, finished off with neon sneakers, their treads so thick he looks like he's in a monster truck rally. The laces are untied, but the sneakers are as crisp and as new as the old guy is worn and blurry. He is so not what Courtney would call "old person cute," which is a version of cuteness that has nothing to do with hot guys. By the way there is a stain over his crotch, which I point out to him, mean girl and reject from the Miss World swimsuit competition that I am.

"This little thing?" he gestures. "It's just urine, young lady. You try peeing through a Zimmer frame."

If Courtney was here she'd pretend to throw up into her Michael Kors purse (this new thing she does), but Courtney is probably sitting round a campfire, singing the dirty version of some Kumbaya-type number and running her fingers up the inside of that hot counsellor's thigh (this new thing she's planning to do).

If Kat was here she'd text me *wwwwwww*, which is Japanese for LMAO, but Kat is far below us, at ground level. I can see her platinum head ducking and weaving although not, obviously, in the interest of avoiding mall crawlers and window shoppers and little kids who drift across her path. The problem with Kat is that she's so beautiful nobody believes how evil she can be.

"It wasn't even me who bumped into you," I say. "It was my friend."

He makes an elaborate 360-degree turn, cocking his head this way and that. He even puts his hand up to visor his eyes so that he can pretend to look into the distance for this invisible pal of mine, but all he says is: "Some friend!"

I shrug, and immediately feel about ninety years old. I mean here I am standing in front of Orthotics Galore and shooting the breeze with an old guy in a smoking jacket and unlaced sneakers. Someone whose age my own is the square root of.

"If that's a smoking jacket, where's the smoke?"

"You want to smoke, young lady?" He brightens as if the slow, dopey blood in his veins has suddenly turned phosphorescent. As if he's a slot machine landing *thunk thunk thunk* on a triple row of double cherries.

I do want to smoke, and I say so. Smoking is the thing I'm really good at. Everyone has a thing, Kat says, and this is mine. I'm talking smoke rings and torpedoes, I'm talking loop de loops. I'm talking exhaling through both nostrils at once like a street-festival dragon.

We start ambling toward the exit. Glaciers thinking about the possibility of moving could not be more cautious.

"Call me Milt," the old man says when we finally Zimmer our way to the exit with its practically immovable pneumatic doors that seem to want to trap you in the Mall of Desolation forever. I wrestle one open for him and he gradually inches himself through, blinking into the sunlight, his weak eyes tearing up behind his fishbowl lenses. But even a beat-up old guy in a walker isn't allowed to stand and smoke within fifteen metres of a public building, so we're forced to dawdle across the parking lot to the bus shelter where you're not allowed to smoke either, but everyone does. There are a couple of food court ladies in hairnets already in occupation but they move over when they see us coming. *Take a load off, fellas, there's room for everyone in the smoking hut!*

Out on Empress Street, the road crews are using jackhammers to break up the asphalt. The sound keeps getting louder then fading away then ramping up again, like the corny soundtrack to a movie about giant earthmovers coming alive and taking over the world. I tell him my dad's theory about there being only two seasons in this city and he nods as if he's heard it before.

"Call me Milt," he says again, over the noise. "Milt, short for Milton. A terrific poet but not such a good father, if you don't mind me saying so."

"Call me Ida," I say, just for the hell of it.

"Still, he had some very nice daughters. Fine girls," he says. He opens the bag he's been clutching for the duration of our acquaintance and fishes out a packet of Marlboros.

Whoa! I think, but do not say.

Milt seems to know what I'm thinking, though, because he knocks me an enormous wink that involves both his eyes and half his face. I'm praying that he doesn't light a cigarette by puffing at it and then handing it over, all saliva-ed up and mouth-germy. I don't mind when Kat does that, even when she gets lipstick on the filter, but this guy? He has old man spittle zigzagging at the corners of his mouth. But he doesn't gum up the cigarette, just lights it off of his own, like a normal person.

Smoking has put Milt in a rambling mood. He starts to tell me about his friend, Mr. Tergusson, who has a daughter he sees maybe once a month. She has enormous feet, this daughter of Mr. Tergusson's. In fact, whenever his daughter visits, Mr. Tergusson just cannot get over her feet. Where did she get such big feet? his friend often wonders to himself. It's difficult to believe that he's fathered such a Labrador in human form. Then Milt who, get this, used to be in men's clothing and apparel, whatever that is, kindly fills me in on Mr. Tergusson's waist size (32 inches) and his shoe size (8 in a men's narrow).

"Ah well," Milt concludes, "that's just how it goes with parents and kids."

I ask him how, *how* does it go? For some reason I'm mad as hell but Milt just shrugs and blows a perfect smoke ring then shoots an arrow through the middle. The food court ladies clap and he nods in solemn acknowledgement.

"Break's over," says one. They grind their butts out and fling them into the long grass beneath the trash can. We watch them dawdle back to the mall, adjusting their hairnets and yawning.

Milt turns back to me. "What about your father?" he asks. "Just a for-instance."

"An instance of what?"

"For instance, is he a good father, a kind man, a faithful husband?"

I snort. "None of the above, but he's super fit, so."

"And into what does he fit?"

I think of all the things my dad fits into: his loft apartment above the gym, his new car, his shiny new life. Everything, I guess, except his old family: my mom and me.

Milt is gazing at me from behind the magnification of his enormous spectacles. His eyes are curious and bleary like the eyes of a sleepy, but intelligent, burrowing animal, a gopher or a chipmunk. "And what about your alleged friend?" he burrows.

"Yes, he fits with Kat," I say. "He's her boss at the gym, but they're good friends too."

"Your father is a friend of your friend?"

"Yeah, well, I don't have any friends so he gave me one of his."

"Huh," Milt says. "A new world."

I think of Kat — her latex skin and her nylon hair and her double double Ds. She is ten years older than me and fifteen years younger than my dad. She fits in between us, where my mom used to be.

"Yup, yup. Being a father, it ain't easy. If you don't mind me saying."

"How many kids do you have?" I ask.

"One living, two dead," he tells me.

After that we just smoke for a while. Milt blows three smoke rings in a row, the first one already beginning to waver and break up before the last is fully formed. A bus comes by but doesn't stop. There's no one at the bus stop anyway, except us two, and my natural tendency toward invisibility is enhanced by the presence of this old guy beside me. Two dead, I keep thinking. How did he manage to lose two kids? Tragic, my mom would say (hand over her mouth). Life, eh, my dad would say (shrugging). *OhEmGee!!!* Courtney would text, spelling out the letters (her thing), three exclamations minimum. But Kat would probably just go, "How careless is that?" and be on her merry way.

It's hot out, after the air conditioned mall. The sun is like a pinball, zinging off every windscreen and side mirror and metallic surface in the parking lot. I'm trying to wriggle out of my hoodie when Milt puts out his hand and I think, *Here it comes.*

"Easy does it, Ida," he says.

I am so grossed out that I want to vomit. I flick my cigarette away and get up to leave. The old man is clutching at my tank top. The veins in his hands look like they've been badly knitted, and his nails are thick yellow ridges, like rinds of hard cheese. Which is when I realize that, benefit-of-the-doubt-wise, he was probably only trying to prevent my tank top from riding up over my head. I'm flooded with shame and guilt and wish I was dead. Luckily this is such a familiar feeling that I'm immediately comforted.

"Slow down there, Lady Godiva," Milt says. He lights us both another cigarette and passes mine over. We sit there in the noisy, dusty, fumy parking lot, staring into space and smoking. I don't know how I'm going to get home and I'm just considering hitting up Milt for bus fare when he points. "Lookie, lookie, here comes cookie."

"So you did see her," I say, and he taps the side of his nose with his finger. Kat comes skipping toward us.

"There you are, my adorable Dora. *Vamanos!* Let's blow this two-bit Popsicle stand."

"A pleasure to meet you, young lady." Milt shuffles to his feet and holds out his hand. "You can call me Milt."

"*Milt!*" yells Kat. "Milt, Milt, Bo-Bilt, Banana-Fana Fo-Filt, Fee-Fi-Mo-Ilt, *MILT!*"

"Ha, good one," says Milt. "And I'll call you Hit and Run, eh. I'll call you Locomotive."

Kat cottons on. "You can call me the Reaper," she says. "You can call me Euthanasia." She takes him in, from his monster-truck sneakers trailing their fraying, knotted laces, to his smoking jacket that looks bald and shabby in the sunlight. Milt flourishes his green silk handkerchief and wipes his forehead.

Then he grins, as if to indicate that she is an unreliable child but ho-boy, one smart cookie.

"O indignity, O blot!" he exclaims in a quotey sort of voice. He goes on for a long time, one hand on his red velvet breast. When he's finished, he beams at her. "My namesake, Mr. John Milton."

Without missing a beat Kat starts to sing our current favourite song: "You *jerk*, you *jerk*, you are s-uu-c-h a *jerk*!" She blows through the chorus twice, really belting it out, then takes a bow. "My idol, Ms. Kim Stockwood," she deadpans.

"Stockwood…Stockwood…Do I know her father?" Milt asks.

Kat catches my eye and makes the international sign for *This-guy-should-be- locked-up*, or perhaps it's the one for *That-is-one-totally-rad-smoking-jacket*. Who knows? The thoughts that used to flash between us, fast as text messages, are on a half bar, and the signals have begun to waver and break up.

"O-*kay*," Kat says, cracking herself up at the memory of a long ago joke. "*Je suis désolée* but it's time to go. *Allons-y*, Chop?" She's standing in front of the sun with her long legs and bright hair that, just this minute, has burst into flame. Her fierce and terrible beauty. She looks like the mannequin angels of my remotest longing.

I stand up and shuffle after her.

"Goodbye, Ida," Milt calls. "Maybe we'll bump into one another again."

I'm halfway across the parking lot and Kat is going on about Ida — "I'da thought you had better things to do than pick up dirty old men, Chop!" — and yakking about her bra status, when I remember something. I turn and run across the parking lot, swerving to avoid toddlers and traffic and old women driving their dead husband's enormous cars. My heart is pounding and I can feel the blood jackhammering at my temples, but he's still sitting there, leaning forward on his walker and staring into space.

He doesn't say anything and neither do I. I balance on my haunches before him and grab hold of his right foot in its giant trainer. With one knotted, trailing lace in each hand, I make two loops, tie them in a butterfly, then double knot the bow. When I've finished one foot I get busy on the other.

DOG DAYS

SEVEN

THE CELLULOID MUSEUM

1.

Loping. Sams is *loping.* He likes the sound of the word because of its loopy, jerky, slightly jolting yet satisfyingly stride-along shape. It is the talisman that gets him safely past two-dog house and its black roar. Which is what he has to pass on his way to the movie rental store — there is no other way, strictly speaking. Speaking less strictly, there are other ways and plenty of them — detours, back lanes, alleyways — it's a neighbourhood after all. *Loping loping loping*, thinks Sams with each loopy, jerky, slightly jolting, satisfyingly stride-along pace, and two-dog house and its black roar recedes into the distance.

2.

Weary and restless are the two main feelings Sams feels. Mostly alternating but sometimes doubling up, so that a day of weariness will be followed by a night of exhaustion. Or else a night spent loping through the city streets, faster and harder as morning approaches and he grows desperate, will somehow fail to tire him, and he'll spend the next day spinning on his bed beside the dying creature and the phosphorous glow cast by his dying. But worst of all are the times when weariness and restlessness meet in the middle like ancient lovers running toward one another from opposite ends of the bright jerky screen that is projected directly into his head from some unassailable God-like source.

Sams squeezes his eyes shut to escape the terrible movie. But all afternoon the lovers Weary and Restless embrace and part and reconcile and die in each other's arms.

Tonight he knows he has to get away before the midnight screening, so he's on the road by well before. *Well before* is because he doesn't wear a watch. Nights like this a watch wouldn't work anyway — time slows or stops or starts to tick backward. Pages tear off the kitchen calendar, the sun yoyos across the horizon, moons wax and wane in the Etch-A-Sketch sky. His blood turns magnetic and time hangs heavy as a row of knives on a kitchen strip. The last thing he wants is to be responsible for the world's endless fall. But *well before* means he has to wait a spell because the days are lit at both ends and burn down swiftly. And all day, light pours out of things, out of the mouths of things (dogs, people on the other end of the leashes of dogs, cars, birds, kids in strollers crying, windows, Imee pointing at the mad, light-breathing daffodils, kids in strollers laughing, mailboxes).

3.

But mainly dogs.

4.

Sams throws a blanket over the creature and bolts. Tries to bolt. The creature is dying but not swiftly or with grace, decorum, good sportsmanship, punctuality, avoirdupois, or any appreciation for the comfort of others. Not with wisdom gleaned from experience or joy snatched from pain, either. So it goes, so it goes.

5.

WHO HE IS

- A creature, a thingummy. Dying.
- Sams doesn't know why or even, strictly speaking, who.
- A found creature, a lost soul.
- Found him in the corner of his room one day.
- Not dying fast enough.
- Finders keepers.
- Resembles a crow with a rook's head.
- Call me anything you like, it says.

6.

The problem of his hunger still consumes him. (Ha-ha, good one, Sams.)

Lazar comes home from school hauling a carrier bag full of groceries. He munches Pop-Tarts from an open box while he fries something on the stove, stirring and salting, rustling a recipe torn from the *Riverview News*. Scratching his chin and chewing his bottom lip. The sweet pink chemical smell of the Pop-Tarts makes Sams's eyes water.

"Oh, right," says Lazar when he lifts his head from the stove. He throws the box of Pop-Tarts into the freezer where all the terrible smells are stored and thumps a couple of plates onto the kitchen table. His brother's been dragging home groceries every night, fretting over vegetables and oozy packets of butcher-wrapped meat. Bottles and jars of Sams doesn't like to say what. It reminds him of a movie he's seen. Two brothers in a kitchen.

"Hey, Sams," says Lazar. "What's eating you?" (Ha, good one, Lazar.)

7.

So, two things then, thinks Sams, still loping.

There is *always* food.

He is *always* hungry.

Do these two things cancel each other out? Are they a contradiction or a syllogism? What would Lazar do? Sams tries multiple choice.

a) There is always food *but* he is always hungry.
b) All men are hungry.
c) Sams is a man.
d) *Therefore* Sams is a liar.

Sams is vexed, his spirits brought low. Long story short — nothing seems to fit anymore. Not his blinds that fail to keep out the seeping day, and not his bedroom window that, every evening, transforms into a rectangle of swarming light. Not his room or his bed or his pillow, not his jacket or his jeans or his skin. Everything is too big or too small, too hot or too cold, too smooth or too lumpy. All of creation has boiled down into a lukewarm bowl of *Not enough* and *Too much* and *Try again later, pal.*

8.

Hopelessly confused, Sams, still loping. The sky has cracked into a jigsaw that won't fit together, quite. One piece always missing, some bit of cloud no one can find. The wind crackles with electricity; gravity is losing its hold on things. Hence, the drifting trees. Also, some houses are beginning to detach from the street and float upward. Those ones, at the end of the block.

9.

LIST OF THINGS THAT DON'T FIT

- too much light
- words into word-holes
- hands into pockets
- photo in magnetic refrigerator frame (keeps falling)
- doors in doorframes (keep banging)
- *Greetings From Your World Vision Child* into envelope provided
- skin and skin's faulty shrink wrap
- dog into god

10.

A crow moves in a branch above Sams. Caw, it says. And then, White food.

Oh, thinks Sams, of course.

It's Strictly Speaking come to the rescue again. Occasionally Strictly Speaking manages to transform himself into a raggedy old bird and fly reluctantly to Sams's rescue, but mostly he is a sick and dying creature panting in the corner of Sams's bedroom. Where did he come from? Heaven knows. Heaven or its counterweight, Hell.

Old crow, old creature! No faith in human nature, no wishes to bestow. And the mouth on him! But he's useful every now and again. Today he bundles himself awkwardly from branch to branch beside the loping Sams, come to remind him, come to say —

White food.

Oh yeah. Sams shudders as he recalls the ferocious clashing colours that tumble in Lazar's grocery bags. How they hiss themselves to a frenzy in hot oil then languish hideously on brown rice.

All the bright and quarrelsome food! He's forgotten that he only eats white bread, white cheese, white meat, and the albumen of hard-boiled eggs whose poisonous-looking yolks he knocks out with the tip of a spoon. His gaze averted, his breath held. His favourite meal is a glass of milk.

That's just the way things are.

11.

"Oh, leave him alone, Max," Maggie would say. "Pick your battles, sweetheart."

"Okay," Max would pretend to give the matter some consideration. "I pick food, I pick goddamn nourishment. I pick normal hemoglobin levels and vitamin intake and the kid not dying of rickets. I mean *look* at him, just look —"

The two of them would both be staring at him now. "He can't help it," Maggie would try to explain, but by then Sams would be long gone. Sometimes this elsewhereness was physical — sometimes he'd manage to grab his leather jacket in time and slide out of the room, the house, the world, shrugging off their attention with an impatient movement of his shoulders. But at other times he was just too damn weary or clumsy or lead footed, and then he was left high and dry, stranded with the two of them in their fond argument. So it behooved him to think fast and act faster.

Like white on rice, says Strictly Speaking.

Sams knows what he means.

You gotta act fast or they'll be on you, says Strictly Speaking. Like —

Yeah, says Sams. (White on rice.)

12.

ONE DAY, BACK . . .

. . . in winter, Sams woke unexpectedly, his eyes clicking open in the dark. What had roused him? Was it silence? Was it time?

The all-night-falling snow stopped falling the moment he opened his eyes. Perhaps it was dream snow all along. Sleep snow, a white weather system drifting through a blank white mind. This was the first time he saw him.

The creature was crouched in the corner of Sams's room, picking at the lice in his pin feathers. He had a rode-hard and hung-up-dry look about him.

Hard day's night? asked Sams.

Strictly speaking, the creature replied.

He looked like a devil on a chain but said he was a guardian angel. In the end it turned out he was only a crummy bastard, sick as hell. His eyes were yellow as liver failure and his wings were peeling off his back as if he didn't deserve them. He claimed that high living, booze, and dames were the cause of his dereliction but that was just bravado. He was always a game bird. Sams brought him cigarettes to smoke and Scotch to drink and day-old horoscopes to read. No matter how bad the predictions were, the future was already the past by then.

Spring arrived with a terrible sleep hangover. The creature was dying. He looked chewed up and spit out and he stank to high heaven. That old squatter, death, had found a home in him.

13.

Strictly Speaking is still following Sams, flying from tree to tree with an awkward flap of his perforating wings. Although flying isn't the word for it, not exactly. More like a weary gathering followed by a ragged bundle outward. More like a Hail Mary pass into the vanishing future. He launches himself from branch to branch and somehow sticks, somehow holds. Dandruff drifts from his wing sprouts and a smell like ancient bandages precedes him. The ointment on old, blackened bandages.

Scoot, says Sams kindly.

Strictly Speaking opens his cracked beak to reply but what with all the dying he is doing, finds he has no energy for his cursing. Caw, he mumbles weakly.

Scoot, says Sams but less kindly. Obviously.

The creature has been practicing his scorn. He is scornful of anyone who might outlive him. (Point: Everyone.)

Buy a vowel? he offers. The only thing keeping him alive is *Wheel of Fortune*. It's mainly Spin Girl, Sams suspects, because whenever she appears he caws himself into a frenzy, trying to buy vowels and solve puzzles.

14.

Black Bird Shot, says Sams, and Strictly Speaking flies away.

15.

Sams lopes past the high school sports field. "Go Ravens!" reads the scoreboard. "Have a Safe Summer!" Sams hopes to God the summer wins. He is heading to Café D so that he can do his thinking and compile his monthly movie selection. His list.

"Sams's Picks" is late again so he has to goddamn hurry up and get it done which is what his boss at the Celluloid Museum told him, in so many words. Actually, in those exact words, also adding some others but stopping when he remembered the circumstances that might have extenuated Sams's tardiness.

Thunder Clap Hands, Sams mumbles.

The café is only two kilometers away, as the crow flies. Strictly Speaking is waiting for him when he gets there. What took you so long? he cackles. One day that crow will die laughing, *mort de rire*.

Café D is Sams's favourite place to do his thinking. He often remains at his table all afternoon, working on his list and occupying valuable retail space. But Dieter is resigned to him. Sams is his guarantor, the tithe he offers up to God. Dieter even allows the kid to buy a glass of milk instead of a cup of coffee, if he has money on him, which today — feeling frantically in his pocket — for some reason, he does.

Sams slaps down a dollar coin on the counter and Dieter nods hello and pours him his milk. To which Sams smiles his thanks, waving away any fugitive offers of change, as if to say — and grandly — *keep it, my good fellow.*

In truth, the price of a glass of milk is greater than your average dollar and has been for some time. But in his heart Sams is a splendid tipper and Dieter, a generous man, bears him no ill will.

16.

Because there are so many ways to be sad (obviously), Sams knows he has to be damn careful. Sorrow isn't what he means and anguish is the opposite. Also melancholy, also unrestrained weeping.

Sams drums his fingers against the table — a word is coming to him. This is how all his lists begin. (They *begin* and then they *begat*.) The word begats the list, the list begats exhaustion, exhaustion begats visions and monsters, visions and monsters begat sleep.

Liquid trembles at the rim of a slightly rocking glass. He downs his milk in a couple of gulps. His head still thrown back, he wipes his mouth against his sleeve and blinks up at the ceiling of Café D.

What is a list? A reminder, an autobiography, a chronic disability. A cross-hatching of pencil marks stippled with grubby pink eraser flecks. Time jerking through its sprockets at twenty-four frames per second. For Sams, lists are what keep him from cracking into all his shiny pieces.

He likes to have his word in place before he begins, although (obviously) the object of the list is to conceal the word from view. Perhaps the word will come to him if he continues with his list and his thoughts and his milk. Unfortunately his milk is finished, but maybe?

Sams cocks a hopeful eye at Dieter who either pretends to, or does not pretend to, ignore him, but either way.

17.

Or a list can be a method of elimination. A hit list.

18.

The man at the next table smiles at Sams as if he recognizes him from somewhere. He wears a heavy coat and his shoes are soaked. It's summer, not a cloud in sight, no rain for weeks. He's like a visitor from another time (winter) and place (again, winter), carrying his own weather system around with him.

The man smiles at Sams but his sadness streams out of him like tickertape. His sadness is a long white scarf looped around his neck. For a moment Sams thinks he recognizes him, but no.

19.

Bernadette stops by his table to drop off a coffee, compliments of the house.

"Hey, Samson, *ça va?*" Sams and Bernie have known each other forever, having both grown up on Magnolia Street although, as soon as she could, Bernie fled that neighbourhood of leafy trees, and after-school piano lessons, and kids playing street hockey, shouting *Car! Car! Car!* in the dusk.

"Hey, Samson. *Ça va?*" she repeats in case he hasn't heard her.

Sams is mightily startled and mightily pleased although — as always seems to be the case — the second doesn't cancel out the first but merely lopes along beside it.

"Hey, *Je m'appelle Bernadette*."

She bursts out laughing, the way she always does when he calls her Bernadette. She's Bernie, has been since she could swing her first punch, although she eventually got tired of beating him up. Sams is Sams: a leopard with permanent spots, an old dog resistant to new tricks. Sometimes he calls her *Song of Bernadette*, and sometimes, as today, she is *Je m'appelle Bernadette* (both movies), and sometimes he sings, "There was a child named Bernadette," or "Bernadette, people are searchin'," (both songs), because he has known her forever. In retaliation she calls him Samson, although she won't let anyone else do that. And sometimes she just sings the chorus to that song, he knows the one. Very softly: *If I had my way, if I had my way, if I had my way…*

"Whoa, haven't you finished your lineup?" she exclaims. She means his list (obviously), which Sams is scribbling on a paper napkin, both sides. There's a stack of paper napkins beside him, at the ready, because you never know.

"Working on it," he says.

"Utopian Game Theory?" she asks hopefully, trying to guess the theme of his upcoming list. "Heat Wave? Misplaced Patriotism?"

Misplaced Patriotism is because of Canada Day, just passed, and American Independence Day coming up, which Sams understands (he almost always understands Bernadette). Alternately, she could be thinking of the weather, Hermann Hesse's birthday, or the exact midpoint of the year, which today just happens to be.

You never know.

20.

There are exactly 182 days on either side of July 2nd. Today is a drain the year has been circling. If it was a leap year the middle would be July 4th, but no.

Sams likes middles, perhaps to excess. Movies have taught him to be wary of the darkness that waits in ambush on either side of the year or the screen. Instead he tries to live inside his head, that bright lozenge of flickering light. But sometimes the light gets out and escapes, *c'est la vie*.

He's given up trying to figure out where the story ends and he begins.

Perhaps that's why he likes middles. They are the no man's land where the angels are still working the angles in the service of wings, and Darth Vader is nobody's father yet, and the zombies are merely on their way to being up to no good. Sams lives in the exact centre of the North American continent, in no danger of falling off the edge of anything, least of all reason.

21.

Bernadette is still puzzling over the key to his list. The one that will explain everything. Also, she's mad as a hornet about the upcoming American election and the low-life, no-account Republican candidate who doesn't stand a chance but has the power to arouse anger. Sams ought to do a list on resistance, she tells him, resistance in the movies. She immediately looks abashed. Sams's list is not open to debate or interpretation, everyone knows that.

But Sams doesn't take offence. She is just Bernadette; she likes to act tough and mostly succeeds, but she has a weak spot for the way history tries to wedge itself inside time. Either one or the other is the wrong shape, he wants to tell her. Either history or time.

Give her credit, though — she never goes Dead Fathers? She never goes Highway Accidents? She never goes Strange Passengers? Ever since her mother died last year, Sams can see that something has broken in her.

Not open but apart.

Now she squints, craning to read his list upside down, so Sams turns it around for her and Bernadette goes, "Oh, sad movies."

It isn't, but *tant pis*. Nobody's ever gotten the point of his Picks, which is how Sams likes it. They all think they have — his fans — which is how *they* like it.

"What's the saddest movie you've ever seen?" he asks anyway.

"*Umbrellas of Cherbourg*, hands down. No contest." She starts to tell him why, which has to do with unrequited love (obviously) and how beautiful that French actress was. Catherine Deneuve, right? But she can't remember the actor's name. The male lead. Agh! There's snow at the end, so much snow. Deneuve stops at the gas station with her daughter, which is most likely his daughter too, and at first pretends not to recognize him. Or maybe she really doesn't recognize him — is that possible? Bernadette can't remember.

"Which would be sadder?" she wonders.

"Not recognizing him at all," says Sams (obviously). "And him not recognizing her."

"Well, one of them has to recognize the other one. Otherwise what's the point?"

Sams shrugs. Not recognizing is the point. He remembers the movie and the way the wallpaper always matched the girl's dress — sometimes exactly, sometimes with subtle variations. He doesn't know what this means — that the girl is a piece of scenery? That the walls are alive? Perhaps that when you're in love everything coincides with itself, everything is a perfect match.

"Wait a minute," Bernadette says. "They do recognize each other. Of course they do. At least I think they do. Why can't I remember?"

Sams doesn't know. He's never been in love. There is something in him that won't break, or maybe breaks but all the time and in the wrong place.

22.

The snow begins to fall when the lovers recognize each other. *So much snow.*

23.

"Hey, Samson, are you coming tonight?" asks Bernadette. "Come, if you want."

Sams nods. Nods, again.

"Agh," she reminds him. "Nuit Blanche, you goof."

24.

The man at the next table is still staring at Sams. Which would be sadder: pretending not to recognize him or not recognizing him? Sams shrugs. He himself is not the sort of fellow who looks like someone anyone knows.

25.

Bernie has gone off, singing to herself. "If I had my way, if I had my way, if I had my way, I would tear this old building down."

26.

LIST OF WHAT HAPPENED AT CAFÉ D

- Dieter nods at Sams (not smiling).
- Sams goes, Hello Dieter.
- Sams buys his milk and tips Dieter.
- Dieter nods at Sams (smiling).
- Sams drinks his milk, begins his Picks.
- Man in overcoat looks at Sams, but no.
- Bernadette brings Sams a coffee, compliments of the house.
- Bernadette goes, *Ça va,* Samson?
- Bernadette goes, *Umbrellas of Cherbourg*, hands down.
- Come if you want, says Bernadette.
- Goes off singing.
- Sams works on his Picks.
- Overcoat man looks at Sams but Sams is the wrong man.
- Sams gives the man the cup of coffee that Bernadette had brought him. Compliments of the house, he goes.
- Sams wishes he could get more milk but —
- He doesn't have his three wishes yet so —
- No more milk.

27.

Sams is back in the flow of time, back in his dolorous mind, back on the street. A girl in an evening dress and gold sandals floats by. She looks like someone he ought to know. At first he thinks, Bernadette? But, no.

Was that Spin Girl? asks Strictly Speaking, appearing suddenly from nowhere.

Whoa! thinks Sams. Why didn't he recognize her? *Electric Eel Pie! Surprise Blow Fly! Stun Gun Shy!*

Buy a vowel, says Strictly Speaking. Rolling his *Eye Ball Bearings.*

28.

"What now?" asks Sams, trying to keep the exasperation out of his voice. Trying but not succeeding (obviously), because Strictly Speaking swoops down from his tree, snatching weakly at Sams's wrist with his claws. It's the weakness that gets to Sams, the way that weakness always does. He bends down and puts his ear to the creature's rotten stinking beak.

Strictly speaking, you get three wishes, he mumbles. Can't beat that with a stick, kid!

Then he starts to laugh. *Mort de rire, mort de rire.*

Sams can't think of anything he wants, not one wish springs to mind. Unless — if the creature would just die in peace. Buy a vowel and solve the puzzle. Cash in his chips, spin the wheel, and disappear forever into the *High Jump Rope*, the *Long Dash Light*, the *Get Lost Horizon.*

His black tongue lolls from his beak. Spittle collecting in the corners. Long loops of drool.

Strictly speaking, he croaks, you get 'em whether you want 'em or not.

Sams wishes the creature would go and, just like that, he does. Whoa, looks like Strictly Speaking can grant wishes after all! Just when you thought he was fading fast, his crooked current growing weaker every day, he pulls this last fast one, this peccadillo, this prank.

29.

So, Sams. Sams pulled back to earth through the funnel cloud of his longing. Sams loping toward the river, hunched in his cracked leather jacket. His long hair, thinner than before, his frame likewise. Crikey, the wrists on him! The way they poke out of his sleeves, red and knobby.

There is a place in the city where two rivers meet. That's one way of looking at it.

Sams makes for this place, the rivers' fork. He stands on the riverbank and watches a boat pulling against the current. Overhead the sun is trying to set, a helium balloon having the usual trouble with buoyancy. He makes out shadows moving in the gloom beneath Railway Bridge: four men, a girl in a navy jacket and hiking boots. Jeers and hisses greet him as he hunches down beside her. She's an unstable sort of girl, coming into focus and then blurring again. Sams squints, frames her between the rectangle of his viewfinder hands, adjusts his imaginary shutter speed. But there is no keeping that wavering girl in his sights. She ducks under the lens and creeps closer to him, clutching at her jacket. He wonders if she's cold.

"On the contrary," the girl says, reading his mind. "I am cool as a pickle." Her words hang in the air. Today is the opposite of winter yet her words hang in the air like breath clouds.

"But thank you for inquiring," the girl adds hastily, and Sams — who doesn't remember asking — understands that she is burdened with good manners, which are a curse and an affliction, as inopportune as blushing.

She's a silent movie sort of girl. Enormous eyes take up half her face and she has the ability to talk without saying a word: *Help, a train is coming! Oh, woe is me! How dare you, you brute!* The girl blushes through the black-and-white film stock. She can't help blushing; it's a reflex, the consequence of being who she is (well brought up) colliding with her circumstances (existential fading).

One cool customer! she assures him (silently). Then she opens her eyes wide, as if she has just regained her sight after years of blindness. *Yes, I can see now.*

"You look like someone I know," the girl explains. Sams is pleased as punch. He's never looked like anyone someone knows before.

Only she can't remember who, she admits, looking as if she is about to cry. She's been wandering the city for so long, she tells him, and forgetfulness is catching up with her.

Sams knows what she means. "What's the saddest movie you've ever seen?" he asks, he hopes helpfully. Helpfully is his aim. But the girl has never seen a sad movie, she has only seen Mr. Groucho Marx and his brothers. Sometimes the missionaries allowed the kids in her village to watch Mr. Groucho Marx and his brothers on a sheet hung outside the infirmary. She is a great admirer of this Marxist Brother family, she tells Sams. They are full of hijinks and shenanigans to do with how many people can fit into a small space. Which she appreciates, having to share a room, as she does, with all her sisters. They are the

Ngunga Sisters, she informs him proudly, although not movie stars. (Point: Girl.)

Sams and the girl crouch beneath Railway Bridge watching the men, four of them in all. Ragged and filthy, their yellow eyes click in the dark like beads. Why are they angry, the men?

The sun finally loses its battle with momentum and plummets into the river.

"Plop!" Sams says, providing the soundtrack as usual.

"Goodnight," the girl mouths, popping her Mary Pickford eyes. *Good Night Cap.* The movie has ended, the film coming loose from its sprocket and flapping against the projector. *Sleep Tight Rope!*

Sams watches her spin away like a dust mote caught in the projector's blue beam.

"*Ftt!*" he says.

Immediately the smell beneath the bridge resumes — unwashed bums and piss and spilled beer and sweet, rotten teeth. The reason the men are angry is a bottle. The bottle is wrapped in brown paper and belongs to one man, although it's coveted by the others. Everyone wants the bottle in voices that boom and echo beneath the concrete overhang of the bridge.

30.

What happens next is that the men begin to wander about.

31.

LIST OF THE MEN WANDERING ABOUT

- The first, robust and shouting encouragement.
- The second, thinly wringing his hands.
- The third, breaking the bottle over the head of —
- The fourth — the fourth.

32.

"Whoosh!" says Sams, as liquid gushes down the man's face.

A jocular mood prevails because one of the men has been vanquished. He lies off to the side, quite still, a new red necklace looped casually about his throat. The remaining three men gather around the fallen body of their companion. They work busily on him, trying to set him to rights, make him good as new. Sams hunkers on the embankment, watching.

But it's already too late. The hit list is a contract between enemies who love one another.

The leader of the group, the man in charge of mayhem, squats beside Sams and wriggles his crazy eyebrows. He pulls a lit cigar out of his breast pocket then passes Sams the bottle in its brown paper wrapper. Sams nods his *thanks all the same*, but looks around to see who's next.

"You bet your sweet life, toots," says Eyebrows, snatching back the bottle and pressing it upon him. Sams shakes his head vigorously and tries to scramble up the embankment but Eyebrows is on him (like white on), roaring his Old Testament God-roar and whacking him with the bottle.

33.

Another way of looking at it: this is the place where the river divides in half.

34.

The creature is fading fast.

Strictly speaking, he manages to croak. Strictly speaking, you still have two more wishes to go.

Another way of looking at it: this is the place where the mind divides in half. List or lost. Hit or miss. Wish or won't.

35.

Eyebrows has him down on the ground and is poking him with whatever is at hand: his cigar, his scorn, even the bottle. Sams knocks his head sideways but the older man pulls the bottle from its brown paper bag and unscrews the cap. The bottle puckers its thick lips and Eyebrows latches it to Sams's lips. Eyebrows wrings his screeching hands and tries to pillow Sams's head on his lap. A terrible odour comes off this man, a brew of all the worst things that Sams has ever smelled.

36.

LIST OF WHAT HE SMELLS LIKE

- old bandages and armpit fear
- cigar butt breath
- sweet pink chemicals

- garbage bag ooze
- walking past Serenity Candles and Soaps
- dishwasher on rinse cycle
- when a light bulb explodes
- bottom of pill bottle
- but mostly dogs

37.

Sams twists his head this way and that to get away from the poking bottle and Eyebrows with his electric, whirring muscles and his borrowed smell. With all his heart, Sams makes a wish. But it's a wish without music, words, intention, hopefulness, conviction, or delusion. If anything it's the white spaces between words. If anything it's the black words between stars.

If I had my way, if I had my way, if I had my way...

Once again, Eyebrows fits the bottle to Sams's lips and pours. Pouring. He's sweating himself into a melting candle. Fat drops of wax ooze from his pores and fall, burning, onto Sams's face.

"Smirnoff," whispers Eyebrows, cradling Sams's head in his lap. Sams swallows the unspooling warmth until he begins to cough. But, ah — the Smirnoff has been a splendid idea. The men clap and whistle and stamp their feet in a circle around him (Point: Eyebrows).

Time to go.

"Not so fast, slick," says Eyebrows, that crazy kid. He reaches over and involves Sams in a complicated handshake. Naturally Sams buggers it up — the grip, the hold, the grapple, the grasp. The tricky turn and the double clasp. To tell the truth, Sams is not partial to hands most days and this is looking to be one of those days. But still, he wishes he'd got that handshake right. That he'd grasped it! (Point: Sams.)

38.

There's a roar overhead and the ground beneath Sams starts to shake. The arches rumble, *thunka thunka thunka*. He looks up in time to see the red-eyed monster come tearing through the night, pulling its segmented body behind. It takes forever for the monster to end and the bridge to begin again, a single rusty arch flexing into the night.

For the second time Sams wishes to be gone, and all at once he's stumbling away from the men in their cages of eyes and ribs and grasping hands. He takes the embankment in a couple of ragged strides and, plunging his hands into his pockets, lopes toward the downtown lights.

39.

"You can come if you want," Bernadette had said. It's her way of saying, "Suit yourself, my friend," although "suit yourself" is what she frequently does say because she's not one to pull a punch. Sams thinks he might as well go. Might as well — can't stay in the house, what with the creature in its death throes and his mother flaring like a match in her dark room with every dry thought. Smoke blue as her famously blue sailor's mouth.

40.

"Insomnia is the devil's white night," she says every morning. Sams suspects the creature of having crept into his mother's room one night and bitten her in her sleep, or at least in her *neck*. Some mornings his mother's neck is pocked with mouth-shaped bruises that she tries to hide beneath turtleneck sweaters or scarves. Maggie is definitely edging toward vampire status in Sams's estimation. He's not looking forward to the day that he will be obliged to drive a stake through her heart in order to save his little brother and the rest of humanity.

Ah, who's he kidding? Sams could never hurt Maggie, and Lazar probably doesn't need rescuing, and Sams is certainly not up to the task of saving humanity, which his dad used to say was going to hell in a *Hand Basket Case*. Sometimes it seems that whatever Max cared about least had the power to rile him up the most, Sams being the exception that proved that rules don't apply in families.

41.

Sams sets off, the alcohol flaring in his veins. He cuts up from the river and heads south, soon passing the Law Courts and the Memorial Gardens. On top of the Legislative Building the statue of a golden boy flaps his golden wings and turns into a crow. Oh boy, Strictly Speaking is at it again.

By the time Sams reaches the art district with its galleries, nightclubs, and open-air restaurants, he is what Imee calls *jumpy*. "Jumpy as a skipping rope," she used to say. Everywhere he looks he sees strange sights. People gathered on street corners, in doorways, or in the foyers of buildings. Some are

clustered around installations: sculptures and wire cages, trees
hung with dead rabbits. Young women lower themselves into
vats of red paint, young men throw knives and swallow swords
and breathe fire. Set themselves alight, then blow themselves
out. Everywhere music plays: bright, jagged shards of jazz, the
paisley swirl of Cuban drumming. Sams claps his hands over
his ears and leans in a doorway, panting.

42.

Sams leans in a doorway, panting. Jumpy, all right.

His disorderly synapses are firing blanks. The soundtrack
isn't quite synched up; everyone's mouthing what they've
already said, snapping their elastic red mouths this way and
that.

"No, no, no!" cries a woman, pulling her lover close. "Yes,
yes, yes!" she entreats, shaking her head in revulsion.

All at once the music separates into distinct syllables of rock,
hip, pop, hop, rap, jazz. The music scintillates like a thousand
points of light that you can only see whole if you stand far away.
Possibly on the moon.

Everywhere Sams glimpses bones beneath skin, wine stains
on gleaming teeth, tattoos shackling ankles and wrists, punctu-
ating the spine's long sinuous sentence. Oh pale green fracture
of the world's sprain!

He hears the woman say, "Come here, darling." He hears
the man say, "Get away from me, you whore." Sams recognizes
Weary and Restless, those ancient lovers, running toward and
away from each other. *Come, go, stay, leave, but sweetheart, you
bitch you bitch you bitch.*

"Excuse me, what's the time?" someone asks. Sams flashes

and flashes and flashes his wrist (no watch). But time keeps being asked of him.

43.

BOUQUET OF NUIT BLANCHE

- exhaust, exhaustion
- acidic wine breath
- perfume like a rose headache
- old smoke, old lungs
- dust burning off
- wafts of intergluteal cleft
- scalp, feet, groin

- adrenal glands
- gutter fruit
- scratch and sniff of the mind
- bright food frying
- electrical circuits
- like dead flower water
- pheromone stink, stink, stink

44.

"…*la nuit blanche*," he hears, rising to the surface of his oceanic lostness. "Or as they reported in the *Sun*, blanched nuts."

"Don't let me get started on the cutbacks! But at least we're finally doing something for the arts. It's nice there's a night like this for the community, *bien sur?*"

"It's all about how to connect. Do we discuss art or literature? Politics? No, we exchange a small obscenity."

"If you go down to the Exchange you'll catch some kind of unauthorized lovemaking troupe. Yeah, totally spontaneous."

"Hey, dude, watch out for the —"

45.

— *oops!* Sams nearly gets clipped by a city bus, the lit-up words *Sorry Not In Service* blazoned across its unapologetic orange forehead.

46.

"Gone," he mumbles. It's Sams's third wish, his last wish. He wants to find somewhere dark to hide, a burrowing place in the *nuit blanche*, the terrible white night. Somehow he finds himself shambling, headed for the alleyway behind the video rental store.

47.

Done! cries the creature from inside his dying.

48.

La nuit blanche can't penetrate the darkness in the alley behind the Celluloid Museum. Even the moon is too high above and far away to see between the buildings with their rounded edges like playing cards. He sits with his knees drawn up and his arms braced about them. Patiently, he goes through an entire deck of cards in his head but comes up deuces. He rocks and rocks until he finds ballast. Until his body is an empty sieve for his mind to pour through.

49.

The truth is he hasn't finished his list. Nowhere near. The truth is he doesn't care a *Dam Burst Balloon*. His boss is the *Hell's Angel Cake*, and he — Sams — is *Dead Man Cave* for the next hundred years.

Well, okay, he thinks, rocking. Okay Corral.

50.

Gradually he realizes that he's not alone in the alley. Further along on a loading dock, squatting, his pals from the railway bridge are playing strip poker. Groucho, Chico, Karl, and Harpo throw down their cards and jeer at one another over poorly executed bluffs and badly played hands. Groucho is the worst, with his dollar store mask and corny patter. Only his cigar is real and he twirls it with gusto, blowing smoke rings and wriggling his eyebrows.

"Too rich for my blood," he keeps saying. "My blood ain't the heiress it once was."

Each of the poker players wears a nametag on his shirt. *Hi I'm Groucho! Hi I'm Chico! Harpo! Karl!* Chico's name is upside down, and Karl's is scrawled in the invisible ink of history, and Harpo's is obscured by his dripping red necklace, but Sams knows who they are. He's been watching them all his life. Whenever Groucho makes a joke he twirls his cigar and stares hard at Harpo until the poor fellow obliges him by taking up a plank of wood and hitting himself, or falling head over heels from his perch on a crate, or just wearily banging his head on the ground without creativity or the zest to inspire it. Pain is what Groucho requires of him, a dulled spirit, blood if necessary.

Sams is enjoying the movie. It's a hit, as far as he's concerned. The Marx Brothers are first rate in his book but Chico is his favourite because of accents and a talent for beseeching. Truth to tell, he's long suspected Groucho of this subterranean river of cruelty. The beetling brows, the sharp tongue, the twirl of his glowing red ember. Sams leans forward, for once neither restless nor weary.

51.

"Two pairs," yells Karl. "I'm out!" He yanks off his corduroy pants and is down to a wife beater and a pair of Y-fronts.

"Ring ring," says Groucho, twirling. "The boys' department just called. They want their underwear back."

"Ha, ha," yells Chico. "One-a more-a dumb-a play and you'll be down-a to your crooked-a yellow worm-a."

"Nah," says Groucho. "He's still got his vest, his beard, and his ide*ology*." He stares hard at Harpo but the poor son of a gun is fresh out of innovative self-mutilating ideas and merely bangs his head with the flat of his palm, pleasing no one, least of all his brother who shoves him into the cards and flicks cigar ash at him.

"Fuck you!" yells Harpo, silent no longer. He launches into Groucho and begins to pummel him (*a hit!*). Meanwhile Chico, who has misplaced his accent in the melee, hollers cartoon encouragements from the sidelines. *Biff! Bam! Kapow!* Karl pulls down his Y-fronts and dances around the fray, yanking his member and threatening to piss on the proles.

Sams suddenly becomes aware of scattered applause from the open windows of the Celluloid Museum, where faces cluster, and even in the darkest reaches of the alley strange voices shout *Bravo! Encore! Da Capo! Splendid!*

"Okay, boys," says Groucho. "One more time."

52.

In the endless *nuit blanche* in which Sams wanders, the white night without end, Strictly Speaking dies again and again. The lovers, Weary and Restless, stir from their ennui and run toward each other with open arms. Dieter slams down another glass of cold milk. It's exactly the right colour, and exactly the right temperature, and as Sams tilts his head back to get the last drop, he hears that sick old dying creature flapping its black wings one last time.

53.

Fade to white.

54.

SAMS'S PICKS

- *The Wrong Man* (1956)
- *Le Retour de Martin Guerre* (1982)
- *Singin' in the Rain* (1952)
- *Darby O'Gill and the Little People* (1959)
- *A Kiss From Mary Pickford* (1927)
- *Dead Alive* (1992)
- *It's a Wonderful Life* (1946)
- *A Night at the Opera* (1935)
- *Star Wars: Episode V — The Empire Strikes Back* (1980)
- *City Lights* (1931)
- *The Song of Bernadette* (1943)
- *Big Night* (1996)
- *Les parapluies de Cherbourg* (1964)

55.

SAMS'S WORD

— — — —

56.

Buy a vowel, dummy, says the crow.

EIGHT

CAMP BEAVER

NATHAN WAS TOUCHED by the way that kids always got sex slightly wrong. He'd been camp director for ten years now, so he'd seen some things, but the looming sum of what he'd seen could never quite topple those moments when he slouched, transfixed, hands in pockets, before some kid's screwy version of what adults got up to.

Inside cabin #3, the walls were a snide cross-hatching of names and initials and telephone numbers, of speculation and intention, of hearts, arrows, exclamation points, and the occasional well-endowed stick figure. At the end of August when all the kids left, the last motorboat chugging its allowable quota of sun-blasted, over-oxygenated children to the mainland, Nathan and his cleaning crew took occupation of the island. They were the Oompa-Loompas of Pleasure Island — nobody saw them arrive and only Gunnars, who owned the motor launch, was witness to their departure. They trawled the paths and cabins and outbuildings, roughly setting the island to rights, hauling the canoes to their winter grounds (the shed), dry docking the vast inflatable water slides, emptying bottles of bleach into the latrines, heaving in the docks, and finally dismantling the banner that fluttered throughout the summer, welcoming children to Camp Beaver.

Beaver was the name of the camp, the name of the island, and the spirit animal that the original counsellors had blithely appropriated in order to exhort campers to patriotic feats of industry and endurance. The camp had been named in an earlier, more innocent era, and now they were stuck with it: Camp Beaver! Naturally, unwholesome variations on the name abounded, but Nathan was the only one who called the place Pleasure Island, and then only in his head.

His head was the same place that he imagined his precisely honed squad of Oompa-Loompas, his ninja cleaners, his crack team of glinty-eyed janitorial staff. In fact, his cleaning crew was composed of a couple of counsellors so strapped for cash that they were willing to stay behind and close up shop. Mostly, though, the burden of camp cleanup fell to good old reliable Nathan. If Nathan had a fatal flaw it was his hankering for the picturesque and his improbable love of Hollywood musicals.

The walls of cabin #3 had been whitewashed so often they were half an inch thicker than they'd once been. All the cabins were like that, their walls growing inwards by increments, year after year. Late at night in his camp director's cabin, after he'd talked to his section heads, after he'd reviewed the day and planned the next, after he'd made his lists and assigned his duties, after he'd texted his girlfriend to say goodnight (phone reception on the island was so poor they'd been forced into an epistolary relationship), Nathan would click off his desk lamp and watch the window-framed rectangle of night sky jump into the room. At moments like this — the darkness both near and far, within and outside — he could almost reach out his hand and skim the cluster of boys' cabins huddled to one side of the dining hall.

The darkness thickening in his living room was full of the sound of frogs coughing up their green phlegm. It was possible that Nathan was growing fanciful. His girlfriend hardly ever wrote back anymore. "I'm not a narrative girl," she explained.

The lights of the cabins were doused and the campers were sleeping, sleeping and dreaming, dreaming and growing and flourishing like weeds in the vitamin D–enriched sunlight and scattered showers necessary to turn earth to grass and boys to men. Mostly not, though. Mostly the grass was trampled to mud-splatter by the feet of these boys — running, kicking, cavorting — and the boys themselves tended to turn wavy and grow younger as the weeks passed, as if they were flashbacks to some earlier summer. Jump cut versions of their younger selves captured on an eight-track home movie. The sun stopped in its course and ran backward.

Nathan was pushing forty and forty was pushing back with the strength of conviction. He was the only adult man at sleepaway camp, and he hadn't had sex for going on twelve weeks although he'd been on the island for eight.

The not having sex didn't bother him. There was too much of it about anyway. The air swarmed with pheromone musk, the fried onion stink of boiling armpits, the ammonia chlorine of wet dreams. He didn't know what the girls' cabins smelled like. Bubblegum lip gloss, he hoped. Strawberry shampoo and cedar hope chests.

Nathan's girlfriend always seemed to smell of garlic. It was a mystery, yet another one. Either she chewed a couple of cloves for breakfast every morning or she rubbed raw garlic behind her ears. She was his yeasty Italian loaf, his fragrant girl-shaped pizza. Or perhaps it was only a vampire thing — she'd always been a girl who took precautions. Once, back in the city, he'd discovered her on his bed, her knees drawn up, tears streaming from her eyes. "Burns," she'd moaned. Was her soul in mortal danger? Was her heart aflame? No, it was just a garlic clove she'd pushed inside herself to cure a yeast infection. Perhaps the infection explained the rising bread smell he'd been noticing. He crouched on his knees between her legs, sniffing the warm, doughy folds of her vagina as he tried to pry out the clove.

Vagina was not the word Nathan's girlfriend had used. Her name was Riva and she disliked prevarication. "Stop fiddling around with your fingers and suck me, you cunt!" she'd snapped.

The problem with whitewashing the cabin walls, as the two-man cleanup crew pointed out to Nathan, was that the words and their illustrations were indelible. Within hours of rolling on an undercoat, they would rise to the surface again, faintly perhaps but still legible. Someone had made Morgan Dejardins cum three times, *cum all over herself*; someone else had screwed your mother till her tits fell off; and Jason would love Brianna forever.

There was some contention about the identity of the reigning BJ Queen. "Sami Fisher?" one graffitist wondered, but another maintained that Mikey Koslov sucked dick for free. Nathan was intrigued at the implication that dick-sucking had become a potentially profitable camp activity but couldn't help admiring the ingenuity of the interrogation mark after Sami Fisher's name. It seemed to bespeak an unexpected curiosity, a willingness to put forward a hypothesis that might later, and violently, be refuted. Mainly, though, the scrawls consisted of one- or two-word variations upon a fairly specific theme. Obscenity was the lingua franca of these cabin walls; it penetrated deep as the studs that held the wooden frame in place.

Nathan had a fantasy that over the winter months the gossip and prurience that underwrote the walls would rise once more to the surface until, come summer, the campers would be welcomed back by the quaint poems of yesteryear. "Hannah fucks / Anna sucks" and "Ookie Ookie / Who ate the Cookie?"

He was still thinking about kids getting sex wrong. Pleasantly dumbfounded. A girl couldn't cum all over herself, even three times. And no matter how hard you screwed someone's mother, her tits, almost certainly, would not fall off. It was endearing in its way, which way was neither innocent nor experienced.

And not exactly innocent or guilty, either, thought Nathan, jiggling his non-existent change in his pockets. He rocked back on his heels, shook his head, and whistled. *Hoo wee*, these kids.

Behind him, his maintenance crew was horsing around. The launch was picking up the three of them at six o'clock and the island had to be trig by then. Neat and self-contained as a nut in its polished shell. At the moment, though, Hunter was flicking whitewash at Newman and Newman was squealing like a girl and then, hearing himself, his treble shriek, he smartened up and merely pretended to squeal like a girl. Newman had a slight build and pitchy vocals; he couldn't be too careful.

"Who ate the cookie?" Hunter read aloud. "Man, are they still looking for that damn cookie?"

"Darn cookie," he corrected himself, but Nathan just shrugged. Camp was over. He was off the clock.

Hunter and Newman began reminiscing about cookies past.

They'd all been duped by the cookie. It was an ancient summer tradition, a squeamish rite of passage at Camp Beaver, and probably every other camp throughout the thousands of islands and inlets that made up Lake of the Woods. And possibly the World, the Galaxy, the Universe (bottom right quadrant of cabin #3's palimpsest of wonder and solipsism). Islands past had had their donkey's ears, their ticking crocodiles, their Man Fridays, their conch shells, but Pleasure Island was all about the cookie.

As a boy, Nathan had attended this same summer camp where, in the very first week — homesick, dizzy, full of nonspecific yearning — he'd been introduced to Ookie Cookie, a game in which adolescent grossness combined with *Sesame Street* nostalgia. A plate of lust with a glass of milk to wash it down. Daring in conception, prosaic in execution, the game involved a group of boys standing in a circle with a cookie in the centre. Nathan had heard of, but naturally never participated in, a jerk circle: a ring of engorged boys in someone's parent's basement, drawing their weapons, pounding their puddings, counting down from twenty-five. The one who bull's-eyed the cookie last had to eat it.

If you thought about it, which in the intervening years Nathan had certainly done, the game was the perfect adolescent antidote to fledgling fears of premature ejaculation. The game was about cumming, cumming *fast*. The boys in Nathan's cabin had called it a jerk's circle.

"Ready boys?" Nathan turned to his work crew. He grabbed a roller and began slathering whitewash across the wall in unseemly streaks. Hunter glanced at Newman. They'd planned to scrub down the walls first but if Nate wanted to cut their work in half that was the dude's prerogative.

The rhythmic sine waves of mindless labour, the boysy attar of sunscreen and bug spray, unwashed socks and slightly mildewed bedding, put Nathan in mind of Camp Beaver, circa 1986. He'd been a scrawny kid with a nose his mother had assured him he would one day grow into, "the family nose." Perpetually wrong footed, off balance, and skittish, he was envious of the casual intimacy everyone else seemed to share — boys and girls, campers and counsellors, humans and nature.

The guys in his cabin liked to talk about the legendary zombies that roamed the island, the anticipation of Saturday night burgers, and sex. Mostly sex. Many professed an acquaintance with breasts, even nipples. Danny Rubin, a big shot even then, claimed that he'd once persuaded a "hot chick" to sit on his face, and allowed that things would have gotten "out of control" if he hadn't suffered an asthma attack, which necessitated exchanging the girl for an inhaler. The other inhabitants of cabin #3 vigorously debated the probability of Danny's being a son of a bitch bastard liar but Nathan caught a whiff of the collective musk of their envy, since it so perfectly matched his own. The ability to manufacture such an unlikely Playboy scenario and then relate it with unblinking conviction impressed his listeners as an end in itself. Good work, Danny! Better luck next time.

The assorted misadventures of Nathan's first summer at camp included poison ivy, impetigo, a virulent strain of pink eye — possibly exacerbated by bleach in the eye (a cleaning mishap) — a likely wood tick infection, sunburn, heatstroke.

"Nice move, McFly," said his frustrated counsellor the third time he'd had to escort the boy to the infirmary. Everyone at camp, it seemed to Nathan, had seen *Back to the Future,* the previous summer's hit movie. Everyone but him. However, he was not excluded from the famous Camp Beaver Taco Debacle — delicious going down but not, alas, staying down — so there was that. There were so many ways of being excluded, of failing to fit in, that he was absurdly grateful even for the stomach cramps and painful diarrhea that followed. A shared adventure, a bonding experience! In between his various afflictions, Nathan learned to swim in the lake, he successfully completed the ropes course, he had his first crush. A mixed bag.

Molly Leibowitz was her name, she of the beguilingly inward-turned toes, a physical quirk that he imbued with all manner of esoteric meanings. She was shy, she liked him, she was dying of some mysterious pigeon toe–related ailment, she *like* liked him. Also, and in tandem with all of the above, she secretly hated him. Although why the secrecy? he would later wonder. There were plenty of girls who hated him to his face, who were not shy in proclaiming their aversion to Nathan Miller, that stupid little diaper baby mama's boy.

During rousing games of Capture the Flag, Molly would sit on the sidelines with her friend, Leah Silverstein, shouting girlish encouragements that Nathan pretended were directed at him. While waiting for his teammates to free him from jail ("Nice move, McFly"), he would dream of infiltrating the opposition's territory and singlehandedly capturing the flag while savagely tagging opposing players. He could spend entire afternoons hovering at the edges, frozen in place, his mind so full of heroic deeds that actual combat seemed incidental. It was his Walter Mitty period.

"Why don't you ask her to the Saturday night dance?" Danny Rubin asked. The boys of cabin #3 had been wrangling over who was hotter, Melanie Kaplan or Rose Epstein, a good-natured pre-lights-out squabble that had developed into a semi-hostile analysis of competing baseball metaphors. Fourth base was going all the way, "Doing it," a home run, Michael Shayowitz insisted — there was no such thing as fifth base. But Danny Rubin claimed the existence of a hitherto unimagined base, a fifth base, and even expressed incredulity that the other guys were so clueless.

"Haven't you ever heard of the dugout?" he asked slyly. Cabin #3 erupted in the kind of prolonged hysteria that relied on energy rather than assurance and which lasted fully five minutes, petering out only when each boy had convinced himself that his stellar performance — slapping hand to head and falling over backward, laughing until the tears came, begging for mercy — had convinced the others. Convinced them of what? Nathan didn't have a clue.

"Yeah, yeah," Danny finally allowed. "You're all dugout champs." That was when he asked Nathan why the hell he didn't invite Molly Leibowitz to the dance Saturday night. "Hey, maybe she's your density," he offered, a *mot juste* that so delighted the boys that it was some time before anyone could draw breath, after which their counsellor stormed in to say, "Shut the eff up, morons, it's lights out."

It was a quote, Nathan realized, another quote from a comic book he hadn't read or a movie he hadn't seen. A boyhood he had no idea how to live and a life that he suspected would offer the same endless opportunities to sit on the sidelines, dreaming, when all around him his compatriots were capturing the flag and getting the girl and winning the glory. From Nathan's perspective there was no hope of redemption because however much he grew, however much taller and older and wiser he got, there was no way to go back and rescue the wretched kid he'd been.

Yet although he suffered indignities that first summer, Nathan was no longer the small, wobbly creature who'd boarded the camp bus and stared out of the window for the next two hours and 210 kilometres. He had been assigned a cabin, and although runty, lacking in coordination, and inclined to inexplicable rashes, he'd become part of a group, a member of a team, a red T-shirt during the colour wars and the lower half of a cabin #3 bunk bed. He was lousy at sports and unlearned in the knockabout ways of thirteen-year-old boys. He upended every canoe he tried to paddle and had to be rescued from the cabin's traditional, forbidden midnight swim to a nearby island, but he was a cabin #3 boy and they were stuck with him.

During the summer of '86 his world contracted to the rocky configurations of Beaver Island and it was difficult to imagine any other world. Indeed, so profound was his sense of isolation that he failed to write even one letter home despite the five crisp, stamped, and self-addressed envelopes his mother had carefully packed in the webbing of his duffle bag.

"Dear Parents," he had scrawled on the first page of his stationery pad, "We had tacos last night. They were wonderful and terrible."

That was all. He could barely comprehend his experiences, let alone write about them.

In the end he didn't ask Molly Leibowitz to the dance. She was out of his league. A delicate girl with long, piano player's fingers (she was a prodigy, it was well-known, destined for greatness), she wore her hair in a dark, shiny ponytail pulled high so as to reveal her slender, breakable neck.

"Why don't you make like a tree and get out of here?" Leah Silverstein would taunt whenever she caught him staring at the girl. Sometimes she yelled, "Get a room, why don't you.

For yourself!" It was a jibe that made as little sense as the one about the tree, although the contempt behind both insults was genuine. Even at that age, it seemed, he had been compelled to parse the logic behind motiveless teenage derision.

Leah and Molly were best friends, seldom out of each other's company. They made an odd couple, one girl slender and delicate, the other sturdy and indelicate. Everyone called them the Rocky and Bullwinkle of Camp Beaver, which did nothing to sweeten Leah's disposition.

"Hey dickhead," she'd call after Nathan, call loud enough for everyone to hear. "Have you eaten any cookies lately?"

Everyone in the canteen heard (it was lunch time), everyone laughed (maybe not Molly, he couldn't bring himself to look), and the laughter was raucous and convulsive and prolonged. It was the kind of laughter that said: *Better you than me, sport.* The kind that fully acknowledged that there but for the grace of God went some other fellow.

"Hey, don't worry about that dyke," Danny comforted him. "She's in love with Leibowitz. Everybody knows. Not that she'll get anywhere with her," he added after an uncharacteristically reflective pause. "'Cause your girlfriend's a frigid little bitch. Everybody knows."

Once again, the vast chasm between what everybody knew and what Nathan demonstrably did not know seemed insurmountable. One thing Nathan knew, however, was that Danny had laughed at Leah Silverstein's taunt. Laughed so hard, in fact, that he'd swallowed his hot dog the wrong way and ended up snorting ketchup from his nose.

The cookie was ubiquitous that summer. It had not yet acquired its rhyming nickname. It was just *the cookie*, sometimes chocolate chip, sometimes oatmeal raisin. Most of the cabin

#3 boys claimed to have taken part in a cookie jerk, although no one would admit to being the first to cross the finish line, who knew why. Some misplaced notion of sexual endurance, perhaps. Coming last, *cum-ing* last, was no great honour either, all your splattered pals wiping their hands on their jeans and watching your clench-fisted, red-faced huffing. And then there was the matter of eating the damn cookie afterward. No, the trick was to aim for middle place in the Great Cookie Cum, said Danny Rubin. Sometimes being part of the crowd had its advantages.

Being part of the crowd was, in fact, essential. Although the present incarnation of Camp Beaver was inclusive, all faiths welcome, even those of little faith, even atheists, Nathan's Camp Beaver had been a Jewish summer camp although not, in theory, exclusively so. That year a gentile boy had taken up residence in cabin #3, a boy identical in all particulars to the other boys — grubby, boastful, happy-go-lucky, tough. Nevertheless the rumour grew, and persisted, that Blaine Richardson had never been circumcised. It was such an outrageous claim that it just might have been true. Certainly the boy never took part in the endless cookie debates, nor did he volunteer for the great dick measure off, five of the boys lining themselves up along a notched stick. Clearly he had something to hide, a concealment made more conspicuous by the fact that he showered in his bathing trunks and wriggled into his pajamas under cover of a beach towel.

How had it shaken out? Did the counsellors dunk young Blaine in the cold lake so he'd have to strip naked right there on the dock? Did the boys ambush him in the toilet cubicles and pants him? Had one of the slutty girls invited him to the beach one night for a make-out session that would conclusively address the problem at hand? Such hijinks had been endlessly discussed, meticulously planned, dates and times had been set. But in the end nothing happened. Blaine Richardson had departed Camp Beaver at the end of the summer, his modesty intact. Perhaps it had been too hot, too humid, too lazy to work up the necessary investigative zeal. And it was always possible that the boys had matured a little — by the end of the summer they had decided that a man's cowl-necked dick was his own business, best left unprovoked.

Sleepy from their long days in the sun and logy with trying to digest the midweek meatloaf, talk in the cabin would turn speculative, the boys opining in turn as to what sort of cookie they'd be willing to eat despite its provenance. None, was the first choice, Oreo the second.

But it was all just talk, Nathan suspected. A hot ticket to the oldest established, permanent floating, crap game of all time. By the end of his first month at camp, Nathan could just about distinguish bird shit from bullshit. The first dropped out of a clear blue sky, and the second was all around, although you could only smell it when you stepped in it. He was growing up, a disordered innocent no more. The word *cookie* gave him a hard-on, even when it was innocently meant, so that snack time was mortifying and the rest of the day swung between the dual poles of shame and arousal, his penis the dowel on which he hung.

At the end of the summer, Molly Leibowitz began going out with an older boy named Max Binder. The two could be observed walking out beyond the shelter of the cabins and sports fields, to the forbidden no man's land between the counsellor's quarters and the woods where no kids were allowed, where bears roamed free and baseball rules prevailed. He'd never stood a chance with her, Nathan figured, and Binder was a good guy. Nathan was probably too young to have a serious girlfriend, anyway, and besides the cabin #3 boys would have ragged him mercilessly.

It hurt, though, at first. Max and Molly would stroll by, holding hands, and Nathan would force himself to notice the girl's awkward gait, her skinny legs. What had he seen in her? These rationalizations ought not to have worked and no one was more surprised than he was when they did. His father was a great one for boasting of his mind-over-matter capabilities and Nathan, it turned out, had inherited his father's ability to assert his mind over what had once mattered to him. He didn't know then, and certainly wouldn't have cared, that he was exposing himself to certain contagion, to a habit of fatal indifference.

But it would take him years to realize that love was the thing that had licked him, not because some other guy had made off with his girl but because, in the end, he'd decided that he'd never wanted her in the first place. As a result he'd grown into the habit of not wanting anything very much. Certainly nothing that he would have to fight for or anything he was in any danger of losing. In years to come he would finally understand that he had given up the possibility of love, however unrequited, however unlikely, for a Walter Mitty dream of Capture the Flag. Sure, love was the thing that had licked him, but not in the way the song meant, although the outcome was pretty much the same. Either way you looked at it, Nathan was just another victim.

"Lord, how you've grown, Nate," his mother exclaimed when his parents picked him up at the bus depot. Unaccountably, Nathan burst into tears. He wanted to go home but he had lost his compass. Home wasn't his childhood bedroom anymore but nor was it the row of spunky bunk beds that comprised cabin

#3, domain of the lost boys. Embarrassed, his father hustled the snivelling boy into the back of the family station wagon. "Let's get you home, big guy."

Now, finally an adult, his childish knack for dissembling perfected, Nathan could pretend to enjoy the grand illusion of his various childish bereavements. For better or worse, Nathan the Camp Director had come home.

"Whatever home means," he said to Riva.

"It's where you live," Riva helpfully explained. "It doesn't *mean* anything. Meaning is a construct, anyway. Look at maple-glazed donuts. I mean, hello, bacon?"

Did she mean to flaunt convention or was she merely referring to the inconstancy of pastry trends? In any case, Riva was taking the Mickey and taking it better than Nathan could, which he resented.

It was difficult to know where Riva stood on most things. She was a scrappy labour lawyer, pugnacious and devoted to her clients. She thought of herself as a cultural anarchist, she told Nathan, occupying her free time by planning marches and raising funds, arranging petitions and sit-ins and vigils. The trouble was she had a disastrously ticklish funny bone and a talent for malarkey. Sometimes she put aside her high-minded pursuits and engaged in other kinds of interventions, writing fake letters to newspaper advice columnists or phoning in to radio talk shows and pretending to be a transgender teen named Ziggy. She said outrageous things and made outrageous claims but she just might have been who she said she was, was her ploy.

How had the boy who'd once fallen in love with delicate, aristocratic Molly Leibowitz taken up with such a provocateur, Nathan sometimes wondered. An anarchist!

It was an unanswerable question. In the intervening years,

between the boy who'd bunked in cabin #3 and the man now whitewashing its lurid walls, grudges had accrued. All the dopey, bashful, terminally grumpy impulses of Nathan's psychic cavern of inner dwarves had come to the fore. He had become a man of resentment. Even the twinge of arousal he still experienced from the word *cookie*, with its snack-associated memories, irked him.

"Gunnars says boat's coming at six sharp," said Newman hopefully.

"Nice move, McFly," Nathan said. He had long ago acquainted himself with the movie, which like everything else in life, had not lived up to the buzz. Whatever Principal Strickland said and however Doc Brown grandstanded, some things just didn't add up. You couldn't accomplish an impossible task merely by putting your mind to it, history was not going to change, and, most importantly, you couldn't go home again, whether home was thirty years in the past or three hours in the future where Newman was evidently projecting himself. It was clear that the young man wanted to be on that boat and off that island. Eight weeks was plenty. Eight weeks was four weeks too long and another two weeks even longer than that. Eight weeks of tossing kids off the dock and applying sunscreen to grimy napes and escorting boys to the outbuildings late at night when the buddy system was no longer viable. Eight weeks of hearing his name rhymed with *Pooh-man*.

Nathan got where Newman was coming from. God knows he'd been there himself. But there was still something he wanted to do. It was the last thing he set his mind to every year before packing out. Before clicking off the island's imaginary light switch and nailing down its shutters. Something he had to accomplish in order to feel the past flooding in like water in a basement, the old house awash in muddy runoff, sloshy with memory. Back in the city, Nathan lived in a sixth-floor apartment building largely occupied by students. Technically he was a student too, since he'd not yet submitted his dissertation on "Tragic Nostalgia" to the film studies department at the university where he laboured as a sessional instructor during term. The apartment building had a basement, of course, but it was the bailiwick of the janitor and, frankly, none of Nathan's damn business.

When Hunter and Newman left to wash up, cabin #3 filled with the voices that visited Nathan only when he was alone. They were the voices of campers past, the ever-young, ever-loved lost boys who had once pelted down these pathways and swung from their bunk beds and decorated the walls with their ardent, derisive vernacular. The voices spoke singly and in chorus, their words recognizable but their music plaintive and ungainly, like the poorly executed cover of a beloved song.

Nathan listened closely to the rough boys' voices and heard what he always heard: *We're never gonna die! We're never gonna die! We're never ever gonna die!* This was the secret that all the kids shared: they were going to live forever. They were so young that their entitlement, their longing, their *fury* for life had not yet coincided with their mortality. It was sad because it was truthful without being true, which was pretty much the definition, Nathan reckoned, of tragic nostalgia.

The voices eventually separated out so that Nathan could take attendance. Danny Rubin, leader of men, was there, and his best friend, Michael Shayowitz. Harry Naiman and Michael Segal were present and accounted for, also Leo Friedlander, Bernie Rubin, and Blaine Richardson. Last, possibly least, was that hobbledehoy, Nathan Miller, quieter than the others, subdued. There they were, the eight boys of cabin #3, their gaping hearts and cracked voices. Their unkissed lips and luckless spasms and sticky fingers. That long ago summer was the cupboard in which they would spend the rest of their lives rummaging, searching for their younger selves amid the soiled winter jackets and mismatched gloves that nobody had gotten around to discarding.

Molly, sweet Molly, where did you go? Now that she was gone, grown up, married with children of her own, she had become mortal (Nathan had heard that she was seriously ill, dying). Now that mind over matter had become only mind, an automatic tic, now that nothing mattered *that much*, Nathan was able to dip his toes in the lovely shallow goo of nostalgic regret.

He lay down on the stripped mattress of his old bunk bed. Furthest from the door, darkest part of the room. There were two windows in the cabin but he couldn't see much from where he lay, hardly anything. Once he'd woken in the night and crept, in his boy's pajamas, to the window. The moon was behind a cloud, and the cloud was behind infinity. The face of God obscured.

"Boys, boys," Nathan murmured, but they raged on and on. Zombies, burgers, sex. The lousy food and how there wasn't enough of it and the various bases of the sexual batting cage. And always and forever: the cookie, the cookie, the cookie.

He must have fallen asleep because he woke to the sound of the motor boat launching itself at the island. The light outside the window was the syrupy amber that suspends time in its glaze like flies or memory. Nathan sat up and swung his feet over the side of the bed. The boys were silent, long gone. He knelt beside the bed he'd once slept in for two lonely months. Nobody bothered to shift the bunk beds when they whitewashed the walls and the space beneath them was grimy and neglected, with dust bunnies the size of tumbleweed and a dire collection of boxer shorts and socks from years gone by, each one growing its little grey pelt.

At first he didn't see it and then he did, the handprint coming into focus as the years fell away, ripped page by page from a calendar in some cornball movie (the kind he secretly loved), its plot advancing through spinning newspaper headlines and a steam train that plowed through the names of various capital cities. "Nathan Plays to Full House!" "Three Cheers for Local Boy!" "'An Honour,' says Miller!"

It was only a blue handprint that some faithful, heartbroken Kilroy had left as a mark of his there-ness. Nathan had discovered it during his first week at camp in circumstances that included an empty-for-once cabin and a homesick kid sobbing his heart out, on his knees. Some nights he would wedge his arm between the bed and the wall, press his hand to the blue handprint. Other nights he'd turn his back on the whole thing: the wall, the darkness, the bogeyman under the bed, his aberrant yearning for a friend.

When he looked back at his younger self he cringed at the wobbly, hurt boy he'd once been. The hand was part of that messy scramble, that yolky half-formed, unpocketable thing, but it was also entirely itself, a creature apart. By the end of the summer, Nathan's hand was bigger than the other, and when he pressed his fingers against the blue hand for the last time, he had the strange sensation that it was pushing back. The hand shoving against his palm with the springy, over-inflated feel of a new basketball.

Over the years the blue hand had shrunk. Or perhaps his own hand had grown. Who could say?

Hand in hand, Nathan and his younger self lay still. Time passed — a minute? a week? — until Nathan the older, the flesh-and-blood man, the camp director, heard footsteps. Newman and Hunter were hurrying up the path toward him. They were coming to yank him on the bungee cord of his longing, his loopy nostalgia, back to the mainland and his turnstile life and his girlfriend, Riva, whom he maybe loved but who was not a girl to fit conveniently into somebody else's story.

Down on the dock, old man Gunnars was waiting by his launch. "You ready to go home, Nate?" he called. His hair was blowing in the wind and he was waving at Nathan with his whole body, impatient to be off.

FALL

NINE

TREE OF LIFE

THE YEAR OUR sons turned thirteen and became men in the eyes of their people, if not their mothers, was the bar mitzvah year. The previous year our daughters had turned twelve and become women, so we were accustomed to the spin-cycle of emotions that thumped through us like wet laundry as we watched our suddenly tall daughters approach the bimah in their curled or straightened hair, their shiny glossed lips and darkened lashes, and their twitchy new ways of walking.

Our lovely girls — how they sought to disguise hopefulness with irony, sincerity with irony, curiosity, kindness, and confusion: all with irony. How they pulled down their necklines and hiked up their skirts. Oh girls, girls! And a year later our sons would be called to the Torah, their ungovernable voices cracking between notes, and their Adam's apples jerking behind the constriction of their tight collars and sloppy, Windsor-knotted dignity. As we watched, we wondered what sudden switch had been thrown to make them surge with those invisible currents of boy voltage and nervous energy. Oh boys, slow down!

Our children were rosy with excitement or pallid with nerves as they kissed the fringes of their prayer shawls for the first time and allowed their mothers to wrap them in the blinding white silk with its gold embroidery or silver thread. And as we smoothed the prayer shawls around our sons and daughters, we blinked away the tears that doubled our vision for a moment. For the act of tucking and swaddling the shawls reminded us of wrapping our infants in their receiving blankets, and the sound of the years crashing against each other like waves against rock, brought the salt water to our eyes. Every girl and boy was beautiful — not just in the hearts of their parents but in all our eyes. We had known these children since they were born.

Some of them had been homely babies with an ancestral line in noses, or capacious ears they'd have to try to grow into; some had been creamy little puddings you could eat with a spoon. Some discoursed like philosophers before they could walk and some tottered about on shaky baby-legs for months without blowing a wet syllable from the pucker of their raspberry-shaped mouths. Some were scrawny as plucked chickens and some had dimpled knuckles and pinchable cheeks. Some bubbled like tiny kettles when we nuzzled their palms or pressed our faces into their warm, humming tummies; some turned red as baby-rage when we petted them. Some smiled in their sleep, their lips parted in the eternal *Yes please!* of language-less dreaming; some puckered their mouths into a perfect *O*, as if practicing for a lifetime of silent refusal: *No! Not now! Go to the dogs!*

"Pixies and thugs!" exclaimed Mrs. Harvey Silverstein, it being her long-held conviction that all babies fall into one or the other camp. But they were our babies, and we loved them all.

In truth we knew that Mrs. Silverstein loved them too. She was merely exercising her talent for observation and her librarian's fondness for organizing the world into efficient categories. The year that our daughters turned twelve was unseasonably cold, prompting us to retreat indoors, to our weather-sealed houses, and from there to burrow even further until we had taken up residence among the upholstered furniture of our memory rooms. The past played forever on these walls, in jerky spasms of colour without words. The only sound was the hum of the projector and our own noisy thoughts.

There was Leo Friedlander at Rose Epstein's sixth birthday party, pulling the pigtails of all the pretty girls whose mothers would comfort them, saying, "If he pulls your hair he likes you, darling."

"What nonsense!" Leah Silverstein would later exclaim. "Inflicting pain is not a sign of affection. We're preparing our girls for a lifetime of abuse."

"*Pshaw*," said Mrs. Harvey Silverstein, which was the closest she ever came to chastising the daughter she loved and disapproved of. Little Leah, the oldest of three sisters, had been a thug baby (the other two were pixies, naturally), and now she was a malcontent, and her mother still couldn't get over the fact that Leah needed a man like a fish needs a bicycle.

The invisible projector whirred on, threading our memories through the jerky sprockets of our collective past. There was little Molly Leibowitz at her first piano recital, tripping over the opening chords of "Unforgettable" before suddenly — you guessed it — forgetting everything she'd learned in three years of piano lessons. How she wailed and banged her head down upon the keys. We watched as Harry Naiman and Bernie Rubin and Nathan Miller ran in circles outside the community centre, a litter of puppies chasing a soccer ball, while the dads on the sidelines yelled, "C'mon guys, pass! *Pass!*"

In spring the kids were distracted by the yellow dandelions that buttoned down the rumpled green jacket of the field, and in fall they whirled with the wind and the leaves and their own wayward, wind-up impulses. The leaves flipped from green to yellow to red. They were the traffic lights of our disordered longing and we watched, transfixed, as the seasons stopped, then started up again.

"Oscar? Really?" Leah Silverstein had exclaimed thirteen years ago at her nephew's bris. We agreed with her but were too polite to comment. Besides, who were we to judge? We had been given the anglicized names of the ancestral dead by our Yiddish-speaking, immigrant parents, but in the intervening years we had shrugged off our past and named our children hopefully, reclaiming the black, fire-scorched inscriptions of an earlier time.

To the east, in the Promised Land, the Israeli prime minister, David Ben-Gurion, had proclaimed our future: a new language for a new land. We who did not live in Israel but in the dead centre of the North American continent, in a city looped between two meandering rivers, one swift flowing, the other fat and sluggish, we too longed for a new language, a new land. Our names were the names of American actresses and television stars — Marilyn and Linda and Shirley and Barbara — but our children were the sons and daughters of biblical heroes, striding like conquerors across a parched and blazing land.

Rachel and Leah and Sarah: our daughters were ignorant of the hawking, throat-clearing, immigrant tongue of their grandparents. They were neither slaves in the land of Egypt nor shopkeepers in the diasporic cities of North America. They went to high school and summer camp, learned piano, wore dime-store lipstick, dated boys. Overnight they grew up, our little girls. The braces came off and the makeup went on. Then they began to roll their eyes at their mothers. But such pretty eyes! We were exasperated and awestruck. How did we produce such beauty, such intellect? Such willfulness? One by one they went off to university, our darling girls. We who had been housewives and librarians, teachers and bookkeepers, we who had toiled in dress shops and shoe stores — we couldn't get over our daughters' achievements. Doctors! Lawyers!

The world was their oyster, their seafood buffet, as we told each other knowingly. For they had never tasted oysters in *our* homes.

Adam and Daniel and Jonah: our sons declined to attend business school, to take over their fathers' commercial ventures, the Meat Wholesalers on McPhillips or Fine Leather and Furs on Portage. Not yet, maybe never! Instead, they backpacked through India or raised chickens in the austere kibbutzim of the Galilee. For a time they turned their backs on the girls they had known all their lives and dated pretty blonde gum-snappers from the white bread and mayonnaise suburbs and, yes, sometimes married them. It broke our hearts because we had not been raised in the modern way. We did not believe that love conquered all.

Let them marry who they marry, we'll still be their mothers, Minnie Binder would say. In time she even grew to accept her son's gentile wife because her boy — Maxele, she always called him — was such a good son that he turned the words she had used merely to save face into a scientific fact. A proverb, almost! But Minnie was right. Whatever they did and whoever they married they were still our sons in whose adult faces with their newly squared-off jaws and sandpaper cheeks we could yet discern the sweet-natured, puppy-breathed boys they had once been.

And they came back to our city, most of them, fully grown salmon, labouring upstream to spawn in clear northern waters.

It was the kind of city that children often returned to, dragging their memories behind them like a beloved blanket. A summer camp they used to attend, the taste for a particular birthday cake only obtainable from a bakery in the city's North End, the family cottage at a lake just two hours east. It was the way the rivers froze early in winter so that our children could skate for red-cheeked miles or organize a pickup hockey game with their pals.

"It was colder in those days," Leah Silverstein would tell her nieces and nephews. "You kids couldn't have handled it."

And then our children began to have children and we became grandmothers. Once again we made a great big cupboard of ourselves for others to rummage in. Ah, but what a joy to hold a soft-boned newborn in our arms again, to feel the clutch of baby fingers around our calloused thumbs, to glance down and see a fontanel pulse with every heartbeat. They were fragile but they cleaved to life. Such delicacy! Such toughness! If we had known what fun grandchildren were we would have had them first, we joked to one another. One day our children became parents to children of their own, and we watched them suddenly apprehend that the world was ruled by gravity and the democracy of merest chance. That it bristled with sharp objects, barking dogs, and banging doors.

Oh tiny fingers, oh tiny toes! Oh little bones, green and supple as the branches of a sapling. The sun rose and set; not a day had passed but a year, a decade, a lifetime. Day and night we worried about our children and our grandchildren, reminding one another of our rabbi's favourite joke.

"Four ladies sit down to play mahjong," Mrs. Silverstein would begin.

We were used to Rabbi Zalman. He had his faults but he certainly knew how to tell a joke.

Some of our children didn't marry, of course. Stylish, catty boys who were rumoured to be living with other boys. Well, we'd always had an inkling about Mrs. Goldstein's youngest, who didn't play soccer or hockey but would draw up a chair at our kitchen counters and help us pat out cookie dough. Fierce girls who grew up to ride bicycles, avow their allegiance to fish and their independence from men. Beneath their declarative T-shirts even their breasts required no external support.

"But a fish doesn't need a bicycle," Mrs. Silverstein had wondered all those years ago. Nevertheless, when Leah Silverstein eventually became an aunt she was the best aunt ever, losing her heart to her nieces and nephews, although she never entirely lost her critical faculties. "Oscar? Really?" she'd exclaimed, years before, at her eldest nephew's bris. "What, are they all going to own delis?"

Leo and Rose and Molly. Harry and Oscar and Nathan. They were the Deli Generation! The years had come full circle and our grandchildren had inherited the shtetl names that had once shamed our grandparents. Assimilation was no longer the fashion; we were not milk to be poured into the cereal bowls of this gentile prairie city. Disappearing without a trace, diluting.

Ah, but we watched those children like —

"— like lighthouses," said Mrs. Harvey Silverstein.

"A lighthouse on the Prairies?" exclaimed Leah. "No such thing."

It was true that there were technically no lighthouses on the Prairies but sometimes young Leah missed the forest for the trees. Or, in this case, the waves for the rocks! What her mother meant was that we ourselves were the lighthouses. We watched those kids with 360 degrees of vigilance. Our searchlights revolved so fast that we gave the ships seizures!

If anyone had asked us to describe how we felt during the years when our children were becoming adults, our daughters women and our sons men, we would have said, "Busy." There was so much to do, so many chores to finish, so many items to cross off our lists before we could put our heads on our pillows at the end of the day and say, "Done."

Nothing was ever truly done, though. Lists branched into other lists, chores multiplied like brooms in the cupboard of a sorcerer's apprentice. Our children were coming of age, and we could not allow the day to pass without the appropriate festivities. A big hoo-hah, Mrs. Silverstein as much as said, although who was she to talk, her daughter wanted to know. Leah's bat mitzvah had been a ritzy do, one of the most elaborate of its kind in those days. We still remembered the speeches, the candy-themed centrepieces, and poor Leah's party frock that had been ordered from Toronto three months before her special day, and unfortunately as many months before the growth spurt that strained the bodice, waist, and hips of her chartreuse off-the-shoulder evening gown. It was an oddly adult colour to choose — "Especially for such a sallow child," remarked Bessie Naiman — but what is a mother's love if not alert to beauty in all its variegated disguises?

"May she be as lucky as she is beautiful," the late Harvey Silverstein said to all and sundry, all the well-wishers and onlookers and back-slappers.

"Who needs luck when you have such beauty?" Mrs. Silverstein had retorted.

Such defensiveness! Did she finally regret her extravagance in ordering a stylish frock from an exclusive dress store? In another city, yet! No returns and no discounts, she'd boasted. But who could wish the mother's sins piled upon the daughter's slumped shoulders? Leah's ungainliness only made her more precious to us.

"She will grow into her luck," the rabbi's wife reassured us. With all our hearts we wished Leah Silverstein a lucky life, for we could not imagine, despite our sage rebbetzin's certainty, how the child would grow into her beauty.

Meanwhile, we had our own events to plan. We ordered food for our kiddush lunches, and reminded Debbie at Bouquet Boutique to deliver floral arrangements to the synagogue before the Sabbath began. We dithered over luncheon menus — Menu A or Menu B, we wondered, or perhaps we could persuade our husbands to consider Chef Hubert's Premium Deluxe Menu C Buffet, which included tuna lasagna and cherry kugel, along with the party sandwiches and egg salad on bagels that were the mainstay of our Saturday kiddush luncheons. The party sandwiches were the real draw, of course. No celebration was complete without those white bread dainties with their trippy layers of salmon or tuna salad, chopped egg, cream cheese, and sweet pickle relish.

One year, Bella Shayowitz, who made exotic jewelry in her spare time and was always something of a maverick, persuaded Chef Hubert to conceal a maraschino cherry in the cream cheese centre of her party sandwiches, something sweet and unexpected to surprise her guests. Certainly her guests were surprised, as who wouldn't be by the jauntiness of a cherry-centred sandwich?

"Does she think a party sandwich is a cocktail?" Mrs. Silverstein asked.

"Do you know how long it takes the stomach to digest a maraschino cherry?" Shirley Rubin protested. "Seven years!" she replied, before anyone else could hazard a guess.

"Who needs to eat a sandwich that lasts seven years?" someone else, probably Barbara Becker, inquired. It seemed we were all so astonished by that little syrup-soaked sweetmeat leaking its red dye into the cream cheese centre of our decorum that all we could do was exclaim.

"Well, well," said the rabbi's wife finally, summing up the matter in her usual astute manner.

We knew what she meant and besides, she was a saint, the kind of woman who refused to speak ill of anyone. The truth of the matter, as Bella's great friend, Minnie Binder, pointed out to those who would listen, was that Bella Shayowitz had only one child, a thug baby who had surprised nobody by growing up to be a burly, buzz-cut fellow. Minnie too had only one child, one son, her Maxele, and so she understood the importance of getting it right the first time. No do-overs! Bella Shayowitz had one chance to shine and if she thought the cherry in her party sandwiches was enough to put the cherry on top of her celebration, then so be it.

Although he didn't exactly look it, Michael Shayowitz was smart as they come, no flies on that one. But, unfortunately, the brain box had a tin ear, and when he took his place on the bimah that morning, we all hoped he would have the good sense to rush through his portion "like a Ferrari," as the rabbi was inclined to tut. But instead, the boy chanted his Torah portion slowly and emphatically, so that every flat note, every off-key syllable, every cracked scrap of melody, seemed to tumble forever in the high-spinning dust motes of the sanctuary.

The night before, the custodian had — for the first time that year — turned on the heat, which, since it was the Sabbath, could not now be regulated. Oh, how we perspired into our shirtwaists and liberty-print blouses, the sweat trickling into our armpits and between our breasts so that we were obliged to use the weekly synagogue bulletin to fan ourselves. By the time the service was over our tempers, like the sanctuary, were overheated.

However, Michael Shayowitz's unmusical performance was a side issue. What we really meant when we pointed out that he was an only child was that his mother had leisure to spare. Free time! But, as Minnie Binder pointed out in defence of her friend, even one child takes up one hundred percent of a mother's attention. How much more time can two children take up? We were confused, for although we agreed with Minnie in theory, we also knew that the numbers didn't quite add up. Do the math: time is time, but time divided by half is both more than half and less than all. What this meant in reality was that if Michael had had a little brother or a big sister, then Bella Shayowitz would have had no time to craft her unique trinkets and no time to think up her artistically filled party sandwiches.

On the other hand, as the rabbi's wife pointed out, we were none of us physicists, capable of dividing time into matter, or at least into whatever matters most.

True, Minnie conceded. She herself had worked all her life in her late husband's store, Elegance Shoes, and she ran a household and cared for her aged parents as well. In fact, she was so rushed off her feet in those days that she barely had time to have her hair washed and set once a week, her only indulgence. And yet, with all the work, the shopping and cooking, the standing on her feet for eight hours a day — in heels, no less — it was Maxele who had taken up all her attention, she was certain of it. Perhaps time wasn't always a measurable commodity, like the hours in a day or the distance between years, Minnie speculated. Was it possible that time ran along different tracks, one track for all the things we had to do in a day and the other track for all the people we loved?

We all looked at our friend in amazement. What had happened to our practical Minnie?

But whether we chose to believe in love or time, housework or physics, we all agreed that with only one bar mitzvah to plan, poor Bella wanted to make a bit of a splash. Naturally she had chosen the Premium Deluxe Menu C Buffet, to which she had persuaded Chef Hubert to add an extra kugel — strawberry, with a choice of sour cream or applesauce. Debbie at Bouquet Boutique had outdone herself by fashioning five potted trees, which she had artfully distributed around the room. The trees were constructed of silver-sprayed branches draped with cutout menorahs, Stars of David, dreidels, and strings of non-denominational crystals.

"Jewish baroque!" scoffed Leah Silverstein. But we knew that the potted trees, with their gaudy decorations and their tendency to overbalance, represented the Tree of Life, which had given our people their direction and our synagogue its name. Yet even though it was only fall we couldn't help noticing how these trees resembled the artificial Christmas trees that, in another couple of months, would ornament the shopping malls of our suburbs and the living rooms of our gentile friends. Poor Bella, we thought, so much sass yet so little sense.

But who could blame the woman? The truth was, with so many mitzvah celebrations to attend in those years, we

were at synagogue every Saturday morning listening to someone's child babble or mumble or whine their Torah portion.
Afterwards we would sit in our strangling pantyhose and our
tightly belted frocks, with our husbands and our friends, eating
party sandwiches and egg salad bagels, either from Menu A or
Menu B. Who could tell the difference anymore? The coffee
in the enormous stainless steel urn could only be heated once
on the Sabbath, so it was cold as piety and bitter as obligation,
an uncomfortable combination and one that tended to cause
acid reflux. Naturally, we all wanted to do something just a
little bit different.

Sally Segal paid Chef Hubert a surprise visit two weeks
before her daughter's bat mitzvah. She found him taking stock
of his dry goods — bags of flour and sugar, boxes of soup mix
and matzo meal — and since they were already in the synagogue
kitchen, she took the opportunity to demonstrate her skill with
fancy garnishes. Radish roses and carrot curls! Orange spirals
on toothpicks and artfully placed cucumber fans! No more
parsley sprinkles, she told him. People get tired of picking dried
herbs from their teeth.

In a daring break with tradition, Shirley Rubin went ahead
and ordered four baked cheesecakes for her dessert table — one
chocolate, one double chocolate, one chocolate-vanilla mar-
ble, and one turtle toffee — and Shirley's sister-in-law, Marilyn
Rubin, let it be known that she was planning to rearrange the
buffet table altogether. A total overhaul. Put the dessert table
up front, she instructed Chef Hubert, and the luncheon dishes
and heating trays behind.

To all these suggestions, Chef Hubert nodded thoughtfully, or tapped his nose with the point of his wax pencil,
or scribbled notes to himself on his expense sheet. It made

no difference — he was French (his name was pronounced "U-bear") and glamorously confident of his superior judgement. Chef Hubert's Gallic charm certainly lent a touch of class to the proceedings and, it was hoped, mightily impressed the out-of-town guests who had schlepped in from cosmopolitan centres like Toronto, Montreal, and even Minneapolis.

"Huh, let them have their chocolate fountains and their helium balloons," Mrs. Silverstein would say. "We have our wonderful Chef Hew-bert. He's French, you know."

"Francophone," corrected Shirley Rubin, a stickler for geographical accuracy.

Chocolate fountains and helium balloons were two of the prohibited luxuries we had all experienced at events in other cities, but our own stern rabbi had outlawed them since they encouraged feats of clowning (chocolate fountains) or tended to tug loose from their moorings and drift up to the lofty ceiling of the sanctuary (helium balloons). This last was a particular vexation because the balloons were as brightly coloured as they were indestructible. Their silent, gentle drift and bob was strangely hypnotic and proved such a distraction to daily services that the staff was obliged to hire expensive equipment to remove them.

"Francophone," Shirley Rubin repeated. "Not French." And impossible to deal with, she did not say. We knew what she meant, though, and most of us agreed with her assessment. But Chef Hubert was immovable on the question of how things were done since he had been doing them for years. He'd been the first caterer hired by the synagogue steering committee and he meant to go on as he had begun. Which is to say: without changing a sugarless cookie.

"Do you know how many diabetics attend Saturday morning services?" he asked Barbara Becker. "They have to eat too."

Chef Hubert was as knowledgeable of the dietary requirements of the community as he was canny about their greed. He
was of the advanced opinion that no one needed four cheesecakes at their mitzvah celebration since, although all would
certainly be sampled, at least a quarter of each would remain
untouched.

"Don't forget, you've also got your chocolate log, your halva
log, your schmoo torte, your Ark of the Covenant slab cake,
your assortment of dainties, and your fancy fruit platter," he
reminded Shirley.

How much sugar can you people possibly consume? he did
not say and perhaps did not even think. As for the proposed
new distribution of the luncheon hall, with the dessert table
up front and the buffet table crowded in back — well, that was
an accident waiting to happen.

"Nobody will know where to go," he told Marilyn Rubin.
"Not the regulars, not the guests."

"What, so they'll all wander around with empty plates in
their hands?" snapped Marilyn.

Chef Hubert gazed off into the middle distance, silently
but gently, until Marilyn was forced to follow the trajectory of
his gaze into an apocalyptic vision of, yes, her guests stumbling
hither and yon, confused by desserts where there ought to be
warming trays of tuna lasagna and cherry kugel, their plates
in their hands.

It was fruitless to quibble with Chef Hubert. He had seen
everything and was impressed by nothing.

On the matter of garnishes, however, he conceded a point, a
small one, making a staunch ally of Sally Segal forever after. Of
course he would never have considered foregoing parsley altogether. What else could enliven a side plate of olives and pickled

cucumbers or a dish of chilled butter balls? And what but dried parsley could be sprinkled over his bowls of mounded egg salad and heaped platters of party sandwiches? Parsley was the necessary complement to any celebration meal, an honoured guest, even. Indeed on the subject of parsley — its dried and its fresh incarnations — Chef Hubert grew uncharacteristically loquacious. If garlic was the predominant note of French cooking and basil its Italian equivalent, then parsley, that humble but honest herb, that survivor of countless culinary purges, evoked the essence of Jewish cuisine, he told Sally, who reported this insight to us. We were impressed but bemused.

Who knew that the picked-over blandishments of Menu A and Menu B, the flavours that were almost as familiar to us as our children's faces but that nevertheless refreshed us after our three-hour services (longer, if the rabbi had a bone to pick with one of the enemies of Israel), who knew that they constituted what Chef Hubert called "a cuisine"? In his French accent, no less.

"Francophone," Shirley Rubin reminded us. "Not French."

Yet the fact remained that Chef Hubert had conceded in the matter of radish roses and carrot curls, orange spirals and cucumber fans, and from then on we felt that our synagogue was justly celebrated for the perfection of our garnishes.

But for all that we obsessed over our luncheon menus or exhorted Debbie at Bouquet Boutique to design ever more unique yet affordable floral creations — or consulted with Linda of Linda's Linens over our table settings, and ordered gift baskets from Not Only Cheese to be delivered to the hotel rooms of our out-of-town guests — however we distracted ourselves with shopping for clothes, matching shoes to purses, and making sure that our husbands had purchased new suits in time for them to be altered, we could not conceal our real anxiety. All the sound and fury, the mountains poking through our mole-hills, and the storms blowing themselves out in our teacups, in short the endless niggle of our preparations, could not silence the still, small voice that came in the night before we closed our novels and tumbled into sleep or again in the early morning as we took our first sips of coffee.

"The children," whispered the voice. "The children, the children, the children."

Again and again we recalled our rabbi's favourite joke.

"Four women sit down to play mahjong. '*Oy!*' sighs the first. '*Gevalt!*' groans the second. '*Vey ist mir!*' wails the third."

We always began laughing at this point, often so hard that we couldn't find breath for the punchline. But behind our laughter, a persistent worry ticked over, like the second hand on our kitchen clocks. *Maybe, maybe, maybe*, went the worry tick.

Was it possible that our children would grow up over the course of one eventful weekend? We simply couldn't believe it. Such nonsense!

No, we knew that the weekend would pass, and on Monday morning we would wake our children for school, as we had for the last ten years. We would throw open the blinds and tousle the tops of their sleep-tufted heads and say, "Rise and shine, darling!" The odour of slightly sour laundry and unwashed shin pads and hormone-buzzing teenage bodies would reassure us that all was as it should be. On that morning we would feel particularly tender toward our children, patiently coaxing them awake, pouring milk into their cereal bowls, and reminding them to eat slowly. *Don't wolf it down, honey. Do you want to get sick?* We would ignore their scowls and yawns, the implication that we were treating them like children. Didn't we realize they'd been eating breakfast for years?

Of course we did. We knew that they were no longer children. But they were still our children.

Yet even if we succeeded in keeping them close for a little while longer, our children grew up in the end. It was inevitable, like proving a loaf of challah dough overnight. In the morning we would lift up the damp dishtowels and find palpable evidence of the way time passes as we sleep. Look how the dough has doubled! Tripled! But a child, unlike a loaf of bread, cannot be punched back down or beaten into shape. Heaven help us, and why would we beat our children? The truth was nobody made their own challah anymore. Not since the kosher bakery in the North End began distributing their bread to local supermarkets.

So our children grew up — slowly or swiftly, awkwardly or gracefully, with grateful hearts or serpents' teeth — but in the end they all grew up. And we, too, grew older, although we seldom heard the whir of time's machinery as clearly as we did when we gathered at our book clubs or Sisterhood meetings or when we got together to play mahjong. Then news of our children would flash across the synapses of the room like nerve impulses: this one was finally getting married, that one was suddenly getting divorced or having twins or — God forbid — going in for a biopsy. It was like those movies we'd all seen: when the epilogue describes what happens to the characters as they grow up.

Where was the moral? we wondered. What was the lesson of the epilogue? That nothing grows while you watch, that a surprise ending is better than a good beginning, that the future lies in the hands of a Hollywood scriptwriter? Perhaps if we knew the future we would never get out of bed in the morning. Poor Minnie Binder, what happened to her Maxele should never happen to another mother. What mother wants to outlive her child? No, better not to know the end of the movie.

Meanwhile, between the end of the last frame and the slow fade to the credits, our children leapt into the billion scintillating points of light that was the future. Rose Epstein turned the family schmatte business around and eventually went into fashion design. You might even know her label — Is a Rose — which Bev Epstein explained was actually a poem. Harry Naiman became the dermatologist in charge of not letting women age. You can see his face on benches and billboards all over the city with a caption that reads: "Only a Shar-Pei needs to live with wrinkles!" Of course there is also a picture of this dog, this Shar-Pei, with its draped face staring out. Leah Silverstein is also on benches but with her it's a matter of real estate. Between the two of them — Leah and Harry — they have almost the whole South End covered, bus bench–wise.

None of our children grew up to run delis, although the Segal brothers started up the famous Dough Nuts franchise, specializing in fresh cookies which is maybe confusing given the name (no nuts, no donuts), but as Sally Segal pointed out, you don't want to fool around with names when the business is doing so well. If it ain't broke, she would have said, if she wasn't such a well-spoken gal. And, of course, none of our children became soccer stars or movie actresses or famous pop singers either. Molly Leibowitz didn't get to play her piano at the Albert Hall (she's a music teacher, three lovely children), and Leo Friedlander never did learn to drive an ice cream truck or operate an earthmover (he's an orthodontist, bless his heart, and he drives a Saab). Nevertheless, Michael Shayowitz surprised us all by becoming a world-class entertainment promoter. Not one musical production or reunion band arrived in town that he didn't personally oversee. A finger in every pie, an iron in every fire!

"A finger? The whole hand!" Bella Shayowitz would boast, and how could we begrudge her the pride she took in her only son's success? Michael Shayowitz was not himself musical, as we all recalled, but it seemed he possessed the magic formula that transforms dross into gold. The Midas touch, a pocketful of pixie dust, the secret name of his first-born son. (Actually, his first-born son is now called Chloe and is currently living on the west coast with Michael's ex-wife and her new husband, but that's a story for another time.) Whatever talent Michael possessed, only see what glamour it produced! And despite what people said, the trouble he got into later had nothing at all to do with music and entertainment promotion.

"Everything will come out all right in the end," as Harvey Silverstein always used to say. "Perhaps we just haven't come to the end yet."

Ah, but all this was in the future (Molly's breast lump, Max Binder's terrible accident), and in our late-night kitchens the dough was still proving. In short, they remained our obstinate or pliable, messy, rebellious, muddle-headed darlings, and we were so relieved that they hadn't grown up overnight that we forgot the cunning ways in which time could slow down or accelerate, could switchback or even change tracks entirely. Dear Minnie had once wondered if time travelled along two separate tracks but now we realized that time itself was what drove the train. Time was the wily signalman, the flip switcher.

The problem, of course, was Genesis and the dinosaurs.

We had all been through Genesis and the dinosaurs, and we'd tried to prevail with humour and imagination, with patience and even delight. For we remembered our own childish bewilderment at the story of the creation: the animals on the fifth day, Adam and Eve on the sixth. On the seventh day the Almighty took a nap and, hey presto: the World! It was Mrs. Silverstein who broke the news; she related how Leah had come home from second grade with the age-old question burning on her lips. Leah was the first, as always, but soon mother after mother began reporting that the great debate was upon us. Where, our children wanted to know, did the dinosaurs fit in?

Some of us said natural selection and some of us said God. Some of us said survival of the fittest and some of us said ask your teacher. Some of us said a day was longer in those days, about a million years! Some of us tried to explain how Darwin and his monkeys swung through the branches of Genesis while the Almighty created the world in six short sleeps and one long one. Some of us said you can't do it, you have to choose.

Some of us went out on a limb and talked about "interpretation" rather than "truth." Some of us even went so far as to say imagine the Bible is a story, imagine the story is neither true nor false, not in *that* way. Do you know what a metaphor is?

Some of us said well who created the dinosaurs then? Some of us rolled our eyes and shrugged our shoulders. How were we supposed to know? Some of us said forty days and forty nights, some of us said gone in a flash. Some of us said think of it this way, what would have happened to all the birds of the air and the fish of the sea and the beasts of the field? Some of us said if a dinosaur and a whale got into a fight, who do you think would win? Some of us said there are certain things we can never know. Some of us said okay then, where did they go?

But those of us who, like Minnie Binder, were often exhausted after standing for eight hours in the shoe store, said God is God. Have you ever *seen* a dinosaur?

Have you ever seen God? her Maxele immediately replied. He was just curious, she realized later, always such a curious, eager boy, although at the time it had seemed like cheek and was punished accordingly. In fact, she'd slapped him. There, she'd said it. A swift cuff, nothing serious, no lasting scars. Except to the one who had slapped, to the mother who could never now forgive herself.

Oh, Minnie, cut yourself some slack, we told her in the months after the accident, when all the poor woman could remember were the very few times that she had been harsh to her son. How that slap reverberated through the years, how it stung. Not for Max, of course, who had probably forgotten all about it five minutes after it happened (Wasn't that always the way with children?), but for his mother whose hand still trembled when she remembered.

Oh, Minnie, we chorused, you were a wonderful mother! And we would sit with her and try to console her: Eat something, drink something. How are you sleeping? Have you thought about volunteering? They need people at the Inspirational Living Centre. Have you thought of joining a support group? Crying is good, anger is good, grief is good. Here's a cup of tea for you, here's an old camp photograph I found, here's a joke our rabbi liked to tell.

"Four ladies sit down to play mahjong. 'Oy!' sighs the first. 'Gevalt!' groans the second. 'Vay ist mir!' wails the third. 'All right already,' says the fourth, 'are we here to play cards or talk about our children?'"

In truth the joke was so old that it was popular when Tyrannosaurus rex walked the earth. Well, why not? Dinosaurs had children too.

Ah, why bring it all up again, those extinct years when our

children turned to us with starry eyes and earnest, questing hearts? This was the first spiritual crisis of their young lives; they still believed us — they still believed in us. Now, all these years later, they accepted nothing that we said. They rolled their eyes and slammed their bedroom doors on our good counsel. They were laggardly about learning their Torah portions and grumpy at the thought of a weekend full of visiting relatives they hardly knew. Some floundered about in their recently acquired, ill-fitting, nearly adult bodies; others drove us crazy with shopping for fashionable clothes. Suits for the boys, real ties not clip-on. For the girls, modest yet stylish outfits and high heels to tip them forward on the axis of their new femininity, their swelling breasts and rounding hips.

Most of us were happy to purchase the new clothes that our children desired. We were adept at shopping, at flicking our fingers through clattering rails of trousers or shirts, at holding up gowns to our daughters' shoulders to judge for length. We narrowed our eyes and estimated drape and cut, deftly plucking a skirt or a blouse from a row of swinging garments. "Go and try it on, darling," we'd coax. Then we'd wait patiently outside the fitting room although it was always a challenge to keep the younger kids from running amok, pulling merchandise off the shelves or tagging each other with price guns.

"Anyone in there?" we'd eventually call through the change room door. "Let me see how you look, sweetheart." Did we imagine magical transformations as we stood waiting expectantly: our girls in their ball gowns, our boys in their suits?

But they were not those kinds of change rooms. Beneath the new dress shirts and the shiny fabric our children remained themselves, only paler and slightly jaundiced-looking in the lurid department-store light. What were clothes but the disguise beneath which our children's bodies changed, subtly or suddenly, into an idea of the future in its still-wet, waiting chrysalis? The truth was, we did not want to think of those changes — the swellings, roundings, protrudings, the encroaching hair, the hardening muscles. Most of us did not like to dwell too closely upon those growing bodies. Instead, we preferred to focus on the clothes our children were growing out of and the childish games they'd outgrown. But Bella Shayowitz, as always, was shameless.

"I walked into his room one day," she told Shirley Rubin. "Obviously he didn't hear me knock."

"She didn't bother to knock," interpreted Shirley.

"And what do you think I saw?" Bella asked.

We could imagine, although none of us would have dreamed of barging into our son's rooms.

"She saw a forest," Shirley confided to her sister-in-law.

"A forest!" exclaimed Bella, gesturing with one hand at her crotch, the other hand clutched to her heart.

Years later, when Michael Shayowitz was first taken into custody and before his childhood friend, Danny Rubin, even then a big shot in the courts, got him out on bail, we comforted ourselves with the thought that at least his mother had passed on. Little Michael Shayowitz who had once grown a forest was now growing an empire. How could he know that all of a sudden the promotion of boxing matches was not considered kosher business?

"Bare-knuckle fighting, Mom," Leah told her mother. "It's never been legal."

"Michael Shayowitz has been fighting without his gloves?" exclaimed Mrs. Silverstein, as if the boy had forgotten to wear mittens in the middle of winter, which, in her opinion, was just as dangerous.

Not fighting but promoting, is what we heard. In one of the shady hotels near the airport. Michael Shay — for this was his fancy promoter's name — not only organized bare-knuckle cage fights, he had even bankrolled an Israeli (ex-Mossad, it was rumoured) to star in one of his fist-fight productions.

"Alleged, Ma," Danny Rubin reminded his mother. "Alleged promotion, alleged fraudulent immigration practices, alleged illegal gambling."

"Ari the Jew," Shirley Rubin mused. "You say he's good at his fist fighting?"

"The best, Ma," Danny assured her.

It was true: the papers reported that Ari the Jew, a six-foot-four colossus with whirring muscles, was the undisputed champion of the bare-knuckle circuit and had yet to be defeated. Despite our horror, we were impressed: that a Jew should be so powerful, so fearless, so talented in the fist-fighting department, went a little way toward allaying the shame we felt on behalf of Bella Shayowitz who, if she were alive, would have been broken-hearted at her son's imprisonment, although understandably proud of his enterprise. On her behalf — dear Bella! — we too were proud, we too were heartbroken. And, remember, she had only one son, Minnie Binder reminded us. No do-overs!

But this was years in the future, decades! The past blew a gale from the left and the future crashed down on us from the right. The present moment was just a fragile bubble caught in the middle of these cross-currents of wind and water. We dared not reach out to touch that iridescent soap bubble with its oil puddle colours. Instead we waited, as we had always waited, our hearts freighted with misgiving.

The Shayowitz bar mitzvah was held on a Saturday morning during the ten days between Rosh Hashanah and Yom Kippur.

We knew these days by many names: they were the Days of Penitence, the Days of Remembrance, the Days of Judgement, and the Days of Awe. Only Rabbi Zalman, with his customary sense of calamity, referred to them as the Ten Terrible Days.

"Feh, what kind of career is that for a Jewish boy?" Mrs. Silverstein would ask, reminding us of the punchline to an old joke concerning three Jewish mothers who get together to boast of their sons' achievements.

"My son is a famous surgeon and president of his medical association," says the first.

"My son is a law professor at Harvard," says the second.

"My son is a rabbi," says the third.

"A rabbi!" we would chorus. "What kind of career is that for a Jewish boy?"

It was a joke we never tired of, an oldie but a goodie, funny because true. Our rabbi was a shining star in the firmament of his people's glory, yet we did not want our sons to grow up to be rabbis.

The days between Rosh Hashanah and Yom Kippur, fraught as they were with religious significance, our yearning to turn away from deceitful ways toward repentance and forgiveness, were not an ideal time to plan a bar mitzvah. But Michael Shayowitz had turned thirteen in September and that was all there was to it. And we have already recalled Bella Shayowitz's snazzy event with its abundance of food and deluxe décor. Between you and me, I wasn't crazy about the red velvet table-cloths with their black satin runners that Bella had selected for her luncheon and that Linda Shapiro, the proprietor of Linda's Linens, had warned her against, but no one asked my opinion. I was supposed to be Bella's best friend but even to me she was a puzzle.

If I have given myself away then forgive me. These are the Days of Awe when one is obliged to be truthful. And if I speak for myself occasionally, it is only provocation — red velvet, satin runners! — that tempts me to break faith with the community.

Four days after my dear friend Bella Shayowitz's magnificent event, we sat once again in the synagogue on Kol Nidre night, the holiest night of the calendar. Every year our rabbi stood on the bimah and preached to us.

"Think of the changes this year has brought forth," he instructed.

We thought of our children, the grace and awkwardness of their wings. We thought of the memory rooms in which we had lived all this year, the whirr of the projector on the walls, and our hearts — the hearts of mothers — beating out a rhythm of "How did it happen?" and "Where did it go?" and "Not yet, not yet, not yet!" Once there was a crease in time when our children still teetered on the brink of who they would become. That was the year our sons turned thirteen. That was the bar mitzvah year.

"Everything changes," resumed Rabbi Zalman, "except faith and good deeds which bind us to the Almighty." And he also said, as he reminded us every year, "Tonight the world lies open to our wonder. Tonight the universe is waiting."

We would sit in the sanctuary on Kol Nidre night, the hair on our arms standing on end and the blood thudding at our temples. Truly, the world hung in the balance: a word, a prayer, would cause the scales to dip or rise.

Early the next morning we would hurry through falling leaves, the glamour and gold spangle of autumn. When we arrived at the synagogue we'd linger for a moment in the cloak-room, hanging up our jackets and warming our hands on the radiators. In our minds the leaves still spun and whirled in drifts. Usually we had no time to think of leaves. What were they to us but the rubbish we raked from our lawns or the muck we scooped from our eaves? But on this day, we couldn't help noticing the helpless beauty of the leaves.

Then we heard the sound of chanting and hurried into the sanctuary.

All day we bound ourselves to the rise and fall of the cantor's voice. Nothing passed our lips but prayer. Not a sip of water or a bite of food, not a frivolous word. The more we fasted and prayed, the more insistent the voices grew. They were only whispers but their fervent longing was the helium that wafted them up to the temple's high-arched dome. All day the prayers rose until the susurrus of our mingled words became too powerful to be constrained. *Bless our sons and our daughters*, we prayed. *Bless our grandchildren. Bless Leah and Rose and Molly. Bless Harry and Oscar and Nathan.*

The strength of our prayers seemed to lift the temple so that we hung in the limbo between heaven and earth. All over the city, all over the country, we imagined such prayers wafting upward, the air humid with our yearning. What a roar they would make at the portals of heaven. Surely the angels themselves would come forth to welcome our prayers. In the evening when the shofar blew to end the fast, we woke, dazed, as if from a dream. The sacred world had fled, leaving us with our workaday concerns, our ordinary hunger and lightheadedness, the usual jokes that we made at the end of every Jewish holiday. They tried to kill us, we won, let's eat!

And every year, whether we broke our fast with bagels and lox, with brisket and kugel, or with a nice slice of honey cake and a cup of tea, we would resolve to hurl ourselves into the

New Year. The world was waiting for us. All we had to do was begin! There, in the fresh-cut morning, in that wilderness of apple trees and dinosaurs, of Adam and Eve swinging through the branches, the days passed as slow as evolution, taking their own sweet time, but the years were gone in an almighty flash. A million years, an eon, an ice age!

And then it was tomorrow. Tomorrow we would begin.

TEN

GROVER PARK FIELDS FC

"CATCH THE GAME LAST NIGHT?" I say to Coach Bob, but he's too busy setting up a drill for the team. Coach Bob is all about defence, which is a natural outcome of the fact that his kid is the team's goalie and a lousy one at that. "They gotta get through nine players before they score on you," he tells his son after the last game — a rout akin to the sack of Rome if you can imagine the decline and fall of civilization played out in miniature across a choppy green rectangle on an early fall evening. Couple of dozen eleven-year-old boys but only one of them is bawling.

A word about Coach Bob: he's a teacher at Ridgehaven High across the way, and what he teaches is sex ed. That might be why his son is so messed up or it might be that Coach Bob's last name, and consequently the last name of young Cody over there is — wait for it — Bubel. Look, I know all about the heartbreak of last names, being one of a long line of Boychuk men who've gotten used to the nuanced bullying that goes along with unfortunate end rhymes (suck, fuck, upchuck) and lame peckerhead references. But Bubel? Come on. The soccer kids call him Coach Bob, and sometimes just Coach (as in, "Aw, Coach!"), but he will always be Bubel to me. Coach Boob for short.

Back to the game now or its bloody aftermath, and I'm trying to get the kids into line for the traditional high-five, "no hard feelings" walk-through. I know it's going to be painful. Fact is, we are so low in the standings that we can only make the city playoffs if at least four other teams perish in their entirety, perhaps in a tragic air crash over the Rockies or by sharing their germy water bottles. Ah, but nobody ever promised that being assistant coach of a less-than-stellar soccer team would be anything other than yet another punishment inflicted upon me in this, the very first year of my glorious divorce.

A year, according to my ex, that is perfectly suited for making my peace and making amends. Making *time*, as she puts it, as if time is something you can make, like dinner or promises, one of which I consistently failed to make and the other of which I consistently failed to keep. I'm just quoting here so bear with me. Matter of fact my ex —Mrs. Catherine Boychuk as she still likes to be known, although you'd think she'd drop the Boychuk like a hot perogie — is why I'm here now, assistant to the worst soccer coach in the history of the league, even including Coach Whatchamacallit who gets less restrained with every sip he takes from his personal water bottle, but you gotta love a man who'll call out a ref over ugliness. (The ref's ugliness, that is, which he claimed was distracting his boys.) His name will come to me in a minute.

So, anyway, one day my soon-to-be ex tells me that her colleague, *Ro*bert, who is this amazing father and role model, no offence, has signed up to coach his son's rec team. Trouble is he needs an assistant coach in accordance with league rules, so what do I say?

"No offence taken," is what I say.

Apparently the staff at R. H. High are pledged to support one another even if it means making the rest of the world miserable: the folks who aren't lucky enough to work at that lousy battery farm for over-stimulated adolescents, for instance. Ridgehaven High is no sort of haven and it's built on level ground that is as flat as the rest of this two-dimensional city, but that's what I mean by names and the trouble they cause. Anyway, when I asked her why I still had to take instructions from the woman who told me that the only things I could successfully make were bets (my job), and a fool of myself (extra-curricular), she just stared at me as if I was one of her high school students.

"It's up to you G-Damn-It Andrew Boychuk, to make time for your only son now," she finally said.

Making my peace, making amends, making time. I don't know what she's on about mostly, but you gotta love a woman who takes the Lord's name so goddamn seriously.

Coach Louis was his name, by the way. The water bottle tippler? Louis Grenouille, we called him. It just came to me now.

So anyway, there we were lining up, and there was Coach Danny di Secca back of his boys and already moving down the line, giving our team the high five, the odd head tousle, the consoling, "There's a boy." Look, it's easy enough to be the coach of a winning team: you keep your boys in line, you keep your gloat in check. You say, "Keep your grandstanding for the ride home, guys." But we have this saying at work: Winning never feels as good as losing feels bad.

"Never a truer word, eh Boychuk," as my boss often says. Yup, never a truer word, but the truth of the matter is that we folks at Automatic Off-Track don't really care. Win or lose, it's all the same to us — you pays your money and you places your bets. Video horse racing is a clean game, and the way to keep it clean is indifference.

Anyway, what I was trying to say is that when I looked around for him, Coach Bob was still on the bench patting down his brat. He's a short guy, Coach Bob, with a short guy's chippiness, a marsupial paunch, and an unfortunate regard for sweatpants. He comes by it honestly, being, as I mentioned, a high school sex ed teacher with a minor in "guidance" and a corresponding four-pack-a-week habit. The kind of man, as they used to say, who can neither do nor be. Luckily he can't teach either, so the kids are mostly unaffected by his lousy, tuneless existence. Yup, you got it, he's a bad Sinatra cover in a pair of stretched-out sweats and a cheap haircut. Do be do be do.

As for me, I'm proud to say I've never worn a tracksuit in my life. I come to practice straight from work so I'm always suited up, which makes me look like the coach of a professional soccer team. "Fake it till you make it, eh Boychuk," is another thing my boss likes to say. So I wear my suits, and yell at the kids for turning up to practice with grass stains on their jerseys, and bench them for trash talking. Try to, anyway. Kangaroo Bob has seniority over me, coach-wise, and what he likes to say is, "Cool your jets there, buddy. They're just kids."

True that, I want to say. They're kids, not crybabies. But Coach Bob is still on the bench cuddling his very own crybaby, the amazing diaper boy. I mean, Cody's eleven years old and you can see the snot-rope from here.

The only thing I can ever think to tell my boy in the way of what you might call a life lesson is, "Never let them see you cry, son," and God help me if it isn't the only thing he seems to remember because he sure as shooting doesn't give a thought to slide tackling or automatic red cards for swearing at the ref, in both of which he's kind of made a name for himself. I don't mean a real name, obviously, just a general blur of aggression and speed, a short red fuse blowing himself out on the field, a *Look out, here comes the kid!* kind of thing, which is both flattering and insulting insofar as all the refs have him on a short leash.

His real name, by the way, is Frankie.

By this time, Coach Danny di Secca has moved all the way down the line to get to my boy and you can see he's getting ready to compliment him on the two goals he scored: top shelf, left foot no less. They were damn good goals, had a beautiful arc to them, the kind that threads the needle high over the keeper's head and before you can say, "I think it's goin' in, boys," it's already there. There's a ball bulging out of the far corner of the net, and our team is rushing the kid, and their team is hanging their heads and kicking at the grass.

I know di Secca. He's a good coach, the kind of guy who can see potential in the beauty of a perfectly curved goal. Even if the ref throws it offside two seconds later and *both times*. And it wasn't the kid's fault that his team was employing their classic knife-through-butter defensive strategy. I mean Frankie's a redhead, see. Like his G-Damn-It provoking mother. You have to take some things into consideration — kids being crybabies is one of them, naturally, and now I see Coach Bob's son, running up to join his team, the tears spackling his cheeks.

"Hey Frankie," Cody says, "congratulations on your automatic disqualifications."

There's this thing Frankie does that thins my blood. He smiles. It's a quick, cold, businesslike smile. It's a smile that measures the distance between himself and the world then adjusts for perspective. It's a smile that says, *What kind of no-hoper expects to win on a three-year-old filly called Well Ya Never Know?* It's a smile that directs itself to the folly of ageing jockeys and bad track records and long shots that pay out once in a blue moon. But hey, what are the odds of running off-track in blue-moon season?

At the airport hotel where we run Automatic Off-Track, we see all types come and go, but there's only one type of punter has any traction in the long run. He's the sort with a face like a clock, bland and symmetrical but no expression to speak of. He studies the form and he places his bets and he watches the races on the video monitors. That's all. After the race he collects his winnings or he tears up his ticket. Stays an hour at the most — he's probably on his lunch — and he's back again the next week. Thing about this type of bloke is you can't tell to look at him what the score is. Win, place, show, or lose — seems like it's all the same to him. Seems like *not* showing what he's feeling is the gamble, although *gamble* is not a word we are inclined to use at Automatic Off-Track.

There's this guy, for instance. Comes in one day with his clock face and his fire-sale suit, and makes a bundle off the Saratoga Pick 4, just like that. Sixty-dollar shoes and bad orthodonture. Scraps of toilet paper still stuck to this morning's shaving nicks. The boss has to come in and cut him a cheque. So, okay. He folds the cheque into his wallet, hangs around for a couple more races, then leaves.

"Bye fellas, see you next week."

"Same to you, Mr. Meek."

That's how we found out his name, incidentally. On account of the cheque: Mr. Gordon Meek. Ha, not a bad start to inheriting the world, Mr. Meek.

My boss once told me this story about the fellow who owns the Airport Inn where we rent office space. Rich bugger, and lucky as they come. You'd know his name if I told you, everybody does, but I'm not supposed to say because of employee confidentiality. Turns out he has a stake in Automatic Off-Track, too. But it seems this guy was once so down on his luck he had to borrow money from his in-laws. And when his father-in-law tried to sandpaper him for being such a terrible businessman, prone to misfortune and an all-round unlucky number, Mr. Lucky just smiled.

"Good luck, bad luck, who can say?" he said.

Next day the father-in-law's dead of a heart attack, the mother-in-law has a massive stroke at his funeral — dead before she hits the ground. They could have rolled her in with him and buried them both together — and the entire inheritance goes to their only daughter who, fortunately, is crazy about her husband.

"Good luck, bad luck, who can say?" My boss shakes his head at this brilliant insight but I want to point out that Mr. Lucky's in-laws weren't so damn fortunate to have known him. Instead I smile and agree that some folks have got more money than they can comfortably say grace over. Anyway, what I'm trying to say is that I know all about men smiling when they don't mean it. Hell, I do it about a thousand times a day. I just did it now, when I was talking to my boss, and I probably do it in my sleep, I'm such an obliging bastard. But it's scary to see that exact smile on the face of a freckled boy with a cowlick the colour of maple leaves.

"Now then, fellas," says di Secca, and he wisely chooses to tousle the boys' heads, because who knows where Cody's hands have been. Halfway up his nose, it looks like.

So that was the game against Northern Pirates and here we are at practice again, me making small talk with Coach Bob, something to pass the time, while a dozen eleven-year-old boys sweat man-makers and burpees and star jumps, before getting down to the serious business of all-out defence drill, which is the only way we're going to win a game this season. Strengthen the defence line so that nothing but offside passes and mosquitoes can get to our big boob between the posts. Ollie the Goalie, over there.

That and a kick in the pants.

"Catch the game last night?" I ask Coach Bob again, but he just looks at me as if to say, *One game at a time, sport, and this is the one.* I watch Coach Bob setting up the cones for his patented Lutz two-on-one defence drill. He keeps glaring at me, as if to say, *Why don't you start the boys on their warm up?* But I wait him out — personally, I'm against the unspoken bond between men. If he wants me to do something, let him go ahead and ask.

It's fall and there's a seam of cold running through the afternoon, ready to break open at any moment. I look over at the boys and they're goofing off, as usual, hitting each other over the head with their water bottles and kicking up grass, which pisses me off so I send them on a ten-lap sprint of Grover Park Fields FC, all four fields, which, in turn, pisses off Coach Bob because now he's finally ready to begin practice and the boys are tiring themselves out to no discernable purpose.

The boys finally make it back in a huffing, raggle-taggle bunch, my kid somewhere in the middle, and Coach Bob starts explaining the drill when Frankie says, "Whoa, hold on, Coach, we have to wait for Mr. Automatic."

"Wha —?" says Coach Bob. You've got to hand it to my kid: butter wouldn't melt in his goddamn ball sack.

He blinks at Coach Bob for a moment then says, "Um, sorry, *Cody*. We have to wait for Cody."

We look back to where he's pointing and in the distance we see Cody hobbling toward us, holding his side. The rest of the team cracks up, and in their laughter I hear every goal that has trickled through Cody's legs all season, every ball that has slipped from his grasp, every penalty shot that has ricocheted off his unresisting body to hurtle into the back of the net. And more than that. In the laughter that breaks then gathers again, I hear the echo of Coach Bob yelling from the sidelines, *Good try, Cody! Step it up on defence there, guys*. I hear Coach Bob talking the team up after their last straight loss in seven games: *Good game, guys. You're really improving.*

It's not my place to criticize, but if you ask me, there's a fella who could really benefit from sitting down and having a beer with the truth. By the end of a game he always looks like he's dying for a smoke but he's persistent, give him that. "There's no *i* in team," he tells them, "there's no *u* in win." I'm sorry to say that he makes air quotes around the letters *i* and *u*, just as I'm sorry to report that he then snaps the elastic on his waistband and gives the boys the old thumbs-up. Both thumbs, as if this is a game he can highly recommend.

There's no *y* in *because*, I want to say to him. There's no *gee whiz* in *dammit*. But there's a couple of lousy *o*'s in open goal, if you're interested. And another big fat *o* in Cody.

Whenever Coach Bob begins his spelling bee routine, the youngsters look at him like he just crawled out of a spaceship. Who *is* this alien? They're only eleven but already they prefer to take their medicine without the spoonful of sugar, or the song and dance about sugar and spoons that goes with it. Strangely, Coach Bob seems to favour all-out losses over dead heats. At the next game, where Cody, disoriented, runs into the post and has to be retired at halftime, our midfield, Mateo, takes over and proves himself to be something of a ball wall. We have a pretty decent second half and manage to tie it up with the dreaded Western Windigos. But during the after-game team talk, Coach Bob allows that he is disappointed.

"Look guys," he says, "a draw is like kissing your cousin. It's like driving a Honda."

I'm driving Nagamo and Mateo home that night, and the boys are intrigued by the whole cousin-kissing deal. Mateo, it turns out, has in fact kissed his cousin. His mom made him do it last year when the cousin had her first communion, but he prefers playing soccer, even losing. My boy and Nagamo express their appreciation of Mateo's ordeal with a lot of hooting and hollering and seatback kicking, but it's difficult to know whether they're ridiculing his innocence or its exploitation. Eleven-year-old boys are a mystery to me and I'm still sore at Coach Bob. Who's he to sneer at my non-existent Honda, the Honda my ex drives now, the ghost Honda that I would accompany to Ed's Wash 'n' Wax twice a month, reading the sports page in the mechanic's lounge while she had her hubcaps detailed. These days I drive a secondhand Chevy and I imagine poking Coach Bob in the ribs and asking, "So what's a secondhand Chevy like, eh Bob? Losing? Forfeiting? Breaking your leg in the first half?"

We're still at practice, though. All this time the boys have been whooping it up and calling for Mr. Automatic, and when Cody finally limps up, he's got himself a new nickname. Coach Bob says, "Guys, guys," but there's nothing he can do, and he knows it. A nickname is bigger than a kid or a dad or a coach, a nickname is bigger than a soccer field and more enduring than the memory of a hat trick. A nickname is vast and inescapable: it is the *weather*. And the strange thing is that I'll bet none of the youngsters even remembered that moment in the lineup last week, when Cody congratulated my boy on his disqualifications.

That's Frankie for you, patient as they come.

And you might say, so what? It's just a name. Yeah, right. Remember that you're talking to the guy named Boychuk, assistant to Coach Bubel over there. Besides, where I come from, I'm used to folks trying to pick the names of winners based on what some stud farm came up with five years ago. In eighteen characters or less. In other words, no horse called Chicken Run ever won the Kentucky Derby. It's not rocket science.

My own feeling is that every soccer team has to have a Dante or a Mateo on the bench. Doesn't matter if they're star players or no-hope ball-whifflers. That's just the way it works. Hockey teams now, they're all about the Aidens. My boss's kid plays triple A and his team is all Aidens in one form or another: Brayden, Hayden, Jayden, and a couple of — yup, you guessed it — classic Aidens. Come to think of it, Bubel's boy might've done better on the ice. Nah, probably not. There's only so much a name can do for you. The wife and I had endless grief over what to call our boy. Being a social studies teacher, she was all for Winston, after her favourite prime minister. But I just played my Sinatra CDs over and over until she finally threw up her hands.

"That's how Noriega fell, I guess," she said.

And Frankie it was.

The boy can't sing — won't, actually — and he's no smoothie, no blue-eyed sultan of swoon. But damned if he doesn't do things his way and always has.

Back on the field it's turning out to be a bad luck practice.

Two of the players are injured in the first half hour, and Cody gets a concussion when he tries to dodge his opponent during the final scrimmage. Suspected concussion.

"Damn it, Boychuk!" yells Coach Bob. "Was that your kid again?"

I don't bother answering him. Any fool can see that Frankie is way over on the other side of the field, has been all along.

The fall has set in and I feel that seam of cold tear open. The chill in the air makes my heart contract. Or maybe it's just the sun hanging low in the sky, turning everything hazy and lovable, even the boys who are hopping on one foot and then another to keep warm, shoving their reddened hands in their jerseys. I tell them to run a couple of laps, and walk over to help Bob with his son.

Cody has an ice pack clasped to his forehead as he lunges to follow his dad's finger.

"Not with your whole head, son," says Coach Bob. "Hold your head steady and move your eyes."

But the boy is too cold or too frightened or too confused, or perhaps he really is concussed and his father's words make no sense. He clasps the lumpy ice pack to his forehead and moves his head from side to side as if it's an ancient piece of machinery, creaky and grotesque. His head looks too big for his thin boy's body and I feel sad, the way I always do, when a horse wipes out on the track, and the camera swerves away, and you have to imagine the marshals sweating to haul that broken-legged animal upright and into its box.

"They don't shoot horses anymore! My God, woman, what do you take us for?" I used to ask my ex.

"I don't plan to take you at all, mister. You're not exactly a bargain," she'd say.

So I don't bother to tell her about the vet and his oh-so-kind Ketamine shot, and how the trainer is allowed inside the box with the dying horse although fuck knows what he does there. Whispers in his horse's ear, I guess. Of the endless blue furlongs of heaven and the weightless jockeys who never use whips.

Coach Bob is cradling his son, but the boy jerks abruptly to one side and vomits. Gotta give him credit, he manages to avoid his father's lap, if not the netted bag of soccer balls that lies to the right of the bench.

"That does it," says Coach. "I'm running this boy to Emergency." He hauls Cody to his feet and the two make for the car park, Coach half carrying the boy. And he doesn't look back, and he doesn't wave, and he doesn't say, *Take over, pal*, but then again, he doesn't have to. We have an unspoken bond.

Mostly I enjoy ball duty. It's the assistant coach's responsibility to retrieve the netted bag of soccer balls from the clubhouse before practice and, after practice, having counted them, duly return the bag. There's always a couple of balls missing or one too many added in, but counting is a ritual like anything else. On brisk autumn days you walk across Grover Park Fields with the net slung over your shoulder and the clouds racing like Seabiscuit across a sky as wide as your incredulity. The clubhouse smells cool and dry, as if summer has finally sweated itself out, and every nostalgia station in the city is playing "October." Although you're nowhere near a radio, you can just about hear the opening chords.

On days like this I make bets with myself: Five to one for a decent practice. Three to two Coach Bob calls it early, the lazy son of a bitch. Seven to two, Frankie gets reamed out for not passing. He's a breakaway kid and tends to wrench at the reins, if you know what I mean. Not so much a ball hog as a ball stallion, is what I always think when I see him racing through the other team's defensive line, taking those wide Frankie strides. As always, I call it (bad practice, ends early, Frankie bawled out for not passing). As a forecaster I'm hard to beat on a turf course but I only wager on practices because no coach worth his salt would ante up against his own team in a league game.

Which reminds me of something my boss always says, which is that you can't play the slots well, you can only play 'em *more*. The same goes for betting on a horse or a kid, if you ask me. You can study the form, and trace the lineage, and calculate the odds, but in the end you might as well pick a colour off the jockey's silks or double down on your lucky number. When Frankie was born my ex used to advise me to get my head out of I won't say where and pay attention, G-Damn-It. Kids don't come with a racing form or a stud book, she liked to say.

You can only take an analogy so far, I'd tell her. You being a teacher should know that. Yeah, she'd say, I did know that once. Back when I was a high school social studies teacher and not some baggy-assed mare chosen for selective breeding purposes.

I guess I could have told her that we were just going through a stage, all marriages have hard times. Or that Frankie would settle down, he was just high spirited. Or that she still looked pretty good to me; I liked her ass the way it was (I'm a man who appreciates a certain amount of heft). And I tried to, kind of, only she said, Take your hand *away*, G-Damn-It, that's not what I meant.

I was always getting it wrong in those days, and I'm not saying it to boast. Like the song says: Regrets, I've had a few.

And, yes, I'm drawing this out for as long as possible because there is nothing in me that wants to confront whatever is glopping from the net, and trickling down those balls, and collecting in a vile-smelling puddle on the pitch. The boys are still larking about and pretend gagging, which, in the way of these things, soon leads to real gagging, and practice is over anyway so I send them home. Then there is just Frankie and me, and I tell him to go work on his goal shots, both feet, because I have yet to meet a coach who doesn't appreciate a really fine left-footed striker, but it doesn't hurt to have right foot back up.

I approach the bench, imagining all the lousy things the kid could have eaten before practice. *Please God, not pasta in tomato sauce, not a Big Mac, not anything with cheese.* When I finally stop praying and open my eyes it's as I always suspected. The world is a rubber ball bouncing through a godless void. Or else somewhere there's a God, but he's holding his sides and laughing. He's yelling, *Ha, no free lunch, mister, and while we're on the subject of lunch . . .*

So I take off my jacket and roll up my sleeves. I tuck my necktie into my shirt pocket like some downtown loser on a smoke break.

"Okay, Boychuk," I say, because I'm faking it real hard now. "Okay, Boychuk, you can do this."

I try to wipe the soccer balls on the grass, breathing through my mouth and training my eyes away from the mess of cheeseburger chunks and chocolate shake curds. On the other side of the field Frankie is a blur of a boy, hammering the ball into the net, first with one foot and then the other. Each time, he patiently retrieves the ball then steadies it before turning and jogging backward a couple of feet so as to take another good run at it. *Tock, tock, tock.* The ball plunges into the net like a tongue poking a cheek, and I am oddly cheered by the impudence of this gesture until my hand slides along the treacherous curved surface of a soccer ball and into the still-warm mess of Cody's half-digested sick.

You know how it is; you start gagging, can't help it. It's automatic, like what you do when some bloke yawns in your face at the office or an asshole cuts in front of you in the six o'clock traffic then flips you the bird. When Frankie was a baby he used to throw up, just for the hell of it. Every time he saw me, it seemed like. I started to feel real bad about it, if you want to know the truth. I mean I loved the little fellow, I was his dad and all, but by God he was a putrid ball of poop and spit-up and projectile glop. Mashed peas is what I remember, still can't face 'em.

"Godfrey! Maybe you shouldn't come home at all," says my wife this one time. I'd just walked through the door after a day at the off-track when the kid pulled his knees up to his gut and blew. I swear I saw his head swivel.

"My name isn't Godfrey," I say, just to rile her. You've got to love a woman who won't call on the Lord in vain, even when she's standing there holding a kid covered in its own multi-coloured bodily fluids. There's orange magma bubbling from its diaper and dark brown lava running down its thighs and up top is the head twisting around on its little Frankie neck, spewing out pea soup. I mean, you'd think if ever there was a time to God-bother it might be right about now. It's not "in vain" if we get something out of it, I want to say to her. It's not blasphemy if we're begging.

Instead I hold out my arms and she shoves the kid into them and I think, *It's okay, I can do this.* I'm so damn proud of myself — big daddy come home, the kid still bubbling volcanically but settling down, and his mother flinging herself into a chair and glancing up, yes, gratefully. And I think, *Yup, I'm doing this, by Godfrey.*

That's when the gagging begins.

The gagging is vast and impersonal and omniscient. At first I can't even tell who the anonymous retcher is. It's certainly not little Frankie, who is asleep in my arms but who wakes up as soon as I give this enormous tectonic shudder and spew all over him. *Oh*, I think, and then, *Huh?* That's about all I have time for folks, because then the heaving begins in earnest. It's all I can do to yell, "Take the goddamn baby, woman!" before this same baby is fully covered in his father's half-digested lunch (burritos from Five Alarm Takeout) and about two gallons of coffee that burnt like acid coming up and didn't feel that good going down either, if you want to know the truth.

"Christopher!" yells the wife, by which I know she has just about had it with me. I don't blame her, I really don't. *Andrew Boychuk, you have hit rock bottom! Boy, you have nothing left to offer!* I think between spasms, but each time it seems that there is indeed a little more left to offer.

"Dambusters, give me the baby!" she hollers, and I do.

I bend over and clutch at my knees and breathe through my mouth and for a moment there is silence in that apartment. The stench is something dambusters awful and the look of the place, when I open my streaming eyes, is even worse, but the quiet is the quiet of angels dancing on their holy pins and threading themselves through the eye of heaven's needle. The quiet is the best thing that has happened to me since I walked through the front door. None of us moves: I crouch there, hands on my knees, the baby halted in mid-howl, the wife clutching at a crystal vase that some fool gave us for a wedding gift and — bless her heart — she is as quiet as can be when she vomits quickly and efficiently into its open glass mouth.

There's no us left, just my ex and the youngster and me

in different combinations that have to do with whether I've screwed up, and how recently, and so on. It wasn't exactly the days of wine and roses but that's how I remember us when we were all together. Don't ask me why because it wasn't what you might call a perfect day, and it took forever and about three more involuntary yaks on my part to clean up. We lost the damage deposit on the apartment when we moved, but by then we had a name for that day, "Throw-up Thursday," and Frankie was sleeping through the night, and Catherine had gone back to being a teacher and stopped giving me grief about being a bookie, which I never was anyway.

I'm still hunkered down, rubbing my hand clean on the grass, over and over again. Thinking about how one thing leads to another — you don't see it coming, so you can't stop it. Your kid throws up and then you do. Your wife gets sick to her stomach every time she lays eyes on you, and next thing you know she's serving you papers. You start off coaching the Little Team that Could, but by the end of the season your boys can't get through a practice without braining each other and you're kneeling on the ground wiping vomit off your hand. The thing is, you begin by thinking you were born lucky and then you realize that luck isn't genetic or earned; it's not a reward for good behaviour. Luck is a whore, like the song says. She comes on to you, she fools around for a while, but in the end she leaves on some other guy's arm.

Across the field I hear the *rattle, tock, tock* of my kid's famous left-foot strike. Mostly he gets the ball between the posts but sometimes the ball flicks off the crossbar and a couple of times it bends so far wide of the mark that I have to whistle through my teeth. Once, when a horse called Automaton came in at twenty-five to one, and we were all sitting around stunned, my boss said he'd seen it before with three-year-old bays.

"You can never tell with a redhead," he said.

Frankie looks up so I wave, but the afternoon sun is in his eyes. I think I see him smile his curt smile but there's something in my eyes too and I can't be certain. Then Frankie turns away and steadies the ball with his cleats. Patient as ever, he jogs back a couple of feet to allow himself to take a running start.

ELEVEN

A HOUSE ON MAGNOLIA STREET

VISITING HER FATHER was a short trip down the highway and twenty years into the past. When Bernie pulled up, she noticed that the house on Magnolia Street had a shuttered look, which might have had to do with the fact that the storm windows were finally up and the blinds were still drawn and had been, she would lay odds, since the last time she'd visited her father. Mostly, though, it was the look of mourning that sometimes settled over a house when the person who'd loved it most was gone. This was a theory she'd been working on that took into account the Binders' house next door, as well as her own. In different ways, both houses looked forlorn and unkempt, their shoulders hunched against the cold.

On the other hand, her perception might just have been a consequence of the weather (November), the time (too early), the place (too late), or, most likely, the uneasy combination of melancholy and anticipatory dread that always beset her on the drive to her father's house. The drive *over*, the drive *back*. Never home.

When Bernie first left home and the Heights, she'd gone as far away as she reasonably could, which wasn't nearly as far as she would have liked but was at least outside the city limits, to a ruined nunnery once run by the Sisters of Mercy. A group of her friends were trying to restore the place. Their plan was to farm a little, raise chickens, buy a goat, become self-sufficient. Her father found it hilarious that his daughter had finally ended up in a nunnery, a nod to what he'd have called her "promiscuous ways" and her mother's perverse insistence on naming their daughter after a Catholic saint.

"Maybe you'll have one of those holy visions," he joked. "You were always a fanciful kid."

Saint Bernadette, he meant.

In fact, her mother's people had mostly been Catholic, beginning with their forcible conversion by Jesuits coming into the Great Lakes in the wake of the voyageurs-turned-settlers. Bernie had first learnt the word *Métis* in a high school social studies class, and when she'd worked up the courage to ask her mother, Theresa had said, "More like *half* Métis, honey," then laughed in that open-hearted way she had: head thrown back and devil take the hindermost. Given what she took to be her mother's secrecy, Bernie had grown skittery about her religion, her identity, and her place in a world that seemed to require endless visions and revisions. Somehow her mother could live without declaring herself, her selving, but Bernie needed a border around her quivery, soft-boned self.

In the end the mystery, as far as Bernie was concerned, was why so many of the Revoir family had remained Catholic. For as long as she could remember, her mother had always referred to herself as lapsed. Not so much fallen as falling, perpetually and forever. Perhaps it was Theresa's way of retaining her hold on the old religion, however tenuously, however perversely. If so, it was a position that her daughter might have sympathized with if she had not mistaken the word her mother had used.

Lapsed. The gentle murmur of waves. And since Bernie had no wish to spend her life lapping gently on the edges of some distant shore, she renounced her mother's religion along with her given name. She was Bernie now, just Bernie. And she was nobody's saint.

These days it seemed that whenever she visited, the old man was on the phone with someone from Elk River, Minnesota, or Bronxville, New York, or Taddlecreek, Diddlysquat, for all she knew. Today, when she let herself in through the screen door, her dad was canted back expansively in his chair, his bare feet with their hair-scribble toes and cheese-rind nails propped on the kitchen table. A *heh-heh* look on his face.

"Nope," he said into the receiver. "You heard me right first time, old timer."

"No more moose this year," he said. "Wolves must've ate 'em."

"Wolves are fierce this year," he confirmed. "But at least they're keeping the population down. Moose-wise, I mean."

"Yup, yup. Circle of life kind of thing. Trouble is —" The old man swung his feet off the kitchen table so Bernie knew he was about to launch into the grand finale: "Trouble is, who's gonna take down the wolves now?"

Grinning like a Halloween pumpkin all lit up by trickery, Riley Tergusson gave his daughter a double thumbs-up, his ear still cocked solicitously over the receiver. Halloween was a week past and all the pumpkins in the neighbourhood resembled slow-leaking inner tubes, as if the bonhomie and high spirits initiated by a week-long sugar high were finally beginning to seep away. The constant rain didn't help either, dripping from the trees and the eaves, uttering little hissing sounds as it fell, adding to the general sense of universal deflation.

"Good morning, Bernadette," her father said, making the sign of the cross or his cockeyed version of it. This habitual greeting was meant as an homage to his late wife, to Theresa, but, as with all things Riley Tergusson–related, it was more like a poke in the eye with a sharp stick.

On the table beside her father was a mug of "regular unleaded," recently poured from a machine called Mr. Coffee. It seemed to Bernie that her dad lived an increasingly denotative life, as if old age required constant reminders, introductions to one's appliances in the name of courtesy or the effort to waylay dementia. The coffee machine was still breathing stertorously into the last inch of coffee sludge at the bottom of the carafe.

"Fill 'er up," said her dad, handing Bernie a mug and motioning for her to pour herself a slug.

The coffee mug was printed with the phrase: "That's What She Said!" Bernie recognized it as a novelty item from the gas station's "Collect all Six" range of bawdy ceramic ware. Oddly, the word *Said* was picked out in red lettering, as if the manufacturers, having thrown in their lot with prurience, were regretting their hasty decision. Really? She *said* that?

Her father had drunk regular unleaded all his life but was finicky about the type of gas he chose for his beloved Chevrolet pickup. "Old Gal," he called her at times, and "Chevy Chase," at other times. Named for that fellow with the dent in his chin, he took the trouble to explain. Not Spartacus, the other one.

In honour of the Old Gal, Tergusson claimed not only to have watched the entire Chevy Chase oeuvre but also to have memorized all eight minutes and thirty-three seconds of

"American Pie." Bernie had no cause to doubt him on the first of these claims, and nothing but an overpowering desire to divert him on the second. Tergusson and his Chevy: it was a buddy movie, a love story for all time, a ballad about a man and his horse in the absence, strictly, of either. Bernie's mother had always declined to ride in the pickup, complaining that she felt ignored, although she never explained which of the two — man or machine — had excluded her, had made her feel like a fifth wheel, she'd said with a straight face.

Instead she walked when she could and caught the bus when she needed to. The sight of Theresa waiting patiently in all kinds of weather for the 18 bus was a familiar sight in the neighbourhood. It was just one more way that Bernie's parents failed to get along because the fact was Tergusson doted on his pickup. He insisted on Super Premium gas only because Super Duper Ultra Premium hadn't yet been invented, supervised an oil change twice a year, and personally oversaw the annual spring tire rotation. Come the whiff of bonfire smoke in the fall, come the first appearance of bulk boxes of Halloween candy at Costco, and her dad was already hauling the winter tires out of storage, kicking at them and running a speculative finger over the treads. Reminiscing about the days when they'd have to use tire chains just to reverse out of the driveway. "Black ice," he'd say. "Don't tell *me* about black ice."

"Let's see — that's a ten four, buddy," Tergusson was barking into the receiver.

"Nope, yup, nope," he confirmed.

"That's seven, seven, nine, zero," he said, still grinning his crazed jack-o'-lantern grin and pretending to scribble something down on a pad, even going so far as to lick the tip of his non-existent pencil before completing his final flourish. He looked up at Bernie and gave his daughter a double wink, closing both eyes at the same time and squeezing his face into a rictus, then repeating the whole procedure: close squeeze grimace, close squeeze grimace. Had her father ever been able to wink one eye at a time, she wondered, or was this facial spasm — more reminiscent of palsy than roguish twinkle — the best he could do? She could no longer remember and there was no one left to ask.

Tergusson put his imaginary pencil behind his ear and listened intently for a moment. "Yup, that's the correct number, all right. Congratulations on drawing a winner, sir, but I'm sorry to inform you that we've had to cancel the Moose Lottery this year. *Whoa!*"

Her dad yanked the phone away from his ear as if he was pulling taffy. At the same time he made a series of funhouse mirror faces in response to the squawking diatribe on the other end, by which Bernie intuited that the *whoa!* was inadvertent if not unsolicited.

"Got a live one on the line, kiddo," he muttered. "Would you listen to this?" He swivelled the receiver in her direction, generously offering to share the caller's tinny fury. Bernie waved him away as if to say, *None for me thanks, I've had enough.* As if to say, *You go ahead, though.* As if to say, *Be my guest.*

Tergusson shrugged and pulled the receiver to his own ear. He listened dreamily for a moment then snapped to and pointed accusingly at his daughter's feet. He was indicating either that she had failed to remove her socks and must promptly do so, or that his daughter had gigantic feet, which was a crying shame but certainly not Riley Tergusson's fault. Nosiree, Tergusson could not be blamed for the fact that his daughter had grown to Amazonian proportions, with feet to match. He, himself, was a size 8 (men's narrow) and had been since his voice broke.

Unsurprisingly to anyone who knew him, Tergusson's assessment of his daughter was oddly skewed. Yes, she had large feet but the rest of her was slim, even girlish. She had Theresa's warm smile, a delicate yet pugnacious chin, and a shock of dark stand-up-ish hair that was cut short to make her look fierce but somehow only made her seem more fragile. However, Tergusson was adamant in his claim that his daughter was a lummox and this had been a constant of their relationship for as long as Bernie could remember.

"Rowing boats!" he'd exclaimed whenever the young girl had needed new shoes. "Are you descended from Labradors?"

"On your mother's side," he'd add. And yes, it was true that Theresa Tergusson had been blessed with large feet, both for her size and gender. She'd been a handsome woman with a comically warm smile abetted by dimples and an endearing gap between her front teeth. Her heart was the normal size for her body, her daughter supposed, but in all the ways that mattered — emotional, imaginative, metaphorical — it was by far her largest organ.

The caller, having poured his invective into the phone, duly slammed it down. Tergusson was free to let out a long, self-assessing whistle. "Jeez Louise, would you get a load of Fargo, North Dakota?"

"Moose Lottery been cancelled again?" Bernie said, trying to keep the sarcasm out of her tone. Never having succeeded before was no excuse for not trying.

"You betcha, kid. Shitty day in Paul Bunyan Land." Tergusson pointed at his daughter's feet, snapped: "Off." Her socks, he meant, and not her feet, she assumed.

The reasons — gleaned by Bernie over the years — to account for Riley Tergusson's hatred of socks were manifold.

They itched, they confined, they compressed. They caused the foot to sweat, to swell, to stink. Secretly anarchic, they concealed themselves in the lint catchers of oversize dryers, waiting their chance to escape, to disappear into a nappy limbo of unmatched socks. It was well known that socks were promiscuous and uncommitted, declining to mate for life.

"They don't *toe the line*, heh heh," he'd once confided.

Since his retirement from his job selling advertising space for a men's fashion magazine, her father was always looking for a slogan he could live by. Tergusson's image of the afterlife was of a mountain of socks in which the recently dead were obliged to rummage forever. Searching, in vain, for what they had lost on earth.

Get your rocks off! Take your socks off!

Further reasons for Tergusson's lifelong disdain of men's hosiery included the following: discomfort, dismay, formality, and in certain cases, death. He did not trouble to explain this final dire outcome but pointed out, instead, that dry socks caused electric shocks, wet socks caused pneumonia, and all socks made a man look like a pussy — a sock-wearing, white-pawed, son-of-a-bitch goddamn *pussy*.

Since socks were sold in inconvenient yet cunningly packaged bulk sets of three or six, and occasionally five, it proved impossible for Tergusson to purchase a week's worth of socks, although the outlandish mathematics of dividing seven days into multiples of three or six, and occasionally five, did not prevent him from trying.

"Always too much or too little," Tergusson would mourn, the Goldilocks standard forever eluding him. "Why *is* that?" he'd demand of his old crony, Milt Johnson.

But Milt, whom Tergusson had nicknamed "Second Floor"

because he'd been a purveyor of men's clothing and apparel, always claimed ignorance of the nefarious world of men's hosiery. It didn't matter. Tergusson required an audience rather than an answer to his questions, which were, in any case, rhetorical, insoluble, and verging on the existential.

White socks were for kids, he'd inform Milt. On the other hand, black socks emasculated a man unless he removed them first, heh heh. And as for stripes, checks, and diamond patterns, Tergusson remained scornful. They made his feet look big, he claimed.

Bring the world to heel. Go sockless, young man!

The primary characteristic of socks, Tergusson liked to conclude, all makes and sizes and patterns, all colours and mixtures and percentages of Lycra to cotton, was their tendency to wear out in the heel. A consideration not mitigated by the fact that the womanly art of darning had been lost to the ages. Bernie's mother being the exception, Bernie the rule.

By the time she'd peeled off her socks and laid them on the radiator to dry, her father was dialling another number, peering nearsightedly at the pad in front of him yet scorning to pull his spectacles down from where they balanced, insect eyed, on top of his head. The reasons why Tergusson hated spectacles were as thorough-going and comprehensive, although more forcefully expressed, as his intolerance of socks. It was certainly a more perverse prejudice since — declining eyesight or not, glaucoma and macular degeneration and persistent black floaters notwithstanding — Riley Tergusson drove his Chevy to the levee most days, and twice on Sundays when the Legion Hall opened its doors at midday for their weekly veteran's lunch buffet that always included two types of Jell-O salad and some form of marshmallow-enhanced side dish.

Bernie had once asked her dad if he actually was a veteran but if she thought to trip up the old man with this cunningly phrased question, she was mistaken.

"Not per se," Tergusson had replied. "I'm more what you might call a 'veteran of life.'"

Her father, having finally squinted his way through the chicken-scratch pencil markings on his notepad and dialled his number, was listening, aggrieved, to the mechanical wind-back of an old-fashioned answering machine.

"Leave a message at the sound of the tone," he muttered, then, perking up at the promised tone, he cleared his throat: "State of Maine, Department of Licensing here. I'm returning your call regarding hunting and fishing permits for the coming season." Tergusson would always pause at this point, presumably for effect.

"Unfortunately, all available permits have already been claimed," he'd continue, contriving to sound regretful.

"Better luck next year and remember, the early bird gets the moose," he'd sometimes add. Then he'd pause once again, pretending to reconsider. But no, the law was the law. "Have a nice day and don't forget to floss," he'd say.

"Et voilà!" he turned to Bernie. "Suck it, West Paducah, Kentucky."

Tergusson was nothing if not a showman but lately he'd been drawing out his effective pauses to improbable lengths. His effective pauses had become pregnant pauses, and Bernie feared that her father's late trimester comic timing was in danger of exceeding the gestation period of meaningful satire.

She asked Tergusson if he thought he was being fair. It was one thing to deny hunting licenses and fishing permits to blunt-thumbed Midwesterners who misdialled the long-distance code on a regular basis. It was another matter entirely to take the trouble to phone these beleaguered fools expressly to deny them the hunting and fishing rights it was their constitutional privilege to exercise.

The fact was it was no one's fault, and Tergusson's sheer cussed good fortune that the phone number he'd had for years exactly corresponded to the new customer service line at the State of Maine Licensing Department. The area code was different, of course, but only by one number, the number in question being situated directly below the other on the keypad. As a result, *chez* Tergusson had become the favoured dial-up destination of hasty-fingered Americans from every state in the Union, on the prowl for hunting and fishing permits, who would find their way, via fibre optic cable, electronic switchboard, and blessed human error, to what they would no doubt have considered an obscure province in an unimaginable country floating somewhere above their own. It was a mug's game.

Riley Tergusson not only took every request seriously — although naturally he was obliged to deny them all — he also took it upon himself to return calls regarding claims to the winning tickets of the annual Moose Lottery. It was anybody's guess as to what exactly the Moose Lottery was, but it was pretty clear that all Tergusson's callers were anxious to secure a stake in it.

"Uh-huh, uh-huh, uh-huh," he'd say when he got a customer on the line. "Numbers sound right. Congratulations on the numbers, sir. Yup, seems like you've got yourself a winning ticket, pal. It's just — no lottery this year," he'd announce. "On account of what happened up at Grand Forks. You didn't hear? You're kidding me, right? That's Grand Forks, North Dakota?"

"Huh."

His regret was sincere even if his cover story was dodgy. But in Tergusson's opinion a good story trumped verisimilitude every time. It was one of the many conflicting creeds he lived by.

Sometimes the problem was declining moose numbers, sometimes roving wolf packs whose penchant for snacking on a tasty moose shank compelled them to patrol the outskirts of towns and small cities.

"You don't want to get between a wolf and his dinner," Tergusson would say. "Cooling windowsill pies, household pets, even *kids*," he'd explain.

At other times he'd turn officious, citing vague but pressing bureaucratic reasons for the cancellation of that year's Moose Lottery. Systems failure, computer shutdown, budget cuts.

"Don't even get me started on climate change," he'd say.

"Moose are in decline," he'd say. "Numbers are falling fast. Some sort of internal parasite, brain fever, bone rot. Ever heard of antler, hoof, and mouth?" he'd inquire.

Sometimes he'd go the whole hog, throw caution to the winds, and expansively declare the entire moose nation an endangered species, a bewildered herd drumming their blurred hooves on the edge of extinction.

"That's dead, pal," he'd take pains to qualify. "When they're gone, they're gone for good."

"Like whitetails," he'd say, although when Bernie pointed out that white-tailed deer were plentiful in these parts, a downright nuisance, he'd shrug. Give 'em time, was his attitude.

His ace in the hole, though, his lucky eight ball, the one that always came up "Yes You Can!" was Canada.

"Damn Canucks closed the borders," he'd say. "Herds of

moose trying to get out. Moose droppings all over the place. They've had to rename the Peace Gardens."

"Hah, Poop Gardens!" he'd chortle. "Good one!"

"You know those animal rights activists are trying to get 'em refugee status? Yeah PETA," he'd allow darkly. Taking umbrage at those goons the way he always did, convincing himself of what he'd only just invented. Tergusson couldn't countenance their interfering ways.

"Ah, well," he'd concede. "I guess somebody has to look after those poor dumb beasts. The moose, I mean. Not the dingdongs from PETA."

"Sure they do," he'd say. "Holy guacamole, you think moose just roam through border control? Ever heard of electric fences, ever heard of security barriers, ever heard of long-range surveillance techniques?"

As always, Bernie's father had rhetoric on his side. Rhetoric and his listener's apparent willingness to ride shotgun in the runaway vehicle of his conviction, his visionary account of the ground-pawing moose hordes sequestered in the frozen hinterland. Stranded, heartbroken. Also, and perhaps mostly, Riley Tergusson counted on a certain dumbfounded "you mean to say-ishness" based on arrogance, pie-eyed American gullibility, and geographical ignorance.

"No, that's Mexico," he'd say, rolling his eyes in delight. "Canada's up, Mexico's down. Canada's moose, Mexico's unregulated labour practices and illegal immigration."

"You heard me right, old timer," he'd say. "Damn Canucks think they control the world. Just because they've got the Queen's ass on their twenty-dollar bill."

"Yeah, but you got to fold it right, buddy," he'd say. "Let's see, you got twenty dollars on hand?"

So far no American in the history of the State of Maine Department of Licensing had ever had a Canadian twenty-dollar bill on hand, but Riley Tergusson was always happy to be the voice-over in the described video called Punked.

"You fold the two halves of Her Majesty's face together," he'd say. "Right over left, then under."

"It's a question of perspective," he'd say. "If you locate the sweet spot and then fold into the crease you turn the royal kisser into ass cheeks."

"No offence to our nation's figurehead," he'd say. "I mean, God bless Her Majesty and the twenty bucks she rode in on."

"Who knows?" he'd say. "Trying to reason with these people's like pissing up a rope. Seems like they want all the goddamn moose for themselves. Seems like they got more on their minds than the thrill of the hunt or the taste of prime rib moose steak."

"What am I implying, mister?" he'd say. "No implication. Stands to reason, though."

Appealing to reason was like catnip to Tergusson's inner tabby. It settled him, made him dozy and expansive. In fact, it was usually at this precise point in the story that her father would abjure reason for implication, the heady switchback of slander and slander's swoopy nosedive into libel.

"Ever hear the one about the Saskatchewan farmer who couldn't walk straight?" he'd ask. "Heh heh, neither could his sheep."

It had the opposite effect on Bernie, however. Whenever her father appealed to reason, she took an involuntary step backward. Held her breath and looked to the heavens where volleys of Canada geese were honking like truckers, perhaps in response to her father's lame joke. When the geese and

their raucous humour finally disappeared, the neighbourhood fell silent.

Still gazing from the window, Bernie noticed how trim and
well-tended Magnolia Street looked, even in the rain, even at
this tail end of the season. The householders had long ago raked
their leaves, bedded their perennials, and planted their spring
bulbs. In her time her mother too had secured windows and
bedded perennials, raked leaves and put in her spring bulbs.
It was Theresa's way, which was also the city's way, to choose
these small pragmatic habits of acclimating to the cold that was
a-coming. Bernie saw that the tree band kids had already been
through the Heights, inoculating the trees against Dutch elm
disease and the idealism of the city planners who'd loved elms
so much that they'd planted great unprotected avenues of them.
Even the city forestry crews had come and gone, singling out a
diseased elm here and there, tagging its trunk with a splash of
orange paint. When she was little she'd imagined the marks as
skull-and-cross-bones, as emblems of death.

"It's just nature," her mother told her. "To everything there
is a season."

She was either quoting the Bible or a folk song she'd once
sung to her daughter. Who could say? Theresa was as complex
as the next person and twice as smart.

Her father was still going on about illegal border crossings
on the part of renegade ungulates and Bernie shut her eyes for
a moment, resting her forehead against the cool glass of the
window. When she opened them again she was just in time to
catch the last of the Canada geese arrowheading their way into
unrestricted skies, south of the border but no passport required.

*   *   *

THAT WINTER THE American president would call for a ban on Muslims entering the United States and refugees would begin striking out for Canada, making their way across frozen fields and unaccustomed terrain. When Bernie discovered a Somali refugee hiding in one of the unfinished outbuildings, she thought she was seeing things, experiencing a holy vision just like her namesake, Saint Bernadette, had done. But he was just a freezing man gazing up at her from a corner of the shed where he was huddled, his head on his knees. Outside it began to snow again.

So much snow, Bernie thought, the phrase snagging in her mind briefly before the man closed his eyes and receded once more into his darkness.

Bernie and her friends rushed him to hospital then set up an impromptu refugee station at the nunnery. They had been struggling all year to create a sustainable garden but it was simply too cold for too long. Now they could create something better, more enduring: an underground railroad that would usher refugees to safety. Bernie herself undertook to drive their communal van down to the border every morning.

The border was only a couple of hours away but sometimes there was blowing snow on the highway. High winds and low visibility. The van's heater was unpredictable, either blowing gusts of hot Chinook-like wind in her face or refusing to engage. Overheated or shivering with cold, weary with squinting down the highway or jumpy with nerves, her stomach sloshing with too much thermos coffee, always hungry, Bernie would idle in the van on the outskirts of Emerson. Through the deep freeze of February and on into March, she waited to pick up fleeing refugees. The stragglers, the stumblers, the frostbitten men limping through thigh-high snow in their sneakers, the women carrying children on their backs.

Bored and cold, dangerously sleepy, Bernie would droop over the steering wheel, stamping her feet to keep warm. Where were the moose? she wondered. Her father's imaginary herds stampeding for the border, galloping toward freedom. Or at least the freedom to be hunted down and shot. She hardly knew anymore whether she was thinking of the refugees trying to get in or the moose trying to get out. It was all a lottery, she decided, too cold to make sense even to herself. The border hovered somewhere up ahead, across frozen white fields, and Bernie would wake with a jolt, believing she'd heard footsteps. Hoofbeats.

TERGUSSON HAD FINISHED telling his favourite joke about the Saskatchewan farmer and his sheep, so he started right in on another. He had an endless supply, Saskatchewan being the unfortunate butt of an entire country's lame-assed joke. Bernie often speculated that her father just liked shooting the breeze with other seniors, ancient cranks and codgers, contrarians to a one. They were the only folks who called the customer hotline, since they cherished a belief in personal service and appeared to have no idea that permits, hunting licenses, and tickets to the annual Moose Lottery could be purchased online. Blurred vision and trembling fingers were a factor. And the phone calls he returned were usually answered, often on the first ring.

It seemed that Tergusson had finally gone through his call-back list, ticking off every Barnum-inducted sap with a flourish. He was signing off on his last call — Wisconsin Dells, Wisconsin — with an impromptu shtick on the subject of free trade, customs regulations, and the importation duties on edible wildlife feces.

"Schmuck," he said as he put down the receiver.

"You're taking advantage of them, Dad," Bernie said, who the hell knew why.

"You're right," Riley Tergusson said. "There's this hole in me that can't be filled."

Tergusson's masterful plan to conceal the truth of his inner emptiness by pretending to lie was a double feint. Sure he was empty inside, hollow as a well, but he was also *full of it*. He could city hall it all the way to the pearly gates, although once he got there he'd likely provoke Saint Peter on the issue of border tariffs.

In the year after her mother died, Bernie sometimes glimpsed the pathos beneath her father's knuckleheaded pranks and merry ways. But not often — pathos was only a couple of frames in the stop-go motion picture of her old man's life, barely registering.

It was still raining, the rain blurring the windows, giving the world a half-finished, improvisatory look. Tergusson had evidently completed his call-backs. He took a resonant sip of coffee and leaned back in his chair.

"What happens when we die?" he addressed his daughter. "Explain."

For some months now, her father had been receiving pamphlets from the Milford School of Continuing Education, his age and his retail profile apparently placing him in a demographic that veered, ever so subtly, toward mortality. If Bernie were to hazard a guess at the potential overlap between Riley Tergusson and the pleasures of the unexamined life, she would imagine a couple of Venn diagram circles neatly looped one over the other. But her father was a fighter, a brawler. He would not give in to the apparent meaningfulness of existence. Parody, as always, was his ally. As a result, Tergusson had begun to couch his conversational gambits as bullet points in a glossy brochure aimed at retirees:

- Come Study Comparative Religion With Our World-Renowned Experts! Discover the Great Existential Bugger All!

- Who's That Hiding Behind the Curtain and Talking Through a Megaphone? A Musical Journey!

- Why Do We Spell "God" With a Zero in the Middle? An Inquiry!

Bernie wanted to offer her father solace, but was it her fault she'd grown up without a scrap of religion? Religion was the bone that had been fought over and then gnawed clean by her parents. By the time she came along it wasn't even a bone of contention anymore.

"Does the soul continue after death?" her dad said. "Discuss."

"Dead is dead, Riley," Bernie said, quoting her mother.

"Ay yup, she were a spitfire," Tergusson conceded. The further in time he travelled from the fact of his late wife, the larger she loomed in his memory. It was the opposite with an automobile, he'd once taken the trouble to explain to his daughter, objects in the mirror appearing larger than they did in real life. Or, how about this, he offered: you're driving away from someone and they're standing there in your rearview mirror, waving goodbye. Most of the time they shrink, shrink right down to a tiny rectangle of goodbye and good luck. But your mother now, she was no shrinking whatchamacallit.

Violet, he meant. But Tergusson could never remember the names of flowers. All his analogies, all his examples and rationalizations and expressions of love were car related. And about as accurate as the odometer on a secondhand pickup at the local Ford dealership. But he'd had a lot of experience in driving away, so Bernie took him at his word.

"I'm thinking, though" — Tergusson kept his head down as if addressing his coffee — "What I'm thinking, kiddo, is would it be so crazy? Soul-wise, I mean."

Bernie thought that it would be and said so.

"Huh. Was I *that* bad?"

It was a rhetorical question, often advanced by her father, but she answered anyway. Her answer was in the affirmative but she took her time for once, sketching in some of the eternal pains that Tergusson's renegade soul might be expected to suffer on its journey of redemption.

"If such a thing as a soul exists," she finished up, "which let's hope it doesn't."

It wasn't that her dad was an evil man or even, all things considered, a bad one. He hadn't gone and killed anyone, as he'd be the first to remind you. He wasn't a drug lord or a child molester or a Ponzi schemer. He wasn't a rapist or a slave trafficker or a lawyer. Most of his shenanigans weren't even illegal.

"Illegal per se," honesty prompted him to add.

All he was, when it came right down to it, was brash. Bold. Some might say shameless. Shameless was what his wife had called him, using the word as a mirror rather than a club. A bright, showbiz-y mirror lit up by vertical rows of bulbs in some long ago matinee idol's dressing room.

"That's why your father takes such a good photograph," she'd once explained to Bernie. "He doesn't know enough to say cheese when some fool points a camera at him."

Saying cheese was Theresa's version of plastering on the old shit-eating grin, the beggar's cringe. Tergusson could no more say cheese than uncle. What he usually said, under photographic circumstances, was "Hurry up, idiot" or "Are you done yet?" Bernie hadn't picked up a camera in years.

Tergusson was still going on about the broad range of mortality courses on offer at the Milford School of Continuing Education, of which there appeared to be a surprising number. Less surprising perhaps, given the mean age and average blood pressure of their targeted audience.

"Nirvana or Nihilism?" he pretended to read. "Compare and Contrast."

"Worms versus Vultures: A Comparative Study of Bodily Decomposition. Provide Examples."

"This'll Be the Day That I Die: The Prophetic Voice in American Folk Music of the Seventies," he finished off. "Some Singing Required."

Up until now Bernie's father had never shown the slightest interest in dying; his plan was to live forever. He ate red meat twice, sometimes three times a day if you counted beef jerky; took half and half with his Froot Loops; and liked to add salt to everything, even coffee. Shaking the salt cellar vigorously over a plate of bacon and fried eggs was his only form of regular exercise, and macaroni salad was his vegetable of choice. Still, he remained hearty and had beaten his austere, clean-living wife in the mortality stakes, although it was possible that the vindication he felt was seasoned with grief. Bernie was no expert reader of her father's more delicate feelings.

"Miss America," he'd called his late wife, out of love Bernie hoped and not satire. But she had her doubts. For the truth was that Theresa Tergusson, née Revoir, had been neither beautiful nor American.

"Because of the pie," her father replied when his daughter finally asked him. Tergusson had met the woman who would become his wife in a Salisbury House on Boxing Day. "Eating pie," he explained succinctly. He refused to elucidate, as if even such a perfunctory explanation was too revealing. An unnecessary egging of the marital pudding. All he would say was that when he'd first met his wife he didn't know that that was what she was.

"Nope," he'd say with a banana-split grin, "I had to find that out on my wedding day."

There was no one else to ask, however, because by the time she had conceived an interest in her parents' pre-Bernie lives Theresa was in a coma, her fever-thin body rubbed to nothing between taut hospital sheets. Bernie would sit beside her, holding the loose bunch of her finger bones and thinking of all the things she should have asked her mother: What the hell did you see in him? How did you know? What kind of pie?

It was too late, though, and besides she knew most of the answers already. Razzle-dazzle and high derring-do. Lord, girl, how do you know anything?

Cherry. It was cherry pie.

"WHY DO TREES shed their leaves?" her mother had asked once. Rhetoric was the lingua franca of the Tergusson household, but it seemed she had given the matter some thought. "Because they have nothing left to say," she told Bernie.

Like the trees she was a creature of few words, always shedding. Bernie had been shocked at how little Theresa had left behind, how lightly she'd stepped upon the earth. A couple of boxes of clothes and shoes, an old rosary, and a drawer crammed with Mother's Day cards and birthday greetings that her daughter had sent her over the years, from the first bulky, macaroni art collages to the fulsome, pastel-coloured Hallmark cards with rice paper inserts that she'd purchased in later years, merely signing her name. *Love, Bernie.*

Once or twice, she noticed, she'd even specified their bond, as in: *Your daughter, Bernadette.* But mostly Bernie took it on faith that Theresa would deduce their relationship as she had deduced so many things over the years, her daughter's love among them.

A week after Theresa's death Tergusson had already run the clothes down to Goodwill and thrown away the cards. He claimed to have given the rosary to his pal, Milt, who was a fidgety sort of fellow and might benefit from Theresa's string of worry beads. Her dad might have given them to Milt, although it was a long shot. One thing was certain: Tergusson would have done anything to get those voodoo beads out of the house. Bernie liked to think it was grief that had motivated her father, rather than impatience or the *Reader's Digest* article he'd been reading on the can, urging him to simplify his life.

"Yup," Tergusson had said, "that's about the size of it, kiddo."

"Well, I guess we all end up in a box out on the sidewalk one way or another," he said.

"Your mother was a self-contained woman," he said. "Frugal."

She had died in the worst month of the year, the clocks losing their bearings, spinning backward, and the earth creaking on its iron-cold axis. They were spared the metaphoric chill of a winter funeral because, unbeknownst to her husband and daughter, Theresa Tergusson had set her heart on cremation.

This last instruction had been issued, in the form of a request, to the priest of the local Catholic church that Theresa had ceased attending years ago.

"Thoughtful," was how Father Alvarez characterized this final petition from his errant parishioner. But Bernie discerned that he might have had other words in mind. *Headstrong, surprisingly opinionated. Spunky.*

To Bernie, November had always seemed like a place rather than a time. Outside, the trees, having declared their frugal silences, having made their peace with needless chatter, shed their leaves. There were many ways to interpret the trees and their endlessly falling leaves — death, and gravity, and Ecclesiastes. The promise of renewal and nature's cagey profusion.

"Dead is dead, Riley," Theresa had said.

It seemed as if there were more leaves than there had ever been that year, and neither Riley nor Bernie was inclined to bag them. They covered the lawn in thick drifts of *nothing more to say*. In their profligacy they made a mockery of Theresa's lean aphorisms, her skirt-tucking ways, her instinct for invisibility.

However, Tergusson did not approve of cremation, an opinion he wanted duly noted before consigning his wife to the flames. It was unnatural, he told his daughter, ticking the reasons off on his fingers: it was perverse, it was final. It lacked ceremony, sociability, catering. Burning was for leaves, not bodies. Burning was for out-of-date tax forms and cherries jubilee.

"Otherwise you got yourself a bang and a flash and a shitty little bonfire out back of some place called Dignity or Glory," he explained. "Smoke pouring from the incinerator and nobody looking up. At the end of the day, they hand you a box of gravel and hit you up for an urn. What the hell do you do with the damn urn? Stick it on the mantel, stuff it in a cupboard? Best case, I guess, is you could set it up as a hood ornament."

Given her father's sudden interest in hellfire, Bernie suspected that cremation made for uncomfortable associations. But it was what Theresa Tergusson had wanted — no memorial service, no music, no eulogy.

"Spread the ashes somewhere," she'd said. "Your choice."

If it sounded like an afterthought it was only self-deprecation, it was only modesty, it was only her mother's housewifely impulse to excuse her own dust. In the end she had valued herself so lightly. (But what did it matter? Dead was dead.)

"Spread the ashes," she'd said out of a sense of formality. But she might as well have said throw away, discard, jettison. Dump the ashes, get on with your lives.

THE PHONE RANG and Tergusson dived for it but it was a local call, no permits required.

"Might see you tonight, then," he said into the receiver, by which Bernie intuited that it was one of Tergusson's buddies inquiring as to her father's availability for Monday Night Football at the Legion Hall. Apparently Tergusson liked to keep his options open and his buddies guessing, although he'd never missed a Monday Night Football in, well, ever.

"Yes, I have," Tergusson said when she shared this insight with him. "Don't you remember when your mother was dying?"

Theresa Tergusson had been in a coma for two months before she died, which made eight Monday Night Footballs in all, seven of which, by Bernie's reckoning, her father had not missed. Her mother had died on a Monday afternoon, the only inconsiderate thing she'd ever done. Tergusson had indeed fore-gone that evening's sportscast, but he'd got his buddy, Second Floor Milt, to place a bet on the outcome of the Detroit Lions–Redskins game, the Lions narrowly winning their first game that season, squeaking through, and Tergusson, as a result, making out like a bandit.

"I just had a lucky feeling," he explained modestly.

"We should all have such luck," Milt would later marvel. Death was the inevitable outcome of the game of life, was his point, but the Lions hadn't made the playoffs in two seasons.

Bernie wanted to believe that her father's shame over that ill-timed wager was what lurked between them like the shadow of a crazed serial killer in the kind of horror movies that played on all the channels before Halloween. *Don't go into the Radley house after dark, Scout!* But her father was as photogenic as ever, by which she was forced to conclude that the condition of shamelessness that her mother had once observed, isolated, and diagnosed, still prevailed.

Tergusson was flipping through the brochure from the Milford School of Continuing Education, a look of acute dis-gust on his face.

"Have you given the matter any thought, Dad?" she asked because someone had to bring it up and the lake was about to freeze, would freeze by the end of the month. Her mother had loved the beach by Falcon Lake and Bernie had envisioned tak-ing a boat out, just the two of them, herself and her dad. But that had been in summer. It wasn't possible to sail a boat on the ice-sculpted chop of the half-frozen lake, and by now she just wanted to get it over with. The river was still running, so perhaps? The fact was her mother had been on her mind lately, never more so.

"Get me out of my box, Bernadette," she'd say.

"I've never asked anything of you before," she'd say. "I'll never ask anything of you again."

"Remember me, remember me, remember me," she moaned day and night.

Theresa Tergusson would have said none of those things, but that wasn't the point. She hadn't a shred of guile and had always disdained the easy contrivances of guilt. Besides, her mother was too pragmatic to purposefully haunt anyone. But there she was every night, in her flowered housedress and her comfy slippers, her large-knuckled, reddened hands held out before her. Bernie would wake with tears streaming down her cheeks although until then she hadn't cried for her mother, her self-control the only unclaimed gift she could think to give her. There were so many tears they pooled in her ears, making her feel both tragic and undignified, a queasy combination.

It was a year of firsts trailing their little kite strings of heartbreak and banality. She almost phoned Theresa on her birthday, and in the week before Mother's Day found herself at the drugstore staring at a bank of glitter-bespattered cards before coming out of her daze with a pop. An actual if inaudible pop, like a cartoon character in the midst of a jerry-rigged epiphany. Apparently, Bernie's inability to remember that her mother was dead was matched only by her father's inability to remember that she had ever been alive.

"Have you given the matter any thought?" she would ask from time to time, but her father never had. Never had or couldn't bear to or wouldn't say; by now it was all academic and Tergusson had never been one for book learning, which he pronounced "larnin,'" in mockery of the foolishness others thought they glimpsed in him. But if Tergusson was a fool at least he was nobody's fool.

Bernie wondered if she had been relying on her father's willfulness for protection. Not from saying goodbye or the armpit-prickling self-consciousness that imagining such a leave-taking would engender. Not from grief or grief's somatic blowback, her immune system wearing out like the frayed elastic on a pair of sweats, the "stress" psoriasis spreading its patchy shroud over her body.

"Bye, bye, Mama," she imagined herself whispering as she tipped the funerary urn into the flowing water, her mother's gravel spreading out briefly before sinking like the dense flecks of bone and calcified memory that they were. *Bye, Bye, Miss American Pie.*

No, what her father's immunity protected Bernie from was her mother. Her mother's body gathering dust somewhere in the house, in an urn, in a box, in a cupboard. When the funeral director had first handed her the cardboard box, she'd almost dropped it. It was surprisingly heavy, like a cake baked without a rising agent. Was the soul a sort of baking powder of the unleavened spirit?

"Whoa!" her dad had said. "I'd better take that, kiddo." He'd stashed the urn in Old Gal's glove compartment, and on the short drive home she could hear her father straining not to crack the obvious jokes.

"The old gal's riding home Old Gal style," he did not say.

"Two old gals together at last for the first time," he did not say.

"What's the difference between a heap of junk and a box of dust?" he certainly did not say.

When Bernie was little her mother's body and her own had been cunningly sewn together: Theresa was a kangaroo and

Bernie was her pouch toy. Later she could stand apart from her mother for minutes and then hours at a time, but never too far apart. Her mother loomed so large in her life that often she couldn't see her at all. At other times Theresa hove into view, a collection of maternal bits and pieces — hands that smoothed the hair off her daughter's forehead or patted her back or rubbed her stomach, a neck into which Bernie could press her whole sobbing face. It was hard not to draw the conclusion that she'd been a mournful, sickly kid. Her mother's neck smelled of everything to do with her — face powder and cigarette smoke and laundry detergent, Yardley lavender soap and the familiar warm biscuity odour of her skin beneath. When she was sad she smelled wintergreenish; when she was angry she gave off the whiff of electrical circuits burning dust.

How did Bernie know this? Her mother was never angry.

As she grew older, her mother's body became a dangerous and separate creature. Her breasts, especially, were to be avoided. Bernie never outgrew the adolescent chagrin she felt toward Theresa's body, a body that seemed to have nothing to do with her, with modest, seemly Theresa Tergusson, whose familiarity Bernie now experienced with contempt keen as love, a shame that rendered her stiff-armed and rigid-lipped in her mother's presence.

"Lord, Bernadette, what kind of a birthday hug is that?" Theresa would exclaim.

When Theresa embarked upon the concentrated effort of her dying, Bernie became aware of her mother's body in the hospital bed, awkward and unlovely. This dying body was and was not her mother. Perhaps it had always belonged to a woman so self-sufficient that she could afford to give herself away. To her husband and daughter, to every passing dog, to death. But it was difficult to exist in the conceptual crease where belonging folded itself into strangeness. She held her mother's hand, wiped her face with a washcloth, bent to kiss her antiseptic cheek. Theresa was comatose by then, so who knew if it counted?

But when she died, Bernie realized that her mother's body, the body that she'd once loved and avoided and desired and hated and finally, in its last months, tended, this body had one last unsuspected property. It had the ability to be both gone and present, absent yet insistent. The trees had shed their leaves but surely there was still something left to say?

"Nothing to do with me, kiddo," her father said, a short-shrifter to the end.

It seemed that Riley Tergusson's everlasting gripes against death had not abated. Hypocrisy, sincerity, difficult decisions, needless expenses, he complained to his daughter, resuming his finger-ticking list: ill-dressed funeral directors, the odour of lilies, probate. Also religion — religion most of all. People dying when they owed him money. People dying after the football pools had been finalized, the March Madness brackets selected, or — worst of all — during the annual three-day Legion Darts Tournament. Such events never failed to rub him the wrong way. And the misuse of the word *tragedy* when all folks meant was *sad* infuriated him.

Tergusson liked a surprise ending at the movies but took exception to plot twists in the narrative of his own life. He enjoyed attending the funerals of his buddies, the lying eulogies and homemade casseroles, but was distracted by the resentment he anticipated at being forced to miss his own funeral, which would be, he felt, something of a shindig. If he could he would have arranged to return, like Tom Sawyer, to spy on the mourners, taking notes on attendance.

Death was a flimflam artist, an old con, he said. Death, per se, he added. And besides, there were too many bad songs about death and only one good one. Then he'd launch right into it, the one good song about death, the day the music died.

Whether Tergusson approved or not, folks died and worms ate them or fire consumed them and that was the best you could hope for. It wasn't like dialling a wrong number and ending up on the line with some joker who spun you a yarn. It wasn't like winning the Moose Lottery only to find out that it had been cancelled again, pal. It wasn't like signing up for a mortality course at the Milford School of Continuing Education because you'd left it too late and now you were cramming for finals. It wasn't like any of those things, which was why Bernie asked her dad, once more, if he'd given the matter any thought.

Riley Tergusson said he had indeed given the matter some thought, quite a bit of thought, actually. He'd been chasing the matter around, he said, head over tail.

"Ever seen a dog with an itchy butthole?" he inquired by way of comparison. "Here's the thing though — have you looked at the weather recently? Rivers are about to freeze, kiddo, lake's already frozen." To drive out to the beach he'd have to get his transmission fluid checked again, and *ho-ly* have you seen the state of the roads?

It was November, one in a long line of them. By this time next year Bernie would be in love. She had tracked down the Somali refugee who had almost frozen to death in one of the nunnery's outbuildings. After all, she was the one who'd found him, just as her namesake had once discovered an apparition on a garbage dump near Lourdes. Saint Bernadette, patron saint of illness, poverty, and people ridiculed for their faith!

His name was Afrax. His left leg had been amputated above

the knee and he'd lost three fingers to frostbite. He told her he'd been lucky to find work as an interpreter at a refugee counselling centre but that his long hours didn't allow him much time for his real passions. When she asked what they were he'd looked at her for a moment — a perfectly judged moment, she later realized — and confided that he enjoyed a good game of soccer when he wasn't practicing the violin. He reminded her of someone but by the time she worked out who it was, it was too late. Too late to extricate herself from the fate of Afrax Dahir Galaid, who was brave and resourceful but who was possessed of a tragically comic vision that would beguile and exasperate Bernie for the rest of her life. If love was a lottery, a game of chance, how had she drawn the goddamn joker not once but twice? It was a mystery.

AFTER TERGUSSON HAD finished complaining about the state of the roads and the impossibility, the colossal stupidity, the death-defying feeble-mindedness of trying to drive out to the beach in this kind of weather, he paused for a moment.

"What about we just keep your mother around for the winter?" he suggested. "Plenty of room in the house."

He gave his daughter the patented Tergusson double-wink that involved closing both eyes at the same time. And when he was done, he double-winked again — close squeeze grimace, close squeeze grimace — which could have been palsy or forgetfulness, Bernie reasoned, the impulse to waylay boredom or some fugitive reflex of the body's picturesque decline into ruin. It made her a little sad, though, so she said, "Sure, Dad, we'll talk about it in the spring." She didn't feel like another cup of coffee and the phone was ringing again so she collected her wet socks from the radiator and pulled on her boots.

"Goodbye, Bernadette," her father said, adding as he always did: "Get thee to your nunnery, kiddo."

She got into her car and drove down the street and through the Heights and onto the highway. Three quarters of an hour into the future and twenty years out of the past, the kilometres clicking by, adding up incrementally on the dashboard display while the windshield wipers chased a small patch of the unblurred world backward and forward across the glass.

FIRST SNOW

TWELVE

SISTERS OF MERCY

ONE GOOD THING was that it was an unusually mild December. Naturally, everyone had turned on their furnaces by mid-November, but the river was still medium-to-swift-flowing, and in some places only slightly narrower than it had been at the fullness of its summer girth.

"Hardly chunky at all," June pointed out to her sister. She meant with ice.

The March sisters had been named for summer — doubly named, for they were christened May and June, although June was the older by fifteen years — and both had been born in the fall. May and June March! Imagine!

But if they had been named for summer, they were nick-named for blight. When they were children their father, whether impelled by a sense of playfulness or cruelty, had referred to them as May*fly* and June*bug*, the emphasis entirely his. One sister was a middle-aged woman now and the other was — "Oh, older than that, surely?" June had no desire to live to be 140 years old and was too honest to pretend nostalgia for her despondent youth. But while June had long ago resolved to make a good thing of their father's ill-natured jocularity, her sister had changed not only the joke of her detested double-month name, but her genus as well. She was Rose now, by any other name.

The reason it was a good thing that December was unusually mild was tacked onto a very bad thing, in this case the two kids who'd gone missing outside a house on the six hundred block of Lord Balfour Street. Their names were Brittany Thomas and Billy Sinclair and they'd last been seen three days ago, making chalk drawings on the sidewalk outside number 631. The mail carrier had come by at nine-ish and said, "No school today?" But they hadn't been seen since.

The street in which the sisters lived, Rose with her kids in the main part of the house, June in the attic, was a rundown, piecemeal, catch-as-catch sort of place, in a neighbourhood that matched the street in all essentials. We're just across the tracks from the river, Rose would always say, but in truth everything in the city was across from the river or the railway tracks. The sisters had inherited the house from their parents, but it was hard making ends meet, and they'd lately taken on a boarder, a quiet man called Macilroy. The house itself was an undistinguished double storey on a street of houses distinguished mainly by an air of desultory neglect. Every couple of years there were rumours of gentrification but these, it was generally agreed, had been planted by wily realtors with an eye to the main chance.

"But at least you have a madwoman in the attic," Aunt June would tell the youngsters. However, *Jane Eyre* had not yet been parodied on *The Simpsons*, where her niece and nephew acquired their cultural references. Always slightly elderly in her inclinations, Aunt June had aged disproportionately since her stroke. She'd grown so frail and thin that her niece and nephew often stared at her, at their peculiar relation whom they had once called Auntie Junebug.

In those days they'd thrown their small compact bodies into her arms like missiles — ah, but she'd welcomed those ground attacks of love — demanding all kinds of comforts: a kiss for a grazed knee, candy smuggled into a sticky hand. When their truant father came home on a bender they'd smuggle themselves up to Auntie Junebug's attic room, climbing the wooden stairs with wide eyes set in pinched and anxious little faces. In time, she would grow out of the diminutive, jokey nickname, yet she would always be Aunt June to Rose's kids and, as if in thrall to her childless, ageless self, she remained Aunt June to the world although she was unrelated to anyone in it but these closest three.

"A bender!" exclaimed Rose. "Where *do* you get your crazy notions, Bug?" When agitated, Rose tended to scold, which was not the worst of her transgressions, that being reserved for what she had just called her older sister. Bug.

Bug. It was undignified, it was inaccurate, it provoked Aunt June to say, "What do you call it when a man comes home drunk every week? I heard him yelling at you, Rose, I heard him."

But she did not say, "We all heard him." She did not say the children heard him or the neighbours or perhaps — in a merciful world — even God. In any case her sister would only have said, "He wasn't yelling, Junie," which was not true — he had been yelling and banging on walls and throwing what sounded like a hatful of ball bearings down the stairs — but the way her sister would have said it, wearily and with her hand picking at the fragile broken necklace of her collarbones, gave Aunt June pause. Rose was difficult to contradict. Perhaps it hadn't been yelling but something else, Aunt June thought with a shiver. Her sister had so many different names for love.

With the years, Rose had thickened and grown plump. Her name suited her in that she resembled a blowsy, somewhat dishevelled tea rose, a hybrid. She was divorced now and Aunt June was a spinster, an old maid.

The sisters lived on Furbelow Road, in a labyrinth of side streets leading off the grimmest of the city's training hospitals. Sisters of Mercy occupied almost a city block of squared-off buildings and clamp-jawed parking garages connected by breezeways and wind tunnels and a fluorescent-bright skywalk that hung suspended in the air on dark nights like an empty thought bubble in a comic book. Above the Emergency entrance a red neon cross blazed into the sky. The crucifix was a remnant from the time when the four nuns of the Sisters of Mercy Order ran their Home for Abandoned Mothers on the site. The home had become a maternity hospital, and later a general hospital and health sciences centre. All the while the red cross flickered on, although by now it had become a secular landmark. Most people took it for granted, an indication that patients had come to the right place and might exit their vehicles, although parking outside Emergency was strictly prohibited.

But at night when the winds blew the clouds across the sky, shapes changed and re-formed, the neon cross becoming fanciful, a shape shifter. Aunt June, leaning her chin in her palm and her elbow on the windowsill, could almost imagine that the cross had slipped sideways in the sky, become an X marking the spot on a treasure map, or a cursor clicking on points of interest in the night sky. Ladies and gentlemen — the Milky

Way! It's only a landmark, Aunt June would remind herself at these times, it's only the Sisters of Mercy crucifix. But no, Aunt June was unconvincing, even to herself. On windy nights the crucifix was this, it was that. It was:

"The hand of God," said Rose's daughter, who had a dramatic temperament.

"It's just a crucifix, dear," said Aunt June who did not.

"The hand of God holding a crucifix," her niece insisted.

Aunt June sighed. Her niece was a fanciful creature, currently pouting and primping her way through an aesthetician's course at the local community college. Her name was Elvira, neither flower nor bug.

From her high window in the attic of the house on Furbelow Road, Aunt June could see the red cross and even imagine that she could hear its neon hum. The nights were so cold they cracked. You could hear a train whistle from far away, miles and miles away, as if the train was coming toward them out of the future.

The cross hung in the top left quadrant of her attic window, always in the same place, for it was not a moon that moved across the steep acreages of the sky. Nights it hung there, red and insomniac, but by day it was only a sketchy outline of faith against the blowing snow or guttering clouds, the leaves that massed in the summer and fell in the fall. *You are here*, it seemed to whisper to Aunt June. Here in your room, here in the city, here in the breathing, broken world.

But the cross wasn't the only thing Aunt June could glimpse from her window. Looking down, she could take in almost the entire neighbourhood: the cross-hatching of streets near the hospital, the steeple of All Saints Catholic in the distance, and in the foreground the little Filipino church with its timely announcements ("He is Born!"). There was the new refugee counselling centre in the basement of the United Church and Ken's Kum & Go, the oddly named convenience store across the way, and the usual collection of pawn shops and charity stores and hotel off-license drinking establishments. The auto body place had been there forever but the hair salon on the corner that specialized in weaves was new. In winter when the trees were bare, she could even peer into the refuse-strewn park where the older kids hung out on the swings in the dusk. To smoke and canoodle.

"If canoodling means trash talking and dope smoking, then I guess that's what they're doing," Rose sighed.

"Perhaps they're just courting, Rosie," Aunt June said gently. "Don't you remember —"

But what she remembered, or thought she did, had nothing to do with Rose, who had been called the B-word by one of the young ruffians that very morning as she was crossing the park to her bus stop. All day she'd sat in her office at the new industrial park and stewed — stewed in her own juices, as her mother would have said, encouraging Rose to imagine those juices, syrupy and cloying, and she the fat pink peach at their centre.

Sticks and stones, she told herself. Rubber and glue. I know I am but what are you?

But still, it hurt her, that B-word. For why should she be taunted with a word too awful to pronounce in polite society, a word permissible only by the coy erasure of its subsequent letters? And what had she done? she asked herself, as she sat at her desk in the front office of Thiessen's Tiling and Flooring. She had only walked through the park, more briskly than usual (she was late), pulling out her pocketbook so as to have her bus pass handy. She hadn't seen the kids or she never would have reached into her purse in the first place, no fool she.

In the afternoon, Mr. Thiessen came in to sign for a delivery of laminates but he didn't josh her, didn't call her Ring-a-Rosie in his ham-fisted but courtly fashion. Instead, he'd asked if by any chance June March had completed the books for the previous month. He never failed to call her sister by her full name — June March — it was his little joke. But June, who was never late with the books, wasn't late this month either.

"It's only the twelfth, Mr. Thiessen," Rose started to reply but her boss was already out the door, goodbye and good luck, and she was not A Rose Is A Rose, not A Rose By Any Other Name.

Oh what was the matter, what had she done? She slumped in her vinyl office chair, the afternoon's sour trough of boredom and longing washing over her. *Bitch*, she whispered, trying out the word. *Bitch bitch bitch*.

"THE B-WORD?" WONDERED Annunciata when Aunt June told her what Rosie had been called. As if to say: And what word is that?

What she actually said was: "Brittany and Billy? Isn't that odd?"

She meant the missing kids, of course. Brittany Thomas and Billy Sinclair: both B-words, but not in the least odd to Aunt June's mind.

Annunciata had come to Aunt June by way of a friend of Rose's, someone Aunt June had never met. The friend had asked the young girl to look in on Aunt June, who'd grown so frail that winter that Rose was always worried she'd fall and break into pieces.

Aunt June was feeling pretty bad again. The unsettled weather had settled in her bones, she joked. Mostly, though, those poor children played on her fancy. Earlier, Annunciata had climbed the attic stairs to her room, carrying a mug of tea and a packet of ginger biscuits, both of which she set down on the stacking table, sheepish because she knew that Aunt June yearned for a tray with a steeping teapot and a teacup in its saucer and the ginger nuts fanned out in a little plate beside it. Aunt June had once told Annunciata how her dear mother used to interleave a paper lace doily between the biscuits and the plate on which they were served, although now she could hardly credit such fastidiousness. Who could? A doily!

Annunciata was too shy to root through the cupboards in search of a teapot let alone those blessed doilies, Aunt June knew. But the young girl did her best, letting the teabag draw then squeezing it against the side of the mug to extract all of its strength. Adding milk at the end, and then only a drop. Aunt June could certainly taste the effort she'd put into that mug of tea. She always told her to make herself a cup of tea too, but sometimes Annunciata forgot to make the tea and sometimes she merely forgot to bring it up. The poor girl was so tired today that she looked transparent, Aunt June couldn't help exclaiming.

"Oh my dear!" she said, as Annunciata seated herself beside her. "Oh my dear, I know."

The girl looked startled, as if she was wondering what, *what* did Aunt June know. Did she have a vision of Annunciata's forgotten mug of tea steaming on the kitchen counter, or of Annunciata's mother who was refusing to leave the house until the birthday phone call came? She had not yet grown accustomed to Aunt June's odd intuitions.

It was strange, Aunt June considered, that the Bautista family always referred to it as Maria's birthday phone call when the phone call was anything but celebratory. Annunciata had told Aunt June all about the calls that came on her dead sister's birthday. It was always a man. He was phoning to wish Maria a happy birthday, he said. Sometimes he was amiable and would pretend to be surprised that she was out — *Again! Do you know when she'll be back?* — but more often he was cruel. He would say terrible things to Maria's mother — *Do you want to know how she died? Do you want to know if she cried?* — and Imee would listen until he finished then collapse and take ill for weeks. But when Aunt June asked Annunciata why, why in heaven did her poor mama answer the phone, the girl shrugged.

The man had probably killed Maria, Aunt June reckoned. He was Imee's last link to her daughter and she couldn't give him up.

Annunciata began to talk about the two missing children. Last summer she'd bought a paper cup of lemonade from the little girl. At least she thought it was her. Brittany.

"Her mother must be —" Aunt June caught herself in time, blushed furiously, and fumbled at her collar. "My dear," she began again.

AUNT JUNE'S EYES were marmoset in her pale face; the scrawnier she became the bigger her eyes appeared to be. She'd begun to look positively nocturnal, huddled in her layers of cardigan and shawl in the room beneath the eaves.

Poor girl, Rose couldn't help thinking. But Aunt June wasn't a girl, hadn't been one for fifty-some years, she reminded herself. It was just that for a brief time they'd been girls together and she, Rose, still felt like a girl, no matter what she looked like (she knew what she looked like). It was just that Aunt June had a talent for sympathy, her breastbone vibrating like a tuning fork to what others were feeling. It was just the iron lung of the sky breathing for the city, and the office workers and retail clerks and nurses coming off their shifts who resembled sleepwalkers stumbling home through the raw weather, their nostrils and eyes reddening. It was just that the first snow hadn't yet fallen and the whole city was poised for that irretrievable leap into winter.

It was the four o'clock darkness and the streetlights coming on along Furbelow Road. At moments like this, the winter darkness descending, the streetlights flickering bravely, she remembered a song her mother used to sing, although she could recall neither the melody nor most of the words. Something about a child walking home in the dark, whistling. Rose often thought that this was the worst time of year, the days before the snow fell when it was conceivable — just — for the foolishly optimistic to think, "Well, maybe not?" and "Perhaps this year?" But of course, like everyone else, she longed for the first snowfall, the city's momentary release into silence and snow light.

Rose had fallen into a reverie by this time, forcing her sister to repeat herself.

"Was it the tall boy, Rosie? The one who —"

"How should I know, do you think I stopped to chat?" Rose snapped. "Which tall boy?"

"He wears a baseball cap under his hoodie. He's —" Aunt June was about to say the one without gloves. A baseball cap and a hoodie but no winter gloves. Imagine! But she didn't want to sound overfond.

"Do you stand all day and *watch* those hoodlums?" Rose was shocked but not surprised.

Aunt June, who did, in fact, spend a fair amount of her time gazing down at the street, at the little refugee children walking to school in their unfamiliar coats and boots, and at the young people who congregated on the sidewalk outside Ken's Kum & Go convenience store said, "No, no, hardly ever. I think he's called Dearborn."

"Can't be," Rose said. "No such name."

"Maybe not," conceded Aunt June. "Only I thought I heard one of his friends call him that. Dearborn, Rosie."

"His name is Aaron, June." Rose wanted to put an end to the matter of the little thug's name.

"Ah, then, Aaron Dearborn, Rosie. Do you see?"

But Aunt June took a conciliatory tone because she could see that her sister was shaken, had shaken all day at the humiliation of what that Dearborn boy had called her.

Poor Rosie, Aunt June thought. She was worn out, she had no resilience. And then there was the worry about the missing children, one of whom, the girl, lived down the street at number 631 and the other, the little boy, lived in the nearby government housing complex. The older boy, Dearborn, lived there too.

Aunt June had a dim feeling that they were related — the two boys — the missing child and the teenager who had so unsettled Rose. She had the impression of a many-branching tree of relationships unfolding. It was the same feeling she had when she climbed the stairs and paused on the second-floor landing, watching the dark-cornered rooms scuttle off into the shadows.

"Any news?" she now asked Rose, who shrugged.

No news is good news, Rose was rather too fond of saying, by which she meant the opposite of what everyone else meant. *No* news is good news, Rose would say, emphasizing the "no" in the news rather than any good that might come of it, however postponed.

"There's *never* any good news," she answered her sister with her habitual, one-shouldered shrug.

The downstairs door shuddered in its frame and Aunt June imagined one of the kids, Elvira or her brother, Jaycee, slamming against it. The cold weather made the wooden door contract and the house shift on its restless, river-fidgety foundations. The first sign of fall was the key sticking in its lock, a ritual throat clearing for the long winter months to come. By December it was impossible to enter the house without jiggling the key in its lock, just so, until something caught, then hurling yourself repeatedly against the door until the frame yielded. Once the family had been in the habit of leaving the door unlocked but nowadays —.

The red cross in the top left quadrant of the window wavered for a moment, then held steady, as Aunt June fell into a dream of nowadays. Obeying a call from downstairs, "Mom, what's for —" Rose heaved herself from her chair.

"Coming down later?" she asked June. She meant for dinner but Aunt June hardly ever took dinner with the family and didn't think she would tonight.

For years, dinner had been a grab-bag affair, mostly consumed on various stacking trays in front of the television, but lately it had returned to a more formal dining ambience with every night a family-style stew or casserole, and paper napkins at each place instead of the roll of kitchen paper that had once been passed around. The two-litre bottles of off-brand pop that had once dominated the table like lurid centrepieces were gone. Instead, there was water in the water glasses, only tap water to be sure, but Rose took care to pour her glasses when she set her table so that by dinnertime the sediment had settled and the water was clear again.

All this was because of Macilroy, the boarder, whose rent included one meal a day and access to the washing machine in the basement.

When Rose left, Aunt June reached for her half-finished tea so that she could dip her ginger nut biscuit. Her tooth had been giving her trouble again; she couldn't bear to press down on it. The tea was cold but wet, at least, and it did the trick vis-à-vis the ginger nut which had turned so soggy that Aunt June had to scoop it into her mouth with a teaspoon. But even the trickle of tea and mush twitched some tripwire of pain in her jaw, and the tooth began to throb again. As always, when pain and its accompanying panic rang through her, Aunt June twisted in her chair so that she could focus on the crucifix beyond her window. She wasn't, strictly, a believer but the red glow steadied her, allowed her to focus her poor dispersed self.

She stared out at the red cross, stared so long and so hard that it seemed to mutate into two red crosses, the second a faint visual time delay of the first. The jazzy notes of her toothache picked out a delinquent tune in her skull. On and on it played, stranding her in her bright pain.

LATER, THE DOWNSTAIRS phone rang and Aunt June could hear her sister banging pots in the kitchen. It was Tuesday night, so tuna casserole probably. Rose, as she often remarked of herself, was not one to answer a ringing phone simply because it was expected of her or because its aggravating jangle shattered the peace of the evening and tunnelled directly to the root of her sister's tooth.

"If they want me they'll find me," Rose would say although she did not say how, precisely, anyone would find her since her tolerance for installing a phone line did not stretch to the matter of maintaining an answering machine.

"Mom," Elvira yelled from her room. "For God's sake, could you —"

But still the phone rang and rang. Afterward, Aunt June wondered if she had intuited bad news merely from the sound of the phone. She thought she had. She possessed some sort of gift for pale magic, it was generally agreed in the family, and could even perform minor acts of telepathic cajolery. She'd think of someone far away, and within the day they'd phone or write. Or she'd answer the doorbell before it rang, or absently murmur *bless you,* before a nose had even begun to itch. Her talent for growing tricky perennials was legendary in the neighbourhood.

Yes, she thought she'd felt the earth-shift of calamity before the phone call, and all through the clamour that followed, but Aunt June was distracted by her tooth and could not be sure. Finally, she couldn't take it anymore — the phone, the outraged yells from Elvira's room, Rose's stubborn endurance, her tooth that seemed to be delicately wired to the upper registers of the telephone's choral range — and heaved herself to her feet. The phone had stopped by then but when Aunt June got to the second-floor landing the ringing began again and, one hand pressed to her cheek, she was able to grab the receiver with the other.

"who was that?" Rose asked when Aunt June finally appeared in the kitchen. It had taken her days to descend the stairs.

Aunt June clutched at her heart. "It was —"

"Some damn solicitor," Rose said grimly. "You shouldn't answer the phone on a solicitor. Answering the phone just encourages them."

"No, Rose. It wasn't a solicitor." Aunt June's heart was banging in her chest and her tooth was throbbing at its root and the two sensations — the banging and the throbbing — were curiously out of sync so that Aunt June experienced the moment as tachycardic and violent.

"Doesn't pay to answer the phone on those solicitors," repeated Rose. She had a paring knife in her hand and was turning a potato expertly, around and around, until the peel came away in a thick brown spiral. "Answer the phone on them and they never go away."

"No but Rose, Rose listen —"

Rose finally turned to face her sister, her hand full of the skinned, naked-looking potato with its topknot of brown spiral boinging this way and that.

WITH SOME DIFFICULTY, Rose had gotten Aunt June settled on the chesterfield, the crocheted blanket that was the oldest thing the family owned, a legitimate heirloom, tucked around her legs. Rose sat beside her sister, a glass of sugar water at the ready. Their mother had been a great believer in the medicinal properties of sugar water.

"But what *about* the children?" she asked Aunt June who had been trying for a while to tell her about some children. Children who were lost, it sounded like, or had they been found? Her sister was in such distress that she could barely understand her. She handed the glass of sugar water to Aunt June and made her take a sip.

Aunt June sipped and tried to calm herself. As so often happened these days, she felt adrift and circumstantial. Suddenly she put her hands over her face and rocked in anguish.

When she'd first heard Annunciata's voice on the phone, she thought the girl was calling to thank her for the costume jewelry she'd pressed into her hand.

"You're very welcome, my dear," she'd said.

But no, Annunciata had forgotten all about the bracelet and the brooch. Instead she was phoning to tell her that two bodies had been found near the railway tracks. Children's bodies was the rumour. The police weren't making any statements yet, but she didn't want Aunt June to see the story on the evening news. People had already begun laying their offerings of cellophane wrapped flowers and stuffed animals around the children's still-visible pavement chalk drawing. It had become a shrine.

Unexpectedly, Annunciata began to weep and Aunt June started to say, "There, there, my child. There, there, there." But Annunciata said she had to go; they were expecting a call. The birthday phone call hadn't come yet and her mother was beside herself.

"It's those children," Elvira cried, her voice high and excited at the thought of disaster, the swift blood-flex of catastrophe. She had finally emerged from her room to take charge. Her newly painted nails were wet and she waved them through the air then blew on them absently before exclaiming: "It's those two kids who went missing." No one answered and, in frustration, Elvira applied to the boarder. "Don't you think? Don't you think it's those kids?"

"Might be," he replied, startled. "Might and might not be."

The boarder had been living with the family for the past three months while his wife lay dying in the nearby hospital. They had come up from the country in early fall, she to die and he to wait, with grace, upon her dying. Meanwhile they occupied their separate, rented rooms: hers in the Sisters of Mercy Palliative Care Unit, his at the back of the house on Furbelow Road. He was an angular yet not discomforting presence, but he seldom provided commentary on his life or theirs.

"Oh! Oh! Oh!" Elvira keened. "Oh what should we do?"

"We could wash our hands for dinner," said Rose. But the mother's tartness could not stiffen the daughter's resolve.

"But, but don't you *care* about them? Two little kids lying dead in the cold?"

"And only eleven shopping days to Christmas," her brother taunted. Jaycee was crouched low in a chair, his thumbs roving over his phone as he spoke.

"We could wash our hands and we could shut our faces," his mother snapped. She was sensitive about Christmas. A brisk little ecumenical tree stood in the corner, its plastic branches held out stiffly as if awaiting benediction from some benign agnostic source. Now she turned to her sister in despair: "Oh June, what did you think happened to those kids?"

"Maybe she thought they'd eloped," Jaycee said. "Went off to Vegas to tie the knot." He was enjoying himself. He looked up from his phone for the first time since Aunt June had come downstairs and it seemed to her that his glance was derisive. She suddenly saw herself through her nephew's eyes — a bundle of nerves and sinew, an old sick *thing*, a Guy Fawkes on a stick.

"Boy's right," said Macilroy unexpectedly. "There was no hope right from the beginning."

"Surely there's always hope, Mr. Macilroy?" Rose asked, heartened by this evidence of his attention. It was good to have a man about the place, her mother had always maintained. Perhaps Macilroy would turn out to be the man it was good to have around.

But no, Macilroy was having none of it. "Got to go, ladies," he said. "Doc said to come around again after supper." He stirred himself, pulling on his coat and boots at the door. Then he turned to them and his voice was, once more, the hesitant mumble they were used to. "Goodnight ladies and, um, gentleman."

"You haven't had your supper yet," Rose called out as the door shut. "He hasn't eaten anything since breakfast," she exhorted the family. But the kids were giggling together, united for once in ridicule, and June was still huddled on the chesterfield, one hand picking at the crocheted blanket and the other pressed to her cheek.

"Oh, hush now," Rose said. "That poor man's wife is at death's door. Literally at death's door," she repeated, impressed by the alliterative decisiveness of the phrase. Its power to clang shut against mortality.

THE BOY, WHOSE name was Aaron DeVaughan — "DeVaughan," Rose would later tell June. "Not Dearborn!" — was nowhere in evidence when Rose hurried home through the park the next evening. He hadn't been there that morning either, the huddle of teenagers who were doing God knows what barely glanced up as she passed. Rose heard the wind tugging at the kids' swing, the metal links ringing a single cracked chord upon the cold air.

It had been a dull, leaden day — the identities of the children now confirmed, the falling air pressure a clamp around the skull. Outside 631 Balfour, browning flowers in wind-rattling cellophane massed around the small circle of pavement where the children's chalk drawing had long been obliterated. There were cards too now, spiked onto the chicken wire fence where a couple of incongruous Mylar balloons had also been fastened.

The girl, Annunciata, had phoned early in the morning to tell Aunt June the terrible news; she'd heard her sister whispering on the phone. Conferring, comforting.

"And the other phone call?" she heard Aunt June ask. "The one —"

Really, there were too many phone calls these days, as far as Rose was concerned. All day she had to answer the phone at work, and then when she came home, more calls. Rose was not fond of the telephone, or of any news that had, so far, proceeded from it.

No need to hustle, Mr. Thiessen had said when Rose told him that her sister would have the November books settled by the end of the week.

"Oh?" she'd replied, a little pert because he'd never asked about the books before. And really, there had been no call to inquire about them. June was never late.

"Oh?" she repeated. "But with Christmas on the way —"

"Christmas comes every year around this time," her boss said. "Nothing we can do about it." He'd only dropped in to check on an estimate that some fool apprentice had messed up, and didn't even remove his jacket but sat on his desk, his legs swinging as he added columns of figures in his head and scribbled corrections in the margins.

"You're a human computer, Mr. Thiessen," Rose said when he handed her the estimate for retyping.

The wind had picked up in the late afternoon. It tossed leaves and cigarette butts across her path, exhaled into plastic bags, flipped through the pages of stray flyers as if searching for bargains. In the park, the wind played its single broken chord on the metal links of the swing set. Over and over again. It was dark already, and in the windows of nearby houses, Rose could see Christmas lights flickering rhythmically, a semaphore of effortful merrymaking. Except for one crackling streetlight the park was dark entirely, but the lone streetlight seemed to roar with a terrible orange voltage.

All day, Rose had been trying to recall the song her mother had loved and now, when she was no longer picking at it, a phrase popped into her head, summoned perhaps by the wind's oddly tuned chord and her own inattention. *Walk me back home, my sweetheart...* No, not *sweetheart — darling.* The words pierced her. She was nobody's darling, never had been.

Without warning the boy stepped across her path, his hood pulled low. Dearborn, her sister had called him. At first Rose thought he was only a figment of her preoccupation but no, he was real.

"Oh, *you*," she said.

Startled, he looked up then ducked his head. "Do you have a smoke, lady?"

"Lady, is it?"

"Cigarette," he explained as if she was a moron, even going so far as to tap his fingertips against his mouth in an explanatory gesture.

"So what *am* I, then?" Rose was enraged. "What, eh? One day a, a *bitch*, the next day a lady?"

The boy stood still for a moment and the orange crackle of the streetlight roared between them. Then he lowered his head and stepped into the shadows again. From outside the circle of light and noise, Rose heard the word that he called her. It was neither bitch nor lady.

DINNER WAS A desultory affair. Macilroy's wife had died in the night. Her death, so long anticipated, was swift when it came. Macilroy had spent the day at the hospital and later, the funeral home. Making arrangements, he told them. He would be moving out at the end of the week.

"But what about Christmas?" Rose said, immediately

regretting her lapse. "We're, we're so sorry for your loss," she amended, but her children looked ironic and she felt ashamed.

Macilroy, however, took her question seriously. He would be spending Christmas with his daughter, he explained. His daughter had a couple of kids of her own — "Whippersnappers," he called them — so that was Christmas taken care of. The family, to whom the daughter and the whippersnappers were something of a surprise, could not refrain from self-expression. Elvira, especially.

"A daughter?" she asked, skeptically.

"Nope, two," Macilroy replied. One lived in Elk River, Minnesota, the other on Vancouver Island. One had kids, the other no interest in them. One was tall and rangy —he pointed at himself— the other took after his late wife in looks and temperament.

"She's only been dead a day and already she's *late*," Rose would exclaim to her sister.

"That's what *late* means, dear," Aunt June would comfort, although, in truth, she had only a vague notion as to why comfort was required.

But Macilroy, previously a man of few words and those terse, had turned loquacious. Something, perhaps death, had tugged open the catch of whatever was rusted shut in him. Fact is, he told them, both of his girls had been standing by. All that fall. Standing by and holding hard and weighing their options. But one had a young family and the other had a new job and, in the end, neither could see their way to gallivanting across the country at the drop of a hat. Here he caught Rose's outraged expression and hastily assured them that the Elk River daughter had made him swear, swear on their mother's life, that the minute things took a turn for the worse he would send for them. It was unfortunate that the end had come too swiftly for his daughters to say their goodbyes, but that was life, eh?

"More like death," Elvira whispered to her brother, and the two commenced giggling, united as they always were by malevolence.

As he talked, Macilroy cut at his flank steak, shovelling loaded forkfuls of meat and mash and corn niblets into his mouth, and talking through the resulting spin cycle of half-chewed food. For months he'd picked at his dinner, surviving on Timbits and cans of Mountain Dew. Rose knew all about it — she was the one who cleaned his room, disposing of the empty donut boxes with their crumbs and transparent grease spots, the pop can that he balanced on the dresser and used as an ashtray, although smoking was forbidden and he wasn't fooling anyone but Christ on a crutch, Rose had thought, cut the man a break. His wife was dying, and if that didn't give a man a hankering for what he'd once told her it had been the greatest challenge of his life to quit, well then, she didn't know what to say.

But Macilroy was hungry as a hunter now, as if his wife's passing had conjured the starving man inside the dutiful husband. He clamped the meat down with his fork and tore at his flank steak, sawing at the gristle as if the knife was a set of teeth and he a panting dog. In four or five bites the steak was gone and he began to spoon mash and corn niblets into his mouth, all the while talking about his daughters: the Elk River daughter who had married young and was living to regret it, and the Vancouver Island daughter who was old enough now to smarten up and commit to something she'd likely regret in the future. Life, eh?

He held out his plate to Rose and said he wouldn't mind a

refill of whatever she had going on the stove there, particularly that delicious fried steak.

Delicious? thought Rose. Well, here was a man transformed!

There was no extra steak though, there never was. Rose had only fried up four — one for each of the kids, and another one each for herself and Macilroy. Aunt June tended not to eat with the family on flank steak nights. Whether this was a matter of taste or of tact, Rose couldn't say. Steak was expensive and even such a cheap cut as flank stretched the family's budget.

Rose took Macilroy's gleaming plate from him — had there ever been a plate of such reflective emptiness? — and carried it, together with her own dinner plate, to the kitchen. She'd barely touched her steak, so enthralled had she been by Macilroy's radiant transformation from husband to widower. Inspecting her steak now Rose saw that only one small corner bore knife marks. Swiftly, she transferred her own steak to Macilroy's plate, concealing the bite-sized absence with a thick coating of gravy. There was plenty of mash and corn niblets, there always was.

"SO HIS DAUGHTERS never came in the end?"

"Never. How d'you like that?" Rose was sitting with her sister, filling her in on the day's events. Her stomach growled. In her flurry she had forgotten the cause of her hunger but this did not lessen its effect. She suddenly remembered staring into the gleaming emptiness of the boarder's dinner plate before she'd heaped his second helping upon it. For a moment she'd had the impression that the plate, far from being empty, was actually reflecting her own invisibility. But that was impossible, of course, a passing fancy. It was just a dinner plate, why make such a fuss?

"So the children —" Aunt June ventured in a small voice.

"— did not come."

"No, not those." Aunt June didn't care about Macilroy and his unknown daughters. "The other two, the neighbourhood kids."

The B-words, she meant. Brittany Thomas and Billy Sinclair.

"They have a man in custody, I guess," Rose told her. "Looks like it might be Brittany's father."

"Ooo-h, Lord. *Lord!*" Aunt June moaned, but whether at the idea of the murdered children or at the pain in her tooth to which she had finally admitted, her sister couldn't tell. Rose had brought up a length of cotton wool soaked in oil of cloves and brandy, and her sister had pressed it against her gums. Although her eyelids fluttered in pain at the motion, the homemade concoction that their late mother swore by was gradually having its numbing effect, the colour returning to Aunt June's cheeks, the drawstring around her mouth loosening.

"Oh June," Rose said, stirring. "Did I tell you what he called me today? That terrible boy?" She knew she couldn't say the word out loud although she longed to. *Cunt!* she wanted to tell her sister. That little bastard called me a *cunt*. Imagine.

Instead, Rose began to laugh helplessly and after a while Aunt June, as always, joined in. After that the sisters sat for a time in amiable silence. Even though Aunt June had only laughed to keep her sister company, Rose could see that she had cheered up. Yet Rose was beginning to feel that familiar tug of loneliness that often followed a bout of laughter.

"Wind's picked up," she said to distract herself and also because it had.

Indeed the wind had picked up considerably in the last couple of hours and now, peering out the window over the trees and streets of the neighbourhood, Rose could see that the smoke from the chimney stack of the great hospital incinerator was blowing sideways. Usually the incinerator smoke rose straight as the column of the Lord that had guided the children of Israel in the desert, but now it was blowing sideways.

The children of Israel would never leave the desert.

Instead they would wander there with all the other lost children. The murdered neighbourhood kids, and the teenagers who hung out at dusk in the park, no mother's voice ever calling them inside, and Macilroy's daughters who had not come in time. Even the girl who came to sit with Aunt June had a tragic sister somewhere in her past.

Outside, under a streetlight, a little group of refugee kids turned in circles, waiting for their first sight of the promised snow. Watching them, Rose thought of all the world's lost children: her own that had grown up and out of the orbit of her gravitational love, and Aunt June, who had once been a child although there was no one left to witness the child she had been.

All lost, all lost, the wind sighed as all the children — past, present, and to come — wandered in the imaginary desert of their eternal lostness.

Suddenly, the wind seemed to thicken and fill with snow. The first of the year. The streetlight cast down cones of illumination through which snow fell slantways, but the wind caught the snow before it reached the ground and blew it around. A young woman was walking home, small and lonesome. Rose thought she looked like Aunt June's girl but she could have been anyone's. Someone's darling, perhaps. The cross in the sky above Sisters of Mercy appeared then disappeared, shrouded by clouds or snow static or some gusting failure of belief that had lain dormant for years but, just this minute, flared up again.

For a moment the city, all that she could see from Aunt June's window — the hospital with its ugly geometrical blocks and breezeways, the skywalk that floated above them in a harsh daze of fluorescence, the Friends of Mercy donation thermometer creeping up past the halfway mark of generosity, and further away the old railway bridge and the blackness beyond that was only the river in the midst of its coldhearted freezing — the city hung in the balance. Then the wind caught it up again, turning it sideways, and for a long time the horizontal city streamed past the window like the long white exhalation from a sleepwalker's breath.

THAW

THIRTEEN

A HOUSE, A CITY, A COUNTRY FAR FROM HOME

IT BEGAN A couple of months ago, with a bump in the night. Mine, against the headboard where I'd been trying to grind out the same old bad dream like a lit cigarette. I'd fallen asleep reading Max Brod's biography of Kafka and woken with the book tented over my face. Did you know that Brod refused to follow his pal's instructions to burn his life's work? Instead, he saved Kafka's manuscripts and published them. But of course you knew that. You are a Max B, too. There is nothing you won't salvage.

God, men are so predictable. It's like buying a lottery ticket. You never know what numbers are going to come up but you know for damn sure they aren't going to do you any good. You were wrong about so many things, Max, but the only thing I won't forgive is your optimism. It made you vulnerable, it made you reckless. Presumably even God can't resist a sitting duck, a stopped clock, a greying middle-aged fool who can't keep his eyes on the road. And yes, I'm angry. Don't knock it till you've tried it, my darling. Anger is what has kept me upright and burning brightly through all my dark nights, and anger is what has roused me in the morning with the clean iron cut of an axe breaking the frozen sea within. More Kafka. Should have thrown him in the fire when you had the chance. Anyway, back to my insomnia.

I wonder if Sams is home? I thought. I ran to his bedroom to investigate but of course he wasn't. It was only past eleven and much too early for our son, our vampire, to come home. Sams has gone rogue again, retreating into that dark little pinhole in his soul, the one nobody sees but me.

Oh Sams, Sams. My good, my *best* mistake. Do you remember how Imee used to call him her falling boy? I'd come home from work and there he'd be huddled in her lap and sobbing his heart out because he'd fallen and bumped his head or scraped his knee.

"Sorry Mrs. Maggie," she'd say, "I couldn't catch him in time."

I knew what she meant. I used to throw the boys up into the air when they were little until one day — with this one, this particular boy of my heart — his eyes flashed open, and I watched fear like a shower of small hard stars falling through his body. I caught him in time but he fell anyway.

So, Sams. Out all night. Asleep all day. His room reeks of sour sheets and crusty T-shirts and stale, windowless air. But when I sneaked in earlier this evening there was a different smell. That acetone stink. Don't you remember Dr. Raj explaining about bodies and kidneys? "If he doesn't eat his body will shut down, hence the odour of ketones, Mrs. Binder, Professor Binder, of which we have to be especially chary."

I knew I'd never fall asleep again, not tonight, not ever, so I thought, *Soup, why not?* He hadn't eaten in days, you see.

White soup. It's not easy but it's doable, according to the *Lutheran Ladies' Recipe Swap Cookbook.* The Lutheran Ladies are nothing if not a can-do bunch of gals. Onions and leeks and potatoes. I chopped and sautéed and stirred. Something curdled so I began again. More chopping. By then it was three in the morning and Sams still hadn't come home but someone else was trundling down the stairs. *Bump, bump, bump.* Lazar with that Christopher Robin expression on his face. You know the one: intrepid but slightly anxious, brave in the face of danger.

"Butter beans," he said.

I vaguely remembered a conversation we'd had about beans and why he thought I should add them to soup. Protein, was the answer. And yes, I'd toddled off like Mrs. Danvers, a demented but faithful family retainer, to source those damn beans, a can of which I eventually discovered cowering between asparagus tips and hearts of palm in Aisle 3: "Canned Goods and Instant Foods." I don't need to tell you how welcome I felt in Just-Add-Water Land except to say that Aisle 3 might be my spiritual home. But tonight I could not find those damn beans no matter where I searched, or speculate where they'd gotten to, or enter into a discussion with Lazar about why they were always in the last place you looked. Because sane folks tend to stop looking once they've found whatever they're looking for, I snapped at the poor kid.

Ah, Max, to tell the truth I didn't give a hill of beans. But Lazar has lost so much in the last year that my maternal bosom — rather pinched and miserly by this juncture — swelled. Who knows, perhaps there is such a thing as magic beans. So while the two of us knocked about the kitchen, banging open drawers and tossing through cupboards, I drew up this little existential contract, binding as all such contracts are, even between a mother and her son, even in a late night kitchen, even about beans: *If* we found the beans *then* Sams would come home and eat the soup. The soup would nourish him and, sated, he'd sleep in his own bed, and the smell of starvation would waft away from the room, never to return.

"Give it a rest, kiddo," I can hear you saying. "You always want too damn much."

I know, I know. Naggy Maggie, Maggie the hag, the drag, the lone zigger in the world of zag. Eyes too big for her stomach; stomach too small for her appetite.

"Go to bed," I told Lazar finally, and I suppose he did because suddenly it was morning again and Christopher Robin was coming down the stairs, dragging his gaping backpack behind him as if it was his faithful bear. *Bump, bump, bump.* I couldn't face him so I stepped back into the kitchen and laid my head on the table. Just for a moment. When I jerked back into consciousness about a year had passed, and my mouth tasted like bad dental work, and I had a Halloween pumpkin for a head. I'd been woken by the sound of gagging, and when I was able to focus again I saw that our youngest son was in a death match with the soup.

Naturally I told him he didn't have to eat it and naturally it only spurred the kid on because he grabbed a spoon and forced down a sizeable chunk. Then, of course, he got all bulgy and red eyed, the way he would as a wee lad when you made him eat his broccoli. After I'd wiped him down as best I could, both of us dry heaving and gasping, gravity settled in me like sawdust. All I wanted to do was curl up into a ball and go to sleep wedged behind the stove. But the house was giving me that early morning squeeze, that elbow in the ribs, that *get going, get out, be gone* soul-poke that has yanked me out of bed every morning since your —.

Since.

So I pulled myself up and I shook myself out. I waved to the boy as if it was just another morning, which it was.

"Have yourself some fast times at Ridgemont High, Spicoli," I said and saluted.

And damned if he didn't salute right back. "*Semper Fi*, Mom."

Let the record show that I strode off, waving not drowning, shining not burning. Let the record show that he waved back. And I'd like to believe that kids are stronger than what happens to them, that green fractures heal fastest, that for a time boys, like crabapple trees, thrive best on neglect.

But here's the thing, Max. I felt bad about that soup. Because of falling asleep with a book on my face and waking up with a bump in the night. Because of the bad dream and the eyeball-scrunching, lead shoe-shuffling lack of sleep. Because of Sams gone AWOL, and the smell of death in his room, and the panic that drove me into slicing onions and leeks in the middle of the night. Because of misplacing the butter beans, and trying to find them, and not. Because that soup was the worst soup in the history of the world and, by gum, there was a lot of it. Because your mother, who always used to complain about terrible food and small portions, would have enjoyed the joke. Because I haven't seen your mother in weeks; she makes me too sad.

But the thing I felt worst about was what I said to the kid before I left.

"It's awful," I said. "Just throw it down the drain."

And I knew that when he came home Lazar would shrug off his backpack, roll up his sleeves, and begin dividing that pale gloop into individual freezer portions, pausing every so often to wipe down the counters.

He is the Max Brod to my Kafka. I can do nothing so shoddy that he doesn't believe it can be salvaged.

BEGIN AGAIN.

"One can't help feeling that you're quite, uh, quite given over to anger these days, Mrs. Binder." Dr. Raj put his fingertips together and tilted his head. "One senses a certain, uh, resistance."

I call him the Rajah because he is a demi-wit with a grandiose manner and a clinically low threshold for irony.

"No," I said. "No resistance." I looked at his steepling fingers and his head cocked, the better to pluck my confidences from the air. I swear it was all I could do not to smack him so hard that his tight little therapist's head would whip backward and forward forever on his skinny little shrink's neck.

"No resistance," I repeated, uncrossing my legs and my arms to indicate a free and easy lack of resistance. My movements made my stockings hiss suggestively and — with a little help from me — my ample bosoms heave. The Rajah shifted and blushed and tried to ease his involuntary erection. If I say so myself, I clean up pretty good: my hair was up (mostly), my neckline was down, my dander was up, my guard was down. Resolve up, eyelids down, shirt hiked, mouth turned down at the corners. Up, down, up, down. I was a walking mood disorder.

You know me, Max. I'm not one to weep in public. Never have, never will. The occasional sniffle when in the safe

confines of the family, the odd whimper behind closed doors.
I've been known to sob quite heartbreakingly when alone (well,
it breaks *my* heart, anyway). But mostly was not now and I'm
afraid to report that the sadness began somewhere in the pit
of my stomach. By the time it had worked its way past my dia-
phragm and up my throat and out of my eyes and down my
cheeks, it was too late to say, "Now then, Maggie," or "Hold
that thought, girl."

So much for forty years of never have and never will. Thanks
a bunch, darling.

The Rajah looked disconcerted, as those in the caring pro-
fession frequently are when confronted with people who require
care. What had happened to the Ice Queen? I could sympathize
since I too was anxious to get to the bottom of the mystery.
Why the sudden tears? Why the runny nose, the streaming
eyes? Why all the goddamn liquid?

It turns out that tears are a *good* thing, Maggie. (You don't
mind if I call you Maggie, do you?) It turns out that tears are
what dissolve anger. They are a sign of *authentic* sadness. He
spoke slowly as if to a child, and not a smart one.

"That's swell," I said. "Tears and sadness, huh? Wow, what a
reunion show that would make. 'Tears and Sadness: Together
at Last!' Anger left the band for good but who needs him? He
was a real bummer and an all-round creep."

I'm ashamed to say that I went on for some time in this
vein. Really working the metaphor, if you know what I mean.
Ah, Maggie, I can hear you sigh. *He was only trying to help —*.
I know, I know. He was only trying to help and I responded
with my trademark brand of rinky-dink humour and reflex
cuntery. So it goes, so it goes.

Let's leave the Rajah and his unresolved woody shifting

about on his swivel recliner in his third-floor office in one of those newly chic, restored factory warehouses on the river where, in fact, I did leave him, still pouring over our oldest son's brick of a file. His office smells of Nutty Club candy and Union Shoe leather and the sweat of indentured labourers, and he is undoubtedly a dullish prick and a bore *très* colossal, but Sams is used to him, and he thinks Sams is a troubled soul with an inviolable inner light and no, we don't use the word *bonkers* here, Mrs. Binder.

Well, at least I'd got him to stop calling me Maggie. Small victories, tiny triumphs.

But I continued to think of sadness and anger as I banged my way out of his office and into the street, as I gazed at the river, still frozen despite the New Year's thaw, as I hurried downtown, cars and buses sloshing by, spraying me with gutter swill, as I found myself trapped behind pensioners yertling toward infinity and discount days at the Bay. A giant chocolate chip cookie tried to accost me and a panhandler in a duffle coat planted himself in my path and did a soft shoe shuffle on the sidewalk. I thought of cleaning his clock but didn't. So: on a scale of one to ten — one being calm as milk and ten being me — not that angry, my darling. But then I remembered why I was here and that old shard of glass gave a twist and lodged deeper in my heart.

What happened to us, Max, how did we unravel?

Was it the wear and tear, the this and that, the now and then? The dear old ineffable there-you-go-again? Was it the things said in anger that couldn't be taken back or the failure to be taken aback, no matter what? You had the habit of transparency, of disappearing for days at a time, even if you went nowhere (you never went anywhere), even if you were there all the time staring dreamily into space, your hands loaded onto your knees. The absent-minded professor!

"What?" you'd say when you caught me glaring. "*What?*"

"God, Max, you are such a damn ghost."

"Maggie, Maggie…"

"No, I mean it — you're not even here, you don't really exist, do you? *Do you?*" And I'd poke my finger at your chest to indicate the likelihood of its going right through you.

But you always came back to me in the end. After a couple of days of that long-distance stare you'd sigh, give yourself a shake, and travel all the way back to that Max-shaped hole in the world you'd vacated. *You there, you with the stars in your eyes*, you'd sing. And we'd bumble along for a while as the boys grew and the seasons changed and the world swung around on its axis. You always came back to me in the end except, of course, for *the last time*. Which, as I recently told Lazar, is the point at which sane folks stop searching for what they've lost. But where did you go to, my lovely? And where are you now? No, I mean it, Max, because something doesn't sit right. The world is out of kilter and I blame you for it, and not just instinctively.

The thing is, I sense you hovering, hazy and out of focus, waving your arms about. *Look at me! Look at me!* For weeks now, months, I've felt *hailed*. Something, some*one* at the corner of my eye, snapping like bunting. There you go, slouching through the world, hitching up your pants and scratching. Christ, do ghosts itch? I'll bet yours does. Sullied world, eh, sullied world.

Go away, Max, go back to the grave. I mean it.

We don't need you anymore, if we ever did. Lazar is growing up or older at least, which he'd do with or without his father's ghost panting behind him. *Remember me, remember me, remember me.* And the problem of Sams isn't ours to solve, says the Rajah.

POOR SAMS, WOOZY with the new meds and too sluggish with whatever his shrink prescribed to "take the edge off, and I'd be happy to write you a script too, Mrs. Binder, these are difficult times." Poor Sams, slouching at the kitchen table and scratching at his lists. Staring vacantly into space for hours at a time then tugging hold of a passing word and committing it to paper. The medication came with its usual slew of merry side effects, one of which was to intensify the shakes so that by the time Sams had rattled and banged his way down the length of the page we were both exhausted. His jerky movements and inner whirr reminded me of a wind-up toy, and I wondered if Sams was suffering from nothing more than mechanical failure, if he was merely *broken.*

"Come now," I said. And I held his wrists. But they were awfully thin wrists, Max, mere twigs in the wind.

"Come now," he replied, so softly that I knew he was no longer talking to me.

I poured him a glass of milk and helped him angle it to his mouth. But two pairs of hands create twice the mess, which was what your other son pointed out when he came crashing into the kitchen to investigate. Down he plunged with a dishtowel in one hand and a bin liner in the other. So damn irritating that I had to stop myself from hauling him up by the cowlick.

"Stop that, Lazar," I yelled. "Just relax."

Lazar gave me a reproachful glance but got up, brushing down his jeans and adjusting his manhood. Sams immediately lunged at my cup of tea and carouselled it off the table.

"Christ, Sams!" yelled Lazar, trying to step out of the way.

I was struck by the swiftness of Sams's action, the narrowing gap between thought and its accomplishment. There was something ungraspable in his expression, something I should have understood, as he looked down at his brother who was, yes, back on his knees at our feet, dabbing at the liquid seeping into the rug and glaring at Sams with humid disapproval.

"Twice risen," said Sams. "And once more to go."

We both stared at him and he stared right back, the old clear-eyed Sams look for once. I said "Hmm?" and Lazar said "Huh?" and Sams said nothing at all while the fridge hummed and the basement dryer knocked companionably and all the electrical circuits in the house continued to pull light and warmth into the kitchen. Then he pointed at his brother.

"Him," he said flatly. "Lazarus, twice risen. And once more to go."

And then Sams smiled. A smile that lit up his face like an advertisement for grace. A smile that shone like two eternal flames in the centre of each pupil. A smile that I remembered from long ago but one he'd lost the knack of all these years. A smile that banished the ruin of his twitching body and greasy hair. A just-cut grass and skinned knee smile.

"Don't call me that," Lazar yelled. "Ever, not ever."

Sams flailed from side to side and we both lunged for him but Lazar got there first, wrapping his arms around his brother from behind, his voice soothing. Sams was rocking, trying to shove his fingers and then his hands in his ears, trying to thread his entire body through his ear holes. It was horrible to watch but the Rajah had said he was only trying to comfort himself, the worst thing we could do was interfere.

"The worst thing we can do —" I began, but poor Lazar was finding that out for himself.

Sams was in terrible pain, anyone could see that. He was like a beaten dog, ripples of terror came off him in waves. Lazar was still crooning *don't, don't, don't,* so I grabbed him by the arm, trying to pull him away from Sams who swung out wildly. Lazar, caught off-balance, went down catching his head with a crack on the kitchen counter. He twitched once and went still.

For a moment we were all silent, listening to the echo of the years die away. Then Sams started rocking again and the fridge began to hum. Lazar lay there, his eyes closed. And while that god-awful crack was still ricocheting off the inside of my skull, I remembered a long ago mini-soccer game when this brute of a boy (too old for mini-soccer, surely) decked the ball smack into Lazar's little head and down he went. *Get up, get up, get up,* I thought, wringing my hands beneath my pullover. Barely down when he was on his feet again, our boy, brushing grass from his hair and punching his fist into the air: *I'm all right!*

The crowd went wild. *The crowd went wild!* They roared as one, they laughed and bellowed and chanted. *Go number 21!* He played like fury for the rest of the game, although a goose egg was already swelling above his eye. For the remainder of the season it became our war cry, our cheer. Every time a kid went down: *I'm all right!* The boy struggling to his feet, one arm punching wildly at the air. And, *I'm all right!* the crowd would yell, would always yell, are yelling still in some dog-eared corner of my memory in a bright green soccer field of the mind.

Lazar was lying with his head canted oddly against the kitchen counter but I could see his eyes fluttering. *Get up, get up, get up,* I thought, wringing my hands, always my first line of defence. I knelt beside him, fumbling at his hairline where a thread of blood was spinning out and trickling down his forehead. He shook his head woozily like a boxer after one too many punches trying to knock the ringing out of his head and the sense back into it.

I flew to the faucet to run a glass of cold water and when I looked back he was already on one knee and then the other, pulling himself upright by way of the kitchen table. Sams had stopped rocking. He was looking at his brother; we both were.

"Lazarus thrice risen," I said as he pulled himself to his feet.

"No more to go," Sams agreed.

AND AGAIN.

When the doorbell rang on Sunday afternoon I ignored it. Sams was upstairs in his bed, drifting in his zombie limbo, and Lazar was in the basement, stewing. He appeared to be torn between doing his laundry and setting the house alight. Equally torn. I could hear him lighting matches and flicking them at the walls.

The doorbell rang again. I was reluctant to answer. I'd given up not-smoking one last time and it was taking a toll. My bathrobe was grubby and my breath was sour with the particular anomie of Sunday afternoons: tottering willpower, snow falling, too much coffee, too many cigarettes, more snow. The windows tuned to the static between television channels.

Then the pop-in, the drive by, the *uninvited* — whoever it was — began to rap upon the door like the Gestapo searching for Anne Frank. *Fine, you asked for it*, I thought, banging downstairs and throwing open the door.

"She's in the attic," I yelled.

The man who stood there, his hand raised to knock, cut a formidable figure. It was the raised arm and the utter regularity of his face, as if he'd been folded down the middle to make two identical halves like those paper valentines we cut out as kids. And it was the smooth dark chocolate of his skin, as if he'd been poured into a mould and left to set, seventy percent cacao bean with a glossy finish. He was all in black — trousers, coat, hat, old fashioned briefcase in one hand, umbrella in the other (he would later refer to it as his "brolly") — and this sobriety set against the falling snow gave the impression of a more courtly age, an earlier monochromatic time.

"In the attic," he said slowly. "You keep her in the attic?"

Clink. The penny dropped. "Ah, you've come to sell me another child." I narrowed my eyes at that World Vision lackey. "Well, you should know that the last one didn't exactly pan out."

The huckster hesitated. "No, on the contrary." He spoke formally, giving each word its due. "On the contrary. I have come to find a child."

"Excellent. I have two. You can take your pick."

"Two? But I have come for only one." His accent, I now noticed, was evocative of sub-Saharan Africa with an Oxbridge polish and a liturgical lilt.

"Well, come in and take your pick. Don't expect me to choose." I was bewildered but intrigued, a welcome change from my usual state of out-and-out bewilderment.

He hoisted his rather battered briefcase and leaned his brolly against the front door. Although he carried no brochures, no clipboard, no portable credit card machine, I was suddenly punchy, so angry you could have melted me down and poured me into whatever fight was looming. For no reason that I could explain my life had begun to unravel the day that first World Vision charlatan knocked on my door. My visitor stepped over the threshold and held out his hand, at the same time whipping off his hat. I took the one and shook the other.

"Father Michael Akashambatwa, Missionary of Africa, at your service."

"Huh. A man of the cloth."

"A man of God," he corrected me gently.

"What can I do for you, oh man of the Cloth God?" My rudeness had no effect. He neither smiled nor frowned.

"Am I to understand that you keep her in the attic?" he asked.

"Yes. I keep Anne Frank in the attic with the other Jews," I snapped, wondering when we could drop the Gestapo joke.

"But I have not come for Anne Frank," he said. "I have come for Pat Ngunga."

Clunk. The shoe finally dropped with a thud that was much louder than the earlier penny-dropping incident had been which, if you'll remember, was a mere clink. A tinkle on the surface tension of time. But it would be some time before the other shoe dropped, and the sound *that* shoe made was as loud as the roar of acceleration ripping through the sound barrier. A sonic boom.

ONLY YOU.

Only you in all the world! Who else would think of making a gift of a person? The perfect gift.

Oh Max, oh Max, I could weep. You always believed in her. But, my darling, what did you think we would do with the poor girl? Having hauled her halfway across the world on a wing and a prayer.

Implacable, Father Michael sat at the kitchen table and allowed that a wing and a prayer was a fine start. He didn't expand upon this fascinating insight, although I would have liked to hear his thoughts on wings and prayers, which I had always assumed were the exit wounds of faith and not the flight paths of cockeyed optimism. But Father Michael, upright and spotless as his conscience, was a formidable figure. He'd travelled for a day and a night and then "half again another day," he told me, and come directly from the airport by "taxi cab fellow." Yet he was starched and correct, his edges precise. I was suddenly unbearably tired. One wheel down and the axle dragging, as you used to say.

He asked for a glass of water and I rushed to the fridge, scrounging in a panic for whatever I could find to set before him: a slice of pizza in its smeary takeaway box, two cans of diet cola and a tin of butter beans (so that's where it got to!), the leftovers from one of Lazar's cooking experiments congealing on a plate, and a litre of date-compromised milk. None of it looked very good so I whipped him up one of my Cheez Whiz and sweet pickle sandwiches. He thanked me politely then filled a drinking glass from the tap and, still standing at the sink, sluiced the water down before filling the glass again. He did this three more times — drinking and refilling, his Adam's apple bumping up against his throat — before washing his glass and turning it over on the draining board. When he returned to the kitchen table he retrieved a manila envelope from his briefcase, sliding it across to me as if I would know what to do with it.

He made no comment, only saying that I could look at it later if I wished but if not, not.

I sat across from him in my nubby pink bathrobe, grasping the two sides closed, there being no buttons left with which to barricade my already discredited modesty. My sadly neglected hair (unwashed, in need of a cut) was already tumbling from the couple of wooden chopsticks I'd used to skewer a messy bun to the top of my head. I could smell myself, a heady brew of unventilated kitchen, cigarettes and insomnia, the rankness of my ropey nerves. Too tired to get up and open a window, I limped over to the casement anyway, where I was defeated by the broken catch you'd promised to fix. For a while I struggled with the window but eventually gave up and filed it under one more thing the fuck about which I did not give.

Father Michael told me he was a Catholic priest who had received orders abroad and returned to his homeland to attend to the spiritual needs of his countrymen. Then he put his fingertips together and arranged himself in a listening attitude but since I had nothing to say we sat staring at each other while the afternoon flickered out and settled into evening, the streetlights coming on along Magnolia Street. Like the Rajah he was evidently one of those aggravating people who are as comfortable sitting in their own silence as an untrained puppy in its own muck. Over the rumble of the washing machine on rinse cycle, I thought I heard Sams turn over in his bed. I thought I heard Lazar flick another match at the basement wall.

"Have you taken a vow of silence?" I finally asked.

"I am a Jesuit priest, not a Benedictine monk," he explained, a distinction he must have realized was lost on me because he finally said: "Yes, I can speak."

"Huh. You don't seem to be much of an orator."

Silence.

"You know, a chatterbox."

He nodded as if in agreement. "My people say *Ukutangila tekufika*. It means there are no shortcuts in life."

"Your *people*?"

"The Bemba people who live in the Northern and Luapula Provinces of Zambia." He waited a beat and then smiled. "My other people say the same thing but take much longer to do so. Do you know Matthew 7:13?"

Suffice it to say I did not. "Suffice it to say—" I began, but Father Michael, despite his intolerance for shortcuts, cut me short.

"Enter in by the narrow gate; for wide is the gate and broad is the way that leads to destruction, and many are those who enter by it."

Huh. A bible jockey. Well, then. I gripped an imaginary mic and gave it my best shot. "This for my shortcuts and my dead ends, and my dead friends, and my demons, and my lack of feelins' this evenin'," I sang. Or attempted to sing. You know I can't carry a tune to save my life. And if you're interested in my unexpected grasp of hip hop, you might remember that our youngest son has a carrying voice and a tendency to hit repeat when he's in the shower or the doldrums.

Father Michael stared at me for a long Benedictine moment. His meaning was clear: he was here to discuss a dead friend not a dead end. There were to be no shortcuts and any lack of feeling was all on my side.

"Where is she now?" he finally asked. "Where is Pat Ngunga?"

For a while after the accident, the girl the papers called "the Hitchhiker" had floated in the careless limbo of Jane Doe–land. No one came forward to claim her and she was too battered from the accident to be of use even to first-year anatomy students. I believe the word they used was *compromised*. Eventually some Christian burial society consented to haul her away. Which is what I told Father Michael, not necessarily in those words. He sat very still, his head bowed and his large hands clasped on the table in front of him. He lifted his head and I saw that he was crying, which shocked me. Not the crying so much as his expertise in accomplishing this feat without effort or strain. Two tasteful rivulets of tears descended from the corners of his eyes and flowed down the faint marionette lines beside his nose, but his demeanour remained sanguine. The effect was that of watching a statue weep. Without any warning I began to sob, noisily, messily, and entirely without the sang-froid of Father Michael Akashambatwa.

I was crying for that poor child who had travelled so far from home in order to be shunted off to an unmarked grave in some neglected corner of a municipal cemetery. And I was crying for her mother who would never see her child again, and for your mother who would never see her child again either. I was crying for Imee and all the mothers who had lost their children in the thousand ways it is possible to lose a child. I was crying for Sams and Lazar, the children I'd begun misplacing when they were born so that I would grow accustomed to the pain of finally losing them. I was crying for Father Michael and his huge hands stacked on the table in front of me, and the battered briefcase at his feet, and the brolly outside the door, his foreign defence against the snow. I was crying for the formality of his black suit that had travelled for a day and a night and then half again another day, collecting neither crumb nor crease to mar its matte perfection.

And I was crying because in my rage I had destroyed your computer and trashed your files. I'd given away your clothes and your chair, your *effects*, and locked the door to your office. Then I buried you and refused to mourn you and salted the earth in the wake of your passing. How many ways back to you had I destroyed? Just one stray email and I would have discovered your little scheme, your great surprise, but I was Maggie to the end: a woman scorned, a scold. I had long ago chosen the hill on which I meant to die.

I cried until I had cried myself out, until I was all out of tears.

And then, as if to prove my infinite capacity for self-delusion, I began to weep in earnest because the splinter of glass that had lodged in my heart all year was melting, the anger draining from me like pus from a wound so that my sadness could run clear again. I was crying for you, Max, my lost love, my darling.

All this time Father Michael sat perfectly still until at some perfectly judged moment in the midst of my grief he stood up and went to pour me a glass of water. When he opened the refrigerator the light spilled out, abrupt and yellow, into the dark kitchen. He exclaimed softly to himself. I turned and saw him standing in the square of frigid yellow light, his face gilded, his expression, finally, aghast. He wasn't gazing into the open fridge but at the small magnetic photo frame affixed to its door. I saw that he had travelled all this way, a day and a night and then half again another day, to find Pat Ngunga and what he'd found was what he must have suspected all along: that she was long gone, snatched out of the world so swiftly that there was nothing left to mark her place. All that remained was a blurred face inside a magnetic photo frame on a refrigerator door in a dark kitchen.

In a house, in a city, in a country far from home.

He pocketed the photo in its frame and stood there, his hand on the refrigerator door, for what seemed hours.

AND AGAIN.

Father Michael declined to partake of the famous Binder hospitality package although I offered him the spare bed in Lazar's room or the whole damn room if he preferred. Lazar can sleep on the couch, I told him. For goodness sake, he's only fifteen years old. He asked if Lazar was my youngest son and if he was conscientious at his studies and diligent at his chores. In short was he a fine young man?

I said — back to my old rubber-ball self — "Well, he's certainly two of those things."

But Father Michael, man of the Cloth God, only pressed his lips into the thin line between spare the rod and suffer the little children.

"Our children," he began, then stopped. He opened his hand as if the answer might be written in the lines of his palm but seemed to lose his way and instead sat staring at his empty hand. When I asked him where he planned to go, he said that the Catholic priest at the Diocese of Saint Boniface had offered his guest room. Then he held up that battered black briefcase and damned if he didn't shake it proudly.

"You certainly travel light," I said.

"I travel with God," he replied.

I was about to crack wise on the subject of the Lord's fabled ability to provide toiletries and clean underwear, not to mention 120-volt electrical adaptors to facilitate his servant's shaving requirements, but for once stifled myself so that we parted on good terms.

"God speed," he said, tapping the manila envelope and making the sign of the cross between us. He called a cab and walked out into the snowy night — straight-backed, umbrella held high — leaving me sitting at the table amid the detritus of our untouched meal. The Cheez Whiz and sweet pickle sandwich I'd made him had begun to shrivel at the edges and the cola I'd poured had fizzed out in a thin but constant stream of rising bubbles until only a glass of warm, flat, syrupy liquid remained. Luckily the cold pizza in its grease-spackled box looked exactly the same, proving that some things remain constant even if they are the ugliest and least appetizing things of all.

I heard the washing machine in the basement rumble to a

halt. A moment later, Lazar bounded up the stairs and banged into his room, slamming the door. I knew he was in there for the duration, doing who knows what and how and why and with the assistance of which pornographic web site. I wished him God speed. A little later I heard Sams stir and then he, too, was gone, banging the front door behind him.

Bang! Bang! Both my sons were bullets shot into the ether, the Neverland where even lost boys eventually grow up, stealthily and in their sleep. I had so much to tell our sons about their father who had never betrayed us and the girl called Pat who was meant to have been their adopted sister and my fortieth birthday gift. But for the moment I sat at the kitchen table thinking about, of all things, that damn soup a couple of months back and a hundred years ago. The truth was I still felt bad about the soup. How it had bubbled up and into my life, spilling over into all the people I'd failed and the infinite ways I'd failed them. How it had boiled away into a terrible sludge of betrayal and mess. Lost sons, lost ideals, misplaced butter beans — the whole crumbling bouillon cube of longing and regret. And Pat, the androgynous World Vision child, and Lazar the ravenous hunger artist, and Sams and Sams and Sams.

And you, especially you.

Goodnight, my darling. Don't let the smoke get in your eyes.

ONCE MORE.

I opened Father Michael's envelope and a sheaf of papers tied with dirty string fell out. They were all letters, dated over the course of the past year, and sent c/o World Vision Canada to Nakonde District, Muchinga Province, Zambia.

Area Development Programme
Nakonde, Muchinga Province
c/o World Vision Zambia

Dear Pat Ngunga,

How ya doin' bro? I got your address from the back of
the last progress report you sent us where it also said that
"Communication from sponsorship families is welcome."
That's what we are, I guess. Your friendly sponsorship family.
Which makes you and me half-brothers, in a way. Intense.
They don't give an email address, though, so I hope this gets
to you.

First off, cool brochure! Your village looks awesome, especially with the addition of the Muyumbana Rural Health
Centre and, hey, props on your first polio, measles, and tetanus
shots. Mr. Isikananganda sure looks like a guy who knows his
way around the farm and Mr. Kanyanga's new piggery — also a
righteous sight. Who's the preacher dude outside Saint Mary's
Catholic Church? Talk about American Gothic! Although
in his case I guess you'd have to say Zambian Goth (joke).[1]

Sorry about the floods, and all the crops being washed
away last year, and the rise in malaria casualties and so on.
Bummer.

Okay. If there's anything you want to know about us, feel
free to ask (or write, ha ha). We're just an ordinary family —
mom, dad, couple of kids — nothing special, no disasters.
Although the truth is I wish I had a sister. I have an older
brother and he's righteous, you can ask anybody. I mean he's
the sort of dude who helps you with pre-cal and buys you beer
from the Drake Hotel drive-thru and would totally have your

back if you were his younger brother. Which I am, so.

Anyway, I was reading that you have four siblings only it doesn't say what kind. But it stands to reason that one of them must be a girl. So what I was thinking, bro, is that you could get your sister to like write to us. Snapchat or texting would be great, or even email (see enclosed co-ordinates). But, you know, letters are also good. Just a short letter, say:

Dear Binder Family, I am well and hope that you are well too. I am a girl and enjoy playing with dolls and skipping rope. I eat soft foods like custard and porridge, and my favourite colour is pink. Some day I hope to grow breasts. With good wishes, sister of Pat, [fill in the name].

Much obliged, dude.

Solicitations from your half-brother,

Lazar Binder

1. On account of he's fitted out in black, not his alternative taste in music, which obviously I don't know anything about.

* * *

Area Development Programme
Nakonde, Muchinga Province
c/o World Vision Zambia

Dear Pat,

Haven't heard from you yet, bro, so I thought I'd drop you a line to say *Fulumira msanga*. Intense, right? If you really want to know, I used Google Translate (TM), but with your "fair to excellent grade" in Eng Lang Studs I reckon we should just keep chatting in Eng. The thing is, I was wondering about that sister of yours — how she's doing, does she still like puppies and custard, has she written to my mom yet?

I was going to say no hurry, but actually I've given up lying so what I'm saying is please tell your sister to hurry up and write to my mom. She needs one small good thing in her life, like the story says, and it doesn't need to be cake, believe me.[1] What I'm thinking now is that one small good girl might be enough because she's always wanted one.

The not-lying thing is sort of an experiment. My dad loved a good story so he didn't mind what he called the conveyance required to get there (lies), and my mom said it depended what colour and what size and why (white lies, small in scope, social necessity), and my gran said you need look no further than your namesake for a truly accomplished liar, my boy.[2] Oh yeah, and Imee, who used to be my nanny (do you have those?) said keep spitting into the wind, boy, and you'll end up with a wet face, and when I asked her what *that* meant she sighed and said: Spit downwind, child.

Only Sams (that's my real bro, bro), Sams can't lie, which has something to do with what's wrong with him. Everyone else I know lies big time and so far no one's pants have caught on fire and no one's nose has grown an inch a second, so.

If your sister writes soon I'll fill her in on the details of how my not-lying is going.

I remain, your affectionate half-bro,

Lazar Binder

1. Have you read any stories by R. Carver in Eng Lang Studs? I totally recommend the dude. He wrote this story called "A Small Good Thing," which if you haven't already read it is

about this little kid who dies. No spoiler alert, it happens right in the beginning. After that there's a lot of bad stuff, followed by even worse stuff, and then the ending which is the small good thing that the writer is trying to tell you about all along. Totally kickass.

2. Lazarus, she meant. Who rose from the dead or some crazy shit like that, excuse my Eng. That's who I was named after but no one's allowed to call me anything but Lazar and the kids at school think it's got something to do with light rays and death stars. So, yeah, I can see how that Lazarus character was some weird truth-bender.

*   *   *

Area Development Programme
Nakonde, Muchinga Province
c/o World Vision Zambia

Hey, Pat my man,

I get it, dude. Your sister isn't going to write to us. Hope it wasn't anything I said. I thought I'd keep writing to you, though, if you don't mind. I don't have too many people to talk to and at least you listen. Well, I'm guessing you do. And also because I think I might have given the wrong impression about my mother.

The thing you have to know about her is that her heart beats faster than your average mom-type person and her brain fires quicker than a Google search engine and all the time there's this voice in her head going, *Now! Now! Now!* Well, that's what my dad used to say anyway. She slams books and phones and doors, can't help herself, and she jiggles keys, and drums her fingernails, and taps her feet. God help us when she gets her hands on a pen with a clicker. Your mother is an emphatic woman, my dad would say with honest to goodness admiration, but when he was young Sams would put his hands over his ears whenever he saw her coming. Which absolutely slayed my mom because Sams is her Achilles heel.

Sams has these episodes which I won't go into except to say that sometimes he doesn't go to bed for days and other times he doesn't get out of bed for days. No biggie, either way. Just doesn't feel like it. There's other stuff and it gets a bit complicated diagnosis-wise. Basically, no one can agree with what's wrong with my brother although everyone agrees that something is.[1] Luckily my mom doesn't believe in labels, except in the way of washing instructions for clothing (which she ignores) and expiration dates on dairy products (likewise). But just try to slap an age restriction on a movie or the Surgeon General's warning on a box of cigarettes and you'll hear all about it. I mean they do anyway, I'm just saying.

See, if Sams came with a label it would read "Handle With Care" or "Delicate Cycle." There was this time when he was in high school, he just lay on his bed and stared up at the ceiling for like a week. His mouth was moving as if he was talking, but no sounds were coming out, and anyway there was no one there to hear the sounds he wasn't making. Man, it was freaky. The first morning we found him like that my mom totally panicked.

Kid's got a temperature of 107 degrees, I heard her tell Miss Frölinger, the school secretary.

I could hear the gasp of horror through the phone.

Meanwhile my mom was elaborating: Yeah, yeah. *Sopping.*
I've had to wring out the boy's pajamas three times already.
God, and the sheets!

There was a garble of concern from the phone and my mom
rolled her eyes and flung her wristwatch at me. Move it, she
was saying, because *I* still had to go to school, no question.
So I ducked into the kitchen and yanked the Pop-Tarts out
of the freezer where we've had to keep them since Sams's last
major freak-out, on account of the colour (pink) and the smell
(pink chemicals). From the sound of things, voices and static
and my mom's escalating lies — bird flu, dengue fever, Lyme
disease — Frölinger was working herself into a state of epic terror and my mom was muttering *less is more, less is more* under
her breath which is what my dad always told her was the way
to go, little white lies–wise.[2]

I mean my mom tries, she really does, and what she tries
about, she once told me, is not making the same mistake twice.
Which means making different mistakes all the time, Lazar,
she laughed. But if you really want to know, she sucks at avoiding the same old mistakes although she's actually quite good
at finding new ones to make too.

Yet the thing that persuades you to forgive her is how bad
she always feels afterward. There she was banging the phone
on her forehead and pretending to shoot herself in the head.

No big deal, Mom, I said, but I was already late and all
the time I was picturing that stupid yellow school bus grind-
ing up the street until it stopped outside our house, the doors
whomping open and like *waves* of anger pouring out.

Céline! I could hear the driver yell. Oh Cé—*li*—ine! Get
in here, you great big beautiful doll.[3]

You need a good breakfast in you if you're going to

skedaddle, my mom said, beginning to hum. The hum always put the fear of God in me although it was meant to be a happy sound. The sound of my mom trying to decide what meal to make, what recipe to follow, what havoc to wreak upon whatever innocent family member had wandered into her kitchen.[4] So to stop the craziness, I stuffed a couple of Pop-Tarts in the toaster and said I'd better get going if that was the plan, what with all the Lyme disease that was going around.

All this time she kept darting into Sams's room and taking his temperature and his pulse and telling me not to worry, Laz. Don't worry, kiddo, she kept saying. I've got this. But she was talking so fast that her words swerved into one long skid.

Quit it, Mom, I said eventually.

So then she sat down at the kitchen table and watched me while I tried to stuff down a couple of Pop-Tarts, which wasn't as easy as you'd think. It's not that I don't like *love* my mom or whatever. I mean I remember all the usual stuff — swings and birthday cake and, you know, soccer games — but you have to remember she has a lot on her plate with Sams. I guess when you get right down to it, that's where we have the most in common, my mom and me. Looking out for Sams.[5+6]

Your pen pal,

L. B.

1. His latest dude is the best, though. His name is Dr. Raj and he really likes my brother. He says Sams is who he is, not what's wrong with him. I know, total Popeye, right?

2. On the other hand, my dad's favourite saying is *the more, the more,* which means the more there *is,* the more there'll *be.* The more there is for one, the more there'll be for all. Crazy,

huh? You'd think that only good things have happened to my dad, that he lived a life of abundance and happiness. Which maybe he did. I mean it's not the kind of thing you discuss with your old man, is it? "How's the *abundance* going, Dad?" "Pretty good, pretty good. Ample to profuse, kiddo."

3. Why does he call me Céline (for Céline "my voice will go on" Dion) you might ask? 'Cause we're both rich and skinny, famous multi-millionaire singers? Yeah, or *girls*, more likely.

4. It's like when you wake up in the middle of January and it's bright and shiny and glittery outdoors. Disco ball weather. I mean anyone who doesn't live on the Prairies would be like, wow, what a great day! Yeah, right. Sunny means thirty below and don't try to lick a pole, dude. Don't eat the yellow snow or suck on those frozen brown pellets either. And *that's* the kind of hum it was.

5. Sams took off all his clothes during Nuit Blanche. But he was okay when the police officers arrived and they kind of knew him from before so they drove him home in a blanket which was gross — the blanket, I mean, smelling of all the night's piss and throw-up.

6. Oops. They drove him home in a cop car, obviously. The blanket was what he was wrapped in. Sams kept trying to tell me about it but I stopped listening because sometimes it's easier to cope with the voices in Sams's head than at other times and this was neither of those times.

*   *   *

Area Development Programme
Nakonde, Muchinga Province
c/o World Vision Zambia

Hey stranger,

This is going to sound weird but I was wondering what your people think about dying. I mean, are you guys curious or thrilled or scared to death, ha ha, or what? With me it's the pain thing, like everyone says. But also, I mean what happens if, you know, if it doesn't take.

Like the other day, Ms. Ramirez got us to read this story for homework. Only Jackson Riley (the boy with two last names) threw up in third period on a bet, and there wasn't time for class discussion. And the next day, when Ms. Ramirez said take out your books, people, Jackson grabbed his stomach and started gagging again and Ms. Ramirez said — expletive-expletive-expletive — that was *it*. She's on sick leave, if you're interested, and the sub they got for us is an ancient dude, Mr. Patchett, who wears a lousy toupee and wants us to concentrate on "Commas, ladies and gentlemen, the pause that refreshes."

I don't know if you've read this Poe guy in Eng Lang Studs but let me tell you, bro, he writes a humdinger of a tale.[1] You know more about sisters than I do so I won't go into how freaky that Madeline chick is. I think the best part of the story is at the end, though, when the no-name narrator escapes. When he turns to look back and, just like that, the house splits apart and sinks into the earth.

I don't have strong feelings about commas but Mr. Patchett doesn't have strong feelings about discipline, so we get along fine.

Here are some examples of our getting along:

Heh-heh, so the cat ate your homework again, Binder.

Electricity out in your street? Happens, happens.

Yeah, no, those printers run out of ink all the time. So just try to catch up, eh.

Once I even told him that I was excused for the afternoon on account of my dad's funeral. But didn't he already — em? Yeah, I said. But he rose from the dead and now we have to bury him again. It was a good exit line so I left, and naturally the genius didn't try to stop me. I walked out the door and down the corridor and out of the school. And I didn't look back once. It wouldn't have worked in any case. Just looking back can't make a school building split apart and sink into the earth, so.

Sams and I used to play this game called Would You Rather? Fly or be invisible? Survive a zombie apocalypse or watch all the zombie apocalypse movies ever made? Magically receive one perfect wish or three pretty good wishes with only minor catches? Or how about five tricky wishes but with the option to renew?

Anyway, this whole death thing is a big matzo ball[2] so I've thought of some questions to "focus your thoughts, people."[3] Would you rather die young, no pain, or die of old age but suffer? Would you rather dream about worms or flames? Would you rather go through purgatory with the possibility of heaven or just go out like a light? Would you rather know for sure there's nothing after death or live in misguided hope? Would you rather be haunted by a ghost your entire life or be stalked by a psycho killer for three weeks? If the ghost, someone you know or someone you haven't met yet? If the psycho killer, violent but funny or useless but dumb?[4] Would you rather have the power to go backward in time or forward? And if backward, to kill Hitler or buy shares in Microsoft? And if forward, to turn back time or stay there forever? And if forever — see how it works?[6]

No sweat, bro. Don't worry if you can't answer all the questions. They're what Ms. Ramirez used to call "prompts to get your juices flowing."[7]

Salutations from the House of Binder,

L. (aka no-name narrator).

1. What my dad would probably say.

2. What my gran sometimes says.

3. What Ms. Ramirez always used to say.

4. Think of John Travolta and Samuel L. Jackson talking about eating a Royale with Cheese (funny) vs. Peter Lorre talking about absolutely anything (dumb). [5]

5. What Sams would say, I bet you anything.

6. Answer key: young, none (ugh), light, hope, psycho killer (prob.), haven't met yet, funny (cancels violent), forward, Hitler (obv.), forever.

7. She means creative juices. No relation to what Jackson Riley means when he torments homely chicks by sticking his middle finger in the air, then sucking (the juice, geddit?). Hey, here's another one: Would you rather be surrounded by jerks who hate your guts or losers who like you?

* * *

Area Development Programme
Nakonde, Muchinga Province
c/o World Vision Zambia

Yo bro,

You haven't asked but I wouldn't say she's getting worse exactly, my mom. And not better either, if you really want to know. But certainly more peculiar, which in our family is an adaptive measure. *Binder peculiaris.*

Take soup, for instance. Like I said before, my mom is a nasty cook and the only good thing about her never being home anymore is not having to eat the crap she used to scrape out of tin cans and mix together to the moronic delight of our father who, I might have forgotten to say, is dead and no longer a fan. But just the other night, late, I hear her bashing about the kitchen, and when I go down I find her making soup and digging through the shelves, muttering *butter beans, butter beans* in this way she has, as if something's missing, some damn thing has fallen out of the world again and if she can only find it she can calm down and go to bed. I got the hell out of there because I so did not want to get into a discussion of what she'd actually lost, like the other day when I tried to help her find her reading glasses and it turned out she was really looking for her lost youth.

The huge pot of soup was still there in the morning, curdling on the burner, with a disgusting wrinkly milk skin over top. The soup was what Grandma Minnie would have called a mixed blessing: it was terrible but at least there was a lot of it.[1]

I couldn't deal with the milk skin so I tried to yank it off with a fork but the skin suddenly came alive and began to fight for its life like one of those movies Sams doesn't watch anymore. *Creature from the Black Lagoon* meets The Soup of Death. So there I was, bent over the kitchen sink, gagging and running the faucet at full blast when who should walk in? She stood there in the doorway, my mom. I want to say more in sorrow than in anger, but the truth is they were equally mixed, a neck-and-neck race to the finish line of sorrow-anger. She looked tired, as if she'd been up all night, but also like — I don't know — cracked from side to side.[2]

Here we go, I thought. She was clutching at her throat, her eyes getting that red-rimmed, watery look. Then she gave herself a sort of shake. Like she was a dog and its owner at the same time. Like she'd taken herself by the loose skin at the back of her neck and brought herself to heel.

I felt bad on account of being such a terrible son, the badness rising and trying to get out of my clenched throat. There were these two kinds of badness: guilt and nausea, and my body was saying *choose!*

I'm really sorry, Mom, I said after I threw up again in the kitchen sink. And I was. She was sad because of all the things she'd lost but mostly Sams who was a lost soul. He slept all day and roamed all night, and his room smelled of the lion's cage at the zoo, as if something was trying to die inside it. He was starving again so every morning I put a plate of food outside his door. He wasn't a dog but what else could I do? He was thin as an electric current and his hair was falling out, I think.

My mom said, Oh Laz, in a helpless sort of way.[3] She wrung out a wet dishtowel and pressed it to my forehead and turned the burner down on the soup which was already beginning to form a new wrinkly skin. God, you couldn't stop it — it was like some sort of monster, growing new cells before it sloughed off the old ones. I still hadn't eaten breakfast so maybe it was the hunger that reminded me of this story that Ms. Ramirez made us read last term.[4]

Let's have some soup, Mom, I said.

Don't be silly, Lazar, she said. Just pour it down the drain.

After she left I grabbed a Pop-Tart from the freezer but there was no time to shove it in the toaster because the bus driver, wearing his little yellow school bus, screeched up to the house and leaned on his toy hooter.

Cé—*li*—ine! Get in, Céline! he yelled as soon as he saw me. And, Sit down, Céline! Shut your yob, Céline! No fucking eating in my bus, Céline!

I sucked my frozen Pop-Tart anyway, pretending that it was a Popsicle while he yelled himself hoarse all the way down the block. I mean what was he going to do? He wasn't allowed to stop the bus and pretend to punch out kids anymore on account of his anger issues and shitty distance judgement and what happened to that Daniel kid who also used to get on his thin little oxygen-deprived nerves.

I looked out the window at all the crappy suburban houses with their stupid Home Depot colours and their birdfeeders and their dumb Christmas lights still strung up around the eaves, and their melting snowmen out front. Mr. Tergusson was outside, brushing snow off his ugly old Chevy. He saw me and saluted with two fingers against the visor of his baseball cap like we were goddamn marines or something, but I looked away. The frozen Pop-Tart began to melt so that the frosting came off on my fingers and somehow got onto my jacket leaving this yucky pink trail. The thing is, it wasn't a big deal. It wasn't a Popsicle or a cinnamon roll or the icing from a dead kid's birthday cake. All it was was my life so far — a flare of sugar and a sudden crash.

'K, bye.

Laz

1. This is an old person's joke and my gran's personal favourite. It's only one sentence long. Here goes: The food was terrible and *such small portions!* Cue creaky old person laughter.

2. Ms. Ramirez once made us read a poem by this Victorian dude called Alfred Lord T. and at first it was crap and we all moaned and threatened to prong our eyeballs out every time she put on her poetry reciting voice but then I started to dig it — I really did. It wasn't exactly rap but I'm thinking that Kendrick and Kanye and those guys might've gotten their swagger from being forced to read bros like Alfred Lord T. in high school. Maybe.

3. My mom's been standing there for a while but I haven't forgotten about her and I hope you haven't either. There were just some things I had to get off my chest. Soliloquizing, Ms. Ramirez called it. (See *Hamlet*, Act 1, Scene 5.) Another thing Ms. Ramirez used to say was that *Hamlet* would have unexpected relevance to our lives even in this post-modern age. Jackson Riley said Ms. Ramirez could stuff herself in an envelope and *post* herself to Denmark for all the relevance she had to his life. There was a lot more of this stuff going on during ninth-grade language arts, and if you really want to know, *Hamlet* wasn't one of Ms. Ramirez's greatest successes. Everyone climbed onto their desks and cheered when

Laertes ran Hamlet through at the end and Jackson started this vampire chant — *more blood, more blood* — whenever anybody got killed, which in the final scene was everybody. But guess who turned out to be spot on about relevance?

4. That story by R. Carver I told you about. Absolutely everyone liked the story although it made Courtney Segal cry her eyes out. What I liked about it was that it combined a dead kid with No Pity At All. And at the end everyone shared cinnamon rolls, which was both unexpected and awesome. I mean think of your favourite thing to eat and then put it at the end of a story that doesn't seem to be heading toward cinnamon rolls. Winner.

FATHER MICHAEL CAME by this morning on his way to the airport. He was all in black, spiffy and band-box elegant, with a *Pardon me, ma'am* snap to his hat brim.

He sat at the kitchen table and accepted a cup of tea, requesting two tea bags and wringing both dry. A drop of milk to turn the tea a tawny orange hue, and three heaped spoonfuls of sugar, which he stirred in briskly. I remembered how he'd stood at the kitchen sink three nights ago, downing glasses of tap water, and understood that this cup of builder's tea, made to his exacting standards, was his gift to me in the form of a confidence: I am a man who likes his tea, who likes his tea made so, who drinks his tea in three gulps and wipes his mouth with the back of his hand afterward. To some men even a person is too small and inadequate a gift, and to others a small habit judiciously exposed is gift enough.

He'd had a busy few days, he told me. But he'd accomplished his mission, which was to search out the grave of Pat Ngunga.

He'd said a prayer and sang a traditional mourning song, but mostly he sat beside her and talked to her.

"Aloud?" I asked.

"Of course aloud. She's not a mind reader."

"Don't worry, I'm not going to ask what you two chatted about."

"We talked about the weather, mostly. And snow, a little. She was most enthusiastic about snow. And she asked me to wish you the happiest of birthdays."

"Huh, bit late. But tell her thanks."

He showed me a Polaroid snap he'd taken of the grave. "Now her mother will have two photographs," he said with some satisfaction.

We sat quietly watching the snow fall. It had snowed gently but continuously since I'd seen him disappear into a cab, the snow forming fondant mounds and peaks on the roofs of houses. I asked Father Michael if we ought to prepare for a blizzard of Biblical proportions. I expected him to reprimand me, to remind me of the covenant, but he said only that God had given up testing humankind. No more Noahs, he said. Not even in the district of Nakonde, where three days of rain would fill the rivers and the water tables and the wells but also wash away roads and crops and cause mosquito larvae to hatch in standing pools. He shrugged. What you lose on the swings you win on the roundabout.

I asked him if Nakonde hosted many carnivals, what with all the swing and roundabout action, and he said yes, matter of fact the annual Nakonde District Fair was underway as we spoke.

Whoa, a joke! Father Michael confirmed his levity and my astonishment by grinning, which was when I noticed that he was not the entirely symmetrical being that I'd once thought he was. There at the corner of his mouth, buried deep, a shallow dimple dented his left cheek.

I wanted to see that dimple again so I told him your favorite joke, Max. You know the one although, naturally, you always forgot the punchline. The old Jew haranguing God: I'm so poor, I'm so luckless. Grant me a favour and I'll never bother you again. Just this once, let me win the lottery. On and on, day after day.

Poor, luckless, favour, lottery.

"Yes," Father Michael said, leaning forward. "And what was the Lord's reply?"

Here goes then, my darling. From me to you by way of Father Michael. Once more with feeling.

"There's a clap of thunder and a bolt of lightning and a deep voice booms out. It's God. 'Max,' he says. 'Max, meet me halfway. *Buy a ticket!*'"

Father Michael let out a bark of laughter and flashed me his dimple. "Buy a ticket!" he repeated wonderingly. "Yes, that would be most advisable."

We were still laughing when Lazar, who had been standing in the doorway for who knew how long, cleared his throat and said, "Um, Mom?" He was staring at Father Michael but talking to me, boy code for *Who is this fine fellow and why is he sitting in my chair?*

"Lazar, this is Father Michael," I said, flapping my hand from one to the other. "Father Michael, Lazar." I hadn't yet told him the story, the story being too big, too improbable, too loopy to imagine, let alone relate in the time between when Father Michael first knocked on the door three days ago and his current magisterial presence at our kitchen table.

"Do you remember —" I began then stopped because I had no idea what to say. Do you remember our World Vision child? Do you remember the boy-girl called Pat? (The one you wrote all those letters to?) Do you remember your old man? The more I floundered the quieter the kitchen became — Lazar frozen in the doorway, Father Michael motionless at the table. They formed a tableaux vivant that came to life when Father Michael rose from his chair and stretched out his large, ministering hand.

"Good morning, Lazarus." Father Michael stared at our son. "Since you don't look like your mother, you must resemble your late father." Again, he peered into our son's face so intently that the boy flinched. "He was a good man," he continued, undeterred. "He was a good man and you are in the process of becoming one. Possibly both."

Lazar stared, shook the hand. Stared. I thought he would object to the name Father Michael had called him, that old taboo, but he seemed to be trying to work out a riddle.

"Good *and* a man," Father Michael explained kindly. "Both things."

I looked at my son and saw that he was, indeed, becoming a man, his jaw squaring off and his shoulders broadening, his muscles ropy and hard under the skin of his arms. His acne was clearing up and his face, which had almost shed its sullen adolescent cast, revealed a new sweetness that reminded me of the little boy he'd once been. The one who'd asked me what a good mistake was. "It's something you don't even remember regretting," I'd told him, smiling at the memory. "You have to know you made a mistake, though."

Lazar smiled at me, his face softening. And suddenly, there he was: my baby, my boy, my almost-gone. All three ages in one.

There's not much else to tell, my love. I drove Father Michael to the airport so that he could catch his flight to Toronto and from there a Heathrow connection to Lusaka followed by a twelve-hour bus ride to Nakonde. A day and a night and half again another day. Mrs. Ngunga will be grateful to receive these photographs, was all he said. The gratitude of Mrs. Ngunga being beyond me I fussed a little, offering to buy him chewing gum or a newspaper. He refused all my blandishments, politely but firmly. It was his habit to use whatever free time was allotted him to pray.

"Since I am already in the sky," he told me.

"Give your Cloth God my regards," I teased him. He said he would and I was thankful for no further pieties.

We parted on the most amiable terms. Which seems like a good place to end, my darling. On terms: the most amiable of which I offer you. Goodbye, Max. Don't let the moon break your heart.

ZERO
VISIBILITY

FOURTEEN

OUT OF TIME

WHEN MAX OPENS his eyes all he sees is stock footage: snow falling, temperatures falling, night falling. Snow and the intervals between snow. Faster and faster, like a film sped up over time. Blurred wings, wind, wind-back. Sun dogs snapping at the horizon. Stars whirling in the darkness. When the film comes to the end of the reel, he sits up, trembling, to find himself on Magnolia Street.

Max hunches up, his elbows on his knees and his head in his hands. Who is he? What is he doing here? Why, *why?* His family is dead, that much is certain. How can he go on without them? It doesn't seem possible. But why does his knee still ache, why is he so cold? How can these chafing pains exist alongside the towering loss of everyone he loves? He longs to pray but he can remember nothing: no praise, no song, no psalm, no plea. Not even the words to the mourner's prayer he once knew.

One day, for no reason that he can imagine, he is able to struggle up off the sidewalk. Brush himself down and gingerly put his weight on his knee. Then he begins to walk, limping and cold, turning down the streets of strange and familiar neighbourhoods where dog owners are yanked along on their taut leashes and stroller-pushing mothers dawdle about their weekday mornings, wheels spinning. It's all so beautiful, this broken, breathing world! He forgets himself and stops to pet a beagle, compliment a mother on her crimson-cheeked snow dolly. The mother ignores him, the baby sleeps on. Even the dog steps through him. And suddenly he is nothing again, as thin and vacant as the prairie air.

At night he dosses down beneath Railway Bridge. The river ice creaks and the trains rattle through the night. High above the river, the railway tracks, the bridge, an electric crucifix clicks on in the sky, a broken promise of resurrection. The homeless congregate beneath the shadowy struts of the old footbridge. Fires are lit, thin and insufficient, and the men in their greasy coats huddle around them, paddling their hands. Max peers into the turned-away faces trying to make out a comrade, a familiar. He's looking for someone, a young woman, a girl he once knew. He's waiting for something, but damned if he knows what it is.

In the morning Max gets up again and hobbles away. He walks to ease his broken heart, to heal his pain. He walks to catch up with his family who seem to recede with every step he takes. They are unreachable now, as far away as the painted figures on some vast allegorical canvas. Breughel's Icarus, he thinks, who rose and fell while a doughty peasant tilled the soil in the foreground and the sea flowed impassively onward. According to Williams, according to Auden. When bereft, Max retreats to the aesthetic position and death, it seems, hasn't robbed him of this pointless knack.

"Maggie, Maggie, star of my firmament. Love of my life," he mourns.

Far away his children call out to one another. He can barely hear them. They ripple and waver like mirages. His boys!

"Wait for me," Max calls, breaking into an awkward, limping run.

But they can't hear him and when he puts out his hands to touch them, they disappear. This mourning, this yearning — it's more than he can bear. Ah, grief! They'd once had a nodding acquaintance, just a polite how d'you do and a tip of the hat brim. Now grief has put a firm arm around his shoulders. Hello, old friend, old pal, old buddy, old chum.

Grief is the winter static in the air and the way his skin twitches in response. It's the nail on blackboard screech of packed snow underfoot and the shuffle of crows in the trees. Grief is the yolky, over-easy sun that slops across the horizon. It's the old woman at the bus stop halved by her dowager's hump, and the kids in hoodies who elbow her aside, and the kindly social worker type who takes her firmly by the elbow. *Watch the sidewalk, dearie.*

In all this time, forty-five years next month, Max has failed to notice the great rusty clank of life that surrounds him. Now everything is too bright, too noisy, everything trails its own chain. At the busy intersection of Harrow and Rue he grasps a pensioner by the elbow and tries to escort him across the street. But the old man just stands there, leaning on his walker, his jacket unbuttoned and his laces untied. Again and again, Max tries to help the fellow who gazes listlessly into space, his trembling frame resistant.

And the children he fails to catch! The boys who tumble on outdoor rinks, hockey sticks flying, the school kids he rushes after to tie flapping scarves around their necks. The missing children he fails to recover, the heroin babies twitching in their hospital basinets, the teenage runaways hitchhiking out on the highway, begging for a ride. The murdered girls settling at the bottom of the river, their hearts like stones. All the children he can't catch as they fall out of burning houses, as they are borne away on cresting rivers, broken-hearted and pillaged and lost.

But Max can't catch anyone. Can't throw himself between a collapsed vein and a syringe, can't stop a bullet or a knife from tearing open the city's tender throat. Can't open up the river, can't turn back the current, can't set a net wide and fine enough to recover what's been lost. God knows he tries.

ALL NIGHT THE river creaks like a door. When Max wakes the next morning he is covered in drifts of snow. The homeless men sleeping beside him are also covered in snow. They look like ghosts.

In the morning the ghost men are sociable, he's found. They help one another brush snow off their shoulders and chat about a possible spring flood. Some say yes, some say no. Some say dollars to donuts, some say don't bet your shirt on it, pal. Yup, nope. Maybe, couldn't say. *One thing, when it comes it's gonna be a doozy!* The city, looped in its curly rivers, is vulnerable to flooding.

Max sets off as he does every morning, neither buoyant nor resilient. His knee aches and the cold has made a nest in his bones. He's lost his bearings again. These days he can't even find his way back to Magnolia Street. Also, as puzzling as it seems, he suspects he's being followed by a crow. An ugly black creature, more unkempt than your average crow, more disreputable. It bundles itself from branch to branch as he walks, shaking down feathers and snow, trying to shit on his head. Cawing insults in a rhyming singsong. Get out the *door!* Don't be a *bore!* You've broken the *law!*

But when Max picks up his pace the crow falls behind, too weary to keep up with him, although he can still hear its insults fading into the distance. *Caw! Claw! Craw!* When the terrible creature is out of sight, he slows down again because of his gammy leg. What a pair they are! Rotten and the Gimp. That night he hears a train clattering toward him from two provinces away. It's coming out of the west, which is the future, the about to happen, the nearly there.

MAX FINDS HIMSELF unexpectedly weary, immune to spring fever. That darn crow appears to be following wherever he goes, choleric and impatient.

"Taking your own sweet time, eh?" the crow complains.

Can time be sweet? Max wonders. He picks up his pace and usually manages to throw off the crow by the time he reaches his park bench. He's taken to sitting outside the high school, watching the passing throng, hoping for a glimpse of his boy. Not counting on it. Lately the students all seem restless and exhausted. Winter-pale some of them, with dark smudges beneath eyes that look as if they've been put there with sooty fingers.

Elsewhere in the city, householders look out on their greening lawns and joyfully sharpen the blades of their mowers. One day in early summer, Max strolls through the old neighbourhood in his grubby, post-winter coat to find that every storm window in every house, up and down the block, has been taken down and replaced with screens. That evening the fat smell of barbecued meat wafts through the streets.

Soon after, they begin dragging the Red again, searching for the remains of the women and girls who've disappeared over the years. The river isn't always the culprit, but it has its guilty secrets. The ranks of the disappeared had to reach a critical mass, the waters rising over what had displaced them, before enough people would believe the ones who wanted to bring their children home. For years the authorities refused to believe that the women had really disappeared, and then they refused to believe they were important enough to be missed. Now lack of belief hangs heavy on the city's conscience.

School is out for the summer, the kids dispersing. Max sees groups of them outside the 7-Eleven or hanging around neglected parks. But it's astonishing how few there are. Where have all the children gone? He spends his nights under Railway Bridge and his days on the banks of the Red, watching the boats move with the swift-flowing current, imagining their cruel hooks dragging beneath the surface of the river.

In the old neighbourhood the cankerworms trapeze through a green cathedral of elms. The air is choral with bees. Peonies zoom up out of the earth and burst into messy, tissue paper blooms. Limping through the streets in the staleness of late afternoon, Max can hear the *snick-snick* of sprinklers in backyards, the neighbours calling to one another from their front porches. Each day is a gift, another gold coin falling from the sky. The trick is to shore up the coins for the dark winter months ahead but no one has figured out how to hoard time. In summer the city goes a little crazy, turns grasshopper-ish and devil-may-care.

Can time be sweet? he wonders again.

One day the colour drains abruptly from the world. The trees dim and the grass turns to stubble. It's as if a fuse has blown. He's never noticed this strange waning moment between the thick impasto of late summer and the thin, crinkly gold-leaf of fall. It's an in-between time with a colour all its own to match a season that smells of rotting crabapples and new pencils and the white paint they use to mark up the high school football field. The scoreboard reads: "Welcome Back Students. Let's Make Every Day Count!"

Time slows, sweetens. Max returns to his bench outside the high school.

IN LATE FALL the rivers begin to freeze, the water thickening and the current growing sluggish. They have to dock the dragging boats for the winter. Max watches the men winch a motorboat out of the Red, the muddy river water streaming down its sides. A woman sits on the bank with her head in her hands, weeping. With some difficulty Max kneels down beside her and puts an arm around her shoulders. She doesn't even bother to shrug him off. Overhead the alchemical winter sun turns the water metallic. He stays with her while the men secure the boat on a flatbed trailer.

When the woman leaves, Max remains on the banks of the Red, weeping. He has finally realized that his family is gone. What's more, he hasn't lost them in some apocalyptic spasm of the world's casual malevolence. He hasn't lost them at all. And if he hasn't lost them then he will never find them. No, he is the one who is lost, lost forever in the impossible translation from flesh into spirit. He can never go home again, not ever.

It's getting colder, the terrible unrequited cold that yields only when the first snow falls. Max knows he has to keep moving. He's stopped fighting the crow by now; they've reached a détente. The creature is his companion, more or less. He can swear it's trying to tell him something in the insinuating, slightly deranged language of crows.

You stick in my *craw!* Face like a slammed *door!* Mind like an open *jaw!* That's the kind of thing the crow screeches but it isn't necessarily what the creature means, Max reckons. Because you can only use the words you've been given — even a crow, even a rotten, stinking crow — and if the words aren't what you intended, well you're shit out of luck, pal. It's complicated.

One day the first mitten pops up on a fencepost, a small red mitten some toddler has flung down in stroller-bound rage. After that they begin appearing all over the city, a blizzard of mittens and gloves, knitted scarves, little hats, little socks. Max seems to remember that it's the custom, when one comes across these lost articles, to hang them from a prominent place — a fencepost or a mailbox, the low-hanging branch of a tree — so that their owner can retrieve them. Here on the Prairies folks are respectful of other people's possessions.

These quiet winter courtesies lift his spirits and he roams the streets with a purpose now, his eyes searching.

FOR ONE WHOLE year Max has risen at first light and made his way to the house on Magnolia Street. He limps along the river, traverses a couple of neighbourhoods, shortcuts through the grounds of Ridgehaven High, across Grover Park Fields and the Legion Hall parking lot, turns down one tree-named street and then another, and there it is finally, his house, still shuttered against the early morning light. The house blurs in and out of focus as if Max is crying. He's not, though. He hasn't wept since that day on the banks of the Red. Whether through temperament (stoic) or circumstance (death), he finds that he can't cry anymore, although he would like to, if only to skim off some of the grief that slops around inside him.

He makes his way to Magnolia Street every day, waiting. The house blurs in and out of focus. Max slumps on the pavement, despondent. Maggie opens the door and strides out. A hard bright light surrounds her. Max winces, his eyes watering in pain. Maggie stands on the sidewalk, crackling like fire. He can smell the burn coming off her; he can already see the flames licking at her legs. The heat radiating from her could boil snow, turn ice to steam, melt the fillings from his teeth. She jangles her house keys, winds her scarf around her neck, stamps her feet to get them started. Then she turns on her heel and strides down the street, a woman in flames. Max watches her leave him until she is nothing but a wisp of smoke in the distance.

He watches her leave him again and again. Death, a continuous loop on a blooper reel of unbearable moments or some damn day he's fallen into that's closed over his head like water. Now he can't get out of it, he's lost the knack, and the only woman who could ever talk sense into him bursts into flame every morning. Oh Maggie May, he mourns. Star of my firmament. Love of my life.

After Maggie leaves, the day stalls, turns over a couple of times, then finally catches. Cars hawk into the raw air, blinking red-eyed before reversing down back lanes and alleyways. The school bus turns into Magnolia Street and comes to a halt outside Max's house, flaps out its stop sign and hisses pneumatically until his son's vast backpack emerges and walks itself down the front path on spindly denim legs. His youngest, his Lazarus. The boy is tall and growth-spurt skinny, with the long-distance gaze of wary adolescence.

Max worries, belatedly, about the heaviness of the backpack, the curvature of his son's still-growing spine, the possibility of scoliosis and hernias and compacted discs. Bad posture, even. The boy's head and hands are usually bare, his parka always seems to be hanging open.

Lazar, Lazar, thinks Max, hastening across the icy sidewalk.

He kneels in the path before his son, yanks at the uneven edges of the parka as he tries to align the zipper's metal teeth. Vaguely, he remembers kneeling in front of another young person, trying to wrangle a winter jacket into submission. But that was long ago and in another country.

The boy drops his backpack and roots about, searching for his front door key. Max takes the opportunity to investigate his son's pockets, digging for the gloves or toque that might lie neglected within. Their proximity is heady; Lazar smells unexpectedly of fried onions and toothpaste. Max bends closer, gets a whiff of chemical sweetness, a harsh note of strawberry-frosted Pop-Tart added to the bouquet of early-morning boy. With eyes sharpened by yearning, he notices that the hair at the back of Lazar's head is awry and stand up-ish. Stricken, he puts out his big hand to smooth down his son's cowlick.

But Max can't find a toque or gloves, and he's not having much luck at zipping the kid's parka. The edges of the grimy ski jacket jerk from his grasp as Lazar launches into his backpack. Finally, Max discovers the house key in his son's jean pocket and hauls it out. *Look!* The boy ignores his father, thrusting his whole head into the opening of his backpack.

"*Look!*" Max shouts, tapping the key smartly against the cold metallic air.

The boy looks up. He *looks through him,* his father, as if Max is not there. As if he is a ghost.

The school bus has been tutting against the sidewalk all this time. Evidently the bus driver has lost patience with all this disarray, with tardiness and confusion and what appears to be an altercation between a boy and his backpack. He leans on his horn until the street unzips into the two flapping halves of a ski jacket snagging crazily in the wind.

"Coming!" Lazar yells. He scrambles to his feet, shoving things — *stuff* — ring binders and pens, his phone, a dirty nylon wallet, crumpled pages from a math sheet, a Salinger paperback, into the backpack. "Coming!" he yells, because the bus driver is still leaning on his horn, all his gimcrack patience through thousands of school days of bad morning smells and terrible afternoon noises and picking gum off the bottom of his shoe every evening at the depot has given way to fury.

Lazar scrambles up, hoists his backpack over his shoulder, and lumbers after the school bus that is either peeling away, or pretending to peel away, from the curb. At the last possible moment, the bus driver slows down, cranks open the door, and allows Lazar to haul himself aboard, but Max can still see the man gesticulating, flailing his hands and punching the air. He imagines he can hear the snarl of the driver's invective as the bus pulls away and disappears down the street.

The front door key lies where it has fallen, on the cracked flagstones of the front path, after Lazar, in his clumsy rout, knocked it out of his father's hand. *Didn't even see me*, thinks Max. *What am I, a ghost?*

He limps stiff kneed to the sidewalk and slumps down, his feet in the gutter. He props his elbows on his thighs and lets his head drop into his hands, closes his eyes, tries to sort through his various anxieties. There is the matter of his son's icy hands and no gloves to be found. There is the boy's un-zipped parka, his toque-less head. The backpack beneath which Lazar staggers every morning will do him an injury, no doubt about it. And now the searched-for key lies abandoned. Max picks it up and absently pockets it.

He tries to remember what Lazarus was like as a little boy. A demon on the soccer field, he seems to recall. *Go number 21!* Or wait — wasn't that just a story Maggie used to tell about a kid and a ball. But whose kid? Whose ball? Memory is secretive, it hides behind a door. *Knock, knock.* The door inches shut. *Who's there?*

What death is, Max is beginning to suspect, is being caught in the present tense forever. A grammatical limbo. The past is imperfect and the future is conditional, but every day the front door opens and who should walk out but Maggie, burning, then Lazar, staggering, and then — hours later, but Max has nothing to do except wait — Sams.

Sams in his cracked leather jacket with his long, streaming hair and his hands shoved deep in their pockets. Sams, loping. *Who's there?*

FOR A LONG time Max turns up as he has never, in life, turned up. The truth is, like most of the men in his family, like most Binder men, he's loved his sons and tried to understand them (failed, mostly), and railed against their place in his wife's heart (silently), their foreseeable place in the world after he's gone (subconsciously). But he's never been one to throw a ball or bait a hook. Mostly he's just done what dads do: snooze in front of the television, grumble about bills, kid around, try to pat a passing back, ask about school when he remembers, and hope to God somebody will need something from him someday.

Advice, cash. A kidney.

But turning up is not what he's been best at.

These days he not only turns up but he arrives early, his bones ringing like the iron tracks across Railway Bridge when a locomotive approaches. Some mornings he shakes so hard that the world is a blur until noon. Some mornings the trains that have been running through his head all night keep going. Some mornings he wakes up frozen almost to death on the sidewalk in front of the shuttered house. His feet in the gutter, waiting.

The thing is, he is terrible at death. Face it, a bumbling goof! He can't even haunt anyone, although he raps and bangs at the door between this world and the next. He is nothing — the wind comes off the river and blows straight through him. He was all flesh once, Max is certain of it. Very little in the way of spirit or soulfulness. Clumsy, untidy, an ugly bastard, but impossible to ignore. Now he's gone and mislaid his own death.

As the days pass he grows less hungry, less cold, less short of breath. Less agitated, less lively, less hopeful. His feet are wet and his knee is painful and inflamed. Also — and he hardly likes to mention this — he's begun to smell. Ripening, always ripening.

It embarrasses him, this stink of his bodily corruption. But what can he do with himself, *his body*. This bag of bones and gas and greening flesh. He avoids heated interiors, walks upwind, burrows into his winter coat. Still, dogs tend to congregate around the Max-shaped hole he's hollowed into the world. The dogs snuffle and burrow in a grotesque parody of affection, their ears cocked.

A crow flaps up beside him, settles in a tree. Don't be a *bore!* it advises. That's what death's *for!* Shut the damn *door!*

* * *

MAX POSITIONS HIMSELF carefully on the train tracks just off Highway 9. It's his third try and he's full of ire, pumped up with righteous indignation. He's chosen his position after careful consideration, some on-site observation, and a painstaking study of the CPR timetable. No doubt about it, the Great Western Line is the way to go. Although their trains are notoriously unpunctual and inclined to dawdle at level crossings, they can be depended on to gather speed on the open prairie. Besides, the GWL Express Freight is the only locomotive with enough heft and momentum, with enough *conviction*, to wreak sufficient damage upon a man of his ambiguous stature.

At this very moment, Max can see the GWL Express chugging along the line toward him. He stands with his legs braced on either side of the tracks. He's trying to keep his spirits up because it's his third consecutive day. On the first day, the freight didn't hesitate but barrelled straight through him, resulting in a hollow, nauseous feeling in the pit of his stomach. On the second day, the engine seemed to give a lurch as it hit him, albeit a tentative lurch, a lurch in the shape of a wobble. Then, once again, it ploughed through his middle, the freight train sturdy as ever, belting its way west, apparently unaffected by his ghostly suicide attempt.

Still alive, or at least not quite dead, Max is tired of being a ghost, sick at heart and weary of soul. He wants nothing more than to kill himself, *requiescat in pace*. But this second death hasn't been easy to accomplish. Far from it. At first he merely throws himself off various structures: highway overpasses and trees, a small building or two. But nothing ever happens except for a gentle bounce, the ground rushing up to meet him, and then a slow fade to white.

But Max persists, hurling himself from his overpasses and

trees and buildings, bouncing and fading to white, his knee throbbing. Frankly, Max is afraid of heights. He longs for death but he would rather not die of fright. If he had a particle of courage he'd clamber to the top of the highest bridge in the city, take a deep breath and throw himself into the river. And yes, he's clambered, hung over the railings, shuddering at the thought of that secret riverine current moving swiftly below its thin skin of ice.

How much time has he spent hanging over the rusty trestle of the disused railway bridge while a breeze tousles his greying hair? His necktie blows over his shoulder, stiffening then going limp with every change in the wind's direction. He peers at the water and calculates the impact of accelerating bodies intersected by gravity. Suddenly he remembers the dragging boats of last summer, the woman weeping on the banks of the Red. With every spasm of his heart the river recedes.

As always, Max falls back on his literary resources. That old reflex. He contemplates a bullet to the head (Hedda Gabler), briefly agonizes over poison (Madame Bovary), a sleeping draught (Lily Bart), hanging (Antigone), drowning (Ophelia), arson and jumping off the roof (Bertha Mason), swallowing fire (Portia), or waking up (Lady of Shalott). Why are all his suicidal mentors women? he wonders. And mostly written by you lot, Maggie would have pointed out. Men! You can't wait to kill us off.

He has few resources, is the problem. A shortage of guns, poison, fire, courage. In the end the trains lure him (Anna Karenina), the trains panting and gasping across the Prairies, bearing their clattering miles of boxcars and their bloody-minded spirit of free enterprise. There's something fateful about trains. Perhaps it's their propensity to trundle by on double tracks, swerving neither left nor right. Or their arrowing off-ness into the distance as lines of cars idle at level crossings, their drivers drumming on their steering wheels and cursing. Or the feeling he invariably has on seeing a train disappear down the tracks: that it is he who has grown smaller and irreparably distant.

So here he stands for the third time. Quivering with nerves, legs braced, as the GWL Express bears down on him. This time, Max vows, he'll keep his eyes open. This time he'll lunge open-armed to meet his fate. Perhaps if he tries hard enough he'll get this death right. *I think I can*, he reminds himself grimly, staring down the approaching engine. At once he catches the glance of the engineer sitting up in the cab, who doffs his cap and waves. The locomotive ploughs through his middle but this time to some purpose because in its headlong progress it knocks him off his feet and, with an audible *thwock*, sends him rolling like a bowling pin into the wet ditch. He scrambles up the embankment, soggy and winded, to watch the engineer hanging from the cab, receding into the distance, waving his cap and shouting into the wind.

Good luck, Comrade! it sounds like.

Oh God, thinks Max. *Not another bloody ghost.*

But he's heartened by the impact he's finally made upon the freight. His tumble into the ditch. Maybe tomorrow? What did his mother always say? Something about tomorrow.

Tomorrow is waiting for him. Tomorrow he will begin.

SO HE IS dead, okay. But why does the cold morning air burn in his nostrils? Why do ice crystals glitter like diamond dust? Why does the mica that falls about his shoulders stir him as if he is a snow globe, and shaken? Why does the wind make him shiver and search for the hunch deep within his coat? Pull the water from his eyes and the blood to the surface of his cheeks? Overhead a crow rustles in the trees, refusing to transform into an angel.

Max is waiting for the bus. Up until now he's led a life full of the usual amount of things waited for: his wife to forgive him (again), his sons to grow up (finally), his head-scratching students to confide their reluctant answers. Term to end, summer to begin, the Messiah to come. But all this waiting hasn't prepared him for the toe-tapping boredom, the existential whatnow? of his frequently postponed death. His mind is like an old Polaroid camera, slow to bring memories to the surface. The images emerge tentatively, deepen in colour, finally resolve, finally set. Now he remembers waiting for the 18 bus on weekday mornings. Back then he was always reading, a paperback stuffed in his coat pocket, the pages dog-eared.

When the transit bus finally arrives, he steps aside for a woman to enter, then shoulders his way through the huffing concertina doors behind her. But when the woman sits down and pats the seat beside her, Max is startled. *Who, me?*

"Hey there, neighbour," the woman greets him when he sits down.

Max peers at her — is it? It can't be. "Theresa?" he ventures. "Theresa Tergusson! Well, howdy…"

"Howdy, yourself," she says, a little peevish at not having been recognized earlier. Max has turned so pale that she puts a consolatory arm about him. "No need to startle, honey," she says. "Haven't you ever seen a ghost before?"

His old neighbour is looking well, handsome as ever, and when she smiles her whole face smiles too: her clever, complicated eyes, the funny little gap between her front teeth, and the dimples in her cheeks.

"I've been waiting a long time for you to notice me," she says.

Max is shocked. "Where've you been hiding yourself, Theresa?" he exclaims.

"In plain sight, honey." She smiles again. "Think about it. All you need is belief."

Belief, Max thinks, *belief*? Is that the answer? Should he plant himself in front of the next freight train that comes by, with enough conviction in his heart to make an impact? Stand astride the tracks like a colossus? Fling himself unflinchingly at the single red eye of his death as it thunders toward him? He thinks he can. With each hopeful thought, he imagines the happy little engine of his demise chugging closer. Absently but fondly, he smoothes a lock of Theresa's hair behind one of her neat ears.

"No, it doesn't work like that," she snaps. "Sorry."

Scalded, Max snatches his hand away. But Theresa is talking about death and intention and the ability of the GWL Express to yoke the one to the other, and not at all about absentminded but fond tousling.

"It's not up to you, honey," she tells him. "That's the thing you've got to remember."

But Max is unconvinced. Free will is his thing. He's been teaching *Paradise Lost* for years.

Theresa sighs. "Unfinished business," she explains. "Theirs not ours. Ghosts are what other people can't let go of. Bastards, eh? Turns out everyone has a grudge."

She pats his hand kindly. "Oh, honey," she mourns. They rock together in the swaying interior of the 18 bus. "You think you got problems?" she finally says. "It's been more than a year already and will that bastard give up and let me go?"

Riley Tergusson, she means.

Wisely, Max decides not to inquire into what is no doubt a

long-running and far-reaching marital feud. No good can come of interfering between a husband and his ghost wife. Instead he exclaims: "How's my dolly? How's my singing nun?"

Bernadette, he means. He's always been partial to that fierce girl, who has a talent for survival that her mother once seemed to possess and her father's crazy ten-gallon sense of humour.

"Fine, I guess. I haven't seen her in a while. You know how kids are."

Actually he does, having two of his own, neither of whom seems anxious to welcome his dead father back into his life. "Sams offered me a cup of coffee once," he tells her. Although honesty compels him to admit that his oldest boy had mistaken him for an itinerant at the time.

"Are you telling me that Sams saw you?" Theresa is astonished. She twists in her seat, grabs him by the lapels of his coat, shakes him as if to try and wake him from his dream.

"He actually *saw* you?" She's almost shouting now.

Max passes a hand over his eyes. *Oh God, now what?*

Patience has never been Theresa's strong suit although she hid it well back then, white-knuckling it through all her husband's goading. Now she is actually digging her fingers into the sockets of her eyes with frustration. "You're telling me Sams saw you, he *saw* you?"

"No, but you don't understand. Not me. He didn't see his father — it wasn't a, a Hamlet kind of thing. He just saw some stranger coming at him and he must have thought — well if he thought anything at all. You know what Sams is like. Kind-hearted, but."

Theresa can't help it. She really can't. She clenches her fist and punches him in the chest with all her strength and, ghost to ghost, it isn't half bad.

"*Ooph!*" Max says, the pain overlaying an earlier and more violent pain where once a steering wheel had pierced his chest cavity. He sits for a moment, wounded in body and spirit, rehearsing the highlights of his last reply: Hamlet. Panhandler. Kind-hearted.

Nope, it's a mystery. Theresa is in full spate.

"...bloody recognize you or not. But if he saw you, your own son, I mean that's re*mark*able you, you *fool*. The rest of us — we're ghosts, we just fade away."

"Well, that's what I'm trying to do actually," Max says bitterly.

"Good luck to you, honey," Theresa snaps. "If you figure it out —" She stares moodily out of the bus window for a moment then turns back to him.

"They all harbour grudges," she repeats. "And, by the way, you smell like someone who wants to be left alone."

With that she gets up and pushes past him, slamming out the bus at the next stop. Max can't blame her. As always, Theresa speaks the truth. He stinks.

AND THEN, ONE day, the city falls silent. It happens every year but it's always shocking, as if nobody can quite believe what will happen next. It's the beginning of the silence that will deepen with every turn of the weather's screw until all that can be heard is snow on snow, no footsteps, no echoes.

Max limps through a neighbourhood near the old hospital one night. He hunches into his coat for warmth, his frostbitten hands in his pockets. As he passes he gazes into all the lit houses, living out his lonesome, half-dreaming moth life. He sees families eating supper, women in their kitchens, kids squabbling. The red eye of a cigarette, circling. Flicker of a hockey game on

TV, the blue glow of a computer screen. A father coming home late, sometimes drunk, sometimes violent. Max can do nothing; he can't even walk away. He stands there watching, in agony.

But tonight is different, tonight is still. Instead of flitting from room to room, keeping busy, people stand in their windows like chess pieces. Gazing out. The silence becomes increasingly eerie when, suddenly, the wind gusts and the first flakes start to fall. The snow has finally come to unlock the iron cage of winter.

Nobody is out except for a group of refugee kids in their donated winter coats. The children peer up at the sky and when the snow begins falling they pull off their mittens and hold out their hands. They whirl in circles, shrieking when the snow touches them, but their whoops of fear and hilarity blow away in the wind. Max stops to watch the children, following the direction of their gaze, his head craned back as far as it will go, forcing his eyes to stay open so that he can see the snowflakes funnelling down.

Snow and the intervals between snow. At first it falls like musical notes, the air full of a quivering, atonal pitch. And then it falls like nothing he can name — there are no similarities anymore. Everything is changing, turning from water molecules into ice crystals. Max begins to whirl with the children, his sudden, unexpected delight the last stop in the transformation of snow into joy.

THERE'S AN OILY shimmer of broken dreams in the dawn sky above the Binder residence. A family lived there once, intact, more or less happy. By and large. All in all. Maybe you remember them, but probably not. Best not.

Morning again and Max is waiting. It's all he knows how to do and it's the only thing that assuages his grief. The house wavers in and out of focus. Everything is out of step, out of time. Nothing rhymes.

The trouble is he can't quite remember how it all ended. Bits and pieces come back to him. Snaps of colour and snatches of song. *If you want to bring me down.* Luggage lost, stolen purse. Bunting snapping overhead. *Better get in line.* A young woman trying on jackets, no mittens. Pink plastic puppy, yellow Hydro truck. Sun in his eyes and the dark sobbing of angels. *Who if I cried?* And something stuck in his chest, like a hard crust of love he's swallowed down the wrong way. Heartburn.

Mostly, though, the last days of his life have been erased. He is a book with its final chapter torn out, a calendar missing a month, an autobiography whose writer has forgotten the end of the story. He presses his hand against his chest, as hard as he can, hoping to feel the iambic rhythm of his heart. But he feels nothing — no tremor, no beat, no flutter, no thump — until, all at once, his cheeks are wet. Max is weeping. He's mourning the death of Max Binder. Did you happen to know him? A hopeful fellow, a fool.

As far as Max can tell, no one gives a damn about his untimely passing. Day after day, Maggie shines in her inscrutable anger, a matchstick, a flint striking sparks. That iridescent blue halo around her head. And his sons remain as inexplicable as ever. Lazar: toppling over, scrambling up, fighting and falling. A nervy kid in both senses of the word. And Sams? The wrong kind of nervy, the wrong kind of everything.

Max longs to stand and brush the snow from his trousers, walk up the path to the front door. This was once his house, these were the porch steps he pounded up and down, shovelled in winter, swept in fall, hosed down in spring, and on summer evenings lingered on with a Scotch in one hand and a can of

Off in the other. Knowing when to sip and when to spray was his greatest challenge in those days, but one he accomplished with flair. Now he can't even walk up the stairs, can't yank at the screen door, can't fit Lazar's latchkey into the lock.

He hunches on the sidewalk with his big head in his big hands. Why does a ghost need a key? The ghosts in the books he's read walk through walls, materialize as the spirit moves them and the occasion demands — Marley and Banquo and Beloved. That old tell-tale heart. Have all the books been lying? But it's a theoretical question since Max Binder, late householder and current apparition, can neither dissolve into ether, nor glide through walls, nor magically open the front door of the house on Magnolia Street. It's just one of the many things about being dead that remains a mystery, although a more grievous one than amnesia or hunger or his flamboyant problem with dogs.

Mourning his life, mourning his death. Max hunches on the sidewalk, aching. Maggie walks past, no longer in flames. She's grown softer lately; a haze has settled over her. Sometimes she even sings to herself. Out of tune and out of time, but it's a happy sound. Max catches a word or two before she fades out of earshot. *Something something stars, something something eyes.* Later Lazar comes flying out of the front door, hits the ground, scrambles up, his backpack yawning open, its burden of paper and wadded sums spilling like a careless and unimportant blizzard. Much later, Sams. Not walking on cracks Sams. Not lifting his head Sams. Not crossing the road until he's counted three white cars Sams. (Max counts with him.)

In between are walkers who slouch or amble or stride past and occasionally through him, and dogs who snuffle at his fragrant ripeness, and Hariharan the mail carrier, chatting with Imee on the doorstep. One day his mother visits. She looks old and sad as she climbs out of her car, almost too weary to put one foot in front of the other. Max's heart breaks. Oh, what has he done to his mother! He tries to put his arm around her and hug her close. When she ignores him he feels like a child again, abandoned. But a moment later, his mother yawns and Max yawns in response, a secret pact. Is it his imagination or does Minnie Binder straighten up as she walks down the front path? All around them, schoolchildren josh one another on the sidewalk, pushing and cavorting and butting horns in the rising sap of an unexpected thaw. Minnie Binder begins to hum.

Max sits and days pass. Ice floes melt, species become extinct, rainforests die, weather changes. Then it's the afternoon. He sits through it all, hopelessly, because he'd like nothing better than to step over the threshold and into his house. Sigh gratefully and toe off his wet shoes. Undo his belt and release himself into the burly luxury of his recliner. Watch a little football, hockey. Whatever's on. He was fussy once. Flicked through college basketball games and hooted at the curling championships. If only he could have it all again. Once more with feeling.

EARLY ONE EVENING Max is sitting on the sidewalk outside his old house, hawking up phlegm on account of having caught a chest cold. The unfairness of his predicament assails him. It's bad enough to wake up every day, homeless and queasy with nerves, to find himself bereft of wife and sons, to be condemned to limp the slippery streets and thawing boulevards of a once-familiar city, to provide succor to every passing mongrel — but why all this and a fever too? Might as well be dead and buried, he thinks, sneezing convulsively.

Some time later, a silver Accord pulls up to the curb and idles, as if trying to make up its mind to stop or go, stay or flee.

From where he slumps, Max can reach out a hand and stroke the old girl and then — why not? — does. He's begun to notice that as the warm-blooded mammalian world recedes from him objects advance, shine their eerie inner lights, beckon him on. Automobiles and streetlights and parking meters flicker as he limps by, power lines and outdoor ice rinks throw off a chemical radiance. He waits at crosswalks while traffic lights cycle rapidly through their intervals. At the end of the street, in the neighbour's front yard, a snowman glows weirdly as if it's swallowed an incandescent bulb.

He touches the rumbling silver Accord. The car feels warm; there's a spring and give beneath his palm, almost as he imagines a horse might feel, although God knows he's never been anywhere near a horse. While he's petting the flanks of the huffing automobile, a man emerges from the car. Ho, and not just any man either! It's Shapiro, Maggie's boss, that patriarchal son-of-a-bitch pissant.

Grinning from ear to ear, Max lumbers to his feet, his arms outstretched. He wants to grab Shapiro and hug him and shake him. He wants to tussle with him, and thank him for stopping by, and apologize for being such a stranger. He wants to fall upon his neck and weep, and he wants to wrestle him to the ground. He wants to kiss him on both cheeks, enfold him in a bear hug, feel the old so-and-so squirm in embarrassment. He wants to challenge him to an autographic piss-up in the snow, and he wants to pull the lazy bastard down on the sidewalk beside him, confide all his troubles then punch him on the shoulder. *So okay, that's life eh, what you gonna do?*

Because death's like that, he's found. A seesaw with a fat man who keeps changing sides. An up-and-down proposition, a bit of a ragged ride.

Shapiro is looking sharp. An astrakhan coat, no less, and freshly shaven. A muffler, by God. He ambles around the side of his car, slouching as is his way, hands deep in his pockets. Without cutting Max a glance he walks right through him. An ill wind gusts up. The sort that blows nobody any good.

Hello, hello — somewhere behind Max a door slams shut and Maggie, in ankle boots and suede jacket, appears. Max, who has scrambled to his feet, blanches, ghost-like, at her transformed beauty. She's cut her hair short and it sticks up around her head in beguiling, childish tufts. No more tumbling locks, no more quick-wristed yanks to skewer her hair in place. She looks shorn now, shriven. But the change in her is more than a haircut, although he's hard pressed to say what it *is*. It's not the toffee-coloured suede or the ankle boots. It's not even the general air of cinch and strut, of denim stretched across well-rounded hips. Something has given way in her, some taut sinew of principled outrage. Her edges are hazy again, and she seems to be singing to herself, tuneless as ever.

"Well, if it isn't Maggie the Cat!" Shapiro steps forward to open the passenger door, gallantly offering his arm to assist her over any icy puddles and roaring gutters and dead husbands that might waylay her progress. Maggie smiles as she walks down the path, singing. Max opens his arms and closes his eyes. When he opens them again she's still smiling as she saunters toward her patriarchal son-of-a-bitch pissant boss. Max suddenly remembers what a pain in the ass he is.

But Maggie is nobody's cat and merely steps straight through Max, her erstwhile husband. She strides across the sidewalk, over the roaring gutter, and into Shapiro's arms, allowing him to bury his nose briefly in her hair before shaking him off and climbing into the car. Shapiro has a goofy look on his face, a helpless grin. *Uh-oh*. Max recognizes the look of a man whose fondness has snuck up on him. *Good luck to you, pal*, he thinks, but he is pierced with helpless rage.

Shapiro waits for Max's widow to arrange herself in the passenger seat before easing her door shut, striding around to the driver's side, and gunning the engine.

"Wait!" yells Max, stepping forward, shoving one inadequately shod foot into the gutter. But he is too late. The patriarchal son-of-a-bitch pissant lays rubber to road and the silver Accord peels from the curb. Max feels the shock of the icy water travel all the way up his leg to lodge painfully in his knee.

He returns his head to his hands, his elbows to his knees, hunches his shoulders about his ears. Gingerly, he takes a shallow breath but it still hurts too much and he decides not to take another. Maggie is leaving him, he realizes. First the flames died down; then she began to waver and break up. Lately he can barely make out her features although the soundtrack is still clear. The click of heels on sidewalk and a snatch of song in the distance. *Something something stars, something something eyes.* With a start, Max realizes that the pain in his heart is easing. He too is thawing out.

So deep in thought is he that he barely notices that someone has settled down beside him. Then someone taps on his forearm to get his attention and when that doesn't work, sits drumming idly and irritatingly, until he glances up.

"Buy you a drink, Mr. Macks?" says Pat Ngunga, sliding a hand over her thick braid.

Pat's hair has grown since he last saw her, and now it's a knotted rope, the sort of rope a man might climb in his dreams, intricate and shiny. Max notices that his old friend is beginning to fade at the edges and glow in the middle. Her silver backing is coming loose and it shines through her pinholes (eyes, the holes in her earlobes, the pores of her skin).

Surprisingly, she is holding out a thermos flask.

"Well?" she asks again. "Do you have a hanker?"

He shakes his head. Right now he'd love a hot drink, but he hasn't tasted one since he died. Death has rendered him invisible to vendors and baristas, incapable of making his wishes heard or his thirst convincing.

Apparently, Pat has no such problem. She extracts her flask and unscrews the top. Max smells the slightly burnt, bitter aroma of fresh coffee. He gazes at the steaming liquid with deep suspicion. Suddenly he remembers that Sams once offered him a cup of coffee. How long ago that was!

"Don't be dubious," Pat tells him. "Believe."

Her words, shining and cursive, unfurl from her silver-backed mouth. *Believe, believe, believe.*

She puts the open thermos flask to her mouth and tilts. *Mmm*, she sighs, wiping her mouth with the back of her hand and making a *your turn* face at Max. He takes a deep breath, tilts and sips, summons belief. Coffee dribbles from the thermos in a thin, miserly stream. But a start, by George! It's the first drink he's taken since dying, and hunger roots around in his belly. Well, well.

Immediately, the smell of rot that's come and gone throughout the day, wafting dogs his way and chasing more fastidious creatures out of it, rises unmistakably. Is he at last resolving to a dew, running like overripe cheese, liquefying from the marrow in his bones to the gel in his eye sockets?

"It's coming from your coat, Mr. Macks." Pat points to his pocket.

He yanks off his coat and turns it upside down, shaking,

shaking. Dust and more dust, lint, a handful of worn-down pencil stubs. A ketchup-stained handkerchief and a latchkey. But nothing to explain the stench. Oh God. He shoves his hand into his coat pocket, wriggling his fingers through the torn lining. His fingers sink to their joints into something so soft that it almost falls apart at his touch. It is — Max is certain of it — his rot. The ghastly liquid beginning of his descent into effluent and worm shit. But Pat is still waiting, tapping her fingers, so he yanks and pulls and scrabbles to divest himself of his rotten, runny core. Something — what? *what?* — finally detaches itself from his coat lining. A sort of oozing lump.

Beneath its furry spores and green mohair sweater, the lump turns out to be a fast food burger.

Distantly, Max remembers pocketing the burger at a long ago drive-thru window. The wrapper, which is still intact, is the only thing preventing it from dissolving into the mush of its constituent parts: bun mangy with mustard and ketchup, the guttery stink of decomposing meat. He gazes helplessly around him, trying to calculate how the reek of his ghostly burger has penetrated the mortal world. He remembers the rising odour of his days. How dogs snuffled at him, at first in joy and then, stiff legged and flailing, skittered sideways at his approach. Finally Pat, her patience fled, pulls him upright.

"Time to bury your dead, Mr. Macks," she tells him. She's been disappearing all the while they've been sitting on the sidewalk, flickering and dimming as if one of her wires has come loose. Now, when he turns to look at her he can only make out a concentrated glow like a light bulb before it burns out.

Max watches her burn, the smell of sulphur-tipped filament in the air.

"Come on, Mr. Macks," says Pat. "I know a place."

* * *

IT TAKES FOREVER, but they get there: Max limping, Pat padding silently beside him. Together they follow their breath through the night. As they go Max sings to himself: *Something something stars, something something eyes.* Pat joins in on the chorus, her voice melodic and deep. *Something something moon, something something heart.* The singing seems to bring her back into focus, back into her jacket, her skin, her shivering girlhood. Max takes her cold hand.

They make their way through neighbourhoods and suburbs and new housing developments, beside schoolyards and hospitals and shopping centres, between office blocks and strip malls and tract housing, past warehouses and storage lockers and industrial sprawl, alongside trailer parks and rivers and railway tracks, over golf courses and bridges and exhibition grounds, across cemeteries and soccer fields and garbage dumps, until eventually they leave the city limits and hit the highway. It takes forever, but presumably forever is what they have.

Then they're stumbling along on the edge of the highway. *Stars, moon, eyes, heart.* Pat and Max, Max and Pat, go their footsteps. *Pat, Max, Max, Pat, pitter pat, pitter pat.* The moon swings across the sky in a high arc and the Joliecoeur Motor Hotel rises up out of the darkness, its blue neon sign still flickering "Vacancy/No Vacancy."

"Here?" asks Pat. Well, why not.

In the neon-buzzing darkness, in a ravine by the side of the road, in a shallow grave scooped out of the snow with a plastic set of cutlery from some motorist's discarded takeout meal, Max buries his burger. Rest in peace. He stands, head bowed, blue light flashing across his face as he listens to the Doppler effect of automobiles and semi-trailers.

Why is it so easy for everything else to die? Max thinks of the burger disintegrating serenely in the sweet earth. Perhaps it's a sign of how low he's sunk that he doesn't feel foolish standing and gawping up at the moon. Once he would've had to be good and drunk, past gregarious, overfond, lugubrious, melancholy, addled, and raving to linger there, his face turned like a satellite to the sky as if trying to pick up signals from a cold but necessary planet.

He is suddenly so lonely he could die. He draws Pat down to the shoulder of the highway.

"Won't be long now," she promises.

He sits with his elbows on his knees and his fists bolstering his chin. He'd like to know who's in charge of this tedious second death of his. Is there someone he can speak to? Pat broods in silence beside him, drumming her fingers on the cold highway blacktop.

"Goodbye, Mr. Macks," she says. "It's time."

After a moment, Max too dims then goes out. But the blue neon sign above him flickers on and on, caught forever between hospitality and the untenanted places of the soul.

NOTES

On page 5 the poem quoted is Rilke's "First Elegy" from *Duino Elegies*, translated by Stephen Mitchell.

The Russian phrases on pages 53 and 67 are from Dostoyevsky's "White Nights" and *Crime and Punishment* respectively.

On page 178 Milt recites from Milton's *Samson Agonistes* and on page 350 Maggie refers to Kafka's famous readerly instruction from his letter to Oskar Pollak (November 8, 1903).

The installation of trees hung with dead rabbits that Sams glimpses during Nuit Blanche is a reference to Diana Thorneycroft's 1999 art exhibition, *Monstrance*.

Although many movies flicker through this novel I've made particular allusion to *The Umbrellas of Cherbourg*, directed by Jacques Demy and *Big Night*, directed by Campbell Scott and Stanley Tucci.

BINDERS UNBOUND: A PLAYLIST

"Get in Line" by Ron Sexsmith
"Ob-La-Di, Ob-La-Da" by The Beatles
"The Ambient Air" by Louise Talma
"Heart and Soul" by Hoagy Carmichael
"Roll on Down the Highway" by Bachman Turner Overdrive
"Red River Jig" by Reg Bouvette
"Which Way Is Home" by Johnny Reid
"Fairytale" by Cowboy Junkies
"Harvest Moon" by Neil Young
"Louie Louie" by The Kingsmen
"January Girls" by Lord Kitchener
"Xmas in February" by Lou Reed
"April Love" by Pat Boone
"Maggie May" by Rod Stewart
"Big Yellow Taxi" by Joni Mitchell
"Hey There" by Rosemary Clooney
"I Fought the Law" by The Clash
"Irreplaceable" by Beyoncé
"Smells Like Teen Spirit" by Nirvana

"*Zog Nit Keyn Mol* (Partisan Song)," by Chava Alberstein

"Jerk" by Kim Stockwood

"Pavlov's Dog XM" (in-store music for retail zoning)

"Nobody Ever Told You" by Carrie Underwood

"Girl on Fire" by Alicia Keys

"Put It in Your Mouth" by Akinyele

"The Name Game" by Shirley Ellis

"Song of Bernadette" by Leonard Cohen

"Bernadette" by The Four Tops

"Samson and Delilah" by The Grateful Dead

"I Will Wait For You" (Love Theme from *The Umbrellas of Cherbourg*) by Michel Legrand

"Chico's Masurka" by The Marx Brothers

"Dinner (from *Big Night*)" by Gary de Michele

"The Oldest Established Permanent Floating Crap Game in New York" (from *Guys and Dolls*) by Frank Sinatra

"Forever Young" by Jay-Z

"Unforgettable" by Nat King Cole

"October" by U2

"My Way" by Frank Sinatra

"American Pie" by Don McLean

"Turn! Turn! Turn! (To Everything There Is a Season)" by The Byrds

"Whistling Away the Dark" by Julie Andrews

"Shortcuts and Dead Ends" by ¡MAYDAY!

"The Ambient Air (Reprise)" by Louise Talma

"Don't Let the Stars Get in Your Eyes" by Dean Martin

"One Great City!" by The Weakerthans

ACKNOWLEDGEMENTS

My profound gratitude to Rachel Letofsky and Janie Yoon; Rachel for her unblinking support, and Janie for much necessary blinking. Janie's visionary zeal was transformative; I feel lucky to have been sucked into her creative whirlwind. Much appreciation to Joanna Reid and Maria Golikova for turning copyediting into art. Thank you to Sarah MacLachlan and the lovely folks at House of Anansi, and to Paige Sisley and the gracious crew at The Cooke Agency.

Thank you to the editors of *Event*, *Grain*, and *Prairie Fire*, where excerpts from this novel, in the form of short stories, were published. Ian Cockfield, Shashi Bhat, and Cynthia Rogerson were early and encouraging readers.

I couldn't have wished for a more beautiful cover. Thank you to artist Miriam Rudolph, transplanted Winnipegger and admirer of elms. And to Alysia Shewchuk for her gracious book design.

My appreciation to the Manitoba Arts Council and the Winnipeg Arts Council. It is my great good fortune to live in a city where writing is celebrated.

Love and gratitude to Shoshana, Misha, Shai, and their father. Thank you for letting me laugh at you, kiddos. And for returning the favour.

Thank you to my father for buying a ticket, to family and friends, libraries, bookstores, readers, and writers. Thank you and apologies to Winnipeg for playing fast and loose with your streets and neighbourhoods, your festivals and railway schedules. Let's just say that all inaccuracies were intended and call it quits.

Author photograph: © Robyn Shapiro

MÉIRA COOK is the award-winning author of the novels *The House on Sugarbush Road*, which won the McNally Robinson Book of the Year Award, and *Nightwatching*, which won the Margaret Laurence Award for Fiction. She has also published five poetry collections, most recently *Monologue Dogs*, which was shortlisted for the 2016 Lansdowne Prize for Poetry and for the 2016 McNally Robinson Book of the Year Award. She has won the CBC Poetry Prize and the inaugural Walrus Poetry Prize. She has served as writer in residence at the University of Manitoba's Centre for Creative Writing and Oral Culture, and the Winnipeg Public Library. Born and raised in Johannesburg, South Africa, she now lives in Winnipeg.